THROUGH THE FIRE

Rachael Treasure lives in a sheep and cattle farming district in Tasmania. She has two young children and a menagerie of farm animals, including stock horses, sheep and working kelpies.

Currently she is working regenerating her property using new pasture cropping techniques. Rachael began her working life as a jillaroo (trainee farmhand) before attending Orange Agricultural College in New South Wales. She also has a BA (Communication) from Charles Sturt University, Bathurst. She worked as a rural journalist for *Tasmanian Country*, Rural Press publications, the *Weekly Times* and ABC rural radio, until she quit her day job for an adventure on a cattle station in Queensland and to begin her fiction-writing career.

For more information see Rachael's website at www.rachaeltreasure.com.

Also by Rachael Treasure

River Run Deep
The Dare
Timeless Land

THROUGH THE FIRE

Rachael Treasure

arrow books

Published by Arrow Books 2011

10 9 8 7 6 5 4 3 2

'Naked' written by Sophie Clabburn, lyrics printed with the permission of
Jimmy Forte Music

Rachael Treasure has asserted her right to be identified as the author of this work
under the Copyright, Designs and Patents Act 1988

First published by Penguin Books Australia in 2009 under the title
The Cattleman's Daughter

First published in Great Britain in 2011 by Arrow Books
20 Vauxhall Bridge Road
London SW1V 2SA

An imprint of The Random House Group Limited

www.randomhouse.co.uk

Addresses for companies within The Random House Group Limited
can be found at www.randomhouse.co.uk

The Random House Group Limited Reg. No. 954009

A CIP catalogue record for this book is available from the British Library

ISBN 978 1 84809 088 0

The Random House Group Limited supports The Forest Stewardship Council (FSC),
the leading international forest certification organisation. All our titles that are printed
on Greenpeace approved FSC certified paper carry the FSC logo. Our paper
procurement policy can be found at www.randomhouse.co.uk/environment

Mixed Sources
Product group from well-managed
forests and other controlled sources
www.fsc.org Cert no. TT-COC-002139
© 1996 Forest Stewardship Council

Typeset by Palimpsest Book Production Limited,
Falkirk, Stirlingshire

Printed and bound in Great Britain by
CPI Bookmarque Ltd, Croydon CR0 4TD

PART ONE

One

When Emily Flanaghan hit the tree and her heart slammed out of rhythm, she didn't hear the rush of hooves as the other bush-race riders belted past her. Nor did she hear her silver-grey mare, Snowgum, roar in agony, screaming out a hideous guttural sound. As the mare's flint-sharp hooves flailed the air, Emily was oblivious to the smell of blood, both horse and human. Instead, she felt herself drifting up through the filter of gum leaves, her panic subsiding. She marvelled at the imperviousness of gum-tree trunks, how solid they were, in all their silvery beauty.

Gone was the surge of fear she had felt when she and Snowgum had taken the full force of the big chestnut, which previously had been galloping beside them, hitting them broadside. Silver stirrup-irons clanked, the horses grunted punch-drunk, and Snowgum was shunted off course. Fleetingly Emily recognised the contorted face of Clancy's mate, Mick Parker, his sneering yellow teeth framed by black stubble. He was reefing one rein across his horse's neck, while the other dangled broken and useless. Bloody Clancy, Emily thought as the tree loomed directly in front of her. She'd never have entered the race if it hadn't been for him.

Images of her two girls, Meg and Tilly, flashed through her mind. They were down at the marquee with their mob of little

3

friends, running amok. Both girls were lean country kids, with messy sun-kissed ponytails and grubby faces. She pictured them now, waiting nervously to see their mum race her horse across the line.

Before it began her youngest, Meg, had clung to her, whispering, 'Mummy, don't go in that horsey race. Please,' her freckled nose scrunching up. Emily had felt her daughter's tears on her neck, prompting the sting of her own.

In the second before she hit the tree, she thought of her dad, Rod, and the pain it would cause him to lose her at just twenty-six. She felt guilt weigh on her for leaving him alone, now of all times, when the stroke of a pen in a far away parliament could soon take their family mountain cattle runs away from them. Then she had a brief mental image of her brother, Sam, on the other side of the world in a Nashville recording studio. Or, more likely, in a bar with a bourbon in his hand, his irresponsibility as plain to see as his too-cute grin.

Finally, she saw her husband, Clancy. In the last split second of the life Emily had known, she remembered the full force of Clancy's rage against her. As she hit the tree, she felt an overwhelming sense of regret that she'd mucked up her life so badly. She had allowed herself to be stolen away – from herself, from her family and from her mountains.

Then came the pain of impact. As Snowgum gave way beneath her, Emily heard the sound of running water, and wondered why that water was slowing to a trickle. She didn't realise it was the sound of the blood in her veins moving slower and slower. She listened to an axe falling somewhere in the distance, quickly at first, then slowing to a few lazy haphazard strikes. She didn't know it was her heart, beating slower. Then slower. Then almost still. Just . . . one . . . lazy . . . hack . . . at . . . a . . . time.

Emily's body lay crumpled and still on a dry rocky creek bank while a frenzy erupted around her. Race officials in fluoro-orange vests clambered over tussocks and scrambled through

4

shallow rocky water. One of them punched words into a two-way radio as he ran.

'We got a rider down! We need an ambulance! It looks bad. Real bad.'

On the golden river-flat where the makeshift tent city of the Mountain Cattlemen's Get-together had been pitched for the two-day celebrations, people were still watching the race. The commentator, oblivious to the accident on the other side of the rise, continued to call the battle for the Mountain Cattlemen's Cup as the field of competitors half-slid down the jagged slope towards the finishing straight.

Horses were sheened with sweat; riders gripped tight with denim-clad thighs and, through gritted teeth, hissed their mounts on. Adrenaline surged through the veins of horses and riders alike. The two leaders hugged the curve of the track tight. One rider's boot hit at the fluttering triangular blue and yellow flags strung between star-pickets as his horse was bunted and shunted home. They flew past in a blur, belting for the line. Only three people in the crowd were ignoring the neck-and-neck finish. Rod and his grandchildren, Meg and Tilly, searched desperately for Emily on her grey mare. As the rest of the field raced home with Emily nowhere in sight, Rod felt panic rising within him.

'Where's Mummy and Snowgum?' Meg said, squinting up at her grandfather.

Rod gripped both girls by the shoulders. 'I'll go find her, I promise. You stay here.' He tried to sound confident as he saw Meg's eyes fill with tears. A friend in the crowd stepped forward and guided both children away. Rod nodded his thanks to the woman and then he was gone, sprinting towards his ute.

A pretty bush nurse was doing up the silver press-stud buttons of her blue overalls in the back of the ambulance. She pulled her long, chestnut hair back into a ponytail and smoothed the rumpled sheets of the stretcher bed, her rosy lips raw from her lover's stubbly kisses. She could still taste the beer, cigarettes and dust from his lips. Penny felt dizzy and giggly all at once, recalling the full force of his lust. Their encounter had been fast and furious.

She knew he had been watching her all day, like a predator stalking its prey. The very moment that Kev, her ambo crew partner, walked away to get a drink, Clancy had run up to her, curved one arm around her waist and dragged her into the back of the ambulance.

He'd kissed her hard on the lips and reefed open the studs on her overalls to clutch at her breasts. Then he'd lifted her on to the stretcher bed as she swiped aside the drip stands and oxygen equipment. He had wrenched down her overalls, tugged at his own leather belt and unzipped his jeans, revealing hips as snake-thin as a bull rider's. He'd set at her in a flat-out gallop, the rhythm of his thrusts rising in crescendo as the commentator called the mountain race outside the ambulance. As Penny thrust her hips against his, she threw back her head and gripped his perfect backside tight. She felt like a sweating, blowing horse, and he, her rider. The ambulance rocked and she wanted to scream, but instead pressed her hand over her mouth and bit down hard into the flesh of her palm.

When it was done, Clancy lay on her for a time, breathing heavily. Penny had shut her eyes and, almost sadly, stroked his muscular shoulders, already beginning to long for the next encounter. They could only ever steal moments like this. She hoped no one had noticed them today – he was not so subtle when he was drunk. But she'd smiled coyly as she'd smuggled him out of the ambulance and he had jammed his big black hat back on his head, thankful that everyone's eyes were still on the race.

In the lead up to the Mountain Cattlemen's Cup, Kev had been watching Penny in the side-mirror, flirting shamelessly with that selfish bugger who acted like his wife and kids didn't exist. Disgusted, he'd eventually tilted the mirror away and taken himself off to find a cuppa. He couldn't bear to watch.

Now, back in the cabin with his feet up on the dash, he was relieved to see the mongrel husband had gone. But suddenly the radio was alive with static and a man's urgent tones, and Kev knew that this was a bad one. He tossed the paper cup down on the dry grass, its syrupy contents disturbing the ants.

'Penny!' he yelled. 'Get your arse in the front!'

In the creek bed, Rod knelt beside a course official who had gingerly loosened the Velcro of Emily's protective vest. He cried out in anguish when he saw his daughter's twisted, broken body. The translucent white glow of her normally tanned skin, the blood seeping from one corner of her mouth and the deathly stillness of her limbs, all sent fear trickling through him. The official bent closer to Emily's face, listening desperately at her pale lips for any sign of breathing. Next to them, others were hauling on Snowgum's reins, pleading with the mare to stand so that they could move her away from Emily's body. Snowgum's cries were so excruciatingly disturbing Rod wished the mare would just lie down and die. He couldn't bear to look at the way her white flanks were running with blood as she writhed with pain. He heard someone scream out, 'Does anyone have a gun?' Not far away, Mick Parker was holding on to his blowing horse, face scrunched up with anguish, murmuring over and over in an odd whining voice that he was sorry.

Rod's world spun. Surely this wasn't really happening. He looked again at the lifeless body of his daughter, whispering, 'Please, God, no.'

She simply could not die. Not his Emily. Before Clancy had stolen her away to the suburbs, Emily had been the lifeblood of their family and of their whole mountain community. This beautiful girl somehow represented the future. For years Rod and his sister Flo had battled to keep the mountain cattlemen's traditions alive in the face of sustained attacks by politicians, bureaucrats and environmental idealists, mostly in the hope that Emily would one day come home to them. Each time Rod had trudged to another meeting to negotiate his grazing rights with the changing guard of government men, he had held Emily there in his heart as a reason not to give up. Her presence revived him, and she kept the weary older generation of cattlemen laughing and hoping. But then she had moved away with Clancy and Rod had watched, heartsick, mute, as Emily's marriage ground down her soul and eroded her spirit. The bright flame of her youth began to dull.

Now here she was, all but extinguished, and Rod was feeling the sting of guilt. *He'd* been the one to encourage her to ride in the Cattlemen's Cup. He had thought that somehow it would signal her return home to him. He laid one hand on her cheek. Instead here she was, leaving him in the worse way imaginable.

'We're gunna have to start CPR,' the official said, glancing fearfully at him. 'She's not breathing and I can't get a pulse.' Rod squinted through the gum trees, looking desperately for the ambulance. As the man gently eased Emily's helmet off and bent forward to breathe life-giving oxygen into her mouth, Rod was shocked to see that her long dark hair had been chopped off, the scissor marks still rough and jagged against the softness of her heart-shaped face.

'Emily?' he cried. 'Emily! Stay with us. Emily . . .'

Two

Somewhere through the haze, Garth Brooks was playing. Sam Flanaghan rolled over, head heavy from last night's Budweisers, downed after his gig. He'd been in honky-tonk heaven when he'd stood on the Nashville sidewalk and gazed up at the giant neon-red cowboy boot and flashing guitar of Robert's Western World.

He strode into the bar, carrying his guitar case, and was instantly immersed in the rowdy nocturnal den of burgers, boots and booze. He was heady from the crush of rhinestone cowgirls done up to the nines in tassels, tight jeans and lairy two-tone dress boots. The smell of deep-fried chicken mingled with the odour of spilled beer and the sickly sweet scent of the perfumed and peroxided women. Sam sucked it all in, in one deep breath. Right from the start, he had known he was going to get carried away.

Now, in his newly rented room, prising apart his long, dark eyelashes, the first thing Sam saw was his guitar case, open. Next to the Conargo Pub sticker, faded now to a mottled shadow, he saw a hot-pink bra hanging carelessly over the metal clip of the case. His gaze roamed towards the bedside table, where the sound of 'Friends in Low Places' seemed to be coming from. There he saw a large black bra curled up beside his bed like a sleeping cat. Not one but two sorry-looking condoms lay on the floor like bedraggled windsocks.

Eyes wide open now, and with a slow, wicked grin, Sam untangled his limbs from those of the naked Texan girls sleeping one on either side of him.

One girl was dark and lean and lay on her back with her forearm pressed against her brow, as if she were having a crisis. Her mouth hung open and she was making gentle snoring sounds from the back of her throat, her breasts sagging a little too far down her sturdy ribcage.

The other girl, a blonde, lay on her stomach with one knee turned out on the bed, her bent leg mimicking the position of her arm. She was dribbling slightly. The peaches-and-cream complexion that had caught Sam's attention from the stage now looked wan and pasty. Ellen and . . .? He couldn't recall. He did remember they were both soldiers. Home on leave from fighting their 'war on terror' and holidaying in Tennessee, sinking whiskey as if there were no tomorrow. Brassy, boastful women in uniform . . . though clearly not in uniform now, he thought dizzily. Sam looked down at the blonde's breasts. He had so wanted them as a pillow last night, feeling far from home as he did, but his cheek had met not the soft yielding of flesh but stubborn plastic. Implants.

Sam frowned. Garth was still playing. He remembered that this was his phone – it played a different country-legend ringtone for every day of the week, just to motivate him. To get him through the humiliation of suddenly being a nobody in Nashville. He'd come here because there were music legends in every recording studio who could be hired to play on new albums. If his Aussie hit song, 'Jillaroo Junky', about a bloke who couldn't keep his hands off the rural chicks, was picked up here, his dream of making it Keith Urban-big in the States could come true. But so far every single producer had drawled, 'A Jilla-*what*?' It seemed he'd jumped the gun – just like his manager had said he would.

'Sam Flanaghan,' Ike had said, tapping Sam's dinner-plate-sized rodeo buckle before he'd flown out of Sydney, 'you're a cowboy from the bush, you're just not ready for Nashville.

You need to get some professionalism under your belt before you do this. It'd be best to grow up a bit, kiddo, before making a trip to the States.' Then Ike had knocked his knuckles on Sam's head. 'But no one seems to be listening in there.'

And Ike Johnson had turned out to be right. Sam had been in Nashville doing the rounds for months, but so far no record company people had called. Only the dodgy rabble of mates he made in seedy bars ever phoned him now.

He reached over the blonde, knocked a glass of water on to the grimy brown carpet, swore, then fumbled to find the slim silver phone. He flipped it open. There was crackly static on the line.

'Hello?'

'Sam?'

'Dad?'

'Oh, thank God! Sam, there's been an accident. It's Emily . . .'

Suddenly Sam's world back home came hurtling back to mind. Not Emily! The big sister he'd idolised all his life. He sat bolt upright.

'What kind of accident? Is she going to be all right?'

'I don't know, Sam. I don't know. It's pretty bad. They're going to chopper her out.'

Sam heard the raw fear in his father's voice, then the line went dead. When he tried to redial, it went straight to the message bank.

'Dad, call me back when you're in range!'

Sam threw down the mobile and sank his head into his hands just as the Texan girls began to groan their protests at being woken. He barely noticed, transported back to Dargo Primary School with Emily by his side, her long, dark hair worn in lopsided pigtails. They sat there at scratched wooden desks, just as their father had before them. Sam and Emily had adored their teacher, Mrs Dongeal, who had also been their father's teacher.

She might have had wattles like a bush turkey's and what looked like a single overripe watermelon for a bosom, but

11

motherless Sam and Emily craved female attention, and Mrs Dongeal was all for giving it to them. She'd taught in the district for forty years, and sometimes Sam and Emily would fake a few tears just to be drawn into the soft pillow of her bosom, ignoring the prickles from the sharp hairs on her chin.

No, it was inconceivable that Sam could lose Emily too. Like the sun, everything revolved around her. He didn't know how he'd have survived the loneliness of his childhood in the rugged mountain country without her. Or how he would have found his heart-place in music.

Emily and Sam were fifth-generation cattlemen, descended from a long line of determined, hardworking, resourceful people. They had grown up on stories about their great-great-grandparents, who had bush-bashed their way to the remotest part of the high country, on horseback, their kids strapped into armchairs hung either side of a packhorse. Great-great grandmother Emily, who had barely ridden before that trip, had carried their great-grandfather, then just a nine-month-old baby, before her on a hired horse.

They had heard how their forebears had pit-sawn timber and carved out a living from the mountains using both brains and brawn. Tirelessly they built their dreams in the most rugged country in Victoria. In the early days, when the Flanaghans weren't packing goods over the mountains with a team of work-fit bush horses, they were supplying miners with food and equipment from their hut on the King's Spur, or droving mobs of cattle over the mountains in search of sweet summer grass. Even on their rare days of rest, the Flanaghan boys were tearing off on further adventures: searching for gold, digging mine shafts, climbing cliff-faces, leaping horses over fallen tree trunks.

While such stories abounded about their long-gone relatives, Sam found that he didn't seem to thirst for that kind of adventure. With no mother to anchor him, he found himself instead wandering far from home, whichever way the wind blew him.

It had always been the women of the family who had kept

the men in line. According to the stories they'd heard, old Emily was always dishing up a meal or preparing a bed for anyone who had need of hospitality in that wild, sometimes bitter, place. It was she who had encouraged her boys to dabble in poetry and to write stories, painstakingly etching out their letters by the dull glow of a candle flame, in a mountain hut, amidst snow storms. She who'd encouraged them to sound out a tune on a harmonica beside a summertime campfire, to take an interest in hymns and the word of God.

The strong mountain breed of the past was reflected in Sam's sister. This Emily had a quiet strength that seemed somehow to be rooted in the mountain rock on which she was raised. Sam knew he himself had missed out on the hardwork gene that Emily had so firmly engrained in her. At least he had inherited the musical one, but the mountains were no place for a dreamy, lazy boy such as he, and every day of their lives there Emily had covered for him in some way, and made him feel okay about himself.

Now Sam pictured the snow-grass plains where the cattle grazed for four months of the year. Beautiful in fine weather; frightening when it came in savage. But always that country had a kind of majesty to it that even he felt running through his blood. If he sometimes needed to escape for a taste of bright lights and action, it was still a comfort to know he could always return to the mountains.

For the rest of his family, it was seen as their duty to care for those high-country grazing runs that also served them as a kind of insurance policy against drought. Even in dry times, cows that had struggled on winter pastures on their lowland property at Dargo would become glossy with health and rolling fat once they'd grazed on the high-plains government land. The snowmelt and the rich soils that had been spelled for seven months always did the trick for both horses and cattle.

But without access to the high-country runs, the six thousand acres on the lowlands, split roughly three ways between

Sam's father and his siblings Bob and Flo, simply could not support them all. Why did they continue to slave away every year for a meagre, sometimes absent, income, when life could be far easier for them all? Sam just couldn't see how their struggle was worth it. The whole grazing enterprise hinged on the land up top on the Dargo High Plains, and Sam well knew the government could take that away overnight. It had been a noose around the family's neck for generations – ever since the conservationists had first arrived as bushwalkers from the city and begun to make noises about the inappropriateness of grazing cattle in the high country. Now, with a massive campaign in the Western world stating that 'meat is murder', who wanted to live like a man sentenced to hang, reasoned Sam, when you could live easily and anonymously in a city doing your own thing?

As he thought of his gorgeous, funny sister lying injured, though, he suddenly felt totally lost. Somewhere on the other side of the world Emily was fighting for her life, or worse, and here he was acting like some loser using grog, drugs and wild women to distract him from a neediness he couldn't seem to quench.

Looking around the Nashville dive, Sam realised how much he missed home – not his flat in Sydney, but his real home in the mountains. Sure, he had loved living with his road crew on Australian tours. The tour bus with the ice chest that was always kept topped up with beer. The pub crawls from state to state. The bright-eyed Aussie country girls with a thirst for beer and music and a good-looking bloke. But now all he wanted was to be jamming in the Dargo pub. To have life back to normal. An awful dragging fear for Emily gnawed away in the pit of his stomach. He had to go home. If he stayed and carried on the way he had been, Sam knew he was headed for trouble. He'd get himself in deep. Heath Ledger deep.

Three

Clancy stood on the rough-cut heli-pad, shaved like a bald patch on the bushy ridgeline of Mount Ewan, while the dust raised by the spinning rotor blades swirled about him. Unsteady from drinking beer since breakfast, he looked skyward, tipping back his hat as the chopper lifted clear of the treeline, swooping on its way to the city of Melbourne. Kev had refused to let him travel with Emily and was now standing before him, trying to use wanky medico talk to pacify him. Clancy was only just holding back from decking him.

'Number one, you're intoxicated and it's against the law to take a passenger on board in that state,' said Kev, checking off the reasons on his fingers, 'and number two, they're goin' to need all the space in there to work on her. She's in a bad way and you know it. So let them do their job, mate, and we'll get her to Melbourne alive.'

Clancy scowled down at him, taking in his ridiculous wire-wool hair, parted to one side, and the way one eye squinted against the afternoon sunlight.

'Don't you "*mate*" me,' he spat. 'And I'm not intoxicated. Just a bit pissed.'

Penny watched them, her hands hanging limp by her sides, the adrenaline of the past few hours flooding out of her system, leaving her feeling a mixture of exhaustion, guilt and despair.

15

She was grateful that Kev was talking the bear-like Clancy down. Obsessed as she was with him, she knew that he could be a prick. As Kev soothed him, she could see Clancy beginning to relax, the anger in him melting away so that the tight set of his shoulders sagged. He was like a big dumb animal, she thought, but such a gorgeous one. Around him, she couldn't help herself.

'Come on,' Kev said, guiding Clancy to one side of the ambulance. 'Park your bum in the shade.'

Penny stared at Clancy as he passed, but he wouldn't meet her eye. She turned and began to pack away the last of the equipment. As she stepped up into the ambulance she was confronted by the recent memory of seeing Emily lying apparently lifeless on the stretcher bed there. The same bed where . . . Penny ran her palms over the sheets, holding back tears. She flinched when the ambulance radio crackled into life and Kev answered the call.

'I'm sorry, Rod, you've just missed them. The chopper's left.' Emily's father's voice replied with something unintelligible.

'Righto,' Kev said, somehow understanding the mash of words amongst the static. 'See you soon.'

Penny shivered as she recalled the rush to the chopper. She'd tried to assume her façade of professional nursing cool, like she'd done so many times when dealing with the bush patients she knew, but this time it had been different.

In the panic and claustrophobia of the ambulance, with Clancy hovering behind her, Penny was assailed by a rush of contradictory thoughts as she'd struggled to stabilise Emily. Expertly she had drawn drugs into syringes and monitored the equipment. Emily's heart was tracking like a kid's scrawl on the face of the monitor. Despite the urgency of the situation, she'd caught herself checking out the other woman's beauty and was struck by the softness of Emily's even-toned skin, so different from her own sprinkle of ginger freckles. She envied the womanly curves of Emily's body, too. They

16

seemed so beautiful compared to her own angular hips and shoulders. She found herself wondering then what Clancy had seen in her, to take her as his lover for the past twelve months ahead of his own beautiful wife. With her physical opposite lying unconscious before her, Penny had been forced to swallow down the unwelcome realisation that he had just been after one thing.

Kev had started barking instructions then and had brought her round. Penny thought she might hyperventilate. As Kev drove like a maniac round the gravel turns, she had felt the full weight of Clancy's body flung against her. She smelt the beer and sweat of him again, but this time it had irritated her.

'Will you sit down!' she'd ordered him.

'Is she dead? For chrissakes, Penny! Is she *dead*?' She'd turned to look into his blurry drunken eyes, dilated like a panicked dog's. She wished she could say Emily would be fine, but she didn't know. She felt Clancy's strong hands grab her upper arms.

'Tell me she'll be all right!' He began to shake her then, but Penny grabbed at his hands with her gloved ones, trying to prise open his grip.

'For fucksake, Clancy, sit down!' she'd yelled at him. 'You want her to live? Let me get on with my job!'

Kev swung his head round to look at them, and the ambulance lost traction for a second on the gravel track.

'You right back there? If you're being a dickhead, Clancy, you need to come up the front, buddy.'

Still Clancy's fingertips were digging into her, bruising Penny's skin.

'Do you think this is punishment for me? For us?' he said, eyes flickering madly between Emily and Penny. 'For what we've been doing?'

'Clancy, let me go. Let me work on her. Or you *will* lose her.'

'I promise, if she lives, I will never fuck around again,' he'd groaned, casting his gaze heavenward as if he could see beyond the roof of the ambulance. His words had crushed Penny. As she'd turned back to Emily she said through clenched teeth, 'Fuck around, eh? Is that what you were doing with me, Clancy?'

'Oh, God, Emily.' He began to cry. 'I'm sorry baby, I'm sorry!'

Penny heard the despair in his voice and clamped her eyes shut for a moment before drawing on all the resolve she had.

'Sit down, Clancy Moran, and stay there,' she'd told him, using her official nurse's tone – the one she used when dealing with drunks. 'We should never have let you in this ambulance.' She'd just wanted him out of it and gone from her sight. Then she could concentrate on doing her job.

Now, in the listless heat of the afternoon, with the chopper gone, Penny sucked in a breath and realised how stupid she had been ever to think that she and Clancy had been in love. Part of her had always known she was being an idiot, but no matter what she had told herself about him . . . that he was a serial womaniser, he was married, he had children, he was a bastard . . . she was still drawn to him. She craved him every waking minute and dreamed of him every single night.

Even now, pathetic as he was, she wanted to take him home like a stray dog and care for him. She walked around the side of the ambulance to find him crouching there in the dirt, his long, curved back leaning against one wheel. His head lolling forward, hands resting on bent knees, he was the picture of a man afraid and adrift. Penny's heart went out to him. How could she stay angry at him? He was like a drug to her.

She moved over to him and rested a comforting hand on his shoulder.

'Did you hear Rod radio?' she asked gently, 'He'll be here with the girls soon and then you can all travel to Melbourne together, to the hospital.' She moved her fingers towards his cheek. Clancy roared and slapped her hand away. Penny recoiled, shocked, as he stumbled round to the other side of the ambulance. He gritted his teeth together so that his stubble-covered jaw jutted out. Fist raised, he punched at the ambulance. The crack of it against the metal side was sickening.

'Silly bitch!' he shouted.

Penny shook her head, furious now, unsure whether he was referring to her or to Emily.

'Get a grip, you bloody loser!' She grabbed at his fist, raised already for a second punch. 'You tryin' to make more work for me and Kev after we've packed up? I'm not patching you up if you bust your hand. Now don't fuck with Kev's ambulance . . . and don't fuck with me!'

Clancy paused momentarily. Finally his eyes were looking directly at her. He laughed. At first it was just a chuckle. '*You're* saying don't fuck with me?' Then he began roaring with an unhinged kind of laughter. 'Don't *fuck with me*! How funny is that? All you ever do, Nurse Penny, is fuck with me!'

He lurched at her and pulled her to him. Penny was aware of Kev watching them. His narrow eyes were even narrower with disapproval, but he stayed where he was in the cab. This was Penny's mess.

'Clancy, don't.' She struggle to free herself. He grabbed at her again.

'Don't! You're drunk and in shock . . . now get a grip!' Facing up to him, pint-sized Penny drew back her hand and slapped him hard across his cheek. The blow stopped Clancy in his tracks. His jaw sagged. He shut his eyes. When he opened them again he looked directly at her with those baby blues.

'I'm sorry,' he said. 'Pen, I'm sorry.'

She was about to cry when the sound of a car's engine approaching stopped her. Clancy didn't look away. He took her by both hands and said again, 'I'm sorry.'

'So am I,' she said. 'More than you'll ever know.'

As she walked away, Clancy pressed his thumb and forefinger deep into his eye sockets to stop the tears. Exhaling deeply, he took a step towards the car, the ground beneath him shifting strangely like the deck of a ship. He steadied himself and watched Rod pull up under the patchy shade of a mountain ash. When he saw the girls, Clancy nearly broke down. Meg's and Matilda's faces had a sickly smear of dust and tears coating them. They got out and clung to their grandfather's trouser legs, burying their faces in the fabric. Kev stepped forward and crouched down to talk to them both.

'Mum's gone for a ride in a helicopter, so Granddad can drive you down to Melbourne to follow her. Okay?'

He rubbed Matilda on the upper arm and ruffled his fingers through Meg's auburn curls.

'Tell Mum hello from Kev when you see her, all right?'

Meg nodded and Tilly gingerly made her way over to Clancy, reaching out for his hand. He took it and pulled her close, gasping softly before reining in his emotions.

Kev squinted at Rod.

'You right to drive to Melbourne, mate, or do you want me to radio Dargo?'

'I'm fine, Kev, thanks,' Rod said, casting a furious look at his son-in-law.

'They'll take her straight to theatre,' Kev said pointedly ignoring Clancy. 'From what we can tell, she's got broken ribs, and I think the collapsed lung is putting pressure on her heart. They'll be able to tell you more once you get there. There could be more internals . . . possibly head injuries. We did all we could.'

'Thanks, Kev,' Rod told him, swiping a big hand through his snowy hair, massaging away a headache. His grey eyebrows bunched together as he frowned. 'She'll be all right, though, won't she?'

Kev sought to hide the uncertainty he felt, laying his hand on Rod's shoulder to try and reassure him.

'They breed 'em tough up here, don't they, these mountain girls?'

But as Rod strapped little Meg and Matilda back into their booster seats in the vehicle, he winced remembering Kev's answer. All he'd wanted to hear from him was 'Yes, she'll be fine'.

As he pulled the seatbelt across his chest and started the engine, he tried to shut out the stench of stale beer emanating from Clancy in the front passenger seat. Poor Emily, he thought. His poor darling daughter.

'She should never have gone in that race,' muttered Clancy.

Rod didn't reply. Instead he thought furiously, She should never have married you.

'I tried to tell her . . .'

'Shut up, Clancy!' spat Rod. 'I shoulda been with her in that ambulance *and* on that chopper, but how could anyone trust you with the girls? Look at you. If Emily doesn't make it, I'll . . .'

He glanced in the rear-view mirror, conscious that the girls were listening. He bottled up his anger and settled himself down, jabbing on the radio with his thick index finger.

Clancy knew not to argue with the old man. Rod might have been considered a gentle and kind soul, but he had a core of steel. His cattleman's upbringing on the Dargo High Plains had not only taught him to work hard, it had given him a level of integrity in his approach to life that Clancy could never hope to match. He glanced sideways at his father-in-law, taking in the lined face and aquiline nose, the salt-and-pepper hair and the fit and wiry body that was more like a thirty-year-old's than a fifty-year-old's. Clancy wondered if he knew about his son-in-law's affair with the bush nurse.

The way Rod slammed the gear stick back into second around the sharp mountain bends, and the fury on his face, told Clancy that the old man did. He knew everything.

Four

Flo Flanaghan ran her fingers over the ears of her wire-haired mongrel working dog, Useless, to stop her leathery hands from shaking. She was completely rattled after the call she'd had from Rod. Over the crackling of the mobile she'd heard him say that Emily was in a helicopter on her way to a Melbourne hospital. Flo had jammed a finger in her ear to block out the sound of the Hereford calves nearby bellowing for their mums, and concentrated on Rod's voice. Something was said about a collapsed lung putting pressure on Emily's heart, or cardiac concussion, or some bloody thing. Flo didn't know. All she knew was that it sounded bad and she was worried sick for her niece.

She squinted beyond the yards to where her cat, Muscles, sat on a post licking his white paws, and looked towards the timbered rise. Pushing back her cap, Flo searched for any sign of a truck or float. Rod had said they were sending Snowgum home, for Emily's sake. He had told Flo the mare would either make it or not, travelling doped-up and full of painkillers. When she had offered to call the vet in Brigalow, Rod had said they would more than likely need a back-hoe to bury her when she arrived. It was at this point in the conversation that the shock had kicked in for Flo. As she pressed the end button on the phone, she prayed Snowgum would come back here to Tranquillity alive. Illogical though it was, she, like her brother Rod, somehow felt that if the mare lived, everything would be all right. That Emily would come home to them alive too.

In the cattle yards her other brother, Bob, came to stand beside her and followed the direction of her gaze along the dusty gravel road.

'You could have a good feed for the dogs tonight if that horse carks it,' he said. Flo shot him a glance. He was a sarcastic bastard at the best of times. She wanted to knuckle him right there in the cattle yards, and in their younger days she probably would have.

'Ah, piss off, Bob,' she said instead. He always pushed her buttons. Deep down, she knew he was masking his concern with masculine bravado, for even he had a soft spot for Emily and her mare. But couldn't he go a little gentler at a time like this?

She'd already put up with him for the best part of the afternoon as they'd tagged cattle together. It was rare for Bob to offer help, so she had reluctantly accepted it in the hope that he was turning a corner. But she should have known better. He'd spent the entire time grizzling about the government's National Livestock Identification Scheme that was mandatory for sheep and cattle farmers. Nowadays every farm animal had to be electronically tagged so it could be traced from the paddock to the plate. As Flo's notepad flapped in the wind like a panicky bird, she'd waited for Bob, fumbling with his stubby fingers to get the little round plastic buttons into the applicator.

'Fiddly bloody things,' he grumbled. 'If I could find the pen-pusher who invented this system, I'd like to get him out here and tag *him* with one of the fuckers!'

'Just get on with it, Bob. What number?'

He peered at the tiny print.

'Is that an effing E or an 8?'

'Effed if I know,' Flo sighed, 'I'll get my glasses.' She climbed

23

the yards and made her way over to the ute. For the past eight years she'd fought hard not to resent Bob for inheriting the most and the best land when their parents died. He was the eldest son and that was his entitlement, as was the old-fashioned way, but looking at him now, with his belly pushing out his blue singlet and his nose raspberry-red from too much grog, Flo wondered yet again how her parents could have left the best of their land and livestock to a man like him. Tradition, she thought huffily. Blind, stupid tradition that said the farm must be left to the eldest son.

At least they had been sensible enough to will her and Rod a third of the lowlands each to scratch a living from, and they still shared the high-country licence. As long as Flo could pay the bills, have a counter meal now and then and maybe buy a new ute every ten years, she was happy. The Flanaghans had never carried themselves like landed gentry. They were workers who, over generations, had built themselves up to be the largest graziers on the mountains.

Each generation had gradually enhanced their lifestyle, from hut-dwelling to homestead, but no Flanaghan would spend money on grand furnishings or cars, preferring instead to splurge on the best bulls and stock horses. Their Dargo property, Tranquillity, had a beauty all of its own; six thousand acres of grassy hillsides and bush-covered ranges flanking rich river flats that meandered beside the Dargo River. Creeks had carved their way through granite cliff-faces that captured the evening and morning light like a masterpiece. The waterways were alive with trout and tiny native aquatic creatures. The river gave this whole place its heart and soul.

Because Rod was the only one of them to have children, he had been left the white rambling weatherboard homestead that had been built in the early-1900s. It was set above a river-flat, cooled by breezes running over a large spring-fed dam, and sheltered from fierce sun and icy winter winds by a deep bull-nosed verandah. It was a lovely old home but now had a faded air about it, like a beautiful woman past her prime.

Every year Rod said he would paint it, and every year, with money tight, the job slid back down the list.

The same could be said of Flo's home. She lived farther along the track, near the cattle yards, having made the former workman's cottage cosy with her parents' treasured old things. She was settled and happy there with her working dogs and her fat tortoiseshell Muscles, the animals taking the place of the children she had never had.

Beyond the houses rose the spectacular backdrop of the mountains that made up the other part of the Flanaghan property. Eighty kilometers away, along a sometimes dusty, always rutted, mountain track, Bob now owned another nine hundred acres of the best alpine meadows to be found. They still shared a hand-split timber homestead that had survived one hundred snowy winters but Bob's mountain inheritance was still a sore point between them. Surrounding the Flanaghan land were the stunning Dargo High Plains. At least Rod and Flo still shared a licence to graze a hundred thousand acres here. It was secured by Flo's great-grandmother Emily from the government one hundred and fifty years before and had set the family pattern of droving cattle from the lowlands to the high plains every year as the seasons changed. Of course, not all the mountain run was suitable for cattle, but it gave the family access to summertime grazing when the snow had melted and the native grasses, rested and revived, shot up from the fertile soils.

Flo and Rod loved the land, both the riverside country on the lowlands and up in the mountains, but Bob seemed only to endure it. He rarely stayed at the homestead they all shared on the Plains. In fact, despite inheriting the family's alpine country outright and a third of the best lowlands country on Tranquillity, Bob was feeling more and more cheated by the year. He had all that land, all those cattle . . . but no money to show for it!

Instead of working like a dog, he began to drink like a fish. As he unravelled, so too did the farm: the fences slumping,

25

land crumbling from overgrazing, the coats of the cattle turning dull and dry from grazing on depleted soils. His high-country runs were gradually overtaken by weeds and looked sour from overgrazing. Bob was the type who gave cattlemen a bad name. No matter how often Flo and Rod tried to help him, so as to help the land that their parents had once kept in top order, they were always stung by his arrogance.

As Flo drew her hand away from Useless's ears she realised the dog had rolled in a fresh pat of cow dung.

'Ah, shit, Useless.' She frowned and wiped her hands on her grimy jeans.

'Shit's right,' Bob said, rolling a smoke. He lifted his leg, scrunched up his purple face and let out a long, noisy fart as he lit up.

'Christ,' he said from the corner of his mouth, 'I'll blow meself up if I'm not careful.'

'Please, just rack off, Bob,' Flo said. She realised now it wasn't tea he'd been drinking out of his thermos that after-noon. She could tell by the way he narrowed his eyes as he drew deeply on his cigarette, wobbling slightly as he did so. No wonder he was being a prick. Grog and Bob were a bad mix.

'What's up your bum?' he said, blowing smoke out.

Flo shook her head and surprised herself when she began to cry.

'Emily,' she said, as tears washed tiny rivulets of dust down her cheeks. She moved over to a rail and leant on it, resting her head on her forearms and shutting her eyes.

An image of her niece came to mind easily. Flo had prac-tically raised Emily, at Rod's request. The little dark-haired girl with shining cocoa-coloured eyes had toddled into Flo's life pretty much full-time after her mother, Susie, had died. Flo had never exactly been the mothering type so she'd been uneasy at first when Rod had silently placed the newborn baby boy, Sam, in her arms and had ushered Emily to her side. Flo had stood there, panic and grief threatening to overwhelm her, as she watched her broken brother turn away to take care of Susie's funeral arrangements. Now it was all happening again. While Susie had bled to death in a bush hospital with no doctors within cooee, Em was now fighting for her life in a chopper on the way to a city hospital.

'Aw, geez, Flo! Don't go acting like a woman on me, cryin' like that,' Bob growled, 'She'll be right. She's a tough nut, that little Emily.' He thumped one hand clumsily against Flo's shoulder. She sniffed and nodded, relieved that he was at least showing some sympathy. Swiping her nose with the back of her hand, she laughed at herself and at him. Yes, she thought, looking down at her own wiry body clad in men's clothes, she was more bloke than sheila.

Flo Flanaghan wasn't unattractive, just wiry and steely, as if metal-plated beneath her weathered skin. She had an angular build, a striking face with glowing almond-shaped eyes, yet she swaggered like a man, sat like a fella and held a teapot as if it were a spanner. Some people who didn't know her well said she was half-bloke and she must have a set tucked between her legs. She looked funny in a frock and, whenever she wore one, couldn't seem to find the walk to match it. Her sinewy legs bowed out from years spent in the saddle. But every now and then she'd throw her bandy leg over some stock agent or overweight 'dozer driver, just to prove to all the bloody rogues at the pub that she wasn't a lezzo.

'You're right,' Flo said, 'Emily's tough. But I still want you to piss off. We'll finish the tagging tomorrow.'

Bob shrugged, sucking in the last of his smoke before treading it into a cow pat. 'Suit yourself. I'll be off home.'

Flo watched as he ambled away like Shrek, all shoulders, no bum and skinny legs, over to his mud-splattered ute. On the back, DD, short for Dickhead Dog, began barking like crazy as soon as Bob fired the engine and revved away.

Home for them was the new brick house built for their parents' retirement. It was not far from the original homestead, but was at least out of sight. Flo's mother's garden had once been welcoming and green; now there was only a tangle of long dead grass and twists of wire in it. There were broken bottles on the front porch and rubbish blowing in the yard.

Flo was just letting go the last of the cattle from the holding yard when a truck rolled in, rumbling to a halt outside the sheds with a loud 'choof' of its air-brakes. Old Baz Webberly jumped out. Flo braced herself for what she may see in the back.

'Thanks for bringin' her across,' she called to the old cattleman.

'You mightn't thank me if she's not made it,' he said, limping slowly towards her. 'No one held out much hope for her. But we decided we'd try and keep her goin' – for Em's sake.'

The mention of Emily's name left a cloud of fear and uncertainty hanging between them in the still evening air. Flo knew Baz would be thinking of Emily's generous quick smile and easy way with everyone. The world without her in it was unthinkable. They walked slowly to the back of the truck. As they dropped the door they stood in silence, both of them expecting to find the mare keeled over and dead.

'I'll be buggered,' said Baz.

Snowgum stood with her legs splayed and head hanging so that her nostrils touched the rubber matting of the truck's floor. She was still breathing, laboured sorry intakes of air that caused her to grunt rhythmically. Her flanks looked as if a cheese grater had gouged the skin away, her snowdrift-white sides now bloody, weeping and raw. As the light found her, she turned her head gently and half-whickered, half-groaned at Flo.

Tears filled her eyes at the sight of the broken, bloodied mare.

'Good ol' girl. You're home, you're home.'

She entered the truck, laying the palm of her hand on the mare's sweat-crusted neck. God, what had the poor horse been through? How had she stayed upright in that truck? For a fleeting moment Flo thought it had been cruel and selfish to make her take the journey over the mountains in this state. She should have been put down. And if the horse was in this much of a mess, what would Emily be like? Flo stifled a sob. Baz shuffled in next to her, took her hand away from Snowgum and held it in his.

'They say that where there's life, there's hope.' He patted her hand. 'C'mon, darls, let's get her off the truck.'

Moving Snowgum was no easy task. The mare had no flex to her. Her torn muscles had swollen and stiffened so that she could barely turn to walk from the truck. At the ramp top she baulked and let out one long groan, as if she could go no further. Flo raised one hand to her mouth as the evening sun revealed the raw truth of Snowgum's injuries. Her skin had been peeled back in places and there was a deep gouge in it, probably from a tree branch. A vet at the Cattlemen's had obviously patched her up but the ugly brown iodine stains on her grazes did little to improve the look of the wounds that swept across her chest and along one side of her body, with a nasty gash opening and closing like an evil clown's mouth near her girth as she breathed.

'Cripes,' said Flo. 'What did the other horse look like . . . the one that crashed into her?'

'Got off Scot-free, not a mark. Mick Parker is gutted, though. Real sorry he is. Rough nut that he is, he feels terrible about slamming into Em. I've never seen him so undone. He said to tell the family he's mightily sorry.'

'I bet he is. Still, an accident's an accident.'

Flo shook her head. Emily should never have been in that race. She was ill prepared, had been too long away in the suburbs and out of the saddle, but everyone in the family recognised she had to take the plunge. It was her way of running away from that mongrel husband of hers.

'Silly bugger,' Flo muttered.

As Barry and she coaxed poor Snowgum inch by inch down the ramp, Baz rattled off what the course vet had told him.

'He reckons she might have a fracture somewhere in the

rib or shoulder – that's why she's heavy breathing like a whore in a brothel. The other wounds will heal fine if we can keep the infection out. Manuka honey for that deep one. I said that, not the vet, mind you.'

Flo nodded as she agonised over Snowgum with each and every step. She thought of Alfie Jones, the horse vet from Brigalow. She'd give him a ring tonight as soon as she was settled. He'd be up first thing. You could rely on Alfie by day, but by night he was usually too full of grog to make farm visits. The thought of dealing with Snowgum on her own during the night to come daunted her. She'd nursed many injured horses in her time, but the situation was different. It was imperative that this mare should live. She *had* to.

Just as Flo resolved on this, Snowgum stopped moving. She let out a sigh and began to bend her hoof up under her chest, as if to lie down.

'Oh, no, you don't! Don't lie down on me, girl!' Flo flicked at the lead rope desperately and waved her arms, making clicking sounds in her cheeks. She knew that if the mare lay down now she would give up the ghost. They'd never get her up again. Both of them in a panic, Baz clicked at Snowgum too and slapped her on her good side. 'Up, girl, up. C'mon, baby. Hah!' On both knees now, the mare groaned deep in her throat as her nose rested on the ground, the breath from her nostrils raising tiny eddies of dust, her rump pointing up in the air as if she were bowing to Mecca.

'Please, Snow,' said Flo, her voice cracking, 'Up you get. For Em. *Please.*'

A moment passed. A crow called. Snowgum closed her eyes. Flo waited for the mare to thud sideways. But then Muscles jumped down from the fence and nonchalantly walked over to Snowgum, rubbing his body against the mare's cheek. He let out a long cat's hello before weaving back again to rub his other side against the horse.

'Oh, piss off, Muscles,' groaned Flo. 'As if Snow wants your tiny little cat's arse shoved in her face at a time like this! Well,

Snowgum, is that going to be your last memory? A cat's dot?' Then she found herself laughing, albeit hysterically, and Baz was laughing alongside her.

'Well, c'mon,' she said to the horse. 'Make up your mind. Live or die? What's it to be?' Then she knelt down and pressed her cheek to Snow's neck, whispering in her ear, 'Live, Snowgum, *please*!'

Just when Flo thought the mare was going to spread herself out on the ground to die, Snowgum let out one mighty grunt and heaved herself upright.

Flo cast Baz a 'Thank God' look and gradually they covered the short distance to the stall, Muscles leading the way, tail pointing straight up to the sky.

After they had settled Snowgum into a deep bed of straw and again thumped a needle into her neck to inject more painkillers, Flo sighed from the stress of it all. The mare was still refusing to eat, and only took a couple from the short draughts of water Flo offered her from a bucket.

'That's not a good sign,' Baz observed.

'Dunno who's worse off, the mare or Em.'

'Any word?' asked Baz from the corner of his mouth.

Flo shook her head and then the emotion swelled up in her so that her whole body crumpled and once again she surprised herself by crying. She felt Baz's arms go around her, which surprised her further still. He was a profoundly short man, made shorter by age, and Flo had to stoop a little to rest her head on his shoulder. She thought it must look pretty comical, a broad-shouldered woman being comforted by such a short-arse man, so she let the laughter splutter out of her. Then she pulled away, embarrassed by the emotion she'd revealed. She swiped her face with her big hands.

'I'm good now, Baz. All good.'

'You'll be right, love.' He patted her hand.

Suddenly not wanting to be alone, Flo forced a smile. She couldn't face phoning Alfie without Baz there, nor could she endure waiting by the phone alone for Rod's next call with fear for Emily lurching in the pit of her stomach. A solitary all-night vigil over Snowgum, waiting to see if she made it or not was something Flo simply could not contemplate; not with the same worry over her niece as well.

She looked down at Baz and did her best to seem friendly.

'Fancy coming in for a cuppa? Maybe you could stay the night. Drive your truck over the steep pinch in the mornin'. If you like.'

'If I like? Aw, come on, Flo,' he said, eyes glistening. 'You know me. I'm a mount'n man who loves mount'n women. 'Course I'd love to stay.' He sidled closer to her. 'And how 'bout a little touch and feel too for a sad old bugger like me, eh? A fella gets lonely on my side of the mountain now the missus has passed.'

Flo laughed. 'You dirty ol' fart,' she said, thumping him on his arm.

He pulled his face into a parody of dejection. 'Oh, all right then, if I can't tempt you with me body, we'll just have tea. And I'll stick in the spare room, I promise.'

As they walked back to the house, arms linked, Barry wobbling slightly on his dicky hips, he muttered, 'No harm in asking though, eh, Flo? When you get to my age, you know what they say . . .'

'And what's that, Barry?'

'Never trust a fart and never waste an erection.' He wheezed with laughter.

'Oh, Baz,' she sighed, 'it's gunna be a long night either way I go, I can just see it. Stuff the tea, let's just get straight on the whisky.'

Five

Emily had seen herself being carried across a mountain clearing. She turned her eyes away and drifted up into the sky, hovering over the canopy of gum trees. A narrow stream of black clouds pulsed towards her. The intensity of the approaching storm sent a charge of electricity through her. The world around her seemed to vibrate and shimmer into a blur just as she felt the first frightening rush of storm clouds over her face. But once Emily found herself immersed in the eye of the storm, she knew she need not be afraid. She was calm instead; knowing that she was everything, and everywhere, and had nothing to do but feel love and peace. For the first time ever, she had a clear understanding of the spiritual. The truest notion of what those on earth called God. She saw beyond the word that had confused her all her life. She was entire and complete and it was a joy simply to drift as an energy of life.

But suddenly the clouds pulled back and Emily looked down to see a valley spread out beneath her, its tall green grass dotted with cattle. Weaving through the valley's centre was a silver river, flanked by lush trees. She recognised the landscape as Mayford, the site of the Flanaghan family's homestead, but somehow it looked different to the photos she'd seen. On a small rise above the valley, in a clearing, Emily saw a hut and a woman standing beside a smouldering fire.

Emily knew she must go to her. She drifted downwards. As she neared her, she saw that the woman wore a high-necked navy work dress that was worn and faded. Her skirts fell all the way to the ground, dusty at the hem and resting on the toes of her scuffed lace-up boots. Her grey hair was parted at the centre and pulled back into a bun piled atop her head, but her deep-set dark eyes were bright and youthful. She had a long, strong nose and a kindly expression on her oval face.

The sturdy hut to the woman's right was made from thick logs, laid horizontally, topped with a steep shingled roof and a thick square chimney. Behind the woman a man had appeared, arms folded across his broad chest. His braces hung down beside his thighs and his open woollen work-shirt was stained with sweat. He too had grey hair, balding across his brow. His eyebrows had remained dark, as had his bushy moustache, but his trimmed beard was snowy white. He had deep brown eyes, youthful and alert-looking. Emily noted his hands, which were huge and square, in contrast to his short stocky stature. Her own father had hands just like that. To the man's right a glossy chestnut horse with white socks dozed against a hitching rail. A shaggy black dog with a sliver of white running the length of its nose and across the dome of its head stood on the verandah outside the hut and barked once at Emily, then wagged its feathery tail before settling down at its master's feet.

Not far from the hut she noticed a planting of tall, floppy-leafed corn, with next to it a stone enclosure holding a lazy sow sleeping prostrate in the sun. Somewhere in the bush high above the hut she heard the tinny jangle of a bell and the bleat of a goat. With her hands on her hips, the woman stood and watched Emily taking in the scene.

'What are you doing here, Emily?' she asked. 'It's not your time.'

'It's not?' she said, still searching the older woman's face.

34

'Are you looking for your mother?'

'Should I be?'

'Go back,' the woman told her gently. 'You have work to do.'

'Work?' said Emily. 'What work?'

'Mother Nature's work, maybe.'

Emily frowned. 'What do you mean?'

The other woman laughed softly.

'Go back, Emily, and perhaps you will find out.'

'But I want to stay here. That's a beautiful horse. This is a beautiful place. It's our place, isn't it?'

'Go back to your children.'

Emily frowned and the woman gently urged her again, 'Go back to your children, Emily. I'll be there for you.'

She stooped and threw a few sticks onto the lazy fire, then gathered her skirts and turned away. She walked over to the man and together they went inside the hut, letting the heavy curtain of canvas fall over the doorway. Emily somehow knew that this woman was her great-great-grandmother, Emily Flanaghan, and the man her great-great-grandfather, Jeremiah. They were the ones who had first carved out a life for the family in the rugged mountain terrain and had remained there after all the goldminers left. They were the ones who had begun her family's journey here on the moutains.

She wanted to follow them inside the hut but suddenly felt a shock of pain, as if someone had clasped her ribcage with steely claws. Pain ripped through the red string of her muscles and gripped her bones so hard they snapped into shards of white. She felt herself being dragged backwards through the sharpness of the fallen branches of snow gum that speared the ground around her. Then she was struck by a pain so strong it blinded her.

Emily could hear voices shouting over a rhythmic 'whump-ing' noise.

'She's gone again!'

'Clear!' someone shouted.

35

A pulse of electricity caused her body to spasm, legs jerking straight, spine pressing down hard on the stretcher where she lay. Gone were the smells of eucalypt and horse sweat and fear. Now there was only the scent of engine fumes and a roaring in her head. She tried to see where she was but the pain was too much. There was no way known she wanted to come back. Not to her old life. Not to Clancy. All she wanted was to find her valley in the mountains and to see her family again.

Six

Even though Clancy liked nurses he sure hated hospitals. In the sanitised waiting room, he looked down past his boots and thought that whoever had laid the vinyl here had not done a good job. The dull glow of streetlights fell through steel-framed windows on to the warps and dips of the floor.

He wondered if there was a KFC nearby still open, or even a pub that did toasted sangers. A hangover was kicking in. How long were they going to be here? He wished Rod would stop pacing. It was giving him the shits. The girls were crapping him off too – they would not stop asking questions about Emily, and wriggling, and wanting to play I Spy in a waiting room that had only three things in it: chairs, a table, and a pile of old magazines. The little buggers didn't even know how to spell, so I Spy never worked for them anyway, he thought, annoyed. It was Emily who had had the patience to teach them the letters and humour them along. He groaned as Tilly clambered on to his knee.

'Do you have to sit there, Tils? There's plenty of chairs in here.' Rod shot him a look and Clancy cleared his throat uncomfortably and shifted his weight to accommodate his daughter, who snuggled in against his chest.

'You stink, Daddy.'

He kissed her on the head. 'Shut up, you little snot.'

Meg sat across from them in a wide blue chair that was far too big for her.

'Is Mummy going to be all right?' she asked.

Clancy pulled a face.

'Dunno, rug rat. Dunno. Will you stop asking that?'

Rod scooped her up. 'Of course she is, sweetheart. She'll be just fine, you'll see.'

'Should you tell them that? What if she isn't?' Clancy said.

The look Rod gave him then had fireballs of fury in it and Clancy sank back in his chair as an Indian doctor swept into the room and introduced himself. He didn't fully catch the doctor's name but noticed he was the size of a jockey, with massive teeth like a horse's. The Indian made Clancy think of cricket. He wondered how Australia was going in the Test. Surely they had a TV in here? If he could just watch a bit of cricket it would solve everything. Help take his mind off things.

Suddenly his emotions rose up in him. He didn't know what to do with what he was feeling. He knew he'd made a balls-up of it all, but something in his head told him not even to think about that. It was all Emily's fault. She'd ridden in that race. If he could just sneak away for five minutes, he could call Penny. She was a nurse. She'd know what to do . . .

'Well?' Rod said, breaking into his thoughts. 'Are you coming?'

'Coming . . . where?'

'To see Mummy, silly,' said Meg, frowning at him. The doctor was standing waiting for them in the doorway.

'No.'

'What do you mean, *no*?' his father-in-law protested.

'I can't.'

'You *can't*?'

Clancy shook his head. 'Hate hospitals,' was all he could manage.

Letting go of the girls' hands, Rod lurched forward and dragged him up by his shirt front.

'Your wife needs you.' The men stood locked together for a moment, staring at each other.

'Gentlemen,' the doctor sang, 'if you please, I do have other patients.'

When they got to the doorway of Room 27C in ICU, the doctor abruptly spun around and held out his hand, indicating they should go in. This time they all hung back, Clancy glancing uncertainly towards Rod and back to the doctor again. He sensed their apprehension.

'She is still unconscious,' he explained. 'An induced coma, in case there are head injuries. She's also on a ventilator. Perhaps you may like to explain that to the little ones before you go in? That their mummy is sleeping so that she will get better, and the machine is helping her to breathe. Maybe the husband would like to go first? Yes?'

The man ran his words together very fast, and Clancy only caught half of what he was saying. He frowned and imagined pinning him to the wall by his neck, his little legs dangling a foot from the vinyl floor, like a puppet's.

'I'll wait here with the girls and explain to them,' Rod said tiredly, 'You go in first.'

Clancy looked at him almost desperately. He didn't want to go in first. But Rod had already thanked the doctor and was steering the girls away, whispering to them in comforting tones.

The doctor stood waiting. 'Mr Moran,' he said to Clancy, 'if you'll excuse me, I have rounds to do. Shall we?' He held out his arm towards the door again, as if ushering Clancy in to dinner.

'Yeah, right. No worries.'

As the doctor stood with his hand on the curtain, ready to pull it back, he whispered to Clancy, 'Now remember, even if a patient is unconscious or sleeping they can still hear you in their subconscious, so you can do a lot to help your wife simply by talking about the positives. Yes? She's still a long way from coming back to us. But she will hear you.'

Clancy nodded, and swallowed nervously as the doctor drew the curtain. And there she was. Emily. Her pretty heart-shaped face with eyes closed. Her lovely high-arched eyebrows. Long black lashes lying against the pallor of her cheeks like Sleeping Beauty's. Only her long hair was not spread out on the pillow as it usually was. It was sticking up in angry tufts all over her head, and her lips instead of their usual rosebud pink were pale, pulled slack at one side where the tube in her mouth was taped.

The doctor saw Clancy's eyes slide towards the creepy machine that was pumping up and down, making Darth Vader noises.

'We're assisting her breathing until the lungs and ribs heal a little. We want to give her a good long rest before we bring her round properly. Don't we, Emily?' He patted her unresponsive hand.

Clancy looked at the equipment all around her. Nozzles hanging from the wall, switches and signs he couldn't decipher. She looked so strange lying in that bed. He moved over to her, laid one hand on her arm and felt it cold to the touch. He hung his head and a splutter of grief erupted from him.

'Emily, I'm sorry,' he managed to croak. The intensity of his own emotion confused him.

The doctor clapped a hand on his shoulder and stood there for a time, his small palm radiating heat and energy against Clancy's broad shoulder. Then he noted down something on the clipboard at the end of Em's bed and quietly left the room.

Clancy stared down at his wife, and all the bits of tubing and tape they'd put on her. She was already beginning to bloom with bruising across her collarbone and over the top of her left arm. And then he saw, with shame, the other bruises blooming too. The bruises he'd given her the night before the race. The night before the Cattlemen's Cup.

Seven

In a dark old cottage in Fitzroy, Luke Bradshaw stepped out of the shower and slung a towel around his hips. His shoulder-length black hair curled in loose ringlets, dripping water on to his broad brown shoulders. He swiped away the mist on the mirror with the palm of one hand. The reflection of his own dark, almost black, eyes met his gaze. He opted not to shave. All he was doing today was going to the uni gym. Without lectures, tutorials and exams, this city life was stupefyingly boring, he thought miserably. But until he got a job, he was spending a lot of his time pumping weights or swimming laps of the pool.

It wasn't out of vanity, more frustration at not knowing what else to do with the pent-up energy flowing through him. His was a farm-boy's body: used to doing, used to moving, used to being stretched with hard physical work. For the past three years, while studying for his Environmental Management degree, all Luke had used was his head. Not his hands, nor his brawn. Sometimes, when the lectures had drifted into more esoteric realms, he'd even doubted whether he was using his brain.

Now Luke itched to get out of the city. But where would he go? He swiped more mist from the mirror, turned side-ways on and tried to push out his belly. Nothing. It was

41

sculpted to perfection, his skin the colour of dark caramel, his body carrying no fat, a throwback to his dash of indigenous ancestry. His colouring was not a good look for the son of a western wheatbelt boy. At the tiny local primary school he'd attended, his peers, other farmers' sons, repeatedly called him 'coon' or 'boong'. At least here in the city no one seemed to give a damn about skin colour. The population of Melbourne was made up of all types.

Opening the bathroom door, he emerged from a waft of steam and sauntered down the cluttered hallway, squeezing past road bikes, kayaks, backpacks and camping gear. In the kitchen, his girlfriend Cassy was eating organic nine-grain toast smeared with tahini. She was reading *The Age* and didn't look up when he came in.

'Good morning,' he said.

She grunted and went on reading. Luke wondered for the umpteenth time why he put up with her. He shut his eyes, long dark lashes resting on his high cheekbones. He knew. What else was there to do? Now that his dad had sold the farm, what else was there for him? Cassy Jacobson made the time fly. She was one out of the box, and she had pushed him out of his own comfort zone.

'Suck shit,' she said at last after finishing the article.

'I'd prefer Weet-Bix, thanks,' he said, eyes glinting.

'Huh?' she said, glancing up.

'You told me to suck shit,' he said, smiling, a dimple showing on his cheek.

Cassy gave him a dirty look. 'No, not *you*. *This*.'

She tapped her skinny index finger on the paper. Luke propelled himself away from the bench and leant over her to see the article better.

'"A mountain cattleman's daughter was involved in an horrific race accident at the Victorian Mountain Cattlemen's Cup on Jumble Plains yesterday,"' he read in his best anchorman voice. '"Emily Flanaghan, 26, of Brigalow, hit a tree while riding in the Cup. Ambulance officers revived her at the scene and she was flown to Melbourne with suspected internal injuries. She remains in a critical condition. Race officials were unable to comment on the outcome for her horse."'

Luke looked into Cassandra's intense blue eyes. 'You're saying suck shit to this?'

'Yeah. Stuff 'em. Bloody cattlemen! Serves them right. That tree was trying to tell her something . . . Get off the mountains!'

Luke nodded. 'Maybe, but you can't help feeling sorry for the girl. Pretty rough to hit a tree.'

'She's not getting my sympathy. I'm more worried about the horse. Poor thing didn't have a choice, did it?'

'Oooh, Cassy, you're so harsh! You are so mean, especially to me.'

'Am I?' she said, spinning round and running her fingernails down his bare torso.

'Ow!' He pulled away from her but she had hold of his towel.

'C'mon, pretty boy. Let me bite you.'

He felt her pointy teeth on his skin and he turned his head to bite her back, nibbling at a long thin neck that was starting to bristle some weeks into her Demi Moore-style buzz cut. She smelt of lavender and sandalwood oil. The scent had remained on her skin from their slippery lovemaking by candlelight the night before, when she'd emptied a whole bottle of massage oil over him in the bath. She'd only half cleaned it up, giggling as she bent over naked before him, wiping a towel over the oil-smeared enamel.

'What's Karla going to say when she gets back from her bushwalk? She'll go ape.'

Luke had shrugged. He didn't really give a toss what Karla thought. Instead he watched Cassy, her small, pointed breasts swinging down like a bitch in pup and the waggle of her tiny white backside. She was so uninhibited about her body. Luke had seen more of the female form in the past two years than he'd ever expected to see. There were still times, though, when he was pulled up short by Cassy's aggression and selfish ways, which sometimes left him wondering if she was really a gutsy, intelligent girl – or just fucked in the head. Still, she made life exciting and she had turned his farm-boy ways inside out since he'd met her two years earlier.

When Luke had first come to Cassy's house, after they'd skipped a tutorial at uni, he'd been confronted by a bookshelf filled with feminist theory. As she whipped up a vegetarian risotto for him, the boy who'd been raised on chops and three veg on a wheat and sheep farm in the west, ran his fingers over the spines of her books: *Stone Butch Blues*, *Cunt*, *Lesbian Ethics* and *Herland* were just some of the titles.

'Whoah,' he said to himself, as if steadying a nervous green-broke horse.

After their first-date risotto, washed down with cask wine, Cassy became like a lioness. Eyes focused intent on Luke, she pounced. He felt her nails dig excitingly into his skin. She made him go down on her that first time they made love. She seemed culturally exotic. Her body had patches of thick, dark hair in places most Australian women waxed, shaved or hid. None of the girls from Luke's hometown in the wheatbelt had been this uninhibited. They all had long hair and shaved legs and had sex by the rules. Country girls, although fun, liked a little bit of romance.

Unlike Cassy who, five minutes after they'd met at the uni library, said, 'Fancy being my flatmate and fuck buddy? We can save on a room and rent.' It turned him on and turned him off and challenged and excited him, all at once. So for the past two years uni life with Cassandra had been interesting in the extreme. She was the antithesis of the type of girl his mother wanted him to bring home. And at the time they met up, that suited Luke perfectly.

He recalled the day he first led Cassy into the Bradshaw family kitchen – it was as if he'd brought a footrotty sheep into the place. Luke had been delighted by his old man's reaction. His father was in the process of gradually selling off their farm to a tree plantation company and Luke felt his old man was literally selling the ground from under him. As each fresh title was sold he felt more and more bereft, in limbo, with nowhere left to go in life. He figured his parents deserved a dose of Cassandra.

It had been so funny to see Cassy drying the dishes for his mother while lecturing her on feminist theory and how most men were 'terrified of being swallowed up by the vagina'. His mother nearly dropped her prized china teapot! It was Cassy's refusal to stifle her screams during sex later on, on the basis that she was entitled to 'self-expression' no matter where she was, that had seriously undone his mum and dad. His parents had suggested they would be better off going straight back to their share house in Melbourne rather than staying a second night. And a haircut would be good too, his mother had added. For Luke, that was, not Cassy.

Now Cassandra pulled away from him and glanced up at the kitchen clock.

'Shit!' she said suddenly. 'My batik course. It's on in fifteen. Can I borrow the Datto? You can get the tram later, can't you? Please!' She slipped a small cool hand inside Luke's towel and twirled her fingertips in the hair there. 'Pretty, please?'

'Okay.'

'Great! But make sure you're in the city by one. The rally's on.'

'Rally?'

'Yes, I told you about it. Remember?'

Luke looked guiltily blank.

'The wind turbines. They want to put them on the Prom . . . right where the parrots fly. It's just plain wrong.'

'Parrots? Yeah, that's right! Parrots.'

'You'll be there?'

'Yeah, sure.'

She grabbed a satchel made from recycled tyres and turned to go.

'But just one thing,' he said. 'Couldn't the birds learn to fly *around* the wind towers?'

45

Cassy looked at him as if he had just vomited green slime.

'Shit, Luke. *Shit!*' she said, as she exited the kitchen with an irritated stomp of her Doc Marten boots. 'You *are* taking the piss. Geez, I hate that.' She slammed the door and he smiled and looked down at the newspaper. Then he heard the door open again and Cassandra pelted an orange at his head.

'Ow!' he said. 'That really hurt!'

'Well, imagine how the parrots feel, running into those bloody great spinning blades!' And then she was gone.

The house fell silent, apart from the constant drone of traffic on the freeway behind the back fence. Luke rubbed his head as he listened to the stream of trucks, sedans, utes and vans making their way to work or the shops or somewhere. City life, pulsing on in its own constant, ever-hungry energy system. Luke sighed. He missed the country. Here he was, a graduate in Environmental Management. But what environment could he manage? Where? He didn't know. Back out where his home had once been, the farm that was now managed-investment-scheme trees as far as the eye could see? He thought not. It broke his heart knowing all the land that had once produced food was now being taken over by pines and blue gums, mutely demanding nutrients and water in great hungry mono-cultures. Land that no one loved any more.

He glanced again at the newspaper article and silently wished the cattleman's daughter and her horse well, then turned the page gloomily, wondering what other horrific stories the media were dishing up for breakfast this morning. Then an advertisement caught his eye.

Department of Land Sustainment, Conservation and Environmental Longevity (DLSC&EL) requires a Victorian People's Parklands (VPP) Ranger for the Heyfield–Dargo Plains region. University qualifications essential.

He'd often heard about this region from the grandmother whose genes were responsible for Luke's dark colouring. She and her people had come from that place. He felt a tingling sensation on his skin.

The mountains, he thought. Yes, he loved mountains. Perhaps the excitement now coursing through his veins was a sign he was being called back to a home-place. After loving then losing the flat landscapes of the family wheat farm, and then being absorbed into the vibrant energy of a big city, the idea of living quietly in the mountains was balm to him. Luke had never been to the high country, despite Cassandra's half-laid plans for a bushwalking trip. But the Victorian Alps sounded rugged and beautiful . . . He looked up at the clock. The government office phone lines would be open by now. He would ring right away.

Eight

Emily was sure she could see angels. The blue-white light before her seemed to drift and shimmer. She tried to tug something from her face but could barely lift her arm. It took her a while to register the pain that was raging through her body, making every one of her muscles taut. She gritted her teeth and heard an animal sound, a whimper and a groan, then she realised it was herself she could hear. Underlying it she could detect a slow hiss, in and out, repeating itself over and over, and feel something tugging at the skin of her ribs, just below her heart. It felt like she wasn't breathing at all. When she tried to drag air in through her mouth, she couldn't. That scared her beyond belief. She tried to cry out but only a strange 'Elephant Man' noise came from her. She wondered if she had died.

From far away, she heard a voice.

'Emily?' Was it her great-great-grandmother again? 'Emily.' A cool hand on her arm and a bright light in her eyes. 'You're in hospital. You've had a fall off a horse. Emily?'

Horse? Snowgum! thought Emily with a jolt. Then she foggily remembered she had left her girls somewhere. She struggled to recall where.

'Meg . . . Tilly?' she mumbled, agitated, her words lost in the mask that covered her nose and mouth. Again the woman's voice soothed her.

'Your girls? Yes, they've been here to see you. Look.' She held up some bright paintings. Emily's vision was blurred but eventually she recognised Meg's familiar wild brushstrokes in vivid colours and Tilly's neat pencil lines under pastel shades. Relief flooded her. Then the nurse held up an unruly bunch of everlasting daisies and roadside flowers.

'They brought you flowers, too, from the mountains.'

Emily watched the nurse move to the end of the bed, the room spinning in and out of focus around her. It terrified Emily. She frowned and made a small murmuring noise. The nurse moved to stand beside her, carrying a clipboard. She laid one cool, comforting hand on Emily's arm.

'You'll be fine, sweetie, just very laid up for a while and sore and groggy. We've got a machine helping you breathe because you've got some broken ribs in there. Do you want me to tell you what else you've done to yourself?'

Emily blinked. She tried to nod. It felt like every part of her, her skin, her internal organs, her everything, was broken.

'You've a fractured collarbone, a fracture in your arm and there's some internal bruising. The doctors had you under sedation at first, to make sure your heart was tracking right and to see if you had any head injuries. You're a very, very lucky girl! That heart of yours must be pretty smart and strong – it just got right back on track beating for you. You've been given a second chance, my darling.'

Second chance? Emily tried to fit together the pieces of how she'd come to be here. She thought of Clancy and felt a lurch of despair – the last memory of him was a cruel one.

'I'll go find Doctor to tell him you're back with us. Won't be long.' And the nurse was gone.

As Emily tried to lift her arm she noticed a needle taped to the back of her hand, clear fluid running through it. Pain ripped through her. She lifted her other arm – it was in a cast, and Meg and Tilly had drawn little faces and flowers on it in bright-coloured pens. When had they done that? Where were they now? How long had she been here?

49

Emily scrunched up her eyes and a tear slid down her cheek. She just wanted to see her dad and her girls. She wanted to go home. But where would home be now? There was no way she was going back to that squat brick house in Brigalow she had shared with Clancy. No, she thought, home was one hundred and fifty kilometres away from there. Home was Dargo. But not just Dargo. The Dargo High Plains.

As she stared at the back of her hand, Emily thought of the mountains shown to her in that strange vision. Her little finger became the Long Spur, her ring finger with the plain gold wedding band became the main Dargo Spur. Her middle finger, the one she liked to raise at Clancy's back, was the White Timber Spur. Her index finger, which she also used to point at him accusingly, was the Table Spur, and her thumb the Blue Rag Range. The back of her hand was the Dargo High Plains, where the Flanaghan homestead nestled on sub-alpine meadows, surrounded by a screen of white-grey snow gums. Her whole beloved mountain run was mapped out on her hand. Gingerly she lifted it further to scratch her scalp that itched and burned. She was shocked when her fingertips met with the short tufts that stuck up at all angles. My hair! she thought. They've cut my hair! But then she remembered . . .

It was the day before the Cattlemen's Cup. She had been sitting on the edge of their marital bed, gazing at herself in the mirror, waiting for Clancy to come back from his truck run and take them away for the weekend. Her long dark hair looked lank and greasy, even after a wash. Her jeans felt too tight and her tummy rolled over the top of her leather belt.

She poked at the fat roll with her finger.

'That's no muffin top,' she said to herself. 'It's more like a bloody double-sponge cake.'

She looked about the room, bored with it. She'd slept here every night for six years but it had never felt like home. The bedspread fell neatly to the clean carpet, a clock that had been a wedding present, ticked in a civilised fashion beside the bed. Stacked on her side were Hereford cattle and Australian stock horse magazines. On Clancy's side were truck mags on top of a stack of girlie mags, featuring rank-looking, under-nourished women with huge breasts and no class. A tacky, tempting headline read, *Boobs Galore*! Emily glanced down at her own breasts which had sustained both her children in the first fifteen months of their lives. Breastfeeding had seemed the most natural course for Emily, but for Clancy it was not. His brain was wired to think tits were for blokes, not children, and he was jealous of the attention Emily gave the girls. Over time, he had stopped touching her. Nowadays he rolled away from her in bed every night, his back like a wall.

She flicked open one of his magazines to see a girl pouting, her lips parted in a suggestive 'O'. Emily looked at the girl's pert, round, surgically enhanced breasts. Her blonde hair tumbled down over her shoulders. She imagined what Clancy did while he was looking at this picture . . . It made Emily shudder. As she flicked through a few more pages a piece of paper fluttered out like a butterfly and landed on the floor.

Emily picked it up. It was a receipt from a truck stop near Brisbane. As she read through the items it became clear that this tiny piece of paper and what was printed on it spelt the end of their marriage. Dinner wasn't the only thing that had been dished up for Clancy that night, a truckie on the long haul. Prostitutes had also been for sale.

Emily's cheeks reddened and she felt she couldn't breathe as she read the bill her husband had clocked up. Room hire and a Cherie Sweetheart Special with doubles, plus extras. Extras? Emily's heart began to race, her skin prickled. She felt like she would throw up. She stared at her own image in the mirror and gritted her teeth, biting back a cry of pain so the girls would not hear. Bastard!

She had long suspected what Clancy got up to on the road. She'd seen the magazines about big rigs, featuring dodgy ads in the back, and part of her had always known. She'd also seen the way her husband was when he was around mates like Mick Parker. They called all women 'birds' and spoke about them as if they were good for only one thing. The sensuality she had once imagined she would find in her marriage was denied her. Emily felt fury course through her then: fury against herself as much as anyone. She had given herself over to Clancy in marriage, given him her body, given him two beautiful children, and given up a cattleman's life – and for what?

Even in that first wave of shock and anger, Emily could admit that, after she became immersed in motherhood, she had gradually withdrawn from Clancy. She believed now that she had suffered from depression.

In the past year, to keep herself cheery and a little sane, her one diversion had been loading up the kids in the stroller and trawling the big ugly shopping centres locally, hunting down amusing underwear for herself. It was also a kind of a test for Clancy, to see how much or how little he noticed her.

In the mornings she'd pull on pink, ruffled undies with cloth cherries hanging from them, or slip on a purple and black pair that read on the front *Enquiries Welcome But Knock before Entering*. Her favourites were the green pair with the slogan *Protected Wilderness Area* in a triangle on the front. Surely the Greenie-hating Clancy would comment on those . . . but not once did he say anything. Not once did he notice. The months wore on. Her silly underpants collection grew and so too did her conviction that her marriage was dying. No wonder he didn't notice her knickers, she thought as she clutched the incriminating receipt in her fist. His mind was on women who were very different from her.

Emily stripped off to her bra and her Kmart 'Bootiliscious' undies, and stood looking furiously at her ridiculous self. Her once work-fit body had softened from motherhood and inactivity. Six years she had been here! It shocked her that the time had closed in on her so fast. In the ever-expanding town of Brigalow she was immersed in a world of washing, daytime TV, and the occasional trip to a bigger town twenty minutes' drive away where she felt stupefied by the shopping centres and suburban ugliness . . . while all the time her husband was off with truckstop whores! For years she'd been living like this – or, rather, dying like it.

Her brilliant stock horse, Snowgum was squashed into a weedy, oily, one-acre block amidst Clancy's truck-trailers. Her highly trained working dog, Rousie, was confined to a kennel in a backyard, listless with no tasks and no view to occupy him. These days both creatures rarely got a glimpse of action on her father's cattle farm. Since the birth of her second child, Meg, Emily had found it too hard to pack them all up – kids, dog and horse – and cart them out to Grandpa's farm. Here, behind the high weatherboard fence and beneath the Hills hoist that seemed to dominate the yard, she felt stifled. Trapped. Like her soul had come unstuck.

Looking in the mirror, noticing her own soft white belly and pudgy arms, Emily was amazed by what she had become. It didn't make sense. In the Flanaghan family women held the same status as the men. Sometimes the Flanaghan women wielded even more clout. They may provide domestically, but they also rode alongside their men, camped out in the mountains, mustered and salted the cattle, and worked the dogs. They were raised that way. The kids were the workforce, whether a boy or girl. There was no room for sexism up in that wild mountain world; everyone had to be capable, everyone respected as equal. But in Clancy's world women were objectified: sex objects or domestic servants.

Within their marriage, Clancy had never hit Emily with his fists. Instead he subdued her mercilessly with his denigrating words and negative energy. *Stupid woman. Fat hag. Surly bitch. Nag.* When he talked to his mates he called her 'The Missus' or 'The Boss', and he talked about her in front of her as if she wasn't there. Words as sharp as arrows that stuck, barbed, in her skin.

The Emily Flanaghan who had smiled readily, laughed loudly, galloped horses, cut out cattle and chainsawed fence posts had gone. But, looking into her own eyes in the mirror, Emily vowed that this weekend, at the Mountain Cattlemen's

Cup, she would find that girl again. She tossed the receipt into the rubbish.

'Stuff you, Clancy,' she said. 'You won't beat me.' But even as she said it, she wondered how on earth she could ever win in this mess of a marriage. She rummaged in the bedside drawer, pulled out the scissors. Crying silently, Emily began to hack away her long dark hair.

Nine

Luke Bradshaw checked his watch. He was early. He combed his long, curly hair behind his ears and inspected his face in the rear-view mirror. He'd wanted to cut his hair before the job interview, but Cassy had told him not to.

'Keep your locks. It's an official government position. The more indigenous you look, the better,' she had said as she lay naked on their bed, watching him dress.

Luke glanced up now at the tall, sleek building with the striking green logo that someone had no doubt been paid a squillion to design. He got out to feed coins to the parking meter and, as he did, watched the government staff slot their cars into their allocated spaces and bustle into work. They all looked like fairly down-to-earth types, and their cars were middle-of-the-range. Nothing too flash. Still, Luke wondered whether he'd fit in here, raised by a farming father who was far from approving of the bureaucrats – what farmer was? But if this job was his ticket-of-leave out of Melbourne, he'd be happy. Besides, he'd love to see his father's face if he did get a government job. Giving his dad the shits would be icing on the cake. Pissing his father off was one of the reasons he'd done the Environmental Management degree in the first place. What else did the old prick expect, Luke thought bitterly, selling off the farm like that without any kind of consultation?

A brand-new white diesel Land Cruiser chugging into the car park caught Luke's eye. It was really flash. It had a snorkel for river crossings, electric winch, automatic diff-locks, and, judging from the aerials, three different styles of radio and satellite communication wired into it. The driver had obviously just driven it through the car wash and the bright green logo on the door was slick and shiny.

Luke watched the skinny, ginger-haired man at the wheel steer the cruiser to the spot nearest the building. He reached into the back seat to grab his briefcase, then hit the auto-lock button on the key ring. The cruiser made a little *peeyou-peeyou* noise, like a bird, and flashed its indicators twice. That man clearly loved his new government four-wheel drive, Luke thought. He found it funny that the man had parked in the head sherang's spot in the middle of a dirty great city, yet was dressed in khaki shirt and shorts and lace-up boots as if he were going bushwalking with Bindi the Jungle Girl.

Luke checked his watch again and decided to go in. He caught a glimpse of himself in the glass of the automatic sliding doors as he followed the man into the government office building. His long hair, combed back Antonio Banderas-style, looked slightly at odds with the grey suit and red tie he'd dragged out of the cupboard, worn once previously to his grandmother's funeral. All he had to wear with the suit were his Blundstone boots. He felt like a dork. At least the boots were polished to shining, he thought.

In the air-conditioned cool of the foyer, Luke offered up a smile to the girl behind the desk, but she was already busy with the man who'd walked in moments earlier. Luke stood politely to one side, pretending to browse the brochures on the desk advertising how well the government was doing in all areas.

'Good morning, Giles,' she said brightly to the Land Cruiser guy. 'I believe you're walking a different track today.' She gathered up a bundle of mail and newspapers and passed it over to him. 'Down the corridor. First door on the right, I believe,' she said with a wink.

'Yes, Kylie, a new track. A new track. Thank you.'

'Congratulations,' she said.

As Giles made his way along the corridor, Kylie shifted her gaze from to Luke.

'Yes? Can I help you?'

After signing in, he looked at the slip of paper handed to him. It bore the same flashy logo as the building itself. The fine print asked him to observe all safety signage and occupational health and safety requirements, and told him to follow the instructions of the fire wardens or management in the event of fire or emergency. He smiled to himself. The wording was so 'government'. If he got the job, he knew there was an entire different language within these walls he'd need to learn. He clipped his security pass to his jacket and waited to be ushered along the hall by Kylie, who, once walking and talking, didn't pause to draw breath. She clearly relished her job.

'This is the first time Giles . . . er, Mr Grimsley . . . has been in his brand-new office with his brand-new title of acting region manager for the VPP within the DLSC&EL,' she said, looking at Luke expectantly, as if waiting for him to become as excited as she clearly was.

'He's taken over from Ted Deagan, who's away on long service. Giles may seem a little distracted this morning as he hasn't had time to unpack. Human Resources stuffed up the advertising dates and got you in a week too soon, but you and he will be fine. Normally we have a panel, so you're getting off lightly.'

Luke nodded at Kylie's monologue as she guided him along corridors and past offices that were as yet empty but would soon slowly fill up with the less-punctual staff.

'It's great to see Giles step up a notch. He's been dedicated to his job forever. I think he's had over thirty years in the department. No wonder they gave him a new work vehicle, even if it's just for a short time while Ted's away.'

'Will he ever get to drive it on dirt?' Luke asked quickly.

'Sorry?'

'Will he get out with it much?'

'Oh, no. Ted spends ninety per cent of his time in the office, but every region manager is entitled to a vehicle, aren't they? Now that Giles is acting region manager for the Victorian People's Parklands as part of the Department of Land Sustainment, Conservation and Environmental Longevity, he automatically gets a vehicle and a mobile phone.'

'Oh, I see,' said Luke, not seeing at all.

When they arrived at Giles's new office Luke was ushered in front of the man he'd seen get out of the new Land Cruiser in the car park.

'Our job applicant,' Kylie announced brightly, offering Luke a chair in front of the desk.

Giles Grimsley eyed the strikingly handsome young man before him as he shuffled through his application form.

'I note you ticked yes when asked if you were of Aboriginal or Torres Strait descent. Where are your people from?'

'Well, it's just a dash of indigenous blood,' Luke said, blushing, 'on my grandmother's side. She was originally from the East Gippsland region, but I don't have any contacts there.'

Giles nodded, sliding his glasses on to the end of his nose.

'That's good. We need people with a connection to the land.'

'Yes, it's something I've lost since Dad sold the farm.'

'Oh, I don't mean a farming connection. I mean a spiritual one.'

'I see,' Luke said, a little perplexed by Giles's implication.

'Yes, I read in your application that your father grew wheat and raised sheep, but the farm is now sold. A sensible move, given that our arid land is not suited to those pursuits.'

Luke nodded, wondering if he should mention that most of the land had gone into government-supported pine and blue gum production that would rob the soil more than their farming ever had. He decided not to.

'I think my very practical upbringing will stand me in good stead for a job as a remote ranger,' he said instead.

'Yes, but agriculture is so simple compared to the job we do. Your father was only managing a small area. Our department manages a vast expanse, backed up by scientific knowhow. Not exactly farming, is it?'

Luke was about to point out that they had used science extensively in their farming practice but Giles continued, 'I remember being like you. Coming in to apply for a job as a ranger. I thought it was so simple. I was a wide-eyed Melbourne lad, seeking *Boy's Own* adventures in the bush!' He laughed at the memory, then leant forward and laced his fingers together, resting his elbows on the desk. While his blue eyes looked directly at Luke, his attention seemed to drift far away.

'Of course, I had many hours' practical experience in the bush. I'd bushwalked, backpacked, camped in huts and skied all my life – well, at least in school holidays. And when I was a young uni student, I had a bit of the daredevil in me. I had a stint riding motocross bikes in the bush until I broke my leg coming off on a sharp bend in the Licola Mountains. Oh, crazy times! In fact,' he said, snorting with laughter, 'I sat my Biological Diversity exams with my plastered leg propped up on a chair! The examination supervisors had to check that none of the signatures on it held cryptic answers to the paper.' He was chuckling aloud now. Luke wondered if the man was socially inept or just a complete nerd.

'As a young bloke I loved to escape the city and get back to nature, so it was no surprise to anyone that when I finished my science degree I joined the government VPP service.'

'No surprise at all,' chimed in Luke, almost feeling sorry for this man who had clearly never conducted a job interview in his life before and hadn't even had time to move into his new office. Still, he earned points for conviction in his own cause, Luke decided.

'I've devoted all of my working life to the thousands of

hectares of natural bushland managed by the DLSC&EL,' Giles proclaimed proudly. 'Although the department wasn't called that back when I started.'

'Oh?' said Luke.

'Yes, back then it was the Land and Forestry Department. The land was measured in acres, and the vehicles were pretty rough. You don't mind roughing it, do you?'

'Me?' said Luke. 'Not a bit. I love sleeping out.'

'Well, you would, with your Aboriginal heritage. You know the place you're going is pretty remote? We've advertised the job internally for weeks, but so far no one within the department has applied.'

'Really?' said Luke, amazed.

'Oh, don't let that put you off. I can see why people don't want to move that far into the bush – especially family men. You'll be working alone mostly, and Dargo can be a hostile township . . . full of shooters, loggers and rather aggressive cattlemen. The social life is zero for young people living there, and the small school would probably be inadequate by the standards of governmental employees with families. It's good to have a young single man apply. You *are* single?'

Luke swallowed. 'Yes.'

But Giles was already standing up to look at the map on the wall, his mind on another tack. 'It's a big and complex job.' He pointed to the map with his pen, as if giving a geography lecture. 'The Alpine Park territory is some 465,000 hectares.' He ran his finger down the straight angular lines that divided Park from Government Forestry land and private holding. Luke looked at the dark shading of the township of Dargo, and the massive expanse of mountain country rising from its fringes. It was out in woop woop, but that made it all the more appealing to him. Luke was glad they'd had a hard time filling the position – he couldn't care less if Dargo was a redneck town.

'If you do get the job, Mr Bradshaw, I'm sure you'll come to share my approach to the principles and values of conservation. You'll also need to learn how to cope with the some-times dangerous job of ranger. Basically you're doing the job of a policeman, but without the uniform to confer the same level of authority. We also advise rangers not to become involved with the local community. Given the heated debate currently raging over alpine grazing, it would be best for you to steer clear of the locals, especially the cattlemen.'

He pushed that day's newspaper forward on the desk and Luke read the headline: *Grazing Bans on Political Agenda*. Within the text of the story was a short boxed paragraph. He looked at it with interest: *Bush Rider Still Critical*. Giles stabbed his finger at the articles and shook his head.

'The people that irritate me most in this world are these damn mountain cattlemen. I've spent my entire career trying to oust them from their grazing runs. They profess to be the true conservationists,' he scoffed, 'but that's a ridiculous notion, of course. All it's about for them is making money. They don't care for the integrity of the high country. How could bushmen like them hope to disprove what science has shown? That grazing and annual burning off are detrimental to the fragile, natural ecology of the alpine region!'

Luke thought of the girl who'd been injured on her horse and shifted in his seat uncomfortably, but Giles failed to notice. He was clearly relishing having a captive audience. 'It's only a matter of time before the government, based on this depart-ment's recommendations, passes legislation that will rescind grazing licences in all the alpine regions. Perhaps this acci-dent will spell an end to the ridiculous get-togethers they insist on having every year in remote mountain areas, too. Surely the OH&S and insurance costs should by now be making these events prohibitive to stage, not to mention the environmental damage they inflict upon the land.'

Luke nodded as if in agreement.

'Yes,' Giles ran on, 'the cattlemen have caused me nothing but headaches. The day grazing is banned from the high

country will be a happy, happy day for me. And it's coming
. . . soon.'

Giles Grimsley huffed to himself as he stood up, grabbing his cup.

'Coffee?' he asked Luke.

'No, thanks.'

'Ha!' Giles laughed. 'No coffee? You're definitely the man for the job. Finding good coffee at Dargo would be like finding hen's teeth. Oh, what am I doing? I'm the acting manager! I don't have to get my own drinks.' He buzzed Kylie.

Smiling at Luke, he said, 'You could get to the top of the tree one day like me, son. If you work hard.'

As he continued his monologue Luke glanced again at the newspaper article and wondered what 'critical condition' meant. Would the cattleman's daughter make it through, or die, or perhaps be hideously injured for life? He felt sorry for her, whoever she was. But his wandering mind was jolted back on track when Giles abruptly perched himself on the edge of the desk in front of him.

'I like you, Luke Bradshaw. Of course there'll have to be a formal offer, but I think you're the perfect man for the job. What do you say?'

Ten

'Congratulations!' The pint sized Indian doctor was beaming as he sailed into Emily's room, white coat billowing behind him. 'You've been moved off our critical list and you can now vamoose from ICU on to the regular ward.'

For days, Emily had felt like a pilot flying on the brink of disaster. Now, at last, she was being told it was safe to land. She'd been in this same room, this same bed, for ten days now – five of them conscious, all of them Hell. She was going insane from the horror of this place, as she heard the constant drama of new arrivals in the corridors and caught glimpses of the strained faces of people ushering in the seriously ill or injured.

She was also driven insane by the pain in her ribs, her back, her head, her everything. But her internal mind games over Clancy were just as painful, as was the ache inside her every time she missed her girls. Clancy had not once been in to see her since she'd regained consciousness. Thank God, she thought, but at the same time, *what a bastard!* She was exasperated by his cruelty in keeping her girls from her for this long. She knew Rod and Flo were holding back the truth from her, constantly saying Clancy would be in with the kids soon. While Emily begged them to bring the girls instead, they tried to distract her with descriptions of Snowgum's recovery, but she could not be swayed from her distress. She'd spoken to her daughters and husband a couple of times on the phone, a nurse holding the receiver up to her ear. Each time Clancy would say he'd bring them in the morning, but they'd never show.

Even Mick Parker had shuffled in to see her, all sheepish and clean-shaven, to give her some rather plucked-at grapes and his apology for riding into her. When she'd asked him about Clancy and the kids, he'd just shrugged and said he hadn't seen them about.

'Can't I just go home?' Emily begged the doctor now, thinking of the chaotic conditions the girls must be enduring under Clancy's so-called care.

The doctor shook his head. 'Not yet, my dear. A few more weeks.'

'Weeks!'

'Your injuries were significant,' the doctor said, without looking up from his clipboard.

She thought about asking him for a transfer to the bush hospital at Dargo but for some reason, one she couldn't place, found she didn't like that idea. Emily looked dejected as the doctor signed some paperwork and handed it to a nurse.

'Come on! Don't look so down,' he said. 'Rumour has it your beautiful girls and handsome husband are in the building, on their way to see you. You've plenty to smile about.'

He exited the room as quickly as he'd entered, and Emily was left bracing herself. Clancy? Here? With the girls? How wonderful to see them! But how could she tell him it was over with their daughters right there? But how could she wait? She couldn't bear to think of life going on as it had done before the accident.

And suddenly they were there. Meg looked like a rainbow hippy angel, dressed in every colourful item she could find to wear. A tiara, blue sunglasses, purple fairy wings, big green beads strung about her neck. Not just one but two fairy dresses in yellow and pink, layered over a striped top and, of course, riding boots teamed with lolly-leg stockings. Tilly had dressed in a Batman suit complete with foam chest muscles, mask and cape plus a string of fake pearls.

Standing tall behind them was Clancy, apprehension visible on his face. Both girls were hovering in the doorway too, looking fearful, but their expressions changed to delight the moment Emily pulled herself up using a bar hanging above her and beamed at them, calling out, 'Hello!'

'Mummy!' shrilled Tilly, and both girls ran to her, clambering up on the bed and covering her with kisses, the collection of drawings they'd brought for her getting scrunched and torn in the process

'Ow, ow, ow!' said Emily. 'Careful. Shift your leg, Matilda. Gently! Mum's a bit sore. Oh, my girls! My little legends!'

'Don't worry, Mummy! I will save you,' Tilly said in a Batman voice.

'G'day,' said Clancy, shuffling forward.

Emily shot him a quick look.

'About time you brought them in. What took you so long?'

'You try doing everything at home!' he protested.

Not wanting to head straight down the squabbling path with him, Emily focused her attention on the girls. She couldn't stop stroking their hair, drinking in their scent, hugging them as tightly as she could through the pain of her injuries. She felt tears rise in her eyes realising the gift she had in holding them again. How close she had come to surrendering this joy for ever. The thought of them travelling through life without her was unbearable. She had endured a motherless childhood herself, grateful for Flo but always with such a void in her life.

'Daddy let us dress ourselves,' Meg explained.

'Yes. I can tell.'

Emily kept asking them questions about Rousie and what they'd been doing, and the girls fired questions back about the needles in the back of her hand and the machines.

Clancy remained hovering a short distance away, wearing

the same checked shirt she'd ironed for him before the Cattlemen's. It had been washed since but was crinkled, the chest pockets turning up unevenly, like a pup with one ear up, one ear down. He was as good-looking as ever, more so with a new haircut, but his physical beauty, his presence here in the room, moved nothing in Emily. Nothing.

'Mummy, we seen a cupboard with food in it out there!' Meg said, tugging on her lolly-striped tights.

'You *saw* a cupboard? Really? Oh, you mean a vending machine.'

'Yes,' Meg said.

'Have you any money?' Emily asked Clancy. He frowned. 'What for?'

She remembered how she hated that about him. His inability to nut out the bleeding obvious. She inclined her head towards the girls.

'For the vending machine.'

'Why? They ate a heap of stuff on the way down.'

'Couldn't you go help get them something so they can sit and eat it in the corridor?' Emily could hear the tone she always used when talking to her husband. Impatient, annoyed, frustrated. She loathed herself for it.

'We need some time alone. We need to talk,' she told him, trying to soften her voice. She knew they were the words he most hated to hear.

'*Talk?*'

'Yes, talk, Clancy. About us.' She cast him a look of such distress he knew not to squabble any further but dug his big square hands into his pockets.

'C'mon, rug rats, let's go to the food machine.'

Meg and Tilly danced around their father, giggling.

In the corridor he tried to block out the thought that he was being gutless. On the day of Emily's accident he vowed he would change. Kneeling before her body the last time he was in this place, he'd whispered to her that he'd be a good man. A good husband and father. He'd stay by her bed night and day, book a place in Melbourne, find a babysitter and bring the girls in to see her every afternoon. He'd even stop fooling around on the side. And give up Penny. But the moment he'd stood up from declaring his intentions, his resolution had wavered. He'd always hated hospitals.

Instead, he'd run. He'd bundled the girls on to the train despite their tantrums and left Rod and Flo to do the bedside thing with Em. He'd told the old man that a hospital was no place for kids. Through gritted teeth Rod had agreed, but Clancy knew the old man considered him spineless. Knew that he was really leaving because he was scared. He was leaving because he had forgotten all the reasons he'd married Emily in the first place.

In a fit of depression, Clancy had hidden away at home. Rod and Flo had called round daily and, like a dog at the front gate, he'd barked at them to steer clear of him and the kids. He'd said he'd take them back to Melbourne when he was good and ready. All he felt now was anger and bitterness towards Emily for busting herself up and leaving him to deal with the girls while the trucks sat idle. He began to feel that fury extend towards her family, too, who'd always looked at him as if he were useless.

Drinking beers at lunchtime, texting Penny constantly and yelling at the girls when they wouldn't let him watch the cricket ahead of *Play School*, Clancy began to weaken in his resolve to hang on to the kids and keep them away from the Flanaghans. His week home alone being 'kitchen bitch' to his kids was the worst he'd ever spent.

If it hadn't been for Penny and her phone calls and texts, he would have gone nuts, punched the walls out or shot Emily's barking bloody dog. Even though Penny refused to come to him while the girls were there she'd sent him photos on his phone of her pretty little tits, just to cheer him up. Clancy decided he really liked her. A lot. She was fun. He'd even, in a moment of drunken weakness, thought about telling her he loved her. But then Emily and the kids would come stomping back into his mind along with the blurry memory of what he'd done the night before the Cattleman's race, the guilt he still felt over it fizzing around his head like a rocket.

As he fished about for coins and put them in the vending machine he wondered why, of all times, he was thinking about Penny now when he should be thinking of his wife, back there looking like crap in her hospital bed. Emily would never send him a picture of her tits, Clancy thought sullenly.

'I want the purple chips! I want the purple chips!' screamed Meg, while Tilly said over and over, 'Chocolate!' Both girls bounced up and down on the spot.

'Shut up!' he said so loudly that an elderly woman passing by with a bunch of flowers cast him a dour look.

'Just give me a minute,' he added more calmly.

'Hurry up, Daddy, with the venting machine!' Tilly shouted. God, he thought, he just wanted out. To be out of here, back in his truck. Off somewhere. Anywhere but here.

As Emily waited for Clancy's return despair swamped her. She knew he loved his girls in his own way, and here she was about to break up their family – no matter how fragmented that family had become. Would separation be too hard on the girls? she wondered. Was it the right thing to do? Should she stay with Clancy and give him another chance? Perhaps if they went to counselling they could learn to love each other again. She needed answers, feeling utterly lost.

She fanned Meg's and Tilly's drawings out across the bed, looking at them closely for the first time. Matilda had painted a picture of Mummy and her horse. Snowgum had bandages around her legs and head. Emily grimaced before shuffling to the next one in the pile. This was by Meg and it pulled Emily up short. Her hand flew to her mouth as she stared at the picture.

It was a drawing of a house – but not just any house. This was a hut with a crude chimney, just like the one in her dream. Meg had drawn trees too, lots of them, and amongst the clumsy crayon slashes was the outline of a woman with her grey hair worn in a bun. She was wearing a long dark dress. Above the hut was an angel. She had short dark hair like Emily. Beside her was a horse that had wings too. A grey horse with a smoky tail. It was all there on the page. Meg had depicted her mother's near-death experience. Emily shivered. The mountains, she thought. Once again she was being shown the mountains.

And there in her mind's eye was another home, the original hand-split timber Flanaghan homestead – the one they still stayed in now when they took cattle up to the high country. It had been built as a summer residence for the family while the Mayford hut, long ago, once served as their winter retreat below the snowline in an isolated valley. The billy buttons would be out there in full force, dotting the snow plain meadows like thousands of little yellow fairy lights at dusk. The wild lupins beside the house would be standing tall in a burst of colour, and the old twisted trees in the orchard would be drooping from the weight of tiny, bite-sized fruit. All around, the bush would be alive with summer insects. She could picture her family riding through the groves of lush trees on the south-facing slopes. Bell birds chimed like magic. She could hear the lowing of a mother cow calling up her calf, the clop of the horses' hooves on the gravel track, the sound of the wind high on a mountain ridge . . .

Emily kept her eyes closed.

'Well,' came Clancy's voice, 'I thought you wanted to talk? Meg's almost through her crisps so you'd better spit out what you're gunna say.'

She opened her eyes and looked at him so intently that Clancy took a step back.

'*I know*,' she said, in a voice like a growl.

'What?'

'I know about the truckstops in Brisbane.'

'What are you on about?' he mumbled, the muscles in his jaw jumping, his eyes sliding away from hers.

69

'The girls. Ones you paid for. Hookers.'

Clancy shook his head.

'It was a mate. He went there. I just waited in the truck.'

'Liar.'

He flinched. A blonde nurse with an upturned nose and spectacular breasts came into the ward. Clancy tried to avert his eyes from her, but both Emily and he caught a waft of her perfume. Oblivious to the tension, the nurse moved over to the bed. 'I'm Simone. Once your visitor has gone, I'll be moving you to a new ward.'

'He'll be going very soon,' Emily said coldly. Clancy blew out his breath, knowing he was sprung.

When the nurse was gone, he looked anywhere but into Emily's eyes. She had expected him to yell; expected him to rant at her, but deep down, Clancy Moran knew he had broken their marriage irreparably so he remained silent, his head bowed.

'It's over, Clancy,' Emily said calmly. 'When I get out of here, I'm going home to Dargo. You can keep the house . . . keep everything. But I'm leaving and I'm taking the girls.'

'No,' he said, moving closer to her. He put one hand on her arm and held her wrist firmly. In an instant Emily felt as if she couldn't breathe. A wave of nausea hit as she recalled in a blinding flash her trip through the mountains in an ambulance. It must have been on the way to the heli-pad. But how could she remember it? she reasoned. She was unconscious at the time. Still, in her mind's eye, she saw Penny's gloved hands ripping tubing from medico-packets. She could hear voices around her. Kev in the front, coaching Penny as he drove. A barking, urgent tone coming from the two-way as well. Then Clancy's voice, angry and drunk – too loud in the ambulance. Penny shouting at him to calm down. Then the whispers – about things forbidden, dark secrets that stabbed hurt through her.

Emily shot a look at her husband, her face white.

'You right? You're not gunna puke?' he said, loosening his grip.

Emily swallowed. 'You slept with *her* too.'

'Who?'

'That nurse. In the ambulance.'

'Get a grip,' he said, 'They need to change your medication. What are you on about?'

'I remember! I remember you both talking. You were standing over me . . . talking.' Emily was shaking her head, remembering. She didn't want to recall them, but the images kept coming and she had this strange sense of knowing. The way Clancy's body tensed and his eyes narrowed, she knew it was true. He'd not only been sleeping with prostitutes, he'd been having an affair. And then there was that last night at the Cattlemen's with him . . . She remembered *that*. The room spun around her.

'Get out!'

'Calm down,' he said.

She lowered her tone again.

'*Get. Out.*'

He began to back out of the room.

'You can't take my kids from me,' he blustered.

'After all that you've done, Clancy, yes, I can.'

He jabbed a finger in the air. 'No, you can't! You won't get rid of me that easily.'

'Get out!' she screamed.

'Make me, you stupid bitch!'

'Mummy?' Meg and Tilly stood in the doorway, clutching their junk food. At home, when Clancy raised his voice they would run to Emily and cling to her while he ranted, burying their faces against her. Well, no more, she resolved. No more. She thought of the grey-haired woman on the mountain. She settled her voice down.

'Give your daddy a kiss goodbye and come sit up on the bed with Mummy now.'

'No, Emily,' Clancy said, over their heads.

'Can we stay? In the hospital?' Meg was jumping for joy.

'Can Daddy stay?' asked Tilly.

'No, Daddy can't. But you can. You can help me move wards. Then I'm going to ring Granddad and he'll come get you. You can stay with him again for a while. Give Daddy the holiday he's always wanted.' She said direct to Clancy, with coldness in her voice.

The girls squealed, shutting out the angry undercurrents from the adult world. They kissed their father goodbye, and clambered on to Emily's bed.

'You're not taking them!' he yelled. 'Don't be such a bitch, Emily!'

'Everything all right in here?' The nurse was back.

Clancy glanced from his wife to the nurse. Emily could see the fury in him turn his body rigid as steel. His eye's blazed.

'For fuck's sake, Emily!' he yelled.

'Tell me I don't need to call security, sir,' the nurse said calmly to him.

'Fuck you!' he spat.

'Clancy,' Emily said, gathering the girls to her, feeling as if they were being swallowed up whole, 'please. Just go. Just leave.'

The nurse folded her arms and stood looking at him. With a grunt, he turned and walked away.

Eleven

L uke watched Cassandra drag off the head of her bilby suit
and dump it on the grass.

'You *what*?' she screeched.

He sighed. Cassy, awkward in the bulky suit, tipped herself
sideways so she could sit on the grass in the park. Her bottom
lip began to quiver. Oh, God, Luke thought, panicked. She
was bloody well going to cry! In the two years he'd known
her, he had never seen her cry. He dropped to his knees beside
her and held one worn and threadbare paw. He leant his head
into her shoulder and just for a moment wished the Wildlife
Society would dryclean the bilby suit. It stank of marijuana
and a rank cocktail of hippy, student and backpacker sweat.

'I thought you *wanted* me to be an environmental protector,'
he said.

'Yes,' said Cassandra furiously, 'but not move to the
country!'

'I thought you'd be happy I got the job.'

Cassy was fumbling with her paws for the mobile in her
bag.

'What are you doing?'

'I'm calling Mum.'

'But you haven't spoken to her in two years. You said you
hated your mum.'

She shot him a look. 'Well, at the moment, I hate you more.'

Luke shook his head, suddenly angry. This job in the mountains was going to change his life more than he had thought. She was all bloody talk, this girl. Environmental crusader, his arse.

'Cassy, this is something I really want to do.'

'How could you do this without telling me? Taking off to bloody woop woop.'

'How was I to know they'd offer me the job straight away? C'mon, Cassy, give me a break. It sounds like a really great opportunity. Besides, Dargo's only five or so hours away. Eight hours by a train and bus.'

By now Cassandra was crying.

'C'mon,' Luke soothed. 'You can come up and camp out under the stars with me. Get back to nature. Use your new Trangia.' For a moment Cassy sank into his arms, the bongo drums of the other protesters echoing around them. Sniffing loudly and using the back of her furry paws to wipe her nose clean, she nodded. He could feel her coming round, but in truth now realised that he was longing for a clean break.

'Cassy, please be happy for me. It sounds like a perfect job.'

'But what about me? What about us?'

'Maybe you'll find a job somewhere in the region too? You can fight for all your causes at grassroots level.'

'What?' The frown was back on her face. 'Move out there? But my home is here. In Melbourne. What could I possibly do out there to make a difference when all the lobby groups are based here? Honestly, Luke, you're so bloody stupid. And selfish!' The tears were back too.

Where had she gone? Luke wondered. That fierce, strong young woman who'd fought against everything bad known to man. She was anti-battery-hen, anti-live-export, anti-dairy, anti-meat-eating. He'd loved the way she'd ploughed over ground she knew little about with such complete self-assurance. The people he'd known previously had always been so measured. So polite. Compared to her, so boring. She was rock-solid in her opinions. Unashamed. It had helped him ignore his own uncertainty. His dad had told him, 'There's no future in farming,' and his peers had joked that leaving your farm to your son was a form of child abuse. So he'd set out for the city, with farming in his blood but nothing in his heart to replace it. He'd been lost and adrift in his life. Cassandra had given him something to cling to.

Now, as she buried her face in the bilby suit's head and sobbed, he realised she was lost, too. He made his voice gentle. 'I'm going, Cassy. Whether you like it or not.' She looked small and pathetic slumped there in the ridiculous costume. 'If you love me, and you love the earth, you'll come too,' he said, not at all certain he wanted her to but driven by guilt. He reached out to clutch her paw. Angrily she shook him off.

'If *you* loved *me*, you'd stay!' Then she was up and waddling over to her pushbike. She jammed on her bilby head and awkwardly swung her leg over the bike.

'Cassy!' Luke warned. 'Don't be stupid.'

He couldn't tell what she said back, her words muffled by the bilby head, but with a mighty heave she pushed the pedal down with one oversized foot and steered her way out on to the footpath and away down the street into the traffic.

Twelve

'Hooly dooly!' said Emily as she watched a girl wearing what looked like a rat suit sitting up in the back of an ambulance that had just arrived at the hospital. Through the open doors Emily could see she had a near-shaven head, numerous piercings, and that one of her legs had an inflatable splint on it like a giant floatie. She was yelling into a mobile, 'Trust you to have your phone off. When you get this, get your arse to the hospital. *Now!*'

This place was a madhouse, Emily thought. She had to get out of here! For the past couple of weeks she'd endured the uneasy rhythms of hospital life along with sudden shrieks of pain from her body if she moved too suddenly or even coughed. The mood of her day was dictated by which nurse was on duty, or if the girls were to visit, or by the crushing pain that lingered with varying intensity in her neck and shoulders.

A run of days without the sunshine or her daughters flooding into her room, combined with a grumpy, unfriendly nurse tugging at her sheets, left her feeling desperate, as if her life would never again return to normal. But what was normal now? For the first week since Clancy had left, he had phoned the hospital daily, wanting to speak to her. Emily had gently coached the nurses to feed him a range of excuses on her behalf. She was being bathed . . . she was sleeping . . . she was with the doctor. When she did eventually speak to him he didn't have anything to say and all she could hear was his heavy breathing like a grumpy bull's on the other end of the line.

Once he'd turned up in her room, looking out sheepishly from behind a big bunch of carnations. Emily hated carnations. But she hated Clancy's insincerity even more. She could tell his decision to win her back had only been taken half-heartedly. One stiff comment from her was enough to bring all his anger and resentment bubbling out again, showing her clearly that their marriage was broken for good.

Instead of talking and working out a way forward, the gulf of silence between them shouted more loudly than words that this really was the end. Emily sat and cried silently in her bed wearing a hideous floral nightie that Flo had bought her from Big W, while he sat staring mutely at the wall in a ridiculously low chair that forced his knees up level with his ears.

'So that's it then, is it?' he said at last, heaving himself up from the chair.

'Yes, I suppose it really is,' Emily answered. Then he left.

But since that day she had vowed that she and the girls would grab at this new beginning. She would heal herself as fast as she could, just to be with them.

She began to make herself walk laps outside the hospital no matter how much her bruised body complained. It was hard to get her breath, her collarbone ached, and her broken arm, strapped across her body, dragged her down like an old widow with a curved spine.

She spent the drawn-out minutes of her day trying to come to terms with a new version of herself. Single mum. Separated. Divorcee-to-be. None of the words reflected the depth of fear she felt about her future and her sense of loss, nor did they capture the fleeting moments of excitement she felt despite these.

Emily craved fresh air and sunshine, but it was debatable

how fresh the air was in this big city and sometimes walking outside made her feel more depressed. She had to hold her breath each time she walked past the cluster of smokers hanging about the front door. Patients in pyjamas trailing drip stands as they hoovered on their fags. Even nurses and other hospital staff loomed around ashtrays, sucking the life out of cigarettes.

Today she'd bypassed the smokers' area and walked a little further, to the hospital's emergency entrance. Her bones ached, her muscles were tender, and her skin was blooming with bruises in an ever-changing palette of colours from black to purple, brown to yellow, gradually fading. Ever so gradually. Each time she lost her breath, the earth beneath her feet swayed and her vision was obscured momentarily by tiny pinpricks of light.

Today the filter of sunshine through the smog was almost beautiful, so she delayed going back inside. Emily leant on a wall near the ambulance and watched the medico trying to pacify the costumed girl, who was surely on drugs or else plain nuts.

'Now, you just sit back there, darling,' said the officer, 'while we get you into the hospital and nice and comfy. They'll take you for X-rays first.'

Through gritted teeth the girl said, 'The Wildlife Society will be billing you for the suit.'

'I had to cut it. You can't be too careful with suspected breaks,' the officer said wearily. 'Besides, that rat suit has definitely seen better days. You could do with a new one.'

'Rat?' said the girl horrified. 'It's a *bilby*. A sacred animal.'

The medico clunked the trolley down from the ambulance with a thud.

'Ouch! Careful,' she said.

'Sorry, darls.' He spun the trolley bed about and fixed her with his dark eyes. 'It looks like a rat to me.'

'The bilby is a threatened species sacred to the Anangu people and it needs protecting,' she said, crossing her furry arms over her bilby belly and jutting out her chin.

'Really?' said the ambo flatly.

'That's the problem with this world!' the girl yelled. 'People like you, who don't care! What sort of patient treatment is this anyway?'

Emily could see the ambo was really annoyed by now. He folded his arms across his chest, matching the girl's body language, and tilted his head towards her as he spoke. 'You want me to go out to the Tanami Desert, do you, darlin', for the little bilby? Plant some habitat for him? Or maybe you think dressing up like a rat and riding a bike through peak hour is making all the difference? Makes sense to me!' He struck his forehead with the heel of his hand, then reached into the back of the ambulance and tucked the head of the costume under his arm. 'You can hardly count that as a helmet, Missy,' he said. 'And it sure does look like a rat.'

'Don't you Missy me. It's Mzzz. And for the last time – it's a bilby!' the girl said emphatically, before turning her angry gaze towards Emily. 'And what are you smirking at? I'm in pain here.'

'Oh, I can see that,' said Emily. 'Lucky you're not a horse. They would have put you down. At least you can be thankful that the staff here are great. You'll be right.' The ambulance officer gave her a wink, and she smiled and began walking back through the hospital gardens, wanting to be away from this place more than ever.

A while later, Emily sat sunning herself on a bench beneath a beautiful white-trunked gum. In her pocket her fingertips touched the folded painting that Meg and Tilly had brought her from Dargo. There was also a photo of Snowgum, out of the shed for the first time since the accident, picking at the green grass of Tranquillity's lawn. Just feeling these items made tears well in Emily's eyes for the misery of this separation.

She tilted her head to look up at the gum tree, and for the umpteenth time thanked God, or whoever it was out there beyond the treetops, for sparing her life. Then she added: But *please* hurry me home to my family and a new life!

It was during this impromptu prayer that she first saw him – a dark-haired man, of about her own age, in an old Datsun. She watched him driving past in his noisy, beaten up car several times as he tried, without success, to find a space. There was something about him that drew her attention and held it. She didn't know what it was.

Eventually he skilfully reverse-parked across the road and came jogging over to the hospital, weaving his way through traffic. He wore faded denim jeans low on his hips, and an olive green T-shirt with the slogan *Save the Tarkine Wilderness* was rolled up at the sleeves to reveal perfectly formed biceps. His Blundstone boots were city-clean, and the thin leather bracelet on his wrist gave him an aura of cool. His longish hair was a rich mass of black curls and framed a manly, clean-shaven face. His large eyes were the colour of dark chocolate. He caught Emily watching him and flashed her a smile. It wasn't vain or flirty. Just friendly. She looked away, embarrassed, but he kept jogging towards her.

'Excuse me,' he said, 'which way to Emergency?' Emily pointed. 'Thanks,' he said, and she watched his broad shoulders and narrow backside as he jogged away from her.

She tilted back her head and looked up at the leaves above her again. She was amazed by the way this grand gum tree had survived, squashed as it was into this concrete-covered landscape. Beneath the city's crust, the tree must have found some generous soil to sustain it.

Emily thought she needed to be strong, just like the tree, though she was in a place that lacked the essence of what the bush brought to her soul. She shut her eyes, wondering why she was even thinking such things. She wasn't usually one to sit and ponder. The accident had changed her somehow; she wasn't sure how she fitted inside her old skin. Eyes still shut, she reached into her dressing-gown pocket and pulled out Meg's drawing of the woman at the hut.

'Excuse me,' came a voice, gentle enough not to startle her. She turned and saw that the good-looking man was back.

'Mind if I sit here for a bit? Hate hospitals.' He shivered.

'Sure,' Emily said, smiling self-consciously and dragging her dressing gown over her cow-print shortie pyjamas with her good arm. She pulled her feet in under the bench, shy that she was wearing R. M. Williams dress boots with no socks, the only footwear her family had thought to pack her, along with the worst of her collection of stupid undies. She looked away, up at the blue sky beyond the tree, noticing a puff of white cloud shaped like a horse. She wasn't sure what to say.

The man inclined his head towards the hospital. 'My girl-friend . . .' he began. Phew! thought Emily. That eased the tension. At least he wasn't some kind of pervert '. . . got hit by a bus, on her bike.'

'Oh, that's terrible. I'm sorry.'

He shook his head. 'Oh, luckily it wasn't anything serious. It would've been much worse if she .hadn't had all that padding. They've done X-rays. Just a fracture in her foot. They're plastering her up now. She'll be out soon. She told me to wait outside.'

Emily frowned at his comments. What an arsehole! she thought. How mean he was to talk about his girlfriend's extra padding like that. 'How about you? It looks like you've had a rough ride.' He pointed to the arm that hung heavily across her chest in a sling.

'Me? Yeah. Horse accident.'

'Ouch.'

Emily nodded and with sarcasm in her tone added, 'Luckily I have a bit of padding too, or so my husband liked to remind me. So I lived.'

The man looked puzzled then asked, 'How long have you been in hospital?'

'I was kept unconscious for the first five days. I'm going into my third week awake, although it's felt like fifty, and now they're saying I have to stay longer, worse luck.'

'So it was pretty serious then?'

'They tell me I'm lucky to be alive. And so is my horse.'

A glimmer of something passed over the man's face.

'Hey,' he said gently, 'you're not the girl I read about in the paper, are you? The one from the cattlemen's race?'

Emily smiled in surprise, half-turning to face him.

'Yeah. That's me.'

'Wow!' said Luke. 'How amazing is that? I've been thinking about you.'

'You have?' she said, thinking how lovely he looked, but at the same time perplexed by him.

'I dunno why. It was just one of those snippets you read about that sticks with you. I suppose I just wondered how you'd got on.'

'Well, here I am.'

'Here you are! That's great. That's really great. I'm rapt to see you alive and well.'

He was looking at her fully now, taking in her pretty smile and stunning dark-brown eyes with long curled-up lashes. Emily stared back at him. He really was rapt to discover she was okay. For a moment she felt a jolt of delight. Then, just as suddenly, a wave of self-consciousness. They both laughed nervously.

He looked down at the drawing in her hands.

'Are you an artist?'

Emily laughed. 'No. But my daughter is.'

'Oh, good! If you'd done that, you'd be crap, but seeing as your daughter did it, it's great. She's got talent. Is that your home?'

'Sort of,' Emily replied.

'Just the one kid?'

'I have another little girl.'

'Two girls. Nice.'

They both fell silent. Nothing more to say then. She glanced back up at the tree. The man was about to speak again when they heard someone calling.

'Luuuuke!'

82

He jumped in his seat and looked around. Emily turned to see a skinny girl, wearing shorts and a singlet, being helped through the sliding doors on crutches by a nurse, who was also carrying a large bag with a rat's head sticking out of it.

'That's her. Gotta go,' said Luke. He sprang up and walked backwards over the small patch of lawn. 'Nice to sort of meet you.' He shot Emily another heart-melting smile and then he was gone.

'Hooly dooly,' Emily said again. His girlfriend was Ratgirl. Her costume was the 'padding' he'd been talking about. She smiled as she walked back towards the hospital.

That night, Emily woke suddenly without knowing why. She propped herself up and looked around the darkened ward. Light from the corridor spilled a slanted rectangle over the floor. She glanced at the clock. It was eleven p.m.

'Bloody oath,' she said, sinking back into the bed. If the days were long at the hospital, the nights were worse. In the silent eerie space of the night, Emily saw the hut on the high plains and again felt the call of the land itself. She didn't even have to be asleep for the visions to come. What did it all mean? she wondered. Why did she keep recalling the face of the old woman in her dreams? Why hadn't she seen her own mother, Susie, when she had hovered there in the ether between life and death? She just wanted her life to get back to normal.

'Hurry up and heal,' she muttered now, looking down at her own body. Then she heard a noise, a shuffling sound, that she was sure came from beneath her bed.

'Hello?' she said nervously.

'Shhh!' It was a voice in the darkness, directly beneath her.

'Holy fuck!' said Emily, grappling for her light switch, the nurse's button, anything.

'No, no, no, you don't!' A man's hand reached up from beneath the bed and grabbed hers. 'Don't let anyone know I'm here!' She heard a familiar chuckle.

'Sam?' she breathed. 'Sam? Is that you? What the . . .'

With a clatter and a clank, her brother emerged from under her bed clutching a pillow and a hospital blanket.

'Sam! What are you doing here?'

Just seeing him caused emotion to well up within her. Emily flung out her arms as best she could and he fell into them as gently as he could. She took in the smell of him. A mix of hard booze and wacky baccy, with that same underlying smell that was his alone. Her brother.

With a sense of shock Sam took in how frail she looked. How haunted her eyes seemed. And her beautiful hair, that had always been long, was all gone. She looked weakened, broken, and Sam felt for her. Still she let out another squeal of delight.

'Shhh! Shhhh! I'm on the run from the law, sis. Keep a lid on it,' he said in a dreadful phoney Nashville accent.

'Oh, Sam, you big dumb idiot.' They were hugging, giggling and crying all at once. 'I thought you were in the States. Dad's been trying to ring you!'

'Got myself in a spot of bother. Busted. But it's sorted now.'

'Busted! Sam! For drugs?'

Sam shrugged and swiped his hand down over his face.

'You know, just weed. But Ike smoothed it all over. It's all cool. No biggy. They held up my passport for a time but I eventually got it back.'

'Sam!'

'At least I got home to make sure my big sis was okay. I like the butch look,' he said, ruffling her hair.

'Shut up,' she said. They fell silent.

'I thought I'd never see you again,' said Sam eventually, giving her hand a squeeze. They sat silently contemplating how it could have been. Sam back for a funeral, not a reunion.

Emily held him at arm's length and took in the prison-style buzz cut, so different from the last time she'd seen him with his sandy-blond hair all long and floppy. She saw he was still boyishly handsome with his five o'clock shadow and cute heart-shaped face, a mirror of her own. His jawline was fringed with dark stubble. He still had that cheeky smile that turned up at one side, and blue-green eyes like the sea on a mild day.

He was wearing the coolest tan cowboy boots, unpolished and scuffed about the intricate stitching on their pointed toes. His jacket looked like an inside-out sheep – the sort Marlboro Men wore when they rode horses and smoked cigarettes. But there was a new air of detachment, even desperation, about him.

'What the frig were you doing under my bed, Sam? Are you really on the run?'

'Nah! I wanted to surprise you.'

'Surprise me? You scared the crap out of me!'

'You looked so comfy sleeping when I snuck in, I didn't want to wake you. I thought I'd get some shut-eye too – it's a long bloody flight from LA, you know.'

'Does Dad know?'

Sam shook his head. 'Ike said to keep it quiet. So the media don't find out what happened.'

'But shouldn't Dad know you're home?'

He shrugged again. 'S'pose. But I need to lie low for a bit. Get my shit together.'

'Are you okay?' Emily asked gently. Sam shrugged, looking down at his lap.

'You've got yourself a little bit lost, haven't you? And a little bit arrested?' she said, noting the pallor of his skin and the dark circles under his eyes.

'Almost arrested. But definitely lost, yes. Seems like you have too,' he said.

Emily hung her head. 'I've split up from Clancy.'

'I kinda thought you might.'

'You did?'

'Uh-huh, one day.'

They sat in silence together for a moment, the moan of an old lady in the room next door underlining their sadness.

They had both felt a gap in their lives without their mother's presence, so vast it sometimes felt like an ocean.

'Hey?' Emily said.

'What?'

'Want to do me a favour?'

'Name it.'

'Kidnapping.'

'Kidnapping?'

'C'mon,' Emily pleaded, 'you've got to get me out of here. Please.'

Their eyes met and brother and sister grinned.

'Are you sure you're well enough? You look like shit.'

'So do you,' Emily shot back.

'Gee, thanks. Well, where to?'

'Where do you think!' Emily jerked her head in what she thought was the direction of the mountains and the Flanaghans' old summer grazing homestead.

'The high plains. The perfect hideout,' she said.

'Yeah?'

'You've got your ute?'

'Yeah,' said Sam.

'Well?'

He grinned. 'Okey-dokey, let's get the flock out of here!'

As Sam helped her out of bed, Emily noticed how slowly he moved and the way he kept vaguing out. He helped her pack her things, holding up a pair of pink underpants that had a cartoon elephant on the front complete with stitched-on trunk and, on the back, a tail.

'These are truly woeful!'

'Shut up,' Emily said, rolling her eyes. He giggled. 'You're really stoned.'

'What if I am?'

'Only losers get stoned.'

'I'm a loser then.'

'That makes two of us,' Emily said, thinking of the mess she'd made of her own life.

Thirteen

'You can be Thelma and I'll be Louise,' said Sam as he helped Emily into the front seat of his sporty royal blue Holden ute.

'No, I reckon I should be Louise. Lou-wheeze. Get it? Wheeze. The ribs!' They both spluttered with laughter. 'Ouch! It hurts to cack myself.'

That sent Sam careening sideways into the ute in hysterics, before Emily shushed him. He glanced around to see if anyone from the hospital had come after them, but sneaking out had been easy. Anyone who was about seemed too busy to notice or care.

In the shine from the streetlights, momentarily serious, Sam looked over at his sister. 'You sure you're right to do this?'

'Sure as sure.' But in fact Emily was far from sure. The world outside the hospital seemed eerie at night and her body was protesting at sitting so upright in Sam's bucket-shaped racing seats. She felt nauseous and frightened as he fired up the engine.

'No funny buggers,' Emily warned. Sam could be a lead foot, particularly behind the wheel of his boy's toy V8 ute. He shot her a Jack Nicholson smile.

On the Monash Freeway, lit to glowing by endless rows of lights, Emily was grateful to be heading away from this fast-paced world. Even in the middle of the night the freeway was still buzzing with cars, trucks and vans, all hurtling along in a four-lane vortex of speed.

She shut her eyes and suddenly a picture of her forebears came to her. They were travelling across foot tracks in the high country, dressed in heavy felt coats and hats pulled down low, their packhorses making slow progress through the snow drifts, guided only by the moonlight. There was just enough to illuminate the snowpoles and the blazes carved on tree trunks to mark the way. Emily could hear the winter wind and smell the damp bush all around.

She heard a man cough. Emily gasped, a sudden painful intake of breath, and woke to find herself travelling through the city at 110 clicks, with fear clamping her chest tight. She wasn't sure if the panic arose from the strange visions that came flashing into her mind, or from the surreal feeling of suddenly being out of hospital.

'How can you stand this place?' she muttered, peering out of the window at Melbourne's sprawl, but Sam didn't hear her. Beneath bright spotlights another massive billboard loomed, advertising a new country housing estate. Suddenly Emily's thoughts were catapulted back to the night before the race.

At the Cattlemen's bar she'd found Clancy easily under the shining spotlights. He'd been standing tall in a crush of sweat-stained hats and singlets, hairy backs and tats. He looked like a peacock in his colourful shirt of green and blue check, and she had felt so much the plain pea-hen in her oilskin, a brown hat hiding her dull, short cropped hair. Underneath she wore her aeroplane undies with little red and green biplanes buzzing over them, and the words *Landing Strip Under Repair: Proceed with Caution*. Clancy wouldn't be getting the joke tonight.

Simmering with resentment, Emily drew in the smell of spilt beer. Overhead the summer rain careened off the marquee. She was angry with her husband for not helping her set up camp before the storm blew in. She still carried the knowledge of the receipt she'd found earlier that day like a loaded gun close to her chest. Ready to fire. Sprung. Meg was slung on her hip, sulking and tired, and Tilly clung dripping wet to her coat.

She could see Clancy talking to an Amazonian bottle blonde. Her boobs were plumped up in a low-cut top so that her cleavage formed an inviting line down her chest. Her eyes were sparkling. Emily didn't know much about makeup but this girl was coated in it. Black stuff round her eyes, and shimmery stuff on her lids and lips that glowed red. Now Emily knew more about the inner workings of Clancy's mind, she knew the woman's red lips would remind him of the parts of her he'd really like to know.

Emily felt jealousy and inadequacy spike within her. Anger about his infidelities bubbled beneath the surface, like a volcano that could erupt at any time. Despite her jealousy, Emily acknowledged that the girl looked awesome. Slightly trashy, but totally at ease with her far from magazine-perfect body. She was almost as tall as Clancy, with shoulders as broad as Lisa Curry's. She was big and curvy, Wonder Woman in jeans and a tanktop. Her wrists jangled with gold bracelets and glassy baubles, and her white-blonde hair was caught up on top of her head, the dampness of the stormy air curling the ends slightly. She looked like she'd snap a man in half in the sack, thought Emily and perhaps if his wife hadn't come along then that's what she'd been planning to do with Clancy.

Emily looked at the men and women behind the bar who were busy topping up the booze baths with bags of ice to keep the cans cold. They tossed them down from the truck like army volunteers throwing sandbags into a flood. It had been the same scene when she and Clancy first met at the get-together seven years before . . .

Clancy Moran stood six foot tall, and was so impossibly good-looking that women of all ages found it hard to draw their eyes away from him. He was something like the cowboy in a Wrangler jeans advertisement. In Melbourne, with his manly jawline highlighted by flecks of stubble, his indigo-blue eyes and short dark hair, he'd been 'spotted' several times and asked to model for photo shoots, but Clancy had always responded the same way.

'Modelling's for poofters. No way.'

But when he had first hit on Emily, she made sure she wasn't going to react like all the other women. Instead she kidded and joked along with him like she would with a big brother, and teased him mercilessly. It had driven him mad to meet a girl he hadn't won over in an instant with his looks.

'I swear you'll end up infertile with dacks as tight as that,' she'd said to him dryly as she leant, drinking legally for the first time, against the cattlemen's bar. 'They're so tight I can near see your goolies. Did your mum shrink them in the wash or did you plan it that way to pull the chicks?' Clancy had met his match.

Ever since she was sixteen Emily Flanaghan had filled out a pair of jeans like only a fit, strong country girl can, the thick brown leather of her belt hugging a tiny waist. She often wore checked shirts with press-stud buttons that Clancy had liked to rip right open in one hit. He'd also liked the way she wore the buttons partway undone, so that there was always a glimpse of blue singlet and a hint of the gentle rise of her sun-kissed breast beneath. She was nearly ten years younger than him, which back then had turned him on.

He'd told her that he'd always had his eye on her, even when she was a little tacker. He'd noticed the way, years ago, she'd claimed the junior cattlemen's cup on her nuggety little buckskin, by a whisker to a big loping thoroughbred bay. He'd observed her each year after that as she blossomed and grew, cracking stockwhips like a pro in the junior whipcrack, her mouth set firm in a determined line, a soft frown on her face beneath her wide-brimmed hat.

He liked the way her tanned and grubby hands stroked the snakes of plaited leather on her stockwhips as she expertly curled and hung them over her caramel-coloured shoulder when she was done. How she swung lithely on to the back of her stock horse and rode off like an exotic princess, with her dark, wavy hair falling down her back. He had treated her like one, and eventually she had fallen for him.

Now here they were again at the cattlemen's bar and he was treating her not like a princess but like shit. Rage surfaced in Emily. She pushed her way through the crowd, kids in tow, over to Clancy.

Before she could fling angry words at him, the girl he was with turned towards her and beamed at her.

'Emily!' she said.

Emily looked blank.

'You don't remember me?' The girl laid her ringed fingers aginst her chest, 'Bridie. Bridie McFarlane. From Dargo Primary?'

'Bridie McFarlane! Oh my God!' Emily cried excitedly. ''Course I remember you. I just didn't *recognise* you!'

'Yeah, well, the boys did call me Pudden Guts back in school. I was a total dag.'

'Come here!' And with that the girls hugged for a long time, memories of their friendship in the tiny school flooding back. Emily bent down to introduce Tilly and Meg. 'This is Mummy's best friend from primary school!' She stood up again, 'My God, what are you doing back here? I thought you'd moved back to Tassie.'

'Mum and Dad are still there, but I've been away in Brizzie at *bewdy* school. You know, facials, waxing, tints . . . That kinda stuff.'

'Good for you!'

'And you?'

Emily shrugged and inclined her head. Clancy was standing beside them with two drinks in his hands, looking very uncomfortable.

'Just being a slave to my husband. But I see you've already met.'

'*Husband?*' Bridie said, narrowing her eyes at Clancy. She took both the cans from him and very deliberately handed one to Emily, keeping the other for herself. She cast him a frosty look without thanking him.

'Is he looking after you well in Dargo?' she said pointedly.

Emily shook her head, 'We're not in Dargo. Clancy runs a trucking business out of Brigalow and we've got a house there.'

'Emily Flanaghan in Brigalow! Geez!' Bridie said, turning back to Clancy. 'How'd you get her out of the mountains?'

'Looks and charm,' he said with a nervous wink.

'Wouldna worked on me,' Bridie said dryly, then turned her back on him and faced Emily and the girls. 'That's a shame you don't live there no more. I'm movin' back to Dargo. Settin' up me own bewdy business. I coulda really spoofed you and the girls up a bit. It'd be fun.'

'In Dargo? Geez, why set up there?'

'A broken heart makes a girl do funny things. I guess I wanted somewhere familiar for a bit. Plus I don't want to be rushed off my feet with work anymore.' She swigged on her drink. 'You'll have to stop by.'

'I'd love to! I could do with some TLC.'

Clancy looked put out to hear it and Emily realised how much he'd quashed her friendships with other women over the years. Suddenly she saw clearly that her life was not her own. She remembered that receipt and hurt spiked her again.

The clouds had drifted away by now in the wake of the storm, and the evening star was shining brightly in the east. The white silhouette of a new moon was on the rise as the pale sky began to darken to ink. Purple and pink rays from the sinking sun fanned out, illuminating the west. The warmth was back in the air again, but this time it felt steamy, as if they were in a jungle.

'Oh,' Bridie said, ducking her head to look out of the marquee, 'would ya look at that sunset! It's bloody beautiful up here. C'mon.' She linked arms with Emily and grabbed

Tilly's hand. 'Let's take a walk, girls, and leave old Dad here to get sozzled on his own.'

Clancy looked pissed off, but Bridie had such a commanding air he didn't protest. Emily gave him a sideways look for good measure before moving away into the crowd.

She relished walking beside her childhood friend again. She and Bridie had been wild girls going feral in the creeks, rivers and all about the bush tracks on their bikes and ponies. Bridie had been a blob of a kid, but now her wide shoulders were tanned to a tasty cinnamon colour and she carried her weight well. Her tight-fitting aqua tank-top defined a waist that was wide but curved enough into an hourglass shape to be inviting. She moved her ample arse like a slinky cat, which Emily guessed was a trick she'd learnt at beauty school. Despite her heaviness, she walked like she was sex on a stick. Emily longed to take a leaf out of her book. Bridie oozed confidence and strength. But despite the broken heart she spoke of, she also seemed full of the joy of life. Like Emily used to be.

They sat on a steep grassy bank lit by generator floodlights. Beside them, Meg and Tilly joined the pack of kids who had taken to tobogganing down the slippery incline on flattened beer cartons. As they laughed at the kids' antics, Bridie leant her head towards Emily's and rested it on hers.

'It's so good to see you again.'

'Likewise.'

'Sorry I never wrote.'

'Same. I'm crap at letters. Thumbnail dipped in tar kinda stuff.'

Bridie turned to face Emily full on, 'I know it's been a long time, but can I get up close and personal again?'

Emily nodded, unsure what she meant.

'It looks as if you need some sorting,' she said, lifting her friend's hat and surveying the roughly hacked hairstyle.

'I do?'

'Your husband just tried to pick me up at the bar.'

Emily felt tears rise in an instant. Of course he had.

'Doesn't surprise me,' she said, her voice cracking.

Bridie slid one arm about her shoulders.

'Hey! Shush! Don't worry, Auntie Bridie's here! Beauty consultant by day, trained counsellor and drinking partner by night.'

Emily nodded gratefully.

'I've been thinking about leaving him.'

'Only thinking about it!'

Emily cast her a hurt look.

'Sorry.' She tilted her head, 'When?' Emily shrugged.

'I know I've just met him, but he's an arsehole, Emily. And I know 'em when I see 'em.' She tried to read Emily's reaction. 'Geez, sorry. Tell me if I've said too much.'

Emily smiled. 'No, you're absolutely right. He is an arsehole. I'm gonna ride in the race tomorrow. After that I'm telling him that I'm leaving.'

'Really?' Bridie asked.

'Yes, really.'

'Good for you, girl!' she said, toasting Emily. 'There's no turning back!'

Later that night, as Emily quietly unzipped the tent, she felt Clancy's presence behind her.

'You think you're so fucken smart, don't you?' he said, grabbing her arm. 'Pissing off with that fat bitch and treating me like shit.'

She shook his grip off.

'Shhh!' she said, aware of the other campers and the girls she'd just settled in the nearby tent. She moved away to the creek.

In the darkness she looked up at the stars through the river gums and tried to summon up the courage to tell him that she knew about the truckie prostitutes. That their marriage was over. But no words came. Clancy slid down the bank after her in his cowboy boots. She could smell the grog on his breath and the pungent stench of his sweaty underarms. Still in her boots, she splashed through the shallows away from him.

After that her memory became fractured, parts blotted out like shadows in the night. She remembered his fingers biting her soft underarms. His grip was too tight. His fingers were burning her as he shoved her back on to the jagged creekbed. She tried to cry out but he held his large hand over her mouth. The strength of him was frightening as he tugged her jeans down and forced himself into her, grunting into her like an animal. Her eyes were scrunched tight, her head held to one side by his big hand. Rocks pressed into the aching muscles of her back. She remembered the angry bites of ants against her thighs. Then the stillness afterwards when he had rolled off her and swayed drunkenly away. The smell of his warm semen trickling out of her made her want to retch. She remembered crying, hugging her knees to her chest in the dust beside the creekbed, wondering how she could ever go on from here.

Sam's voice above the deep throb of the V8 engine woke Emily. Opening her eyes, she painfully used her good arm to grab the seat belt, pulling herself up from where she lay slumped between the door and window.

'Well?' her brother asked.

'What?'

'Are we going straight to the high plains? Or shall we call into Dad's and get the girls first?' Sam asked.

'I don't want to disturb the girls tonight – it'll be at least three in the morning by the time we get there. And I know Dad'll be furious. He'll probably try to send me back to hospital.'

'Okay, straight there?'

'But I really, really want to get Rousie tonight. I know Clancy won't be looking after him properly.'

'What if Clancy's there?'

Emily shrugged. 'You'll have to sort him for me.'

'You sure?'

'I'm getting my dog.'

The sight of the Brigalow house prompted a fresh flood of bad memories. Emily had to clamp her lips shut so she could slow her anxious breathing. She began reliving her past here: the day they'd first brought Matilda home as a tiny baby; the night feeds, with Clancy fuming because the baby had woken him and he had an early run in the trucks. The way he'd joked about her stretch marks when she was eight months gone with Meg. Emily pictured herself, weight ballooning, body clad in shapeless T-shirts and sagging tracksuit pants. She couldn't believe what she had become, shut in that tiny house.

Sam pulled up and backed the ute into the drive. He turned to her with a cheeky grin. 'For a fast getaway, Louise.'

Round the back, Rousie was going nuts on the end of his chain. His barks prompted lights to flick on in the house.

'Shit,' Emily said. 'He's here.'

Sam got out. 'Don't worry.'

He ran behind the house and Emily swallowed nervously. She saw the bedroom curtains being drawn aside. She saw Clancy's naked torso. Then she glimpsed another form in the bedroom. A woman. In their bed.

Emily felt a strangling sensation in her throat. Her body tensed, every muscle contracting with hurt and anger. She sat in Sam's ute, holding back tears, trying to be strong. It was only to be expected, she said to herself, chanting it in her mind like a mantra. The curtain fell on the scene.

Then Sam was back and Rousie was bounding around the ute, standing up on his back legs and sniffing the air for scents of his mistress. Her faithful dog. Emily smiled and wound the window down. Rousie, too polite to jump up on the ute door but too excited to contain his joy, bounded on the spot and whined with delight, his whole body wagging along with his tail. Emily's smile faded when she saw in the dull gleam of the streetlight, the dog's ribby frame. His stomach was concave and his normally glossy black coat looked dry and frizzled. She felt anger twist inside her. Sam commanded him on to the back of the ute, flipping open a gap in the tarp for him to nestle into.

The front door opened and there stood Clancy.

'What do you think you're doing, Sam Flanaghan?'

'G'day, Clancy,' said Sam. 'Just helping Em pick up a few things. Clothes and that.'

'Fuck her.'

'Hello, Clancy,' Emily said mildly, trying to contain the tremor in her voice.

'You can take your stinkin', barkin' dog, but you're not setting foot inside this house. You chose to leave – so leave!'

'Well, could you just chuck a few of Em's things in a bag, mate, and then we'll go,' Sam said.

'No friggin' way, mate. Stuff you.'

'Clance,' Emily tried to soothe him, 'please don't be angry. We've got to get on. For the girls' sake.'

He roared like a wounded animal then and came hurtling off the front steps towards her. She flinched as he started pummelling his fists on the roof of the ute.

'Just piss off! Get out of my life!'

Emily could smell the grog on his breath. Spit was gathering at the sides of his mouth as he yelled, and she hunkered down in her seat clutching her head in her hands. Then Sam was dragging Clancy away, eventually flinging him down on the lawn.

'Leave her alone!' Sam yelled as he stood over him. Clancy lurched to his feet but Sam was already in the driver's seat, revving the V8 and fishtailing it away down the street.

Six years' worth of distress began to pour from Emily. She sat crying, her brother's hand resting comfortingly on her knee. The tears wouldn't stop. He kept saying over and over, 'We'll be right, sis. We'll be right. We'll get to the plains and we'll be right.'

In the darkness as they drove, Emily looked at the glow from the dash. It reminded her of the first time she'd ridden in his truck with Clancy. She remembered the rush of excitement when he'd pulled up on the drive at Tranquillity, and how she'd climbed up the steps to open the heavy door. It had been five-thirty in the morning and still dark. The moon in the dawn sky was gently illuminating the frosted paddocks. The first thing Clancy had shown her on the complicated computerised dashboard of dials and buttons was his sleeper light.

'I call it the sexy light.' In the dimness, he had cast her an inviting look. 'Do you want my sexy light on?' With a teasing smile, his finger jabbed the tiny cherry-red square with a half moon sign on it. The light above their heads gave the cab a seductive red glow. On that first trip, they'd barely travelled five kilometres down the road before Clancy had pulled over. Emily had shuddered as he kissed her softly above the lace of her bra. The sensuality of that first time in the truck with him was intoxicating.

As he'd undressed her in the cab, she had seen the cattle prodder propped behind his seat, the prongs looking as if they belonged to Satan himself. She'd never met a boy as bad as him. It thrilled her. All her life she'd been so good. So responsible. The glue holding her family together. Now here he was, this wicked man who made her laugh and cry and lose herself in the sexual oblivion of lust. 'Want to get lucky with the truckie?' he had said, helping her up into the sleeper and drawing the curtains shut.

On that first dawn trip, with her body zinging from Clancy's lovemaking, Emily had revelled in seeing the other trucks coming towards them, all lit up like Christmas trees. She was falling in love, surrendering to the gentle sway of the cab, its modern interior snug and clean. For the entire trip she had longed for Clancy to reach over and touch her again. She watched his sexy hands drape themselves over the big round steering wheel, and the way his middle finger teased the split-shift button on the gearstick. As he double-clutched round bends, the sigh of the air-clutch reminded her of her own desires. Everything within that truck was plush and phallic: from the purple polish the men used to shine their silver stacks to the way the truck let out a sound like a 'whoosh' of steam when Clancy pulled up at the truckstop. She was addicted to him. And, back then, he had treated her as if she was the only one in the world for him.

Slowly, though, the truck had begun to take him away from her. More and more he left her alone with the babies. On the rare occasions she rode in the truck in the later years of their marriage, she found herself staring into the giant side-mirror, watching the white line fall away behind her. It felt like her whole life was running backwards, their love slowly turning into something toxic. Now, on her way back to the plains, Emily realised she might never be free from Clancy. They had children together. No matter where she ran to, they would always be linked by that thread. She hunched over in the ute, leaden with sadness for what their marriage might have been.

PART TWO

PART TWO

Fourteen

On the Dargo High Plains the snow gums glowed white in the light of a full moon. The gum leaves glistened liquid-silver, like a million tiny fairy lights dancing in the tree-tops. Long grasses shone in the stillness of the night. As Sam hit another rut in the meandering gravel road and scudded over corrugations in the bend, Emily reached out for the door handle to steady herself, wincing with pain.

'Careful!' she said, casting a glance at her brother, who was happily swinging on the wheel.

'Sorry, mate.' He braked and swerved suddenly to miss a Hereford cow and calf that were dozing on the road. 'Oops!'

Emily glanced in the side-view mirror to see Rousie dig his claws into the tarp of the ute, as if surfing the crest of a wave. She smiled to see how happy he looked to be off that suburban chain and in the scrub again, nose to the wind, where a kelpie should be.

When she saw the town boundary sign at Dargo Emily almost asked to stop so she could visit her girls. She imagined herself tiptoeing through the house and climbing into bed with one of them, but something inside told her to keep going, to take the climb up to the mountains. Sam seemed to sense the crossroads of her thoughts and slowed as they passed Tranquillity's gateway, white in the glare of the headlights.

'You sure you don't want me . . .?'

'Stop asking me if I'm sure! Tomorrow,' she told him, 'I'll see them in the morning.' But as Sam revved on, Emily's heart lurched at being so close to her babies without seeing them, yet knowing she was compelled to make it to the High Plains tonight.

And so her journey back to the mountains began, past the Cherry Tree yards and up the Long Cutting. As they climbed, Emily began to feel better. She felt lighter, stronger, happier, as the mountain air grew thinner and the vegetation, caught in the headlights, changed from straight-trunked woolly butts and brown sallees to twisted snow gums growing on the rocky basalt.

Over a cattle grid and they were there at last: the Flanaghan High Plains Station. They veered off the main gravel road and parked at the station's front gate. Few other people, save the locals in Dargo, knew that this was the gate into the homestead. It was just a regular farm gate set among the snow gums, except that this gate was far from straight. Its pipe frame was bowed out from where a bolting young horse had once hit it in Emily's grandfather's day. No one had ever thought to straighten or replace it.

Sam looked at his sister. 'Home sweet home,' he said, jumping out.

Emily wound down her window and breathed in, savouring the smells of grasses, cooling after a day in the late-summer sun, fat-leafed clovers, eucalypts and clean mountain air. Relief rose within her. This was the place that would help ease her pain; soothe the memory of Clancy's angry attack. This place would wash away the stagnant sadness that seemed to weigh her down. She was home. And soon her girls and her horse would be home with her too, and then surely their lives could begin again.

The old track to the homestead was like a tunnel, lined with silver snow gums. The moon filtered through the canopy of gum leaves and illuminated the yellow everlastings and billy buttons and white paper daisies. The scene was so beautiful, Sam and Emily sat in contemplative silence as they rumbled slowly down the hillocky road towards the hand-split weatherboard homestead.

Sam left the ute idling and got out.

'You sit in the warm while I get a fire going.'

'No, bugger that. I'm tough. I'll help.'

'Don't be a dick,' Sam said, opening the door and helping her out slowly, 'You are going inside. You're groaning like a nanna when you move!'

'Whoah!' Emily tried to ignore the stab of pain from her shoulder as she clambered out of the ute and began to uncurl her body. Her sling tugged and her arm beneath plaster itched. Grabbing for the ute, she steadied herself, trying hard to slow her breathing. She focused on feeling the solid core of ancient basalt soil and rocks beneath her feet. Found herself asking this place to ground her there, so that she would never leave again. The earth seemed to pulse beneath her. As she shut her eyes, it felt for a moment as if time had stopped altogether. Then a gust of wind raced through the trees and passed across Emily's face. With the moon above and the dark earth below, she felt both giddy but strangely purposeful in the midst of her agony. She was meant to be here, though why she didn't completely understand. What was the old Flanaghan woman asking of her?

Emily stared up at the icing-sugar dusting of stars against the velvety black sky. Her trance was broken when Sam threw a swag on to the deep old boards of the verandah and Rousie leapt joyfully from the ute. He came to press his dry nose into the palm of her hand.

'Hello, my boy,' she said, stooping to hug the kelpie. His coat smelt rancid and felt greasy. As she ran her hand across his back she was once again shocked by how thin he had become during her time away in hospital. Emily smiled sadly. It seemed Rousie too was in need of some healing on the High Plains.

As they opened the front door and Sam helped Emily shuffle inside, a rush of memories of summer droving days returned to her. Just the creak and bang of the old wooden flyscreen triggered images of all the comings and goings from this place. Used only in the summer and autumn months as a base for tending their cattle on the mountains, the homestead was like a living museum of Flanaghan family history.

In the hallway, under a rustic bench seat, stood a line of boots moulded by the feet of several generations of Flanaghans. Old coats, still worn when unexpected snow came in at Easter time, made Emily remember her grandfather. She thought of him wearing one of those coats as he slid down a rain-soaked embankment to help a calf up out of the scrub, and how her five-year-old self had stood watching, rain running off her cowgirl hat, her fingers red and cold as ice. As she walked on the old lino, Emily felt the house stir itself awake to their presence.

In the kitchen, Sam reached up to the mantel for matches. The crack and fizz and smell of the match gave Emily a feeling of comfort as her brother lit a row of candles that had been stuck in Auntie Flo's empty whisky bottles. He heaved open the door of the old woodstove and tilted a candle inside so the flame caught the corner of newspaper already laid under some dry kindling.

'Sit tight,' he said. 'I'll go turn on the gas and get a load of wood for the night.'

Emily nodded. Gingerly, she pulled out a chrome and red vinyl chair that had been all the rage in the sixties, and sat down at the kitchen table.

'There you go again,' Sam said, ducking his head back round the kitchen door.

'What?'

'You just groaned like a nanna again when you sat down.'

'I did not.'

'You did!'

'Oh, all right smart arse,' she called after him.

Emily stared through the crack of the stove door, watching the bright flames dance. She listened to the roar of air in the flue and stretched her fingertips towards the growing heat. She ran her hands over the heavy wooden table. Etched on its surface were many stories from the family's past. The dull light from the candles cast flickering dark shadows on to the table's pockmarked landscape. Her great-great-grandmother had had it brought up from the original hut in the Mayford gully, and here it had remained ever since. Emily felt a flash of new energy run through her, the tiny hairs on her arms lifted and a tingle ran over her skin as she saw an image of olden-day Emily, her sturdy boots treading the dirt floor as she stuffed a rabbit at this table and turned to place it in a camp oven for baking. Emily blinked and the image was gone, just as Sam came back through the door with an armload of wood.

'Bit quieter than Nashville out there,' he said.

'Do you good,' Emily told him.

'Do you good too.'

'I just want my girls with me and then I'll be set.'

'We'll ring Dad first thing.' Sam raised the old kettle in the air. 'Cuppa?'

Emily shook her head.

'No, thanks. I'm going to crash.'

As she carried the candle along the narrow hallway, cupping her hand about the flame, Emily felt the comfort of the house wrap itself around her. She was aching all over now, and part of her was scared, but she knew leaving the hospital had been the right thing to do. *This* was the place for her to heal.

Wanting to shed the pyjamas that reeked of the hospital, she opened the old wardrobe and held up the candle to cast more light inside. Whenever the Flanaghans came up to the homestead, they lived out of their bags, never staying here more than a week at a time. It had been different in her grandparents' day. The clothes in the wardrobe had been there since they had lived up here full-time in the summer months, to salt and muster cattle, fix fences and combat summertime weeds. It was easier that way than making the winding eighty-kilometre journey back into Dargo in their little old spring-suspension utility, or on horseback as they'd preferred. Pa always chose horses over cars.

Part of his routine then had been riding out and dropping a match here and there along the tracks to trickle fire through the landscape when the weather was just right, in the way the Aborigines had done. But over the years this ritual of burning to encourage regeneration had been restricted and eventually banned by the government, and the landscape had gradually changed. The beautiful open-treed country of Victoria's Alps had become cluttered with a mass of bone-like fallen limbs from trees weighed down by winter snow. On the lower slopes, dogwood and wattles, once kept in check by the cattlemen burning patches of bush in a mosaic pattern across the mountains, now choked the landscape. Places that were once gently cool-burned and periodically grazed were now inaccessible.

Life gradually changed for the Flanaghans too. The once-isolated family living on the plains had become a thorn in the side of the government men, who did not believe the Flanaghans should profit from pristine wilderness. As the infrastructure improved, interference from the city increased. The more bushwalkers, skiers and rubberneckers that arrived, the more rules the cattlemen faced. Emily's grandfather had died a sad man. Sad for his mountains. Sad for the loss of a simple life, and for the loss of his privacy and freedom.

Emily ran her fingertips over two coarse woollen dressing gowns – her grandfather's brown check and her grand-mother's soft blue one. An image came to mind of Grandpa and Grandma sizzling chops in a pan in the pre-dawn light, while a pot of strong tea sat on the kitchen table under a woollen brown-and-yellow tea-cosy – the one they still used.

At the very back of the cupboard, she found a nightie she didn't remember at all. It was long and white, with intricately stitched blue flowers and tiny buttons at the scooped neck-line. The sleeves were long, ending in a thin ruffle. Emily smiled. The nightie was so old-fashioned compared to the gauzy negligees Clancy always wanted her to wear. The angrier he had become over her cosy flannelette pyjamas, the more she'd dug her heels in. She'd only ever slipped into bed blissfully naked on the nights he was away, enjoying then the sensual feel of her skin beneath the sheets.

She pulled the nightie off its hanger, which was stitched with the same tiny flowers pattern, and decided to put it on. She did so slowly and painfully, then stared at her ghostly reflection in the mirror. The candle's light did not reach far, her legs and feet disappearing into blackness.

'Bloody Joan of Arc!' Emily said, taking in her cropped dark hair, the shadowy sockets around her eyes and the nightie's creamy glow. She sniffed at the sleeves but smelt only moth-balls – not a trace of her grandmother's scent was left. She looked again at her reflection and carefully turned around in front of the mirror, fancying herself as an old-fashioned heroine.

Then she clambered between the icy sheets, feeling relieved to be out of hospital and strangely happy to be 'on the run'. She lay for a time twirling the hospital wristband around and around on her arm, looking at the ornate cast-iron of the old double bed. Instead of thinking about the aches in her body, she thought again about her grandparents. They had lived self-sufficiently, with God and Mother Nature and the spirits of the land as their guides. She thought of the simplicity of their lives, and the core of happiness they always carried within themselves. She'd felt it as a child, and she was sure she could see that same trait in her girls, particularly her youngest, Meg. She would lay her hands on her mother's skin and Emily could feel something special in her touch. An odd child, Meg never seemed to fit in with others, preferring to play alone and talk to imaginary friends, making no sense to anyone but herself. Tilly, on the other hand, was less dreamy and got on with the practicalities of life. In the hospital, it had been Tilly who fetched water for her mother and plumped her pillows and straightened the sheets, while Meg had sat with her warm little hands on Emily as if trying to heal her. In the darkness Emily longed for both her girls.

'Goodnight, Tilly and Meg,' she said to the empty room, conjuring up an image of them peacefully asleep in her old bedroom at Rod's house. As she drifted off to sleep, Emily thought again of her vision of bringing her girls up here full-time, even when the snow came. Was it possible? Even the Flanaghans from three generations ago had retreated to their winter homestead on the lower valley of Mayford when snow draped itself over the mountains in thick blinding drifts of white. Was she strong enough to endure a winter here?

'Emily,' came the whisper.

In her sleep, she frowned and stirred a little.

'Emily.'

That voice again . . . Emily's eyes flashed open. She sat up in the pitch-dark room. The candle stub was extinguished. The moon had slunk away behind the treetops; gone was the glow it had created behind the old lace curtains.

A faint, eerie light drifted in from the hallway and she could hear music playing gently. It couldn't be Sam. There was no radio here. No power to run anything. Before she had time to feel afraid she got up, the lino cold under her bare feet. She struck a match and the skerrick of candle that was left offered up a pathetic, wax-drowned flame. She tiptoed along the hall and gently pushed open the door to Sam's room. Just as the candle petered out, she saw him sleeping soundly beneath old grey woollen blankets.

And still Emily caught the sound of music again. The finger-tips of her good hand pressed to the uneven horsehair-plaster walls of the old house, she blindly felt her way along the hall to the kitchen where the fire still glowed. The music was clearer now. Emily could hear an old piano accordion, and voices, too, being carried along with the tune. The voices were both male and female, and they were singing a hymn. As she walked through the kitchen to the old dining room, she saw a cluster of rough working men in their well-worn Sunday best. Emily stood in the doorway, holding her breath.

They didn't look up from their leatherbound hymn books as they stood in front of makeshift pews of flat slab-cut timber propped up on bricks. At the front of the congregation stood a handsome young minister, his dark hair worn slicked back and with a straight side parting. He was wearing a three-piece suit, his brilliant white priest's collar catching the light from the oil lamps. Could this be Archie, the Flanaghan son who had eventually left his preaching and returned to the plains to work with his young bride Joan? Emily wondered. She looked around. Next to the adults sat a cluster of children of various ages – Flanaghans, Emily somehow knew instinctively, for at their side were the same two people she had seen in her previous vision of the Mayford hut: Emily and Jeremiah. Together with a rough-looking group of goldminers, they were singing songs of thanks to God.

Without fear, Emily stepped into the room, wanting to join the gathering. As she did, the woman with the greying hair looked up. She tilted her head to one side and smiled gently at her. Emily smiled back. Then she, too, began to sing the hymn, the words foreign to her, yet somehow known . . .

'Emily! Emily!' came a voice from the darkness, and she felt the pressure of hands on her arm. She awoke suddenly to see Sam standing above her, his face catching the light from a small kerosene lamp.

'What?' she said, propping herself up on her elbow.

'You woke me up.'

'But I was in the dining room . . .'

'What? No, you weren't! You were in here, talking in your sleep. Well, not talking exactly . . . You were singing. Trust me, *I'm* the singer in this family. Sounded like two cats in a bag.'

He held the lamp closer. 'Geez, what are you wearing? You look like flamin' Julie Andrews in *The Sound of Music*!'

'A nightie. One of Nan's.'

'A passion-killer more like. It's a wonder she had *any* descendants!'

'Get over yourself,' said Emily. 'And I'm not *that* bad a singer. And what would I want with passion anyway!'

'So, you're okay? You don't need more painkillers?'

'Why do you keep asking me that? I'm fine, really I am. I reckon it's you who needs the pills. Are you hooked on them or something?'

'Nah,' said Sam, but Emily felt a stab of concern for her brother, who'd clearly been pushing things too far recently.

'Don't you go and do a Heath Ledger on me, mate,' she said.

Sam looked off into the darkness of the room, his big, blue-green eyes reflecting the glow from the lamp. He didn't answer her. Instead he turned back and said, 'He's really hurt you, hasn't he?'

She felt unshed tears sting her eyes. 'I've let it happen, though. It's not all Clancy. I let him . . .' Her voice trailed off.

'It'll be all right. We'll both be all right,' said her brother, but she could hear the undertone of doubt in his voice.

She knew Sam had really struggled since his smash single had hit the charts like a storm two years earlier and then blown itself out to silence. It hadn't given him enough momentum to walk away with a Tamworth Golden Guitar that year, a crucial badge of success for any young up-and-comer. His disappointment had been tangible, and it seemed to Emily as though his life had begun to unravel from that night on. Sam had drifted far away from the life they had once shared. He'd gone to the city and lost himself in the hullabaloo of beautiful people, parties and hype. He'd not written a new song in two years.

'What are you going to do, Sam?'

'Clean up my act.'

'What are you on?'

'Just the weed.'

'You're lying.'

He shrugged. 'I tried some heavier stuff in LA. It's really messed with me.'

'Have you any with you now?'

'Just some weed.'

'Give it to me. I'll burn it.'

'No, you won't!' His eyes flashed panic.

'Sam,' Emily said firmly, 'do you want to get sorted?'

'Yes!'

'Then give it all to me in the morning. All your party pills, your dope and smokes, the lot – you're going cold turkey.'

Emily looked at her little brother. She'd seen women of all ages pressing themselves to the front of the stage at his concerts and staring up at him as if he were God's gift. He might act like he was ten foot tall and bullet-proof, but she could still see the little boy in him.

Emily could also see that Sam had a very special gift at his core. When he was younger, music seemed to pour out of him. Outside in the dark, Emily knew there was a circle of blackened rocks that made up the campfire the family shared meals around in the summer droving days. She pictured a younger Sam then, in his flannie shirt, sleeves rolled to the elbows, the campfire illuminating his handsome chiselled features and strong arms as he belted out a tune on his guitar.

The droving team, made up mostly of family, had sat on fold-out chairs, stumps, Eskies and rounded basalt boulders, gazing mesmerised as Sam's music vibrated through their bodies. His voice seemed to flow from the black sky above, sifting down through stars and campfire smoke. It was the voice of a strong, bold angel, singing pure country.

'Tomorrow, you start writing songs again,' she told him. 'You write enough for an album. Write about this place: about the cattle, about the fires we panic about every year, about the snow, about the bloody bureaucrats threatening us all the

113

time. Then we contact your company and you cut the best album yet. Okay?'

'I'm not writing about this place, Em. You know exactly what'll happen if I do. I'll be a bloody pin-up boy for the mountain cattlemen – and the whipping boy for the Greens.'

Emily shook her head. 'So what? This is your heritage.'

'Well, fuck my heritage!' he said, clenching his jaw. 'I'm not jumping through the hoops Dad and Flo have gone through all their lives, just so they can graze a few cows up here.'

'It's not just about grazing cows and you know it. It's about looking after this land the way it deserves. Grazing it. Burning it. Caring for it. Not locking it up and leaving it and classifying it "pristine", like some untouchable thing or giant science experiment.'

'You just won't give it up, will you? Still flogging that same dead horse!'

As kids, Emily and Sam had been taught about this country that had been torn apart by frenzied goldminers in the 1800s, and how it had healed itself over: the same way grass grows over battle-scarred lands to cover forever the bones of fallen soldiers. They had seen for themselves how the land had regained its balance over time. The introduced weeds were now the greatest worry. Each year the Flanaghans, with the exception of Bob, helped check the most ruthless of them – blackberries. Sam and Emily knew that the land on the runs in their care was in great shape, and the light stocking of cattle in the summer months only improved things.

They knew they didn't get it right all the time, though. In tough times, when cattle prices were down and drought bit, the family's environmental work took a backseat because there was no money to fund it. They would see their father up to his ears in paperwork, applying for funding assistance so that they could fence streams or control more weeds. They'd seen his frustration when the use of their cheapest tool for managing the land – fire – was outlawed. They came to learn that signing the name Flanaghan on your application forms usually meant your application was rejected. The Flanaghans, their name synonymous with cattle grazing, had felt the sting of bureaucratic judgement and been branded environmental outlaws – people who destroyed precious wilderness areas, bogging up peat swamps and trampling delicate flowers with their cattle.

Sam found it hard some days, being a Flanaghan, and his time in the city had made him bitter about his heritage.

'You know that none of us cattlemen have the education to take on that gigantic bureaucracy,' he said to her more gently. 'Our skills lie in the care of land and animals, not fuelling the media machine and political debate.'

'But your music, Sam! A song can open people's minds if it's sung from the heart. That's why you have this gift . . . so you can show from your heart that what we do up here is sustainable and even good for the plains.'

He laughed. 'I'm happy to become an urban cowboy and leave the protesting to the other tired old cattlemen.'

Emily sighed. 'Then you're a bloody quitter and a piker.'

'Yeah? So what if I am?' He shivered. 'I'm going back to bed. I'm freezing my nuts off here.'

Just before he shut the door of her room, Emily called out, 'Hey, Sam?'

'Yeah?'

'That dream I was having when you came in . . . what was I singing anyway?'

He paused, head bowed in the lamplight as he thought.

'Dunno, really. I was half asleep. But it sounded like a hymn.'

'A hymn?'

'Yeah. Weird, hey? I didn't think you knew any hymns.'

'I don't.'

Fifteen

From his chain near the woodshed, Rousie let out a deep bark that told Emily someone was at the front gate. She flung back the sheets and threw her legs over the side of the bed. Pain knifed through her and for a moment the room wavered. She shut her eyes, waiting for the giddiness to subside.

'C'mon, c'mon,' she willed herself, determined to remain strong. In the kitchen Sam looked up from an old newspaper.

'Why didn't you wake me?'

He shrugged. 'You must've needed the sleep.'

'What time is it?'

'Nearly eleven.'

'*What!*'

Emily trod the well-worn verandah boards in her bare feet, scanning the track through the trees that stood framed against a perfect blue sky. She caught a glimpse of her father's dusty white four-wheel drive, followed by Flo's red Hilux ute and horse float. A broad smile lit Emily's face.

'*Yes!*' she said as they drew near, ecstatic to see Tilly and Meg in the first vehicle, and then the dark curious eyes of Snowgum peering through the float window, her ears flickering back and forth. The girls tumbled out of the four-wheel drive and ran towards their mother.

Emily stepped from the verandah and stooped to let them

into her arms. She shut her eyes with relief. Here they all were, together at last. She ran her hand over the crown of their heads and stepped back to look into their clear eyes, which held the greens, greys and browns of the bush in their depths. Then she drew them in again for a hug as warm as she could make it with the plaster on her arm. She looked over their heads and met her father's gaze.

'I'm sorry, Dad.'

Rod stepped forward to hug her gently. 'Are you okay?'

'Dad . . .' was all she could say as she buried her face in his rough woollen work jumper.

'I phoned the hospital and explained,' he told her sternly. 'They're not happy. It was a very stupid thing to do.' His eyes travelled to Sam then, still standing a little way off. Rod released Emily and stiffened for a moment, seeing his son's prison-style haircut and the dark circles under his eyes. Then his expression softened.

'I'm glad to see you too, boy,' he said, opening his arms wide and embracing his son in a man-hug. 'It's good to know you're both safe and to have you both home,' he said, clapping Sam's back with his big, square hand.

Flo stepped forward then, squinting at Emily.

'What the hell are you wearing, girl? You look like an escapee from a bloody mental institution!'

Emily looked down at her long white nightie and self-consciously ran her fingers through her short cropped hair.

'Good to see you too, Auntie Flo,' she laughed.

Flo hugged her warmly and muttered in her ear, 'Glad to hear you've ditched him, the mongrel bastard! If I can help you, darlin', you sing out.'

Emily was shocked. She knew the family had bitten their tongues on the subject of Clancy for years. Now, she realised, that silence would be broken at long last, albeit out of the girls' earshot. But before Emily could respond, Flo flicked her head in the direction of the float.

'There's someone else here glad to see you,' she said, and

117

as if on cue Snowgum pawed the float floor with her hoof.

As Flo slung down the door and the mare backed off the float, memories of the race rushed back to Emily. She saw the tree straight ahead; smelt the fear. Cringing, she inspected the raw proud flesh of the wounds on Snowgum's shoulder and nearside flank. The ugly, brown-and-pink meaty welts dug deep into her white hide, and were fringed with purple antiseptic spray.

'Oh, Snow,' Emily said, resting her forehead on the mare's neck. The others watched as Emily, in her long white gown, spent a quiet moment holding the horse around her neck, silently taking in the energy of the beautiful grey mare. They saw how beautiful both creatures were, but also how damaged.

'Thanks so much, Flo,' Emily said, tears in her eyes.

'No wuckers,' she said, her casual tone belying the anxiety of nursing Snowgum back from the brink. 'She's been a bit touchy since the accident, but I reckon she'll come right now you're here with her.'

Then Flo disappeared into the truck. She swung back the divider and there in the front of the float were the girls' two small ponies, Jemma and Blossom.

'Had to bring her mates,' announced Flo. Tilly and Meg beamed at their mother, then eagerly ran forward to help unload their pint-sized ponies.

Emily felt tears of relief sting her eyes. She had imagined her family berating her for leaving her husband, for bailing out of hospital, for coming here to the high plains. She'd even imagined them dragging her back down to the lowlands to fulfil her role as wife and mother. But here they were quietly supporting her – as if they all knew that she was meant to be here.

In the warmth of the kitchen, Flo unscrewed the lid on the brandy bottle and poured a neat shot into a row of teacups.

'Purely medicinal,' she said, passing a cup to Emily.

'That'll go down well with her Panadeine Forte,' Sam chipped in.

'Well,' said Flo, narrowing her eyes at him, 'from all reports, Johnny Cash, you'd know what mixes best with what.' There was an awkward silence then as Sam realised the whole family somehow knew of his slide into drink and drugs. His dad must have been on the phone to Ike that morning.

'C'mon, Flo, I'm good. I'm all good now,' Sam protested.

They looked at him. 'Liar,' they choroused.

'But you'll be right now?' Rod asked. Sam shrugged, smiling nervously. He just needed a little more time to ease himself down.

His father lifted his teacup to his lips, took a sip and winced.

'Tastes like medicine! Which reminds me, Emily, the hospital is sending discharge papers for you to sign and return *on condition* that you check in at the Dargo Bush Hospital each day for the next two weeks, to see the nurse.'

Emily felt herself bristle at the thought of Clancy's little nurse. She remembered the person she'd glimpsed in the bedroom of their house last night. She was sure it had been Penny. Though she was glad to be free from him, Clancy's infidelities still hurt.

'I'm not going to Dargo Hospital,' she said.

'You have to,' Rod insisted.

Emily shook her head. 'I'm not! And I won't!' The girls looked up from their game, hearing the angry tone of their mother's voice. 'I'm fine up here.'

'But they need to change your dressings.'

'Then I'll travel into the Sale hospital. But I won't go to Dargo.'

The family, gathered round the table, looked at Emily in silence, pity in their eyes. She suddenly realised that they all knew. *They knew about Penny and Clancy!* Word had certainly travelled fast. Emily felt utterly humiliated.

'I dunno what we're going to do then,' her aunt said. 'I'm no nurse. Snowgum would tell you that if she could. And your brother's not up to the job – he needs a nurse himself.' Sam flinched and hung his head as Flo went on, 'Rod's flat out with the cattle, and who's to run round after the girls until you come right? The only option is to send Bob up!'

'No! Anyone but Bob,' Emily said miserably.

'C'mon, Em.' Flo put a hand on her shoulder. 'I was joking about Bob.'

An awkward silence followed as they each contemplated how life might move forward from here, until Rousie woofed his loud 'someone's coming' bark.

From the verandah they watched a little blue Suzuki four-wheel drive struggle over the track, a small white-haired woman in the driver's seat.

'That's not Evie Jenner from down the road, is it?' said Flo. 'What's she wanting here?'

'Evie who?' asked Sam.

'You know. That woman who moved into the Gows ruins a few years back.'

'Yeah, I remember,' he said. 'Isn't she a loop-the-loop?'

'As nutty as a Picnic bar, so they say,' Flo told him.

'A few 'roos loose in the top paddock, eh?' said Emily.

'A stubby short of a six-pack,' Tilly added earnestly, and they all looked at her in surprise.

'Where did you learn that, Tilly?'

'Daddy,' she said proudly.

Still, whatever Evie Jenner's mental capacity, she had transformed Gows, a former hotel, from a state of sagging decay to one of homeliness. Stone by stone, she had resurrected the house that lay twenty kilometres from the Flanaghan homestead. Its garden now thrived, and a newly hung cast-iron gate invited visitors along the pathway. One time, droving the cattle past a few years ago, Emily had seen Evie in the garden, fixing up a trellis of ti-tree sticks on which snow peas could twine themselves upwards. Evie had looked up and smiled at her. She wore a floppy straw hat, a long purple dress and a red-striped pinafore. Giant black gumboots and loose green gardening gloves finished the look, which wavered between hippy and dotty old lady. At the sight of the cattle, the woman's little Jack Russell had made a beeline for the old stone wall. It had clambered up on top, front paws spread wide, and stood there yapping at the invaders.

'Jesus!' the woman called. 'Jesus Christ! Jeee-sus!' she called again. When Emily had realised the dog was actually called Jesus Christ, she'd laughed out loud. Was the woman a nut or did she just have a wicked sense of humour?

The cattle stood still to look curiously at the small white dog barking canine obscenities at them. An older cow tossed her head in annoyance, then they ambled on again. In the past, the cattle had liked to walk over the rubble of the stone wall to graze on what was left of the old garden and scratch their backs on the low branches of the walnut tree. Emily had often scooted around them on her horse and sent a dog over to hurry them on. They were lazy beasts when they got the chance and the shade of the walnut in summer had always been so inviting.

But within a year Evie had fixed the boundaries so the cattle could no longer make use of the giant tree and the lush green grass now growing unchecked beneath it. Emily had looked at the pretty, productive garden and the sunny seat on the porch. Nutter or not, the woman was a goer. From astride Snowgum, she waved, but rode on after just a brief, shy hello. There was something about this woman that kept them all remote from her. As if she didn't want any intrusions. She had her own patch of Eden and the Flanaghans would wave as they passed it, but never before had the woman ventured out of her rock-enclosed garden to make small talk.

Now, the entire family watched intrigued as Evie Jenner got out of her little blue car and hauled a large bag from the backseat. Her dog tumbled out, lifted its lip at Rousie and proceeded to piss on anything it could find.

'Jesus! Jesus Christ!' Evie cried. 'Come here, you little mongrel!' The dog ignored her. As she walked towards them, they saw that Evie was tiny, but beneath her oversized clothing fit and wiry. She wore her grey hair in two braids, which framed her small tanned face. She came to stand before them all.

'I'm Evie,' she announced. 'And I hear you folk could use a nurse?'

They stared at her, as amazed as if Mary Poppins herself had arrived.

'Cuppa?' was all Flo could manage and before they knew it they were ushering Evie through the screen door. On the way, she gave Emily a quick wink, with eyes the colour of new-spring growth. There was such a life force in her gaze that Emily felt the hairs rise on the back of her neck. The intensity of those green eyes! In a split second, that look had connected with something deep inside Emily, something she had never felt before. It was as if Evie were *meant* to be here. As if Emily had known her before somehow.

She shook the feeling away and told herself the local rumours were probably right. With her long grey plaits, hippy skirt and homespun wool cardigan, Evie could easily be one of those right-on organic types. The ones who made meat-eating and cow's-milk-drinking humans feel guilty for even breathing. Definitely anti-cattlemen. Emily decided there was no way she wanted to be nursed by her.

At the kitchen table, Flo did a poor job of being mother. She slopped boiling water into the teapot and noisily clanked an old tin of stale-looking biscuits on to the table.

'We've got brandy if you'd prefer.'

'Tea's just fine.'

'Here,' Rod said, 'sit. Please.' He pulled out a chair and gestured to it.

Evie sat at the head of the table and the girls came to stand beside her, gazing at her long plaits.

'Is that your real hair?'

'Meg!' said Emily.

'Why is it white, like Mum's horse?'

'Tilly!'

'Are you a witch?'

'*Meg!*' they all chorused.

Evie smiled. 'It's all right. Most people think I'm a complete nutter. It's just because I'm a woman and choose to live alone on a mountain. At least I don't have a house full of cats and share their food with them.' Her smile warmed not just her face but the whole room. The Flanaghans laughed, relieved. She seemed like a very nice, *normal* person.

'How did you know we needed someone to help Emily?' Sam asked, still a little suspicious of her.

'Oh, word gets around,' Evie said vaguely. 'Which reminds me . . .' she reached into her bag, 'today's paper.'

The headlines loomed large. *PARLIAMENT BILL TO OUST CATTLEMEN.*

'It's not looking good for you,' Evie told them.

They huddled round the article. A bill to ban the renewal of grazing licences, which had been in place for over a hundred years, would be debated in parliament the following week. If the bill were passed, there would be a statewide blanket ban on cattle grazing on all government parkland. The Flanaghans would be one of many high-country families affected.

Emily glanced at Evie. Had she come to gloat?

'We're going to have to get on to this,' Flo said. 'We haven't much time . . .'

Rod looked up at their visitor. 'Thanks for letting us know. We'd better get back down to Tranquillity and crank the computer up.'

Sam rolled his eyes. 'Oh, God. Here we go again. Bloody Groundhog Day!'

'This is different, Sam!' Emily said, jabbing her finger on the article. 'In the past they've only threatened bans. Now, if this thing gets through, it'll become law. They'll kick us off for good!'

'And what if they do?' he said bitterly. 'At least we'd be done with this endless fight.'

'It'll be the land that suffers. They do it every time . . . make one rule for an entire region. It just doesn't work that way.

Not all mountains are the same!' Emily turned to Evie, almost pleading with her, 'You don't think we should be kicked off? Or is that why you came here? To gloat?'

'No need to shoot the messenger,' Rod cautioned.

Emily slumped back in her chair and muttered an apology to Evie. But the news that the bill could become law in a matter of weeks had almost unhinged her. To lose this forever was too much to bear. This was the only place she wanted to be – where snow gums flowered like frothy lace: the summer meadows growing thick with tiny star-like daisies, and purple orchids as pretty as fairy skirts nestling at the base of grey-streaked, twisting gums: where yellow billy buttons dotted the snow grass, and around the soft edges of secret springs, moss grew in swathes of green magic beneath the ferns.

They had all worked endlessly to fence the cattle out of creek crossings that might become bogged. They had split trees and slung the heavy timber into deep postholes, straining wire and pulling taut barbs. If the snow melt was too soon and the country seemed drier and delicate, they lightened the load and took fewer cows up – sometimes well below even the light stocking rates stipulated by the National Parks. And wherever they could in the rugged country, Rod and Flo put in a snaking trail of underground poly-pipe, to create gravity-fed trough systems and keep the cattle from the creeks that ran over the tufted snow plains.

'You don't need to convince me,' Evie said, holding up her hands. 'There's no right and wrong in anything in my world. Life just is as it is.'

Emily took in Evie's gentle words, but at the same time saw Flo's face redden. Emily thought of the landscape across the fenceline, which told a very different story about the cattlemen. Uncle Bob's country, where the paddocks were flogged bare, where he let the cattle wander where they might into creek crossings. He'd spray weeds one year but then, on a booze bender, have no money for spraying them the next. He was rude to the Parkies, vocal with the media, and caused all kinds of trouble. It was that kind of hypocrisy within her own kind that sometimes made Emily shy away from the whole debate. But then she thought again of her family's history, and the fact that city bureaucrats were planning to ignore it and put a blanket grazing ban across the entire alpine area. But Flo couldn't help herself.

'How can you *not* question this?' she blurted out. 'It's a decision based on lines on a map, not the land itself. What kind of management regime is that? We'll be allowed to graze the forestry areas but not the Park . . . but how do you fence an area as steep as this when it's just an imaginary line on a map? It's bureaucratic crap!'

Flo was getting fiery now, and even though Emily had heard it all before, she too began to feel the familiar sense of distress. 'We're tired of being targeted as environmental scapegoats.'

'Yes,' added her aunt. 'All this palaver is to distract people from the real issues – like fossil fuel, water shortages, global warming, mass consumerism. It has nothing to do with the land, it's all about getting votes. *That's* why we're getting our arses kicked!'

'Ladies!' said Rod, holding up his hands. 'We can talk about this later. But Evie came here for another reason. For now, we need to find out what kind of care she can offer Emily.'

'Yes, you're right, Mr Flanaghan,' Evie said. 'I'm here to nurse Emily back to health. I can see at a glance that she's in desperate need, not just of nursing but of healing. And it seems there are others here who may need it too,' she added, directing a mild look at Sam who folded his arms across his chest.

'Who sent you?' he growled.

Ignoring him, Evie rummaged in her bag.

'Here are my nursing qualifications, and here are my fees . . . though I expect you can claim a percentage of that with your government health care.' She pushed a piece of paper over to Rod and Emily.

'It'll be easy for me to cook, too, as I'm not far down the

125

road. There'll be no charge for meals. Just a neighbour helping out.'

Rod surveyed the documents, then looked across at Emily. His daughter looked so beaten, so small and bruised. He wondered for a moment if he should entrust this woman with Emily's recovery . . . but there was something about her that seemed so familiar, so comforting that he heard himself saying, 'Sounds like we should give it a shot, eh, Em?' When she didn't respond he clapped his hands together like an auctioneer. 'Done! You're hired.'

Before Sam and Emily could question the decision, the dogs outside began to scrap, with the sound of much growling and teeth snapping.

'*Jesus Christ*!' cried out Evie.

'My sentiments exactly,' muttered Sam to Emily.

Sixteen

Two days later, with Jesus Christ lying on her lap and Rousie sleeping at her feet, Emily nestled contentedly in a comfortable lounge chair on the verandah. She sat in gentle sunshine, watching Sam and the girls grooming the ponies, grateful again to Flo for bringing Jemma and Blossom to the plains. Emily's grazes and wounds looked ugly and raw in the daylight, but she could feel the air on her skin doing them good. Nearby, Snowgum was dozing in the house paddock, her bottom lip drooping. Like Emily she was still stiff when she moved, but seemed content in the sunny meadows.

In the kitchen Evie was humming to herself and, even though the unfamiliar cooking smells emanating from the open window were disconcerting, Emily was strangely comforted by her presence. After just two days she could feel the pain deep within her start to lift. She put it down to the diet of fresh food Evie was serving up to her. Even Meg and Tilly were enjoying the change after Clancy's limited repertoire of takeaways and Rod's sound, but bland, meat and three veg menu.

The peace and quiet were shattered momentarily as the old green radio-phone shrilled from the kitchen. The sixth call that morning. It was happening again, Emily thought sadly. The frantic phone calls flooding in for Rod and Flo as they planned the cattlemen's media campaigns to defend their right to alpine grazing. Ever since the eighties it had been this way, a long, drawn-out battle that left them all depressed and depleted.

'Do you want me to get that?' Evie called, but Sam was already sprinting to the house.

'Could be my agent,' he puffed.

'Don't get your hopes up. It's probably someone from the Mountain Cattlemen's Association looking for Dad,' Emily called.

The girls wandered over to her. They stared with fascination at their mother's scars, grazes and fading yellow bruising. She felt the gentle pressure of their fingertips and flinched when their touch strayed too close to a sore patch.

'Careful!'

'I'm glad Evie's here,' Meg said.

'Oh? Why's that?' Emily replied absently.

'She's an angel.'

'She is not,' said Tilly, hands on hips. 'She doesn't have any wings.'

'She is too,' said Meg, and they began to squabble until Emily guiltily raised her voice to quieten them then coaxed them to go and gather some kindling for the campfire that night. It would be great to sit out under the stars and talk Sam into playing a tune. The girls wandered off, still debating the finer points of angels.

Just then Sam came banging out the door with a tray in his hands. On it stood a steaming pot of tea and their grandmother's ornate teacups, the ones from the back of the cupboard that they never used. They looked delicate and refined, at odds with the rough beauty of the bush around them.

'You were right. The Association Secretary's looking for Dad,' said Sam, annoyed by the interruption.

He set the tray down and leant towards Emily. 'She's a whacko, in there! You should see all the herbs she's got.' He curved his index fingers in the air when he said 'herbs'. 'I've never seen a bigger stash of hooch. She's probably put it in your tea, in these biscuits she's cooked and that stew she's making for dinner. We'll all be off our heads by sundown.'

'Well, you'd know, wouldn't you?' Emily sniped, then regretted it. 'I'm sorry, Sam. I'm a bit over it all at the moment. Clance, the accident, the parliament thing, my body. I've got too much time to think.'

'Drink your tea to start with,' said Evie as she came out of the house. 'Camomile for calm,' she said. 'And yes, Sam, I have a lot of herbs, but they're purely medicinal.'

'Yeah, *sure*,' he said, winking. '*Sure* they are.'

'Nothing of mine can be smoked or used to get high, I'm sorry. It's either blackfella bush medicine or European herbs. I've got a bit of Chinese stuff, but I find I can't grow a lot of that where I am.'

'I can get you a deer penis, if you like,' Sam offered. Emily whacked him hard on the arm.

'Don't be disgusting,' she said.

'He's fine,' said Evie, settling down on an old chair. 'I love bum and dick jokes. You go for it.'

Emily pulled an amused face at this statement from a seemingly innocent old lady.

'It's medicine that's brought me up to the mountains. That and my own personal crud that I don't need to explain to you. But it's healing I'm most interested in. Health and healing.'

'Really?' said Sam. 'I thought you were the local hooch grower. That's what they say at the pub.'

'Do they now? Well, they've never asked me. And I've never said. Let them make up their stories. It's fun for them and it does me no harm. Most of them say I'm mad. But aren't we all, in some way?'

Sam and Emily glanced at each other.

'But why live on your own on the mountain? Why not in

129

the town and work as a nurse at the bush hospital?' Emily asked her.

Evie shrugged. 'Because I'm a loner. Like you Flanaghans, I love the mountains. Anyway, I've moved beyond that conventional medicine stuff so the hospital is no place for me. It serves its purpose well, but my approach to health lies in what's between the ears.'

'What do you mean?'

'Well, take yourself, for example.' Evie looked squarely at Emily. 'From your injuries, I can tell a lot about you emotionally and about how you think.'

'Yeah, right,' said Emily, laughing. 'I thought: Shit, here comes a tree!'

Evie ignored her jibe and continued talking in her calm, gentle voice. 'The fact you have broken ribs tells me you're having deep trouble being the woman you think you should be in your relationship with a man. You sold out your true self. It tells me you're rebelling against authority in some way – you've had a lifetime of the anti-grazing movement, have you not? And the fact you had an accident tells me you not only want to rebel against this authority, but you have lost your voice from it. No doubt, from your injuries, you're finding it hard to breathe, which tells me that you are fearful, not able to take in life fully. It tells me you sometimes feel that you don't even have the right to take up space and exist in this world.'

'Crap!' said Sam, who was leaning on the verandah post, rolling a cigarette. 'You don't know our Emily then.'

'Fine if you think it's crap, Sam,' Evie replied. She turned her clear gaze on him. 'A person takes on addictive habits when he is trying to run from himself. I'm sure you have that feeling of "what's the use?" in life. I know you feel guilt, futility and inadequacy.'

'Doesn't everyone?' he said defensively.

'Drug addiction and alcoholism,' Evie continued, 'are forms of self-rejection by people who can't see the light of God within themselves.'

Sam's eyes were blazing now. 'So you're calling me a drug addict and an alcoholic? What would you know?'

Evie looked heavenward. 'I'm guided by intuitive energies from Source.'

'See! She *is* a God-bothering nutter.' Sam shot a glance at Emily, then looked back at Evie. 'What right do you have to come here and judge us?'

'I'm here because I was called here. And I don't judge.'

'Ooh! Called here, were you? Direct line to God, eh? He got you on the 1800 Source hotline, did He?'

'No. It was the nursing staff at Dargo, actually. They rang. They seemed to know your family needed more than just medical healing. Simply some support.'

Emily froze at the mention of the Dargo Bush Hospital. Could it be Penny who had orchestrated this whole thing out of guilt? She felt Evie's steady gaze on her as if she were reading her mind.

'Emily,' Evie soothed her, 'you've got a lot to process. It's a time of transition for you. There's nothing wrong with a marriage ending.' Emily's eyes widened. So Evie *could* read minds. 'It simply just *is*. Your journey in life is always solo, from birth to death, and though some people may choose to journey together for a time through marriage, one person may transition and change so that they choose to journey on elsewhere. It's all it is.' Evie shrugged and sipped at her tea. Emily blinked. Was she referring to her own situation with Penny and Clancy? And if so, how much did this woman know?

'So Clancy changed?'

'No, my dear. You did.'

Evie gathered her light floral shawl about her shoulders and shut her eyes, breathing out of her nose like a Yogi. Sam twirled his finger round near his temple and swivelled his eyes, signalling that the woman was whacko. Evie opened her eyes again and leant closer to Emily.

'I know something else, too. Men can be utter bastards and choose never to grow up. Sometimes a trip to the sex-toy shop is a better option for us women than a live man.' And Evie winked at Emily as Sam spluttered up his mouthful of tea.

'That's great, Confucius,' he said swiping his wet shirt-front, 'but why do you need to come here, to our family to dish our your herbal crap and unwanted advice?' Emily shot him a look but Evie seemed unaffected by his rudeness.

'I've been out to enough remote bush-nursing stations to know how a displacement from the land can affect the spirit. You see, the body and its health reflect your thoughts and emotions, and these mountains are your heart-place. The medicos may dismiss it as hippy shit, but the better aligned science and spiritualism become, the better people will heal.'

'And what about you?' Sam asked, resting one foot behind him on the verandah post. 'Do you have any pearls of wisdom about *yourself*?'

Evie smiled. 'Are you asking that so as to avoid reflecting on your own situation? Is that why you haven't yet given up your addictions?'

Sam let out a strangled cry of frustration, grabbed up his tobacco and matches and stormed off towards the stables.

'He's still using, isn't he?' Emily said, watching him go.

'I think so.'

'He said he gave me everything he had. I burnt it in the campfire, but he must have more somewhere. He's not normally so hostile.'

'Do you want me to look?'

'He'll be angry,' Emily said sadly.

'It has to be done.'

'I know.'

'Leave it with me.'

Evie went inside, leaving Emily to meditate on what had just been said about herself and Sam. This woman, a complete stranger, had perfectly summed up their lives. Each painful breath Emily took reminded her of her battles with Clancy over the past six years, and of her family's struggle with bureau-cracy. At first in her marriage she had felt perfectly aligned with him, but then when the babies had come and her life had transformed, it was as if she had no connection to the man who slept beside her. She began to feel wiser and more capable than Clancy, despite his being older. She no longer looked up to him. Instead she began to feel frustrated with his simplicity and narrow view of the world. So Evie reckoned she was journeying in a different direction, did she? Emily took comfort from the notion – it sounded better than labelling herself a failed wife.

Evie came back out, a plastic packet in her hand. 'That should be the last of it.'

'Thank you,' Emily said.

They sat in silence for a time, the buzz of March flies disturbing the dogs now and then. They heard a cow call out from the bush.

'Evie?'

'Mmm?'

'Why has my life ended up like this? Almost divorced. Almost kicked off the cattle runs just when I've chosen to come back to them?'

'My dear girl,' Evie said, 'you can't alter what people think, do, say or how they act. Whether it's people in the cities who live beside factories and motorways yet insist that your grass-fed cattle farts are causing global warming, or whether it's a husband who has stopped seeing the beauty within you, it's how *you* respond to these situations that counts. Not how you react, but how you *respond*. Worrying is a complete waste of energy. You need to work out your own true path and not worry about others. How are you going to respond?'

'Respond to what?'

'The situation you're in.'

'Like losing the cattle runs?' Emily paused, thinking. 'The Mountain Cattlemen's Association is organising a protest ride in Melbourne in three weeks' time.'

'And is that the answer?'

Emily shrugged. 'I doubt it. But we have to make people aware.'

'Sometimes the more we protest, the more we're *anti* something, the more fuel we add to that fire. We perpetuate the negative situation. Better to be *pro*-something instead. It creates a better flow of energy. There's as little point in ranting against your husband as there is in ranting against the politicians. It doesn't serve you.'

Emily sat in stunned silence, staring out at the trees. Evie was right. The more they went head-to-head against the scientists, environmentalists and bureaucrats, the less ground they seemed to gain. The more she railed against Clancy in her head, the worse the situation seemed to get. Emily suddenly thought of Ratgirl in the ambulance and her fury over the bilby. Suddenly, horrifyingly, she realised she was no different from that strange angry girl dressed in a costume (except Ratgirl had had a gorgeous boyfriend). They were both protesting against something, while simutaneously making the problem bigger. They were both angry at their men, yet could easily have chosen not to be.

She frowned and turned back to Evie. 'So you mean I should be pro-environment and pro-grazing? Even pro-Clancy. Is that what you're saying?'

'First, ban the word "should" from your vocabulary. That word is a waste of effort, a noose!' Evie reached out and touched Emily's hand. 'You can be anything you like, dear, but you'll create more change by being pro-something, coming up with answers and solutions, creating flow, than you will playing one energy off against another. '

'Ah!' said Emily. 'But how do I do that?'

'Wait one sec.'

Evie disappeared into the house again. Rousie stood, stretched and settled back on his haunches. He set his head in Emily's lap, nosing Jesus Christ out of the way, and sighed deeply as if to say, Bear with her. Bear with this strange old woman. Have patience.

Evie returned with an armful of books.

'The best way to make a difference and to heal yourself

and the people around you, is to control the thoughts in your mind. I've brought some reading for you.'

She unloaded the books on to Emily's lap. *Beyond the Brink, The Future Eaters, Ask & It Is Given*, and the odd one out – a government publication with a dry, lengthy title.

'What's this one?'

'It's a study of how the Tasmanian National Parks organisation use cattle and the cattlemen's expertise to periodically graze wilderness areas there. It's particularly interesting as it shows people working together, not against each other, to manage the land,' Evie said, tapping the cover. 'It shows that, perhaps, in a controlled way, the cattle do belong here on this mountainside, and that local people are worth listening to.'

'But I thought you were against the cattlemen?'

'I'm not against anything, my dear.'

Evie stroked Emily's head and the energy from her hand sent warmth flowing through her scalp and body.

'I simply believe in balance. Now, you need to get on with your healing and then you can go on that ride in Melbourne. After your time with your husband, it is now time to be with your people. Your family needs someone like you, to give them a new direction. '

'What do you mean "like me"?'

'You don't see it, my dear, but you radiate light. You think you are just a single mother with a broken body, but in fact you are a powerful creature with the world at your fingertips. You are truly light.'

'Light?'

'Yes. As is your youngest.'

'Meg?'

'Yes.' Evie gently placed on Emily's lap the old photo album that was usually to be found in the lounge room, with photos haphazardly added to it over the years, particularly on wild days when it was too rough to ride out on the plains. 'Take a closer look. Children are purer. They haven't had time to disbelieve. She's an old soul, that one.'

Evie left Emily alone to flip through the album. With astonishment she began to see the way the camera picked up a shining white glow around Meg's form. Either the crown of her head was lit as if by a halo, or the outline of her body shone with silver light. In some photos the light was subtle, in others it was clear and strong. One picture taken at the Mount Ewan spring captured Meg looking deep into the camera lens. She seemed one with the spring that gushed out of the ancient rock to sustain the gentle fronds of deep green ferns. Meg crouched beside the silver bubbling water and beside her, caught in mid-flight, was a winged insect. Of course, Emily knew it was a dragonfly. But the way Meg's eyes shone as the flying creature hovered near her made them seem somehow connected, like earth sprites or fairies.

'No,' Emily said, shaking her common sense back into place. She snapped the book shut. Where was all this taking her? Before the accident, she'd been a simple mother of two children. Now, more and more, she was deciding she didn't know herself at all.

From inside, the radio-phone shrilled again.

'Emily! For you,' called Evie.

Reluctantly she stood up from her warm nest in the big old armchair and made her way inside, Rousie's claws clicking on the lino as he followed her in.

Evie handed her the phone and as she did so said quietly, 'Remember, you are light.'

'Hello?' The voice on the other end of the line made Emily's heart sink. It was Clancy's. She looked at Evie in desperation, but Evie only looked heavenward and pulled a silly face.

'How dare you do a runner with my kids!' Emily heard her husband roar over the static that hissed on the mountain line.

'I didn't. I did a runner from the hospital and the kids are where they are supposed to be. With me . . . with their family.'

There was that bull-like breathing again.

'You can't take them from me!'

Emily bit her fingernails as she listened, wanting to explode with rage. As she did, Evie turned out a perfect chocolate cake cooked in the woodstove and gave her a wink, then pulled another silly face. With all her resolve, Emily kept her voice calm.

'No, Clancy, I could never take them from you. You are their father. You are welcome to visit them here. Or we can meet you at Dargo for a counter meal, if you like.'

There was silence on the line. He had been expecting a different response.

'Can't,' he said eventually. 'Got a Brisbane run this week. But don't think you can smartarse your way round this! I'll be back for the girls, Emily. You won't be able to hide them up there away from me forever.'

'Goodbye, Clancy,' she said calmly. But as she hung up the phone she couldn't stop her hands from shaking.

Seventeen

Luke wound the Datsun up to its full speed of ninety kilometres along the four-lane freeway. He was given angry toots and the bird by other frustrated drivers, which made him even more furious than he already was. The fights with Cassy were intensifying. Just as he had vowed to break up with her, she had gone and injured her foot. He'd felt bad about leaving her to hobble about the house fending for herself, so for the past few weeks he had stayed. But it had been an intense and fiery time of tears, tantrums and yelling matches. This latest fight had been over the cattlemen. Luke knew Cassy had deliberately picked it because he was packing to move to Dargo.

He glanced into the rear-view mirror, fleetingly meeting his own eyes. Luke knew he wasn't a bad person, but this last fight with Cassy had revealed his uglier side. The more he pushed her into behaving like a shrew, the less guilty he could feel about leaving. He remembered how she had hobbled into the kitchen on crutches and slapped a newspaper on to the kitchen table.

'It's placard-painting time,' she'd said.

'Now?' Luke had looked up from the stack of papers and books he was putting in a box. 'Cass,' he said wearily, 'you know I'm leaving next week. I've got other stuff to do.'

She ignored him, jabbing a finger at the newspaper. 'Says

here there's a protest ride in the city next week. Thousands of those bloody redneck cattlemen . . . hundreds of 'em riding their horses. Can you imagine the stress those animals will be put under? Bastards!'

She pointed at the small map in the paper.

'They start at the MCG, then down Wellington Parade to Flinders Street Station, then up Swanston and on to Bourke Street to Parliament House.'

'Really?' Luke said. He wondered whether that pretty girl from the hospital would be there. 'Sounds great. I'd like to go. I love horses.'

'I've got to let Indigo and the guys at PETA know. We have to move fast . . .' Cassandra stopped talking suddenly and gave him a strange look. 'What did you just say? *You love horses*? You never told me that. I thought you loved cars.'

'What? I don't even like cars.'

'But you're always tinkering with the bloody Datto.'

'That's because it's always breaking down.' He picked up one of the magazines he was packing and pushed it in front of her.

'*Horse Deals*? You read *Horse Deals*! What for?'

He shook his head then, knowing that in the two intense years they'd been together, Cassy hadn't taken a scrap of notice of what he liked or didn't like. It was all about what *she* liked. Life in the city with Cassy was so in-your-face, with no stillness, he'd somehow been able to stop feeling altogether.

As he looked at the cover of *Horse Deals*, the thought of sitting on a beautiful, perfectly educated stock horse in the mountains gave Luke new hope.

'Have you ever had a working dog lean on your leg and look up at you?'

'What?' asked Cassy.

'Do you know what that feels like?'

'A dog on your leg?'

'No! Not a dog on your leg. That look a working dog gives you. The warmth and love in its eyes.'

'What are you on about?'

'Or the way a horse will bend its body round for you if you simply touch it lightly on the flank.'

'*What*?'

Luke snatched the magazine back.

'You'll never understand. You're too in your own head even to notice!' He had raised his voice. Could feel himself shaking. It shocked him, just how much bubbled below the surface in him. A kind of fury, and a deep, deep sadness that he had lost any connection to the life he had loved. No soil, save for the box of seeded parsley on the back windowsill. No animals, save for greasy-looking starlings and hungry little sparrows that flitted about the back step.

'In my own head? I'm doing this for the good of the world. I'm going to that cattlemen's rally for the sake of the environment. What are you going for? To look at horses! You're going to be a park ranger up there in less than a fortnight and here you are, backing them?' Fury blazed in Cassy's eyes. 'I can't believe your hypocrisy!'

'Me, a hypocrite! *You* protest about everything outside of this place,' Luke was shouting back. 'But what about making a difference here? What about a community garden? Or a backyard battery-hen rehab project? Or teaching city kids about food and the land and the cycles of life and death? Why don't you do something good for a change, instead of continually crapping on other people? Actually *produce* something yourself.'

'I can't believe you. If you've got all the answers, Einstein, why haven't *you* done anything like that? I'm the one doing good. I'm the one making a difference. Lately, you just sit around, not talking. You don't smile. You don't even care!'

'Because I've been dead, Cassy! Dead! For the past two years!'

'What do you mean, dead?'

'I don't know,' Luke said, near to tears, running his hands through his dark curls. Emotion blurred his vision. He sat in

140

stony silence, trying to make sense of the newspaper text in front of him. Anything to keep a lid on the emotions he now felt struggling to emerge.

Quotes flashed up at him from the page. These were the sentiments of rural people on their knees. 'Enough's enough', one read. 'Tired of being treated like second-class citizens', said another. 'The state government think rural people don't count', 'A risk there will be no Australian farmers in the future'.

The words began to swim on the page again. Luke had heard these sentiments all his life. They just depressed and confused him even more. Cassy, shocked to see him break down, placed one hand on his shoulder.

Furious, he shook off her touch with a bear-like roar. He flung the box he was packing to the floor and stood up so suddenly the chair fell backwards with a crash.

From the hallway Karla called out, 'Are you two having wild sex on the kitchen table again? Please move my assignment off the table if you are!'

Luke grabbed his keys. He knew the way he felt wasn't all Cassy's fault. But he also knew he needed to get out of this crazy, faltering relationship.

'I'm going out.'

'What do you mean, *out*?'

'*Out* out,' he said, slamming the front door so hard the picture of Krishna came crashing down in the hallway.

And that was how he'd come to be on the freeway in his buzzing little Datsun with absolutely nowhere to go. He wanted desperately to go back to the house where he was raised, where his mother had cooked the veggies she had so carefully grown, where he was free to go yabbying, chop down a sapling looking for bait, or simply wander in the culverts beside the empty roadside. All that space and stillness.

But he knew he was remembering the place through the rosiness of distance and time. The reality of life on the wheat farm had been a different story. His father was worn down and crumpled by stress, his weathered face prematurely

141

creased with lines. His mother, drab in her work clothes, with very little reason to smile. The day the footy coach came and cried on the doorstep, telling them the team had folded. The way Luke's mother had fought alongside the other people in the town to keep the local hospital open. Then they had closed the school, too, and allowed city-folk to sink their money into managed-investment schemes so that farms like theirs were bought and ripped up for trees.

They, thought Luke. Who were 'they'? All these people driving past him in their comfy, clean cars to their offices? He was about to become part of the massive 'they', wasn't he? He was about to join the big bureaucratic giant that managed the forests, the schools, the roads, the hospitals. He felt daunted and dwarfed by the prospect. How could he ever hope to fit in, with a man like Giles Grimsley as his boss? But at least he'd be living in the heart of the mountains. He'd be able to get away from all the city guff spewed forth every day from billboards, radio stations, newspapers, televisions, shop windows and the painted sides of buses.

Bugger this, he thought. He pulled over into a side lane and dialled the number of the woman he'd spoken to in VPP Human Resources. When he at last had her on the line, he asked if he could meet the outgoing Dargo ranger today, if not tomorrow.

'I'm not sure we can accommodate your request at such short notice, Mr Bradshaw. It's really not my department. Your orientation with the outgoing ranger is scheduled for next week.'

'That's okay,' he said wearily. 'I'll just drive out there myself and take a look at the town.'

Luke steered out into the traffic, his mouth set in a determined line.

'Dargo or bust!' he yelled, banging the steering wheel and suddenly feeling much, much better.

Eighteen

The main street of Dargo was wide and lined with large walnut trees that cast dappled shade across the road. A blonde girl with a big bum walking along the roadside caught Luke's eye. She was hard to miss in her hot-pink top and torn denim shorts, and was walking a Pomeranian with an arse that looked much like its head. Another woman, wearing a fluoro vest, was on a roadside slasher, cutting the long grass beneath the shady trees, while an elderly man sat in a verandah chair and waved lazily as Luke drove past.

Apart from that, the street lay empty. The houses dozed in the afternoon summer sun, protected by their leafy gardens and the tall trees that grew in the fertile river-flat soils. Luke caught occasional glimpses of the bush-covered hills beyond the town, too many to count, wave after wave of steep pitched rises tapering up towards the mountains. He smiled, feeling hopeful that soon this place would be his home, and the people in it his friends. And he would come to know this country.

Within moments he was in the heart of Dargo. One store, and opposite it one pub. He pulled up beside a phone booth and took in the whole of the humble township. The store had a grey corrugated-iron roof with the words 'Dargo Store' stencilled on it in large white lettering, in the same font he'd used once on his dad's wool bales.

The pub had a rusty red roof with 'Dargo Hotel' painted in the same glowing white text upon it. Its thick timber upright beams and slab-cut weatherboards spoke of generations of bushmen and their skills. Luke looked again at the store.

In the deep shade of the verandah, on a bench seat, two elderly men were sitting smoking, not saying much of anything to each other. To the right of the store, a shadecloth was hanging over a lawn, with white plastic tables and chairs set out for visiting tourists and their continual need for cappuccinos and lattes.

He felt like going into the pub for a beer, parking the Datsun next to the row of dusty four-wheel drives and utes. These had all manner of blokey items on their trays, including tatty-eared working dogs, fuel drums, welders and chainsaw boxes. Luke decided he'd better head into the store first for something to eat, and to find out where the VPP office was, then a beer.

The old men on the bench nodded g'day and watched with mild curiosity as he passed. The screen door shut behind him, enclosing him in the store's cool, dark interior. The ceiling fans whopped overhead, and as his eyes adjusted from the bright sunshine outside he saw that the place was a hive of activity.

A lean woman sorted letters behind a postal desk, while a young girl in a singlet top and shorts stacked vegetables from a box into tall glass-faced fridges. In a noisy kitchen beyond, another woman thumped the basket of the deep fryer and drained a batch of chips. As Luke stepped towards the counter a juvenile wombat trundled out and began to chew on his bootlaces.

'Hello,' he said, a smile on his face as he stooped to scratch behind the animal's ears. The counter was crowded with stubby holders, postcards, lollies and community fundraiser chocolates, and the shelves were crammed with camping and fishing gear.

'Are you right?' asked the girl in the singlet, pushing her glasses higher on her nose and tossing a cabbage up and down in her tanned hands.

'Just looking for the moment, thanks,' he said shyly.

'Fine, take your time,' she said, then stepped forward and berated the wombat, scooping it up. 'Rack off, Sophie. You're supposed to be in bed.' She bundled it into a bag behind the counter. 'Sorry 'bout that. She's a real tart. Likes the boys.'

The girl looked him up and down, then went back to her fridge-stocking. Luke felt the scrutiny from the other locals, like he'd just stumbled into a frontier town. He remembered what Giles Grimsley had said about the hostility here and wondered if it might be better not to mention he was the new ranger.

He was relieved to spot a bookstand featuring self-published titles on local history. Perfect, he thought. He could read up about the place before he started the job. He picked up a book with a black-and-white photo of a bewhiskered miner on it, and flicked through it. One passage caught his eye and he began reading.

Time and time again, Emily shines out in the Flanaghan story as far more than just tough. A tireless worker, astute businesswoman, dedicated mother and steadfast no-nonsense friend.

No-nonsense, Luke thought to himself. He liked the idea of that, and, so far, he really liked the look of Dargo too. There were no monster shopping malls with giant superstores, no dozen-bay carwashes, no vast entertainment complexes for children. No glossed-over reality.

He shifted the weight on his feet and read on.

Early in 1878 Jeremiah Flanaghan borrowed some horses and took his wife Emily, his children, and all his worldly possessions into the mountains. Emily rode a saddle mare and carried her fourth child, a nine-month-old baby. Her husband fitted an armchair on each side of the second horse for the older children to ride in. Blankets, rugs and so on were stuffed in around the children, and they were strapped to the chairs so they would not fall out.

> The decision to pin all their hopes on this rather risky-sounding venture and shift the young family and all its possessions to a remote spur in the very heart of the snow country could not have been an easy one to make. But both Jeremiah and Emily were courageous and ambitious enough to give it a try, in the hope that it would somehow lead them into opportunities later on, that other less adventurous types would miss out on.

Luke glanced up from the book. Adventure . . . That was definitely what had been missing from his life. Perhaps here he would find a bit of it.

'Emily!' came a voice from the doorway. 'Emily!'

Luke looked up to see a good-looking bloke calling back through the flydoor. He seemed kind of familiar, but Luke couldn't place him.

'D'ya want a pie?'

A voice from outside called, 'Yeah, thanks!'

'Shut the bloody door, Flanno. You're letting the flies in,' called the girl in the singlet.

'Sorry, Kate. Bossy bag.'

'I'll give you one in the bag,' she said, setting aside her veggie-packing. 'What can I get you?'

'Just Dad's fortnightly order on the tab,' he said, handing over a list, 'and two pies.'

'Sauce?'

'Yep. Thanks.'

When the screen door opened again and a young woman walked in, Luke didn't recognise her at first. She wore threadbare, faded green work trousers. They were several sizes too big, rolled up at the legs and hitched over her waist with some old braces. Under the braces she wore a blue-checked flannelette shirt, one sleeve ripped off at the shoulder, the other tattered. There was a rolled towel under one shoulder of the braces, obviously to stop it rubbing on an injury beneath that was taped heavily, and her arm had a grotty plaster cast on

146

it. The whole look was topped off with an old, oil-stained Caterpillar cap. She looked like a hillbilly, straight out of *Deliverance* country, but under the hat he recognised the sweet face of the woman from the hospital.

As she swiped the grubby cap from her head Luke was struck again by the prettiness of that face. Despite her clothing, this young woman was stunning. From behind the shelves, he had more of an opportunity to study her than he'd had sitting beside her outside the hospital.

As he did so, Kate set down the pies on the counter and let out a long, slow wolf-whistle.

'My, don't you look gorgeous, Emily?'

'Yeah,' she said, 'bloody bewdiful, eh? Trust Auntie Flo to deliver my horse, my saddle, my boots, my undie collection and my stockwhip up top . . . but no other clothes! I considered one of Gran's frocks, but florals ain't my bag.'

'I heard you'd done a runner from the hospital. Apart from the clothes, you're looking better than I imagined,' Kate said. 'Let me deck you out in a new flannie and trousers.'

'Thanks, Kate, but I'll find something at Dad's later.'

Luke sucked in his breath then before stepping out from behind the shelves.

'Geez!' shrieked Kate. 'I clean forgot you were there. You scared the crap out of me!'

'Sorry.' He looked at Emily. 'Hello again.'

'*You!*' she said, eyes widening as she recognised the gorgeous guy from the hospital standing in front of her again. Those dark curls, the worn green T-shirt and the jeans that hugged his fit body . . .

'Yes, me!'

Emily smiled as she spoke. 'What are you doing here?'

Luke wasn't ready to tell her he was going to be working for the VPP. He realised he still had the book in his hands. 'Umm . . . shopping for books?'

Emily saw that he was holding the book about her family history.

'It's a good story, that one,' she said, eyes twinkling.

'An introduction any time now would be nice,' put in Sam, leaning on the shop counter.

Luke and Emily looked at each other and burst out laughing.

'I'd like to introduce him to you but I don't know who he is.'

Sam and Kate both frowned.

'I see,' said Sam.

'I don't,' said Kate.

'We met once at the hospital. This is my brother, Sam Flanaghan, and this is Kate.'

'Sam Flanaghan?' Luke said. 'As in the singer? I *knew* I knew you. '

Sam flashed him a courteous smile. He was used to being recognised.

'Nice to meet you both. And you?' Luke said to Emily.

'Emily Flanaghan.' She held out her hand and he shook it, Emily revelling in his touch.

'I'm Luke. Luke Bradshaw.'

'A pleasure to meet you properly this time, Luke.'

'A pleasure it is.' They held each other's hands for a fraction longer than normal, and held each other's gaze, too, until Sam cleared his throat.

'Time to get on.'

'Yes, see you round,' said Emily, suddenly letting go of Luke's hand, blushing and almost bumbling out of the store, remembering what she must look like.

Luke was left watching her through the dark gauze of the flyscreen.

'Made up your mind?' Kate asked pointedly.

Yes,' he said, 'as a matter of fact, I have.'

'Well, good for you.'

'Pie, please, with sauce, and this book.'

'Reading up on Emily's family history, I see?'

'What?'

'The book. It's all about Sam's and Emily's family.'

'Great,' he said.

148

'Can I help you with anything else today?'

Luke paused.

'Umm . . . yes. Can you tell me where the VPP office is?' He could see Kate was curious as to why he was asking.

'Down the street on the right. Opposite the school. You taking over from old Darcy?'

'I suppose so.'

'It surprises me they've sent someone new. There's been talk that the VPP'll run this side of the mountain out of Heyfield, a hundred clicks thataway as the crow flies,' she said, pointing towards the back of the store. 'But you can ask old Darcy about that. Doesn't agree with what they're doing down there in the city . . . kicking the cows off and that. I reckon that's why he's getting out now.'

'Darcy?'

'Yeah, Robert Crosswell. We call him Darcy. He can tell you all about it, but if you're looking for him, you won't find him around here today.'

'Where is he then?'

Kate flicked her head in the direction of Heyfield.

'He'll be in a meeting. Always in meetings over there. But you can still check out the ranger's office. It'll be unlocked.'

'It will?'

'Sure.'

'Thanks,' said Luke. He picked up his pie.

'Oh,' added Kate, 'Sophie's all good for her paperwork.'

'Sorry?'

'The wombat. We've got the permits now for keeping a native animal. In case you were wondering.'

'I wasn't.'

'Well,' said Kate, 'that's not what the last graduate ranger who came here said.' She rolled her eyes.

Luke bit his lip.

'I might be different from the last bloke,' he said as he began to walk out of the store.

'Let's hope that you are,' muttered Kate, but Luke had heard.

Nineteen

Emily sat in Sam's ute outside the pub, watching Luke as he ate his pie in the shade of the shop verandah across the road. She was just wondering what he was doing in town when Bridie arrived, towing an overweight, panting Pomeranian.

'Emily! Thank God you're alive!'

'Hey,' she said, getting out of the ute and hugging her friend. Suddenly Emily was transported back to the Cattlemen's and the night before the race. It was as if meeting Bridie that night had somehow opened her up to this path of change, this life without Clancy. Just being near her again had given Emily the encouragement she'd needed to believe she could leave him, and she was grateful to her friend for that. She was also overjoyed to see her now in Dargo.

'I heard you'd taken off from the hospital,' Bridie said. She looked at Emily sympathetically. 'And I heard you'd left Clancy.'

'Yep.'

'You doing okay?'

Emily nodded but her eyes had moistened.

'Good for you. Where are the girls?'

'Dad took 'em to the beach for a treat, and to get away from all the bloody protest ride organising just for one day. It's been pretty insane.'

'Didn't you wanna go with them?'

'Me? Nah. Not the beach. Don't feel like I want to go anywhere just yet.'

'That's understandable. You'd look shocking in a pair of swimmers with your hospital tan, and you'd surely get sand down your cast. But how are you, really?' Bridie asked. Before Emily could answer her friend waved her silver-ringed fingers in the air and said, 'No, don't answer that. You look like shit so I don't need to ask!'

'You're the second person today to tell me I look like shit. No wonder I haven't ventured into town till now! All I'm getting is insults,' Emily said, smiling.

'Listen, if you're going to look like shit, I'm the *best* person to bump into. Hey, what are you doing now?'

Emily shrugged. 'Kate's just getting our grocery order ready, Sam's getting a carton, and then we were heading back up.'

'Right, that's it. You've got an hour or so to spare. You're coming to my place. Here, hold this.' She picked up the fluffy dog and shoved it at Emily. 'Get in. I'll drive,' said Bridie, clearly impressed by Sam's sporty V8.

'But . . . Sam?'

'What about me?'

The girls spun about to see Sam with a beer carton under his arm making his way over to them.

'Sam bloody Flanaghan!'

He tilted his head to one side taking in the blonde curvy girl before him, his face blank.

'It's Pudden Guts,' Bridie told him. 'Remember? Dargo Primary.'

Still he looked blank.

'She's changed, hasn't she?' Emily said.

'Yeah. Whoever *she* is.'

'*She* is Bridie McFarlane!' Bridie said, doing a twirl and curtsy, pushing out her large, denim-clad bottom.

'Hooly dooly, *Bridie*! You're . . . you're . . .' Sam was stuttering, hypnotised by the sight of her generous breasts rising up out of her singlet top. He set down the carton. '. . . you're bloody eye-poppingly, amazingly *gorgeous*!'

'Well, that's a bit strong, but I have shaken off my Pudden Guts image and grown up.'

'And out,' he said, quickly adding, '*in all the right places*!'

'And you haven't changed,' she said. 'Still a pretty boy tryin' to get the world's attention.'

'But not the only pretty boy in town today,' Emily said. 'Check out the fella over at the store, Bridie.'

She glanced over at Luke, who was now getting into his little car. He smiled and waved at them. Bridie gave a low whistle. 'Cute as! Well, you've got a bit of competition in town for a change,' she said, tapping Sam on his chest. 'Who is that honey-babe?'

'Some city-boy blow-in,' Sam said.

'Just like you, hey?' she teased. 'What's his name?'

'Luke Bradshaw.'

Before Emily could stop her, Bridie was bellowing out, 'Hey, Luke!' He wound his window down. 'Feel like having a beer with this fella here?' She pointed to Sam.

Luke shrugged, got out of his car and began to walk over to the pub, a big grin on his face.

'What are you doing?' hissed Emily.

'Shhh,' said Bridie, winking. 'Tactics.' She beamed at Luke and said loudly, 'Sam here needs some company for an hour or so. Are you up for a beer while I take his sister to my place to get her minge waxed?'

Emily turned bright red and stifled a mortified scream. Luke laughed. 'Yeah. Sure.' Bridie held her charming smile and directed it towards Sam. 'Mind if I borrow your ute?'

'No worries,' he said, while Emily looked on amazed. He never let *her* drive his ute. 'Have fun.' He and Luke turned and made their way inside the crooked old door of the Dargo Hotel.

Emily slapped her friend on the shoulder.

'How could you? I can't believe you said that about my

minge in front of him! My God, Bridie, what were you thinking?'

'It's my trade. I can't help it. Might as well be upfront with people.'

'Well, let *me* tell *you* about being upfront. You aren't going anywhere *near* my front bum with hot wax!'

'Oh, get in,' said Bridie.

Emily stood her ground.

'*Get in*!'

Bridie drove about two hundred metres down the road, bunny-hopping Sam's ute all the way, and turned the engine off outside an old miner's cottage. A new sign was screwed to the white picket fence: *Beauty in the Bush*.

Bridie smiled as she watched Emily read it.

'Get it?'

'Get what?'

'Beauty in the Bush,' she said, then burst out laughing. 'It gets me every time! Beauty in the bush,' she said again, indicating the bush-covered hills surrounding Dargo, 'and beauty in the *bush*,' this time pointing to her crotch.

'Oh my God!' said Emily, getting it at last. 'That's a classic!'

'Yeah. The fellas at the pub think it's a scream. And it sounds better than Beauty in the *Country*!'

Again they laughed hard, before subsiding into silence.

'It's great to see you again,' Emily said sincerely.

'And you too. It's so good you've moved back up.' They paused, both thinking of Clancy.

'You know Clancy's seeing Penny from the hospital?' Emily said.

Bridie bit her lip and nodded. 'He's been here drunk every weekend. Comes up from Brigalow, Friday through Sunday. Word's out Road Transport are after him most Monday mornings 'cos he's so topped up with booze he shouldn't be drivin' the truck. We don't know if he's here for Penny or if he's hoping to catch you.'

'So he doesn't plan on coming up to see the girls on the plains?'

'He's told people he's done and dusted with you.'

'Do you think I should see him? Talk to him?'

Bridie turned to face her. 'Dunno. Probably. But maybe not just yet. You need to get strong, girl, inside and out, before you take that man on. He is bad news with a capital B.'

'Yes. It's just, I don't know . . . life hasn't turned out the way I thought it would,' Emily said quietly. 'The whole thing sucks.'

'Hey,' said Bridie, 'I know, Em. But I'm here to help you. We can help each other. My life didn't turn out the way I thought it would either. But this is our chance to make it better. C'mon inside. Bring Muff with you.'

'Muff?'

'Yeah. My dog.'

'You called your dog *Muff*?'

'Yeah. She reminds me of one of those old-fashioned things ladies warmed their hands in. You know, those rolls of fur. Look at her, she looks just like a muff.'

'You wax bikini lines and you call your dog *Muff*?'

'I know. Priceless, isn't it? The boys think that's a scream too.'

'I bet they do.'

'I never told them I've got a cat, though. I'd never hear the end of the pussy jokes!'

'Well? What's the cat's name?'

Bridie shook her head and raised one hand to her mouth to stifle a giggle. She muttered the name into her hand, but Emily couldn't hear it. She was already laughing from Bridie's infectious gaiety.

'What?'

'Beaver, okay? The cat's called *Beaver*.'

'Beaver?' screamed Emily and both girls dissolved into fits of laughter. 'You, dear Bridie, are the queen of fur!'

'Well, what are you waiting fur! Let's get you up on the slab!'

For all her gaudy dress sense and brassy blonde locks, Bridie

154

had done up the cottage beautifully. Emily felt soothed just standing in the whitewashed salon with its soft towels, dim lights and scent of roses, but her own reflection in the full-length mirror made her heart sink.

'Oh, my God! That's not me,' she said, turning sideways to check out her backside. 'I can't believe I was talking to that hot bloke looking like this.'

'I know. You have kinda got that quarter-horse look going on, what with your hogged mane and that rounded arse. Those pants really don't do much for you.'

'Oh, geez, Bridie. I don't reckon you can do much for me either. Let's just forget the whole thing.' Bridie grabbed her arm to stop Emily leaving.

'Whoah there! You're not going anywhere. Bridie can work miracles. Bridie is a professional.' She wove her fingers together and cracked them. 'Now, I don't play Enya, or Norah Jones. Can't stand the woeful moaners. I will however do Dolly P. And, at a stretch, I'll play The Corrs.'

'Got any Sunny Cowgirls?'

'Do rabbits like to fornicate? 'Course I have. Now get your gear off,' said Bridie, handing Emily a robe. 'We'll have you Princess Mary'd in no time, darls.'

As Bridie left the room, Emily stripped down to her underwear. She looked in the mirror again and rolled her eyes. Her undies were white full briefs that rose up over her tummy and sat low on her thighs. Printed in black lettering across the front was *Why, hello, Mummy!* There was an angry red scar on her collarbone where the doctors had cut her open to pin the break, and her whole body seemed to list sideways from the weight of the plaster cast. She'd taken to carrying a piece of Number-8 wire in her pocket, just to reach the itches that bothered her night and day beneath the cast. Thankfully the grazing on her face and upper arm had healed and she had lost a good few kilos since the accident, but she still looked a wreck.

'You complete dag,' she said to herself before pulling off

her mummy undies, clambering up on to the table and covering herself quickly with a towel.

Emily let out a scream as pain ripped through her skin.

'Geez, Louise!'

'Get over it, wuss,' laughed Bridie. She set aside the small white strip of cloth and dipped the waxing knife into the pot, then expertly ran the metal blade across Emily's shin again. 'Wait till I do your bikini line!'

'I told you, you are not going anywhere near my bikini line, you sadistic bitch! I don't mind mine looking like Muff.'

'You've been married too long. That thing has to come off! Besides, what's worse? Collecting a tree at full pelt on a horse or having a Brazilian?'

'I dunno. I've never had a Brazilian. What exactly is it?'

'You don't know? Where have you been?' Bridie asked incredulously.

'Dargo. Brigalow. Certainly not Brazil.'

Bridie gestured with the wax knife. 'Where do I begin? Have you ever been to Tasmania?'

'Nup.'

'But you know what the map of Tassie looks like?'

'Yep.'

'Well, after Mum and Dad moved us there for the logging, I got very familiar with the map of Tassie. Are you picturing a map of Tasmania?'

'Yep,' said Emily, 'I'm picturing it.'

'I clearfell the bits down the east coast and west coast,' she said, demonstrating with the knife on her own clothed crutch, 'and I do a strip across the top from Burnie to Launceston, but I stop halfway at the midlands about Campbell Town and I certainly don't wax any further south than Oatlands. And I don't go anywhere deep south, near Geeveston. Got it? All clear?'

Emily frowned.

'Well, if you want it *all clear*,' Bridie continued, patting

Emily's arm, 'that's called a Chihuahua. But I wouldn't recommend it. The regrowth is shocking. I'd sooner selectively log with a Brazilian.'

'Oh, my God. You can't half tell you're a logger's daughter. You really are tragic.'

'Thanks. Once the painful bit's all over, I'll give you a facial and you can really chill out. And I'll do a bit of Reiki on you.'

'Reiki? You're into that? You should meet my friend Evie!'

'You're not the first person to tell me that.'

Later, lying back with cool cotton-balls resting on her eyelids, Emily felt her whole body relaxing. The tension she'd held there began to ease and she felt overwhelmingly grateful to her friend. She had never experienced anything like what Bridie had just done for her.

Scalp massage, face massage, then neck and shoulders, avoiding her collarbone, and a manicure, making her nails look glossy . . . Emily felt like Julia Roberts in *Pretty Woman*. Thanks to Bridie she now had a chance to heal on the outside, as thanks to Evie she was already healing on the inside.

For the past few weeks on the high plains Evie had nourished Emily's body with good food and fed her mind with good books. Emily had read and read, absorbing as much as she could: novels about young girls finding themselves and realising their dreams, magazines on permaculture, information on grasses and how they had evolved in tandem with grazing as a tool for their survival. Emily's mind was opening up like a flower and her body was healing more rapidly than she could have hoped for. Evie had explained to her that near-death experiences could do that to a person.

'It's normal,' she'd said, 'to come out of these situations with an altered awareness of your world. There are lots of cases of people like you who nearly died and then returned with a fresh appreciation of life. They often end up having deep humanitarian and ecological concerns. Your fate always has been, and always will be, interdependent with the fate of the world.'

Sometimes, listening to Evie was like listening to some wise ancient prophet, then she'd swear, or burp, or curse Jesus Christ, and seem so normal. She held Emily in a state of perpetual fascination and Sam in a state of constant annoyance. The only thing that irritated him more than Evie was her feisty little Jack Russell. Sam would lift his lip and growl at it as it walked past, and it would lift its lip at him and growl in return. But, deep down, there was a level of affection in the constant stirring from Sam of Evie and her dog. Emily recognised that her brother was slowly learning and changing too, even though he didn't recognise it.

She saw also that her girls were learning intensely from Evie, and Emily felt utterly supported in caring for them, unlike her long lonely days at Brigalow. Evie took them down to her mountain cottage sometimes and they played in her garden, learning about the plants and the way the power of the moon pulled the roots earthward and the leaves skyward, depending on its wax or wane. At night, she taught them the patterns in the stars. Emily herself knew many plants, but Evie knew more. She knew their scientific names and their Aboriginal names, and she knew whether they were good tucker plants or good medicine.

Although unfamiliar with horses, she went regularly to the stable to dress Snowgum's injuries with herbal compounds and manuka honey. The mare was still unrideable as her wounds lay right where the girth would cinch tight, but Tilly and Meg took her out each day so she could pick at the fresh mountain meadows. One day Emily had found Meg standing with her eyes shut, her hands hovering above Snowgum's wounds.

'What are you doing, Meggy?'

'Reiki,' the four-year-old had answered matter-of-factly. 'Universal healing. Evie showed me how.'

'Meg tried to do it to me, Mum,' Tilly said, 'when I fell out of the tree. But it still hurt.'

Emily had laughed then at her girls and the changes in them. Tilly still sometimes grizzled that she missed TV, but Emily could tell that the child who had once thrown regular tantrums was more settled without having to listen to Clancy's unpredictable rages or their parental shouting matches. Now both girls were out every day with their ponies, grooming and saddling them up themselves, or spending hours just sitting astride them bareback, talking as the animals grazed. Meg, who was prone to live in a world of her own, was now letting her big sister into her daydreams and the two of them seemed closer than ever. Tilly, who'd been hard to coax outside as far as the clothesline at Brigalow, would now barely come in for meals.

It was mostly at night that the girls spoke about their father.

'When can we see him?' Tilly had asked last night.

'Soon, darling,' Emily had answered, stroking her hair. The truth was she didn't know.

Clancy had phoned once more when Emily was sleeping and Evie had taken the call. Since then he hadn't phoned back. Each time Emily rang the Brigalow number it rang out. She tried his mobile and it was switched off. It seemed he wanted them gone from his world.

'I miss him,' Tilly had told her, still confused by his absence.

'I know. We'll try him again in the morning.'

'But why won't you let me go home to him?'

Emily had frowned at her daughter and then pushed back her messy hair from her high forehead. 'It's not that I'm *not* letting you. He's not there to go home to!' She tried to keep the exasperation out of her voice.

'Why?'

'I don't know darling. Mummies often don't have the answers. I'm sorry.'

She'd kissed them goodnight then, furious with Clancy for not showing more consideration towards his girls, but upset with herself too for the situation she'd put them in. Should she have chosen to stay, for the sake of the kids, and endured her marriage like many women did? She would lie awake with such thoughts tumbling about her head, tormented, until she recalled another pearl of wisdom from Evie. She had shown Emily books about how her own thoughts created her future, and how she could learn to direct them. She had a choice: to think good thoughts or bad ones. 'All is well in my world,' Emily had heard Evie repeating like a mantra. At nights Emily tried it and at last had found sleep.

With her legs waxed, tingling all over with ti-tree oil and her face glowing from Bridie's facial, Emily sat up smiling.

'Thanks so much! I feel like a new woman.'

'Oh, I'm not done with you yet. There's hair and makeup still. But you'll have to come into the kitchen for that. Then I'll dig out some of my skinny clothes for you, and after that then we're going to the pub.'

'Oh, no, we're not.'

'Oh. Yes. We. Are. C'mon, I've got my hairdressing certificate . . . or at least half of it. I dropped out, but I should still remember enough.' She steered Emily into the kitchen.

'But what if Clancy's . . .'

'He won't be there on a Thursday. He never comes up on a Thursday. Look, pub it is. I'll call now and let Sam know we'll be there soon. They can line up the beers for us.'

With that Bridie was gone to rummage around the bathroom for some scissors and a towel. As she heard her talking brightly to her cat, Beaver, Emily decided Bridie was the best, bossiest, funniest friend she'd ever known. Surely it had been her own good thoughts that had attracted Bridie back into her life. Maybe, just maybe, Evie was right about that.

Everything did happen for a reason.

Twenty

Luke Bradshaw tucked into a thick rump steak. As he chewed on the tender, locally grown, grass-fed beef, he thought of Cassandra. She'd be spitting chips if she saw him eating beef, and that somehow made the steak taste even better.

Beef was buggering the world, she'd told him once, horrified that his family had at one stage run cattle. She'd given him her spiel about how everyone should become a vegan to save the world as they stood outside a giant Direct Factory Outlet. Then she'd dragged him inside to buy new runners, made from leather in some sweatshop in China. She was so full of it.

But then Luke started to feel guilty. Cassy had supported him and kept him at his studies in that big strange city. He did owe her for that. Perhaps he should call her? It had been pretty childish and mean just to walk out on her like that. He decided he'd phone – after he finished his steak.

'You thinking about your girl again?' said Sam, setting yet another beer on the table and sitting down to join him. 'I can tell by the frown.'

Luke shook his head. 'She's not my girl anymore. I'm cutting all ties. Moving out here a free man.'

Sam sipped on his beer. 'You might think that, but women, they think different. From what you've told me, she sounds like the sort of ex who'd boil your bunny in a stove-top pot.'

Luke grinned. 'Yeah, maybe. What about you? Got a girl-friend?'

Sam shook his head. 'In my game there are girls every-where, but they want you for all the wrong reasons. They're lusting after the fella on the stage – not me. So I'm only going to let them down in the long run. I've been the sort to have a girl in every port. But even that gets wearing after a time.' He shrugged. '*C'est la vie*. That's why I'm enjoying being back here so much. There are no women to be distracted by.'

'Good,' said Luke. 'Sounds like a top place.' He swigged on his beer, feeding the bravado behind his words. 'Women are the last thing I need right now. Just give me a block of land and a couple of horses, plus a river to fish in, and I'll be sweet.'

'Just between you and me,' Sam said, leaning closer, looking as sweet as a pin-up poster boy but with a naughty glint in his eyes, 'there's always my sister.'

Luke held up both his hands in protest.

'Whoah there,' he said, shaking his head. 'I don't do sisters.'

'Yeah, sure you don't,' said Sam with a wink. 'She's just split up from her husband. But come to think of it, you don't want to go near that rebound shit. And, luckily for you, I know she won't be interested.'

'Oh?' said Luke.

'She won't go for a *ranger*, mate. It's like dating the enemy round here. Your mob wouldn't like it, and our mob wouldn't either.'

Luke nodded, taking this in.

'*C'est la vie*,' he said, echoing Sam. 'I don't really go for girls in dungers anyway.'

Just then the pub door swung open on the other side of the lounge and Bridie came in.

'Announcing,' she said in a booming theatrical voice, 'Miss Emily!'

She reached outside and dragged in an Emily who had

been transformed. Her dark hair was cut sharply and had that sexy just-romped-in-the-bed look. Her large brown eyes shone and her full red lips looked innocent yet tempting all at once. She was wearing a tight-fitting red top that showed the curve of her breasts and her now-slender waist. Even her plaster cast had had a makeover and was now covered in a bright red horse bandage.

'Hey, chicky babes!' said Sam, getting up. Luke quickly drank in the vision of the dark-haired girl, then swivelled his back to them. He shoved in the last mouthful of steak, keeping his head down, still a little stung by Sam's comments. In this town, he thought wryly, instead of teaching their kids about 'stranger danger', they taught them 'ranger danger'. If he was to be typecast from the start by his job title, he resolved to keep himself to himself, no matter what kind of stunner that cattleman's daughter was.

'What were you were saying about girls in dungers?' Sam said, nudging Luke before going over to the girls.

At the bar he slung his arm around his sister's shoulders and smiled at Bridie. 'You're a genius. Not even the best make-up artists on my music videos could pull off a stunt like this!'

For a moment Emily looked crestfallen, her self-image still bruised from life with Clancy.

'You know, that's very rude,' Bridie said, folding her arms across her chest.

'I didn't mean it like that!'

'I can see you haven't improved much since school.'

'Well, I can see you have,' Sam said, eyeing her tight black top appreciatively. 'You look fantastic too!'

Bridie turned to Emily. 'He's no better than your ex-husband. You poor thing, you've had a lousy selection of males to share your life with. Your father excluded, of course.'

'Oi! That's a bit harsh,' Sam said. 'I just meant Emily looks great.'

'Mr Vanity,' Bridie said, turning her back on him.

'Miss Uppity,' Sam said huffily.

'Come on, you two, be nice. Let's just have a drink. Three beers please, Donna,' Emily said.

'No, make that four,' said Bridie. 'Luke, you are joining us, aren't you? Or are you going to sit over there being a stranger all night?' She winked at him. 'Emily's child-free tonight. The girls are staying at Rod's so you'd best make the most of the local talent. It's pretty thin on the ground round here,' she said eyeing a couple of old codgers at the bar.

Emily elbowed her in the guts.

Looking uncomfortable, Luke picked up his beer. He came over to them and lobbed on to a bar stool beside Emily. He returned her smile with a cute grin complete with dimple.

'Welcome to Dargo,' she said, raising her glass.

'Why, thank you,' he replied, and the four of them clunked glasses. After a short while Emily wondered why Bridie had invited him over in the first place. Neither she nor Luke could get a word in during what had rapidly become the Bridie and Sam Show. Their banter ran thick and fast, and so far there had not been one free second when Emily could ask Luke how his Ratgirl girlfriend was faring or what had brought him to Dargo.

But with Sam and Bridie propping up the bar it wasn't long before they had the whole pub rocking, including Donna, the big-haired, big-boobed brunette barmaid. Emily, not used to drinking, felt blind after the first three beers. She was soon jigging round on the tiny dance floor near the eight-ball table to 'Thank God I'm a Country Boy', her head tossed back, looking up at the hundreds of stubby holders from all over the countryside stapled to the pub's high old walls. She was laughing while Luke swept her about even though her ribs twinged terribly and she couldn't get enough air. But, she thought, at least she was *alive*! And also *pissed*! What would Evie think after all that detoxing?

She grabbed Luke's hands as they danced and above the music shouted, 'So what brings you up from the big smoke?'

'Work,' he said.

'What kind of work?'

'I'm going to be the new VPP ranger.'

Just as he said it, John Denver sang the part about life being a funny riddle and the music stopped abruptly. Luke's words 'VPP ranger' came out so loud even the old snoozers at the bar turned to look at him. Emily dropped his hands, her mouth open, her face flushing red amidst the sudden jarring silence.

'Ranger? Why?' It was a silly question to ask, but she was momentarily dumbstruck. She wanted him to be anything other than a *ranger*. A vacuum cleaner salesman, a sanitary bin disposal man, a gay porn star, yes. *Anything* but a VPP *ranger*!

Emily knew that all the university graduates who came here never lasted long, and looked down on the locals as if they were uneducated rednecks. Was Luke just another one of those over-educated, under-experienced, arrogant young guns? Had he come to work with Darcy, the veteran ranger, just so he could get a leg up to a National Park nearer his girlfriend in Melbourne?

Everyone in town respected Darcy, who had been born and bred in Dargo. But he was one of a dying breed of rangers, those who actually came from the land in the region they worked in. For thirty-five years Darcy had turned down every transfer or promotion offered him just so he could stay in his beloved mountains. The new trainee rangers who occasionally blew in on attachment to him, and the superiors who stepped off the bureaucratic food chain to drop by and criticise his efforts, had not impressed the people of Dargo. As a result the locals were suspicious of newcomers, particularly university graduates. Darcy always said the idealistic young things from the city had what they thought was knowledge of the land in their heads, but did not yet know the land in their hearts or their hands.

'Why be a ranger here?' echoed Luke. 'Because it's a job. And I love mountains.'

'Huh!' Emily scoffed. 'What do you know about them?'

'Not a lot now, but I hope to learn.'

'That's what they all say! It takes more than a few months to learn these mountains. It takes a lifetime! No, more than a lifetime. It takes *generations*.' The music started up again with the familiar beat of Sam's number-one hit blasting from the jukebox. She wanted to finish her conversation with the new ranger now. She was drunk and feeling irritated.

Suddenly the 'Save the Tarkine Wilderness' T-shirt, the girl-friend in the wildlife suit, the bomby Datsun with the left-wing Greenie stickers on it, all made sense. This Luke was coming here to help the process of the cattlemen's evictions. The parliamentary bill hadn't yet been passed, but Emily suspected the government departments were gearing up for change anyway. Old Darcy wouldn't be able to bring himself to carry out the bans, so they'd brought in a younger hired-gun to do the dirty work – start kicking the cattlemen off the mountains.

Tersely, she excused herself and went to the bar for some water, leaving Luke feeling stung. By the CD jukebox Bridie and Sam were having a tussle that was beginning to escalate into World Federation Wrestling.

'You little fox,' he shouted. 'Turn that effing song off!'

'No, you moron!' Sam was trying to flick the switch on the wall while Bridie had him in a headlock, his nose pressed close to her bosom.

'Turn it off!' yelled Sam.

'Don't you wanna listen to your one-hit-wonder song?'

Sam reefed himself away, flicked the powerpoint and the music suddenly died. It was only then that Bridie realised that his eyes were blazing in fury.

In the silence that followed she said sulkily, 'Why'd you do that? I'd just put six bucks' worth of songs into it.'

'Donna will give you a refund.'

'But I wanted to hear "Jillaroo Junkie"!'

'Well, I didn't.'

'Well, I did! I like it.'

166

'Well, I don't! End of story.'

Bridie and Sam stood facing each other, their frustration and annoyance plain to see.

'Party pooper,' she said.

'Shit stirrer,' he said. He turned and joined the other disgruntled man at the bar.

'Another beer?' asked Sam.

Luke nodded.

'You girls can get your own.'

'Sam!' protested Emily, 'What's got into you?'

'I might ask *you* the same question. I can tell from your sour-puss face Luke's told you what he's doing for a living, hasn't he? That's why you've gone all cold and snakey on us.'

'And Bridie's called *you* on the truth,' Emily retaliated, 'That you're a one-hit-wonder because your ego's the size of Texas, yet you're too lazy and fucked up with drugs to write another album.'

Brother and sister glared at each other.

'What about your ego, Emily? Have you even given this fella a chance?' Sam nodded at Luke.

'Hey, don't bring me into it!' he said.

'That's the problem with your lot,' Emily said spinning round to face him, her eyes narrowing, 'you don't seem to realise you are *into it*! By being here, by working here, you *have* to be into it – up to your eyeballs and beyond! You can't come here for work and distance yourself from the community and the land. You have to live it. The mountains don't do nine to five, mate!'

'God, you sound just like Uncle Bob,' Sam said. 'Don't talk shop with the poor bugger now, Emily. Leave that bloody subject alone. He's just rocked into town on a social visit. He's not even in the job yet.'

'No,' Luke said, not taking his gaze from her, 'it's all right. I'm interested to hear this. Really.'

Emily scowled at him.

'Did you know, in Tassie they classify Parkland as having

167

different uses and that influences how it's managed, just the way good farmers do things. Not like the stupid blanket ban they're proposing here! In Tassie they set up committees made up of local groups, from Aborigines, to cattlemen, to conservationists, to fishermen, to four-wheel drivers and foresters, and the government employees facilitate and guide from within the community – but the community has the final say. All you blokes do out here is duck for cover and kow-tow to your Melbourne bigwigs so you can rush straight back to the city as soon as you've done your regional time.'

'Is it any wonder with yobs like you flinging shit at him, Em?'

'Shut up, Sam! You've been out of this debate for years now – in more ways than one. Try living in a rural area where they shut down everything at the grassroots and run it all from the city. It just makes us country people mad!'

'What do you mean, I've been out of it? Last time I looked, Emily, you were a suburban housewife. You're just being a parrot now, squawking all that family propaganda. Wake up to yourself.'

The hurtful words registered with her immediately. She felt her anger drain away.

'Hey,' intervened Bridie, 'that's a low blow, Sam. Don't be a prick!'

'Well don't be a prick-*tease*,' he shouted, then turned his back. 'I don't know what's with you two!'

Emily felt the tears rise. She pushed herself away from the bar, suddenly feeling giddy. Suburban housewife . . . Was that all she was? Was what Sam had said true? Was she just a parrot? Could it be she no longer had any real claim to the mountains?

On her way to the toilets she swiped tears from her face and saw mascara smeared across the back of her hand. The loos were right round the back of the old pub so Emily made her way along the side verandah, past the piles of empty silver beer kegs that were lit by the gleam of Dargo's solitary streetlight.

As she washed her hands she checked herself out in the mirror, carefully rubbing off all Bridie's beautiful makeup. She leant towards the mirror then and tried to look into the core of herself. Where had she gone when her body had lain so still on that rocky bank? What had her eyes within really seen? And why now did she feel so unsettled? It was as if there were a perpetual tussle going on between the old Emily and the new one.

She had a flash, a quick mental vision, of a sawn-slab hotel with a sagging bark roof and sawdust floor. Of drunken miners, Tipperary men, the shysters of the town, two of them down on all fours head butting each other like rams while other men cheered them on. Outside on the verandah a group of young blokes were giggling as they shaved a horse's mane and tail. She saw the handsome young minister from her dream asking for his horse to be saddled. Then a glimpse of the priest being shunted forward on the pub verandah to receive his shorn horse. The other men were drunkenly lurching and laughing as they backed the horse up and presented him with the shaved animal, bridle hung on its backside over what was left of its tail, saddle cinched the wrong way. She saw rough men rebelling against any kind of authority. Very much like Uncle Bob. Like herself too, perhaps? God and grog and rough behaviour . . . this place was founded on them.

Suddenly there was a bang on the door.

'You okay?' came Bridie's voice.

'Fine,' called Emily, 'I'll be right in.'

'Sure?'

'Yep.' Emily heard her friend bustle her way out of the pub toilets, calling back to her, 'What a pair of mongrels!'

Peering at her own reflection Emily recalled how Evie had spoken to her of energies and had given her books on time theory. Could all that goldmining palaver still be going on here, in some other dimension? And the Aborigines . . . were they still here too, gathering moths up on the plains when the seasons were right? Was the angry outburst she and Sam had just exchanged in front of the new ranger connected to what had gone on here before, as if the dark unruly spirit of the place were perpetuated in their very genes? Wildness and unsophistication were the hallmarks of Emily's family history. Maybe Luke was right to consider her a redneck.

She was shocked by her own thoughts. Before the accident, she was a simple mountain cattleman's daughter, who liked to drove cattle, ride educated horses, drink at the pub and eat a counter meal occasionally, just like her aunt Flo. She didn't ask questions about life, death, the universe and everything. But now she was irrevocably changed – and she feared the change in herself. She was learning that having a mind as open as the universe, that searching for a core of integrity as strong as the pull of gravity, could be fraught with danger and downfall in the real world. She was still having trouble believing she deserved the beauty and joy of life, Evie had told her she did.

Evie's teachings came at a price. There were years of family programming to unravel before she could fully assimilate them. When Emily was back in her old world, she no longer seemed to fit in. She could now see herself as if from the outside looking in, and the flaws in her own belief systems were visible. Shocking, even. She thought of Luke, whom she had verbally savaged and judged. She thought of Evie and all her teachings on love and forgiveness. She resolved to make amends. To apologise.

When Emily returned inside the pub, Bridie was deliberately ignoring Sam while she was dancing to 'The Gambler' with old Reg, a crotchety pub regular who collected the town garbage on Thursday fortnights. Both Sam and Luke were still looking hang-dog at the bar, drinking in silence.

'I'm sorry,' Emily said. Luke turned to her, his expression veiled.

'Are you going to say sorry to me?' Sam said.

Emily cast him an annoyed look and went on awkwardly, addressing Luke. 'Would you like to dance? Can I get you a drink?'

'No,' he said, eyes flashing an insult before they turned away from her.

Ouch! Emily thought. She glanced away from him, ashamed of herself, and about to try another apology when she was stopped in her tracks by what she saw outside the window.

An eighteen-wheeler, lit up like a neon sign, was rolling into town. As the truck pulled up outside the pub and the air brakes hissed like snakes, Emily froze. It was Clancy. Respond, she told herself. Don't react. Clancy stood on the road with his legs wide apart and his arms curved out from his body like a gunslinging outlaw from the Wild West. His red truck, like a giant armoured steed, loomed behind him. He watched her through the window.

Emily felt fear slide into the core of her being again.

Then her husband was in the pub and towering over her.

'Good to see you, Em,' he said. 'You look great. Too good really, considering.'

They could all tell he'd been drinking. Emily knew he must be in a bad way. To be caught driving a truck with any alcohol in his system meant instant disqualification of his licence. He must be ripped.

'What do you want, Clancy?'

'I can talk to you, can't I? You're still my wife.'

'No, I'm not. I think you know that.'

He flicked his head in Luke's direction. 'So this is your *new* fella, is it?'

'Clancy,' cautioned Emily, as if trying to calm a savage dog, 'he's not my fella.'

He looked at Luke through narrowed eyes.

'Have you fucked her yet?'

Luke, shocked, pulled a face. 'Mate, no! I've only just . . .'

'Don't you *mate*, me!' Clancy lurched forward and shoved Emily violently against the wall. 'Slut!' The pain in her shoulder left her momentarily stunned.

Bridie moved straight to her side, trying to drag her away from Clancy's savage grip, while Luke and Sam pounced on

171

him from behind. Maddened by rum and misery, Clancy's long limbs flailed the air. He broke free from Sam and swung blindly about. His fist connected with Luke's face. Luke felt the crack of bone and smelt the warm blood trickling from his nose. His hand flew to his face as he doubled over. Then he realised Clancy was coming at him again.

'Get off him!' roared Sam. Donna was there now, barking orders for them to stop. Three logging men in the dining lounge downed their cutlery and rushed around to pull Clancy away and out into the car park.

With him out of the pub, it was as if everyone collectively gasped for breath. In the silence Emily went straight to Luke, offering him serviettes to stem the bleeding while apologising over and over.

'I'm fine,' he said, not looking her in the eye. 'Just leave it, okay? I'm fine.'

'I'm really sorry,' she said again. Luke turned away.

Sam put a hand on his shoulder. 'You right, mate?'

Luke nodded. Breathing heavily, swiping blood from his nose, he got up. 'I'll catch you later, okay?'

'Can I . . .' Emily began.

'No!' Luke almost shouted and ripped his arm away from her touch. Staggering slightly, he made his way out of a side door and over to the cabin he had hired for the night. As he crossed the grass in the beer garden, he felt anger towards them all simmering inside him. He'd walked away from his own domestic dispute into another much uglier one. Emily and her mates, especially her husband, were too rough for him. He remembered again Giles's warning about getting too close to the locals. Now he understood. Locals equalled trouble. From now on it would be best if he kept his distance.

Emily stood feeling dazed, hardly able to believe Clancy was back causing havoc in her life, still wondering if she should go after the new ranger and see if he was okay.

'This is all fucked!' she cried, fury rising in her. She shoved aside a chair and rushed to the door.

'Where are you going?' Bridie asked, but Emily stormed out without replying. She was on a mission. She marched across the road to where the blokes stood counselling Clancy. They were trying to figure out the easiest way of getting him and his truck back home to Brigalow without him raising hell again. He was slumped down on the step, head in his hands. The alcohol that had fuelled his rage was now overwhelming him.

Emily stood in front of her husband, taking in how pathetic he looked. Because they had children together, she knew their bond was lifelong, no matter how much he'd hurt her. But she would no longer tolerate his treating her this way. Respond, she told herself. Don't react. But what a load of crap, Evie! she thought. She *wanted* to react. She wanted to knock his cheating block off!

She put her hands on her hips and her eyes bored into him as she began to shout, not caring if she woke the whole town.

'Don't you ever, *ever* turn up drunk like that again and treat me and my friends that way! You're an *arsehole,* Clancy!' The logging men cleared their throats uncomfortably, self-conscious about being caught in the midst of this ugly scene between husband and wife. They loosened their grip on Clancy and peeled back to hover in the shadows, watching to make sure the rabid-dog version of the drunk did not emerge again.

Clancy looked up, his normally wide blue eyes part-closed from drunkenness.

'Em, I miss my girls,' he slurred.

'Bullshit! You haven't come to see them once! We've been trying to ring you almost every day. You've been off rooting that nurse, haven't you? You haven't even thought about your girls because all you do, Clancy, is think about your dick!'

Emily radiated so much anger it could have been felt a kilometre a way. She wanted to kick him, to claw him, to spit on him. She wanted to scrape the skin from his face with her fingernails. She wanted to sink her teeth deep into his flesh.

If she got started on him, she knew it would take more than three hefty loggers to drag her away.

'Get out of my fucking sight! Now!'

To her surprise, like a dog with an electric collar and no choice, Clancy obeyed. He hauled himself up, wavered as he spun about on the step and tried to clamber up into his truck. The watching men rushed out from the shadows, grabbing him by his shirt collar and dragging him back down.

'Oh, no, you don't, buddy,' said one man. 'You're not going anywhere tonight in that thing. We'll park it nice and safe somewhere for you.'

'Where do we take him?' the shortest logger asked. Emily realised they were all looking at her as if Clancy were her responsibility.

'I'm not his fucking mother! I don't know.' She paused and thought more clearly. 'Sorry. Thanks for your help. Just take him to the bush hospital. The night nurse will know exactly who to call to come get him.' Then she turned and walked away into the darkness.

Twenty-one

'Geez!' said Flo. 'Everyone's geed up at the 'G today!'

From the Flanaghans' horse truck, Emily looked at the amazing scene unfolding before them. The parkland surrounding the giant sports stadium that was the Melbourne Cricket Ground was filled with four-wheel drives, horsefloats, trucks, goosenecks and campers, and tethered to every tree or vehicle was a horse. Over five hundred riders had come to protest against the grazing-ban legislation to be voted on in the coming weeks by the Victorian Government. But it wasn't just mountain cattlemen who would converge on the steps of Parliament House. Other country organisations had jumped on board too, all wanting to voice their dissatisfaction about city-centric government policy. Hundreds upon hundreds of people would be marching on foot, following the cattlemen's horses through the city streets to the State Parliament building.

It was the last place Emily wanted to be, but all of her family had forced her to go. After that night at the pub, her silence and apathy had frightened them. Her dad and Flo, even Evie, had reckoned it would be good for her to get off the mountains and out of Dargo. Emily hadn't even wanted to ride, but once again her family and Evie had insisted that Snowgum would handle it, if Emily rode her bareback. The protest was just a short walk along an even street. They were all infuriating her by being so bossy. It wasn't until Tilly begged for a trip to the city that Emily finally caved in.

'Sam will be glad to be missing this,' Flo said as she helped Meg and Tilly on to their ponies.

'Yes, but I don't see why I had to come,' Emily said. Normally she'd be right into the whole 'cattleman cause' but since the accident she felt on the periphery of it all. She was terrified of losing their rights to the mountains but for some reason all this fuss in the city seemed misplaced to her.

'Oh, stop your moaning, girl, and enjoy it,' her aunt said, 'It's going to be bigger than *Ben Hur*! Sam's better off on the mountain with his new best friend Evie. We all know the Association would've pressured him to sing for the publicity. He doesn't need that crap right now. If he stops home, he's got more chance of staying off that druggie gunk he was on.'

Next to her, Rod's two-way radio crackled into life, announcing it was time to ride.

'You right to go?' he said, holding on to Meg's lead rope and looking down at Emily from where he sat high on his big gelding, Redgum.

'Almost,' she said, shoving a spiral-bound government document into her oilskin pocket.

'What's that you got there?' Flo asked as she bunked her niece up on to Snow's broad back. Emily winced, her body still complaining. She had to pause before she could answer, feeling a little unsteady.

'Just that Tassie legislation Evie was telling us about. She suggested I bring it in case I could put it into the hands of the right person.'

'Oh, yeah?' said Flo. 'Who is the right person?'

Emily shrugged. 'Evie said I would know when the time came. Typical Evie! It's the document that has scientists saying controlled grazing is good for the land. You never know, if they read it our Victorian buggers could actually end up *asking*

176

us to graze our stock in the mountains, to help manage them, not ban us entirely!'

'Well, good on you, girl,' Flo said, settling her toey chestnut. 'We gotta try everything. If today doesn't sway a few minds, we could lose the whole bloody lot!'

'You sure you're right?' Rod asked, looking at Emily. She nodded. She'd been perched on horses almost since the day she was born. She had thought she'd feel scared sitting back up on the mare after the accident, but instead found herself feeling as if she'd come home. Snowgum was steady, calm, and clearly enjoying all the fuss. Once she was settled, Emily felt her own mood shift.

Out of the crowd came a booming voice.

'Let's show the bastards!'

Internally Rod, Flo and Emily groaned. It was Uncle Bob. Evie's parting words to her echoed in Emily's head.

'It's no use being self-righteous, humility is the key. Don't take the high ground. Take the positive, proactive ground. Sow seeds of thought in people's minds that work in the land's favour. This "us and them" mentality won't get you, or the land, anywhere.'

Bob sat heavily on his bay gelding, his big beer belly pushing out over the front of the stock saddle. His nose looked redder than ever. He fell in line next to Emily and Tilly.

'Lucky for you there's bugger all trees in the city, eh, Em?' he said.

'Hello, Uncle Bog,' she said dryly. It was Tilly who had taken to calling him Bog when she was just two. Not surprisingly, the name had stuck and when the girls were about, that's what they called him. He seemed to love it.

'Say hi, girls,' Emily coached.

'Hi, Uncle Bog,' chorused the girls flatly.

'Geez, woman, what have you done to yourself?' Bob said, peering at Flo. 'You're not wearing makeup, are you? And you've dyed your hair.'

Flo pulled her hat up slightly and fluttered her eyelashes.

'Brow shape and eyelash tint. Beauty in the Bush, my darlink.' She blew her brother a kiss.

'Be buggered. You trollop.'

'She looks great, Uncle Bog, don't you reckon?' Emily said. 'Scrubbed up better than I've seen her in a long time.'

Flo leant forward and pulled her top lip down. 'Bridie even did ol' Flo's mo!'

They all laughed, Emily relishing the fact the family was all together, even though she knew Bob would get under everyone's skin, as he always did. Like an army, they fell in step and joined the other riders. Some were holding Australian flags and placards, while others pulled their hats down low and rolled smokes in the light rain.

Emily led Meg on Blossom, who was shampooed to a dazzling white, while Tilly sat well in the seat of a lively Jemma, keeping her cool. The weeks of riding alone up on the plains had brought a whole new level to the girls' confidence and Emily was so proud to have her little ones there beside her. Ahead of them a large green-and-gold banner read 'Mountain Cattlemen Care for the High Country'.

The sound of the horses' hooves fell like heavy rain as both shod and unshod hooves clopped against bitumen. Following the throng was a trailer carrying men and women armed with shovels. When a horse lifted its tail and spilled out a pile of dung, it was flung by the 'poo crew' into the heap on the trailer. A sign attached to it read: *Mobile Parliament – Crap Fed in and Bad Decisions Made.*

A call came from behind them.

'Hey, Emily!' shouted Baz Webberly.

'G'day, Baz!' she said, her face lighting up at the sight of him. 'Thanks for bringing Snowgum home for me.'

He surveyed the mare, taking in the way the red raw grazes had healed to dry grey skin, the hair slowly growing over the scars. Only the deep gash on her girth still looked tender where proud flesh had formed a shiny red patch. Emily, too, no longer had her shoulder strapped. It was only the cast, due to come off this week, that gave any indication of the trauma she and the horse had recently been through. Even her hair was growing back quickly and had a new glossy shine to it.

'She's come up trumps,' Baz commented.

'Flo told me what a trouper you were as a vet.'

He nodded in her aunt's direction.

'She's the trouper. Flo's the one kept her going. Bugger me, it's great to see you here, ain't it, Flo?'

Flo carried her head high, agreeing with a gentle smile.

'Yep, they tell me I was dead,' Emily said. 'But I'm resurrected again. This is the second coming.'

'Oooh! I never say no to a second coming!' old Baz wheezed. 'Your Auntie Flo knows that's right, eh? Hey, Flo!'

'Bugger off, Baz,' she said, clearly loving the attention.

Now the puzzle had come together, Emily thought. That explained why Flo was paying so much attention to the way she looked. Flo and Baz were keen on each other!

Emily smiled. Her view of the whole recent chain of events was shifting. Flo and Baz was yet another good thing to have come from her accident. Buoyed by this thought, she smiled as she looked behind her. The street, lined with elms, their leaves turning from summer green to yellow, framed the crowd of horses and riders for as far as she could see. The horses came in all colours, their coats wet from the rain, ears pricked, heads tossing against the bit or cast low, all riding quietly forward.

She laughed and pointed out to Rod a joker on a horse who had painted on its flank, 'jobless horse'.

'Makes you wonder what our horses will do if the bans come in,' Rod said.

'We'll have to sell most of them, won't we, Dad?'

Rod shrugged. 'No point keeping 'em if you're not working them. Things change. Very few people nowadays have seen a truly work-fit horse or dog. Or for that matter, work-fit people. I think we've been left behind!'

Emily nodded in agreement, thinking of the high plains and the old chaff house, the shingles a little worse for wear. The handle, hard to turn now, would've crushed many a tonne of grain for the horses and the house cows, the pigs and the goats. Back then it was a matter of survival.

She looked up at the ornate façade of Flinders Street Station and across the road to modern Federation Square. The city was so vastly different from the quiet, unpretentious natural world on the high plains. But as she passed the boozers at Young and Jackson she realised that maybe they were all one and the same, as Evie said. Here, just like in Dargo, were honest, hard-working folk still holding fast to that laconic Australian humour that was threatened with drowning under the weight of bureaucracy and political correctness. Emily gave the fellas at the pub a smile. One wolf-whistled back and she blushed.

On their way up Swanston Street they passed a row of police horses groomed to show condition. Their polished and gleaming gear was a contrast to the cattlemen's horses with bridles plaited from hayband and scuffed and worn stock-saddles. As they rode past a coffee shop, Bob called out, 'Can someone get us five hundred coffees? To go!'

Then a woman on the footpath looked skyward and yelled out, 'Sorry about the rain!' Riders within earshot all turned to look at her. Didn't she know that her water supply came from the farming lands surrounding Melbourne and that water there levels had been critically low for months?

A good-hearted old rider called to her, 'Don't you go apologising for rain now, pet. We love it and so might you!'

As they waited the idle traffic lights chimed to each other across the street, alternating their call like bellbirds in a shady summertime grove. Emily wondered how Sam endured it here in the city, but then she heard Evie's words again: 'Each to their own.'

As they converged on Parliament House, politicians and

their staff in dark suits and smart dresses began to emerge onto the steps, to watch the spectacle of two thousand protesters on foot and hundreds upon hundreds of Akubra hats and horses.

One by one, each cattleman speaker reached the podium. Some were in tears as they talked of losing their heritage and access to the land. Others had anger in their voices as they pointed the finger at biased government statistics.

Emily sat silently on Snowgum, her head bowed, her hat pulled low. She listened with fresh ears this time. She heard the passion in the cattlemen's plea, but very few of them gave the simple reassurance the city people needed to hear – that cattle in most cases benefited the environment. It was as basic as that. Emily knew that not all alpine areas were suited to grazing. She knew that in the old days, when environmental concerns didn't rate as highly, the mountains had been grazed bare by stray cattle, horses, goats, and all manner of domestic animals turned loose when the mines shut down. No one wanted a return of those days.

How could she show these people that, in her stretch of country, there was such light stocking of animals on the sturdy sub-alpine soils that grazing was a help not a hindrance to the landscape's health? But she had no scientific backing to prove her point. Emily began to feel the familiar desperation creep back in. What could she do? How could she get the truth through to the people who made the decisions without them seeing the land for themselves?

Suddenly she remembered the Tasmanian legislation she had in her pocket, written in government lingo. She dragged it out and weighed it in her hand. In the midst of the crowd she heard Evie's voice, 'You will know who to deliver it to.' She looked up and saw, standing on the mighty steps of Parliament House, the Premier in his dark suit, flanked by minders and advisers. Her heart racing, she found a pencil in her stockmen's notebook and scrawled on the top, '*Mr Premier, PLEASE read this.*' She looked up at the man on the steps, then back to the page before writing, '*Love from Emily F.*' Wasn't it Evie who had said love was more powerful than anything? She smiled to herself and felt a rush of blood to her head, knowing what she was about to do.

'You right to stay here?' she said to Tilly and Meg, who nodded.

Emily squeezed Snowgum forward, wove her way around the barricades, and popped the mare over the temporary fence that separated the riders from the parliament building. Security men ran towards her as she urged Snowgum up the slippery steps. Arm in plaster, with no saddle Emily gripped as tight as she could with her thighs. All her life she'd heard people say in exasperation, '*That girl can ride!*' Today of all days she knew she had to believe in this, and believe in herself and her loyal, white horse.

'Excuse me, miss. You can't come up here,' one man bellowed, stepping forward to grab at Snowgum's reins.

'Yes, I know. I'm sorry, but this is for the Premier.' Emily held out the document. She was just metres from him. Breathless, she looked up, locking her dark eyes on to his, pulling in all the light and energy she could from above. She cast the Premier a broad smile. G'day, Mr Premier!' she sang out. He nodded and returned a smile to this pretty but obviously crazy young woman. Then, surprising everyone, he stepped forward and took the document from her hand.

'I'll make sure I read it,' he promised. She took in the shine of his eyes, the creases at their corners. Much better-looking live than on telly, she thought.

'Thank you,' she said, nodding her head graciously. Then she turned Snowgum back down the steps. As she did a massive cheer went up before a cluster of cameras and policemen engulfed her and Snowgum. Despite the fuss, the mare stayed calm as the crowd jostled around her. It was no different from the time Emily had ridden her into a cattlemen's bar on her eighteenth, to the accompaniment of flashing lights and music. Snowgum was taking it all in her stride. Emily though, was no longer so sure. There seemed to be quite a mob about her.

'What was it you delivered to the Premier?' one journalist called out.

'Is it true you're the cattleman's daughter who fell from her horse earlier this year?' asked another.

'What's the message you gave the premier?'

Emily looked at the media scrum and drew in a deep breath.

'I gave him the way forward for sensible land management of the alpine areas – unlike the proposed blanket bans,' she said.

The journalists fired more questions at her, but now a policeman was standing beside her, looking frighteningly serious.

'You'll have to come with me, miss,' he said.

From the small crowd of Wildlife Society protesters who hustled nearby, a person dressed as a foam gum tree waved a walking stick at her, screaming out in a shrill voice, 'Get off the mountains!' Emily turned and smiled at the tree. Not a rat today then, she thought, amused.

Even as she was being led away for a stern dressing-down by the Victoria Police, Emily chose to make herself feel exhilarated instead of scared. She had not only proved to herself that her mare and her body were capable of anything now, she knew that she had sown a seed, just as Evie had said to do. And where there was a seed, there was always the chance that something good could grow from it.

Twenty-two

The following week, the new Dargo VPP ranger put his hands on his hips and surveyed his riverside bush block just outside Dargo.

'Paradise,' Luke Bradshaw said to himself. He had bought the block on the spur of the moment with the money his father had given him after the farm was sold. Until now, he'd no urge to spend it. But once he had a place of his own, it was as if a weight had been lifted from him. He wondered how Cassy was getting on in Melbourne. Without the phone connected yet and with his mobile out of range, there was no way she could reach him. Perhaps he should give her a quick call from the Dargo pay phone. It was only fair. The last time he'd seen her she'd become increasingly hysterical over their separation.

He scanned the river that wound in an 'S'-shape for the length of the block, and pushed thoughts of Cassy from his mind. He wanted to savour his twenty acres that ran up a steep hillside towards a dam. His eyes settled on the shabby little cottage facing north-west towards the river. 'Lick of paint,' he said to himself optimistically. He'd paid bugger all for it. The land itself, despite the thick weeds, was brilliant; fertile riverside soil on the flats, rising up to steep paddocks and bush-covered hills. Beside the house stood a shed and, behind that, a good set of red-gum horse-and-cattle yards from the days when the property was much bigger.

Parked in the shed was a secondhand WB Holden ute. Luke knew he'd be supplied with a work vehicle, but after the confines of Melbourne and living with Cassy, freedom was high on his list of priorities and simply owning a ute made him feel free. He'd always wanted a WB. Like the house, the ute needed work, but also like the house, it had so much character.

Luke's final splurge had been on buying two of the best-bred Australian stock horses he could find in *Horse Deals*. He'd trialled them both on his way to Dargo, after packing up and leaving Melbourne. Like the house, he had bought the horses on the spot. He thought he'd ride one and breed from the other, depending on which one he bonded with best. The owner had trucked them up the very next day, throwing in a third horse for only a couple of hundred dollars extra, because he could no longer afford to keep them. The bonus gelding had fantastic stock-horse breeding but was a green-broke baby with no experience. Luke didn't need three horses, and certainly not a youngster. But there was something in the eyes of that young chestnut that attracted him. He could always sell it on. So now he had two chestnut mares with pretty white markings on their legs and faces and the matching three-year-old in his yards.

Today he'd have to fix some of the fences and get the waterlines sorted before he could let the horses out into the paddock, but he was looking forward to watching them discover their new home.

The first night in the cottage he'd barely slept at all as he lay on his back in his swag, taking in the sag of the ceiling and the lean of the doorframe. All things he could fix eventually, or paint over, or tear out. It would take many hours of work, but for the first time in years Luke felt excited, as if his life had some momentum and purpose.

In the past few days he'd spent some time with the outgoing

ranger, Darcy. He had come to see the rotund man of few words as a knowledgeable bushman but one who had become disillusioned with the hierarchy over the years and was now on the complacent and resigned side, comfortable in his government job. He'd shown Luke all over the mountainside, going over the day-to-day tasks like which rubbish bins to empty in the parks, where the huts were, which boomgates needed shutting when snow fell.

Luke sighed. He started work officially next week but didn't want to think of that now, nor recall that first eventful night in the Dargo Hotel. He had three beautiful new horses to get to know and his very own horse arena, set up by the previous owner. With a spring in his step, he set off to the stables to get his new saddle.

Twenty-three

That same Saturday morning, Emily was standing at the bar of the Dargo Hotel while Donna waited, not so patiently, for her to make up her mind.

'Bottle of Bundy rum? No! Carton of beer? No! Bottle of vodka? No! Oh, hell, I don't know what he likes,' sighed Emily.

She had been back from the protest ride in Melbourne for a week now, but the guilt she felt about Luke getting clobbered by Clancy had trailed her all the way from Dargo to Melbourne and back up to the high plains. To make matters worse, Evie had refused to cut her cast off, saying it was a job for the doctor at the Dargo Bush Hospital. Despite Emily's protests, Evie had phoned to make an appointment for her during their once-a-month Saturday morning clinic.

When Emily had heard on the local bush telegraph that Luke had bought a house and some land, she was utterly surprised. No other young ranger who'd been stationed with old Darcy had shown any interest in staying on. They were only ever here doing time to earn points so they could get a job closer to Melbourne. Dargo was seen as a place to bolt from when the weekend rolled round by all his predecessors, so Luke's purchase was the talk of the town. Still, Emily thought, it gave her a good excuse to visit him: so she could give him a housewarming present and an apology.

Earlier that morning, on her way down from the plains, she had dropped the girls into Evie's and continued on to Dargo with the float in tow to deliver for Flo's weekend camp draft. Emily was looking forward to a day just to herself, even though the thought of going to the hospital and potentially running into Penny left her with a sick feeling inside. Some day soon though their paths would surely cross and today was as good a day as any to get it out of the way, Emily reasoned. But still, the thought of coming face to face with Penny made her palms grow sweaty and her heart beat faster.

As she stood at the bar, she realised she was stalling going to the hospital.

'Make it a carton,' she said decisively at last.

'Stubbies or cans?' asked Donna.

'Er . . . Umm . . .' Donna rolled her eyes. 'Cans? No! Stubbies? No! Oh! *Stubbies.*'

'Stubbies,' said Donna. 'Light or full-strength? Draught or Bitter? VB or Cascade? Crown or Blonde?'

Emily squirmed with uncertainty until she saw the teasing expression on Donna's face.

'Beer, Donna. *Just bloody beer*!'

Donna heaved a carton up on to the bar. Emily frowned. It wasn't the most glamorous apology gift.

'Nah. Sorry, Donna. Not a carton. Make it a bottle of Bundy rum. And you don't have a ribbon handy? Jazz it up a bit?'

Donna gave a loud sigh and again fluttered her mascara-caked eyelashes. 'He must be *some* fella.'

Emily sat the Bundy bottle on the passenger seat of the farm ute, complete with blue bale twine as the only decoration she could find, and drove a few metres on towards the leafy entrance of the bush hospital.

She had no sooner walked in than she was confronted by the sight of five hospital staff, receptionist, cleaner and doctor included, all standing around Penny. They were drinking champagne with strawberries bobbing in the sparkling flutes. The mood of the gathering was jovial. Tied to Penny's wrist was a foil balloon carrying the words *Goodbye and good luck!* There was a cake on the counter and a plate of Chocolate Royales. Penny was smiling her pretty little elfin smile and her auburn ponytail glowed richly against the pristine white of her nurse's uniform. When she turned and saw Emily standing in the reception area the smile slid from her face, to be replaced by a look of uncertainty.

The receptionist, Betty Waldron, who was as much a fixture of the place as the light fittings, snapped into work mode.

'Ah, Emily dear! Here for your cast removal with Dr Doreen.' Emily's eyes slid from Betty to the other women. *God*, she thought, as they stared back at her, *they would all know about Penny and Clancy.*

'Oh, don't look so worried dear. Dr Doreen's only had the non-alcoholic sparkly! She'll cut that cast straight as a dye.'

Dr Doreen stepped forward in her Hush Puppy shoes, her ample nylon-clad thighs making swishing noises beneath her shapeless floral frock.

'Come along, Emily, and bring your arm with you,' she commanded in Queen Mother English before looking down over her glasses, assessing the two nurses standing before her.

'Tracy,' she said, 'you can help. We can't have Penny working too hard on her last day.'

Perhaps the business between Penny and Clancy hadn't been disclosed to Dr Doreen, Emily thought hopefully. She kept her eyes fixed on the floor as she moved past the hospital staff, her cheeks flushed pink and a thin layer of sweat forming over her skin despite the air conditioning.

In the consultation room she sat holding her arm out while the doctor and nurse cut the cast, using what looked to Emily like a two-inch circular saw. Soon the plaster cracked open like a shell, revealing a white, rather scaly, arm that was considerably wasted in muscle tone compared to Emily's other strong, tanned arm. As they swiped her skin clean, Dr Doreen asked her numerous questions, lifting Emily's limb, prodding it, squeezing it and stroking it.

'It looks,' she said at last, standing back and surveying Emily like a new piece of artwork, 'as if Evie Jenner is doing a good job of nursing you back to health. You are in fine form.'

Emily flexed her fingers back and forth, saying, 'Fine, yes, fine.'

She couldn't concentrate on Dr Doreen's banter, knowing that Penny was just in the other room. Was she leaving her job at Dargo to go live at their Brigalow house with Clancy? Emily pictured Penny on her couch watching TV. *Her* couch, paid for by the sale of *her* heifers. She imagined Penny and Clancy in the bathroom together, making love in the shower like he and Emily used to when they were first married. She tried to shake her thoughts back into some kind of order – and then Dr Doreen dropped her bombshell. She answered all Emily's questions and more.

'Tracy here will be our head nurse now, won't you?' Dr Doreen said. Beach ball-shaped Tracy's chins wobbled as she nodded, nervous little eyes darting between Emily and the doctor.

'She'll take over from our Penny who's secured a job in Bairnsdale. Mind you, Penny will only be at it a few months before she goes on maternity leave. Silly, really.'

Maternity leave? Emily felt the blood drain from her face while Tracy looked as if she'd gagged on a cricket ball. Oblivious, Dr Doreen prattled on. 'The fellow's popped the question, of course, and promised her a new house, but it's a bit like shutting the gate after the horse has whatsamacalled it. I'm from old-fashioned stock, you see. I just don't understand these young things. Do I, Tracy?'

'Mmm,' was all the nurse could squeak.

Pregnant! Penny pregnant? Emily felt as if Clancy's truck had hit her at a hundred Ks. At reception, she could barely pay the bill. Her hands shook as she tried to recall the pin for the EFT-POS machine. Betty had no sooner handed her the invoice than Emily was scuttling out the door, not sure whether to cry or throw up, or both. She was fumbling with the door handle of the ute when she heard a soft voice behind her.

'Emily?'

She spun around to see Penny standing before her, looking pristine in her nurse's white. The sunshine revealed how pale and freckled her skin was. The tones reminded Emily of a fancy hen's egg – all pretty and mottled. She imagined Clancy touching that skin. And froze.

'Are you okay?' Penny asked.

Emily's mouth dropped open. *Penny was asking her if she was okay?*

'No,' she said falteringly. 'No, I'm not.'

Penny took a step forward, tears in her eyes, a frown creasing her high-arched fine red eyebrows. 'I'm sorry. I . . .'

Emily began to shake her head. She held up her hands and backed up against the ute.

'No, don't! Just . . . just leave me alone.' Breathing raggedly, she got in, fumbled for the keys and drove away, not allowing herself to look in the side mirrors. She didn't want to see Penny standing alone, crying, outside Dargo Bush Hospital. She didn't want to look at her anymore, or think about her and Clancy . . . and the baby.

Emily's hands were shaking so much as she drove towards the old river road that she was tempted to open the rum she'd bought for Luke and take a giant swig. She remembered a warm can of beer that had rolled under the seat and instead pulled over and fished around for that. She yanked it open and skolled the entire can, letting out a loud belch at the finish.

Penny pregnant! By Clancy! She shut her eyes and began to cry, then began to laugh amidst her crying. It was all too ridiculous to take in. To think that Meg and Tilly would soon have a half-brother or -sister . . .

'Shit!' she said. Grabbing up a handful of Tic-Tacs from the dash, Emily shoved them in her mouth as if they were party pills. Then, after jabbing the ute into gear, she pulled back on to the road, telling herself life was all good. All of it. Even the

191

shitty bits. It was all perfection. Or at least that's what bloody Evie had told her.

'Fucking perfect!' she screamed as she bashed the steering wheel. She screamed as she swerved round the corners. She screamed as she dropped the ute back a gear at the hills. Not a girlie scream, but a deep angry scream that seemed to come from a place within that had been locked up and ignored since her mother had died. Emily screamed and screamed until no sound came.

She pulled over again. I'm going mad, she thought to herself. Then she heard a voice say: 'Control your thoughts.'

It wasn't the voice in her head. She glanced at the bush around her. Then she heard it again, in a whisper: 'Control your thoughts.' It was the voice of the old woman in her dreams. 'I am going mad!' Emily said as she clutched her head in her hands. She sat for a time, the engine off, her eyes shut, letting the bitter memories flood in, then letting them go, gently steering her mind towards better days ahead.

Twenty-four

It had been years since Emily had been out past the big bend and she barely remembered the little house tucked away in the bush, but as she drove there she began to feel herself relax. Though her throat felt raw and sore, she continued to focus on choosing a smoother way forward for herself.

By the time she saw the Sold sign Emily had composed herself. She chose not to think of Clancy. Or the baby. Things would get better for her from here she vowed, just as she realised the drive to Luke's house was very steep. She should have thought earlier to ditch the float. This was goat-track country. Not knowing if there was any place to turn around on the other side of the steep rise, she pulled over on to a flat patch of paddock inside the gate and set out to walk the last little way, glad she'd chosen the Bundy and not a heavy carton. She grabbed up an envelope she and Evie had packed for Luke, called Rousie to heel and strode up the rest of the steep hill, her body protesting at the sudden burst of exertion after her long recuperation.

At the top of the rise she saw, nestled in a pretty spot, the rust-blotched tin roof of the house with smoke drifting lazily from the chimney. Dargo was full of these discoveries. Each river bend or hill revealed another patch where some old-timer had died along with their small farming dreams, leaving a meagre mark in the form of a cottage, a shed or two and some yards. These dilapidated dwellings were gradually being bought up by city folk for their bush hideaways. It had begun to give Dargo a transient, seasonal feel, but the tourists also brought jobs, drinkers, spenders and a bit of interest to the town.

The future for Dargo now lay not in cattle or timber or gold but tourism. Though judging from the weeds here, absentee city owners spelled trouble for the land in some cases. This place was a fire hazard. Emily hoped Luke would get it straight before the next summer-fire season.

There was a patch of yellow box gum trees on a levelled knoll just above the house and Emily caught a glimmer of movement there. As she drew nearer she could see it was a horse and rider in an arena.

A young chestnut gelding with a wide blaze and white stockings, *just like the one in her dream of Mayford*, was drifting around the sandy spot on the knoll in a collected canter. Emily quietly moved closer, and leant back against a tree to watch.

What she saw took her breath away. In that moment all her burdens were forgotten. The rider, Luke, sat deep in the saddle, moving as one with the horse. The gelding's effortless movement told her Luke had gentle and skilful hands. He wore a wide-brimmed hat pulled down low and a blue singlet that showed off his muscular arms. His broad shoulders looked as if they would swing an axe well, she thought, and his denim jeans, Wranglers, accentuated his long, strong legs. His boots, held heel down in perfect cowboy rider position, were scuffed and old.

Luke turned the gelding in a dreamy figure-of-eight then dropped his weight back in the saddle so the young horse stopped in an almost flawless halt. Then he stroked the horse. The way he smoothed his palm over the gelding's glossy neck made Emily melt. She tried to keep her eyes on the horse, taking in its conformation and style, but she couldn't stop staring at Luke. He was pure magic on a horse. She felt like a perv, watching him from the trees, and wondered whether she should walk back now and get the float. But what if he saw her leaving? She decided she would call out to him, so as not to startle his young mount.

'Hello!' She began to walk over to him, Rousie close at her heels.

Luke was shocked to see her there. It was as if he'd conjured her up with his thoughts. He rode towards her, his face in shadow under his hat, the gelding's ears pricked and eyes bright at the approach of a stranger.

Emily glanced down at the ground as she walked, so that when she looked up again, Luke was right before her.

'A vision splendid,' she said, looking at the glossy chestnut horse but thinking of Luke.

'He's for sale.'

'He is? But I didn't know you . . .' Her voice trailed away.

'You didn't know what?'

'I didn't know you could *ride*. City boys don't ride like that.'

'That's a bit discriminatory.'

Emily gently stroked the gelding's neck, thinking of Evie and her advice about not pre-judging others.

'Yeah, it is a bit. I'm sorry. I've been really condescending, haven't I? It shouldn't matter that you come from the city.'

'Not any more. Besides, I was only ever a city boy temporarily. I was a Wimmera wheatbelt boy before that.'

'The Wimmera!' Emily thought of the wide expanse of flat farming country, so different from her own farmland. She could picture his dark good looks and lean body in that dry, sun-drenched landscape. So he *was* a country boy! Something inside her lit up. Suddenly Luke was so much more appealing to her, a real possibility. She shook her head ruefully.

'That's *two* apologies I owe you. One for taking you for a city boy and being rude about it, and the other for Clancy's behaviour. Are you okay?'

Luke raised a hand to his face, touching a small scar on his nose.

'Fine now.'

Emily held up the Bundy.

'A housewarming gift and a bottle of sorries. *And* I brought you a copy of that Tassie legislation I was telling you about, and another on an enquiry into the '03 fires.'

He smiled. 'Cheers! I love my Bundy. Nice decoration too. And thanks for the info. I'll be sure to read it. Tonight even. No telly here.'

Emily turned her attention back to the young horse. 'You've obviously ridden a bit?'

'A bit of campdrafting, and I used to get about on horses round the sheep . . . preferred it to bikes. The farm's all trees now, though, worse luck. Dad sold it.'

Emily felt a stab of sympathy. When a country boy said those three words, 'Dad sold it,' he would be dying inside. No wonder Luke had seemed so lost in the city with Ratgirl.

'I'm sorry,' she said.

He shrugged. 'My brother wanted the money, and Dad wanted out.'

Emily looked up at him sitting astride the beautiful horse. She felt breathless and restless and suddenly very shy.

'Feel like a ride?' he asked, smiling at her.

'What?' she said, 'A ride! You . . . I mean, me?'

'The horse, I mean.'

Emily blushed. She noticed the graceful way Luke slid from the gelding and landed close beside her. He was much taller than her, his shoulders so broad. She bit her lip self-consciously and handed him the bottle of Bundy and the documents.

'Be a good way to test this. Got the cast off this morning,' she said, holding up her arm.

'You've got some tanning to do!'

'You calling me a redneck?' she joked.

They both smiled as she took the reins from him and swung up into the saddle. With the beer swilling in her empty stomach, this handsome boy before her and the news about Penny and Clancy, Emily was feeling reckless. If Clancy could have a new baby, surely she could have a new horse.

'So he's for sale, you say? What's his background? How much do you want for him? Can I take him now?'

Luke tipped his head back, laughing at Emily's rapid-fire questions. She cast him a smile, squeezing the horse into a walk. She circled Luke while he explained how the gelding had been thrown in with the two mares. Emily could feel the horse was well educated and nice and forward but needed many more hours to get him beyond the green stage. She urged him on to a trot.

'He had a bit of buck this morning, so watch him,' Luke warned. 'Nothing mean. Just trying to take the pressure off himself.'

'If I do buy him, droving will do him good,' she called back. 'It's the best way to educate young horses.' Then she stopped, realising that if the bill went through there would be no more droving next year. She decided to steer the conversation away from that subject. 'What's his name?'

'I've been calling him Bonus because he was a bonus, but it's for you to choose.'

'He sure is a looker. But a new boy in my life is the last thing I need right now,' Emily said, then blushed, realising how her words must have sounded. Luke just smiled.

'You can take him on trial, if you like.'

Her eyes widened. 'I can?'

'Sure. Take him for, say, three weeks, then let me know.'

Emily thought for a while, her fingers twirling the gelding's long chestnut mane.

'I don't really need a new horse and I don't know if I can afford one either. If the grazing bans go through, we'll be selling all but a few of ours.'

She saw the muscle in Luke's jaw clench. He didn't say anything, just nodded. She wondered if he'd taken her comment as a dig. She squeezed the gelding into a canter, pleased with the way he collected himself up.

Luke watched her strong yet sensitive hands on the reins and the way she sat as if glued in the saddle, at one with the horse. He could see the muscles move in her legs beneath her tight jeans, and he enjoyed seeing the way she talked softly to the horse and how he flexed so well under her. But something about Emily still made him cautious. He wondered what her crazy ex-husband might say about the horse. Would Luke cop another on the nose because of it? Trouble, he thought. As Emily dropped her weight back in the saddle, the gelding stopped abruptly.

'Perfect,' she said, a little breathless from the short burst of riding. 'Oh, hang it! You only live once. I've got the float with me. I was joking when I said can I take him now, but can I? Just on trial. My mare's not too sound after the accident. At least I can get him started, while she's resting.'

'Yeah, sure. Take him now,' said Luke. 'Great.'

Emily dismounted and held the gelding's reins in silence while Luke unsaddled him.

Eventually he said, 'Come inside and I'll grab your number. You'll have to excuse the mess.'

Just as they were about to yard Bonus they heard an engine approaching. They turned to see a shiny new green bubble car come hurtling over the rise. It skidded to a halt outside the house in a cloud of dust, the driver clearly not used to gravel. Cassandra got out, casting Emily a stinging look. Emily's heart sank like a stone in a river.

'Well, hello, Luke,' Cassy said coldly.

'Hi,' he said. There was an awkward silence.

'If you don't mind,' Emily said, too loudly, 'I'd better get on and leave you two to it. I'll just lead him down to the float. Thanks. I'll be in touch.'

She shot a glance at Ratgirl, taking in her strange clothes, and said a quick goodbye to them both. Then she walked away, leading the gelding as fast as she could.

* * *

'What are you doing here?' Luke said the moment Emily was out of earshot.

Cassy delivered her most sultry look. 'I missed you. Plus you'd forgotten some stuff and I thought I'd run it out to you. But obviously you're not missing me. You're clearly not at all lonely out here.'

Luke shook his head. 'You shouldn't have come, Cass.'

'I can see that!'

'It's not what you think. She's interested in the horse.'

Cassy huffed, 'Right . . . At least show me where you're living.'

'Ta-daaa!' Luke sang, sweeping one arm in the direction of the cottage. 'There, you've seen it. Happy?'

She looked mournfully at him.

'Luke, don't act like that.'

'Like what?'

'Like you hate me.'

'I don't hate you, Cassy, I just don't know what you're doing here.'

Tears welled in her eyes. 'But we had a life together.'

'Had is right,' he said. 'Past tense, Cassy. We went through all this before I left.'

'I know,' she said, head hanging. 'At least show me inside. I'm busting for the loo.'

'Loo's not inside. It's round the back. A long drop.'

'Serious?'

'A room with a view. Just watch out for the wombat hole.'

'Yikes! How can you live like that?'

'C'mon, Cassy, you're the one who was always talking about composting toilets and sustainable waste systems and getting back to Nature.'

She cast him a sullen look and stomped off around the side of the house in her Doc Martens. She looked so out of place here, Luke thought. Sure, they'd been bushwalking together a few times, but it was always with a bunch of her enviro-mad friends. They were people who celebrated the environment, spoke frequently of protecting it, but only ventured into the bush periodically to 'commune' with Nature, as if a dose of camping would make them somehow more pure or whole again for the next round of city living.

In the house he briskly showed her through the rooms.

'Bedroom, kitchen, lounge, porch. There. Tour all finished.'

'Luke. Please. I've come all this way.' She stepped towards him as they stood in the bedroom doorway, the bed unmade before them. She reached out, ran her hand along his stomach and hooked a finger into the top of his belt. 'Just one for the road, before I go?'

'No!' he said, pushing her hand away. He could see tears resurface in Cassy's eyes. What had happened to that feisty girl he'd first met? he wondered.

'Cassy, I'm sorry. I really am.' He took her by both hands, and stooped to look into her eyes. 'But we're not going to be together again.'

'Ever?'

'Ever.'

She began to cry.

'You'll be fine. You will be.'

Cassy nodded, smearing tears across her face. She sucked in a breath, looked up at him and jutted out her chin as if trying to summon her strength.

'C'mon,' he said. 'I'll take you to the pub for lunch. Before you drive home.'

She nodded sadly and forced a small smile.

'Hey, do you want to ride the horses down to town?' he asked.

Cassy shook her head. 'No way! Horses terrify me.'

And at that point, Luke knew there was no turning back.

When Emily reached Tranquillity to deliver the horse float to Flo, her dad was waiting on the verandah. As she dropped the float door and unloaded the gelding, Rod let out a long slow wolf-whistle.

'Flash one,' he said. He walked over, ran his hands along

Bonus's gleaming summertime coat, listening to Emily as she garbled out excitedly how she'd seen the horse at Luke's. Then she looked up into her dad's eyes and promptly burst into tears. In an instant his arms were about her. She pressed her face to his chest and breathed in the comfort of his horseman's smell.

'Dad,' she squeaked, 'Clancy and Penny are going to . . .'

'I know,' Rod said. 'He's called here five times already. He knows you know.' Emily looked up at him in shock.

'Penny rang him from the hospital. Then he rang here, looking for you. Said he was sorry. Said he was going to tell you himself.'

Emily drew back and looked into her father's eyes.

'Said he was *sorry*!' She kicked at the dirt. 'Bloody oath, Dad. Bad news travels fast.'

'Well,' soothed Rod, 'it depends how you look at it. It could, in the long run, be good news, couldn't it? A new baby for Clancy could be good news?' He stared into her eyes. She wanted to shout at him that, *no*, it was terrible news! Like a slap. But her dad's eyes continued to look at her lovingly so Emily asked herself the question again, could it be good news? Hurt though it did, she could see the wisdom behind her father's implication. Clancy was now Penny's problem. And a new baby would, maybe, divert Clancy's attention from Meg and Tilly in the future. It could make for a smoother path forward for them all. The tight expression on her face began to soften. Her taut muscles began to ease.

Suddenly she realised why Evie had been so insistent that she should go to the hospital this morning. She must have known it was Penny's last day. Evie had planned their meeting.

'Witch!' Emily said, then laughed.

'What?' asked Rod.

'Bloody oath, Dad, I've been Evied!'

'I think you're right,' he said, gathering up the gelding's lead rope, walking side by side with his daughter. 'I think we all have.' Together they led the beautiful new horse over to fresh pasture.

Twenty-five

At the pub, Cassy frowned at the blackboard, then looked despairingly at the menu in her hand.

'Do you have any vegan dishes?' she asked Donna, who was standing, hip jutting out, tapping a pen on her teeth while she waited.

'We have vegetarian meals,' she said, holding the order pad close to her chest. Luke shifted uncomfortably while Cassy sighed.

'Do the veggie burgers have eggs in them?' she asked.

'I'm not sure. I can read the packet for you.'

'Are they cooked on the same grill as the meat?'

'We can use a frypan if you like,' Donna said, trying to keep her voice light. She was used to the city customers who came in droves during holiday periods and demanded so much more than the locals. It was part of her job to accommodate them, so she shifted her weight to the other hip and cemented a smile on her face.

Cassy looked up at her. 'I suppose I'll just have to have a garden salad. No dressing. And a small bowl of fries *if* they're cooked in clean veggie oil.'

'Fries?' Donna said. 'We can do a you a batch of chips, in fresh oil, if you like.'

'*Yes*,' said Cassy rudely, '*I would like.*'

Donna thanked them as she gathered up the menus, her smile fading the moment she turned her back.

'Cassy,' hissed Luke, 'this isn't Melbourne.'

'I know,' she said. 'Oh, how I bloody well *know*. Why anyone would want to live here is beyond me.'

Luke glanced around at Donna, talking to the cook behind the big bain-marie. Cassy followed his gaze.

'Stop being embarrassed, Luke. It's my right to be a vegan. I don't see what the fuss is about. Don't they know it's wrong to eat animals anyway?'

'Cassy,' he said tiredly, 'you only say that because you've never been hungry in your entire life. You're surrounded by good food and can eat what you want, when you want. Don't you see, yours is such a privileged view? If your family were starving in some third-world country, you'd be grateful to be eating at all. Especially meat – rat, or guinea pig, or dog – you'd be eating all of it, even the entrails, just so you and your family could survive.'

'Luke, stop! Yuk!'

He looked at her levelly. 'I respect your choice, but please don't dump on the barmaid here because she doesn't share your world views. They mean well. They're good people.'

Cassy's eyes flickered. 'Yes, I can see you think that.' Her gaze bore into him and he felt the Cassy of old stick like a barb in his skin. 'These people not only grow beef, they do it on pristine wilderness. That's criminal. Farming livestock ought to be stopped! Those poor cows.'

'Then what would happen to the cows if everyone stopped eating meat, Cassy? Have you thought of that? All the breeding animals would be put down because the farmers couldn't afford to run them on the land for nothing. So the animals you're trying to protect would end up dead anyway. It's the way the world works. Besides, the way they raise cattle here is far more environmentally friendly than all those beasts fed on corn in feedlots in the US. Get some perspective.'

'*Me* get some perspective? If you had any you wouldn't have bought a property in a place you don't even know! I can tell you're trying to pick a fight, Luke, so let's just change the subject.'

'Fine,' he said, clasping his fingers together. 'I hope you enjoy your meal.'

'Yes, Luke. I'm sure I'll enjoy my meal. Our *last* meal together,' she added bitterly.

They were sitting in brooding silence when the door of the lounge opened and a big bloke in an oilskin, beanie, grimy jeans and boots walked in. Donna, coming from the kitchen, smiled at him.

'In for lunch again today, Bob?'

The big man peeled off his coat, revealing a burgeoning blue singlet with white text on it: *Dargo River Inn, Liquor up the Front, Poker in the Rear*. Grey hairs curled over the neck-line. He sat at a table and took off his beanie, revealing messy long grey hair with a bald patch on top.

'Bob's regular, please,' Donna yelled towards the kitchen. 'Salad or veg with your steak today, Bob?'

'Just chips, thanks, sweetheart.' He pushed a twenty-dollar note towards her, and she set off to the bar to pull him a beer.

Luke saw Cassy looking disdainfully at Bob's singlet. Then he saw Bob look sideways at Cassandra. He visibly flinched at the sight of her spiky hair and facial piercings.

'Geez,' he said, 'you fair dinkum gave me a fright, girl. It is *girl*, isn't it?' he asked, looking Cassy up and down, taking in her black, androgynous clothes and chunky kick-your-head-in boots. Cassy narrowed her eyes just as Donna set down Bob's beer.

'Meet our new Park ranger, Luke Bradshaw,' Donna said, 'and his lovely lady-friend.'

'Ahhh,' said Bob.

'This is Bob Flanaghan,' Donna introduced him. Bob made no attempt to shake Luke's hand. Instead he skolled his beer, never once taking his eyes from the ranger as he gulped.

Flanaghan, thought Luke. One of Emily's cattlemen clan. Trouble, too, from the look of him.

Bob set down his empty beer glass. 'So you're the new bloke here to fence us out of the cattle runs if the bans are passed, are ya?' Luke was about to answer when Bob turned to Cassy. 'Be careful hanging out with your Parkie boyfriend, love. You'll be in trouble if you get tangled up in one of his electric fences with all that metal in ya. You'll get a *zap*!' He laughed as he gestured towards the piercings in Cassy's brow, ears, nose, mouth and tongue. She scowled back at him.

'I'm sorry, darlin', but it looks like you ran fair through a fence and you've still got barbs and bits of star pickets in ya.' He leant forward so he could see past Cassy to Luke. 'How do you kiss her with all that metal in her face?'

'I don't have to listen to this,' Cassy protested.

'He's only having a joke, Cass,' Luke said, looking up at Bob. 'We're just here for a quiet lunch, mate.'

'Lunch, eh? Then a bit of fishing after, maybe. Looks like she's already fallen in the tackle box!'

Bob began to wheeze with laughter as Donna stepped forward with a fresh beer.

'Bob, leave the young lovebirds alone.' She turned to Luke and Cassy. 'I think our Bob has had a few before coming in,' she said by way of apology.

'They ought to lighten up,' he said. 'And one way of lightening up would be to take all that metal out of your face. You got shares in BHP Steel or something?'

'Bob, settle,' said Donna before she breezed off to the kitchen again.

Cassy stared at him, fury written on her face.

'How can you stand it here in this backwater town?' she asked Luke.

'They don't ever stand it for long,' Bob said, swigging again on his beer. 'Got no bloody clue, you bloody city slickers. You think you're doin' a good job, do you, eh? You wait till that ban comes through. One spring it'll take, one good spring with no grazing, and then we'll have a fire through that so-called Park of yours and it'll all be buggered. You bloody Greenies have no idea. You'll wreck the lot of it.'

'And you're not wrecking it now with your shitting, farting cattle?' Cassy challenged. Luke shot her a look to silence her, but she kept on. 'When they do pass that legislation and you're banned from the mountains, thousands of people will be celebrating, you hear me?'

Bob's face began to redden. His eyes flared an intense blue. 'You bloody stupid greenies have got it all wrong! You think kicking farmers off the land and planting trees is a good thing for the environment – now we got trees all over the countryside! I'd like to see you find ways of eating the bastards. You townie mongrels take your long showers, shop every day and live in them big houses, then blame *us* for buggering the environment. Well, you can eat the crap from China for all I care. Just stop kicking us farmers in the guts!'

Luke remembered Darcy cautioning him about Bob Flanaghan. He could see the man was fast reaching boiling point. Soon he'd be beyond reason.

Lunch or no lunch, it was time to leave. Luke stood up.

'Where ya going, Mr new Parkie boy?' Bob slurred.

'No point talking while you're full of piss and bad manners, Mr Flanaghan,' he said. 'You come and see me another day and we can talk.'

'Huh!' snorted Bob. 'Talk! That's all you bloody government bastards do is talk! Well, we'll give you an induction to your job you'll never forget, kiddo. We'll see you in the Wonnangatta next week.'

Luke tilted his head quizzically. The Wonnangatta?

Bob rambled on. 'The cattlemen are taking a mob into that park to show what a shithouse job you're doing with the land, and the media will be there to record what a mess you bloody VPP people have made of it. Once that gets out, there's no way known they'll kick the cattle off. Youse bastards are stuffed.'

Luke knew the VPP's Wonnangatta National Park was in an area even more remote than the Flanaghans' grazing runs.

It was the most isolated cattle station in Victoria, and in its heyday had been a thousand acres of beautiful natural pasture, bushland and river flats, nestled in a valley over two thousand feet above sea level.

To evict cattle from the area, the government had bought the property at great expense about twenty years ago. But the logistics and costs of a bureaucracy managing a station that vast and remote were major drawbacks. Luke had never been in the Wonnangatta but his ears pricked up at Bob's tip-off that the cattlemen were planning to take cattle there illegally as a media stunt. Emily may have the face of an angel, but her uncle had the face of an arsehole. Luke Bradshaw had no problem going straight out to the phone box across the road from the pub to ring Giles Grimsley's mobile.

Cassy sat on the back tailgate of his ute, swinging her legs as Luke made the call. She looked like a hyena that had dined well that day, such was her joy at seeing him dob in the cattlemen's plans to his boss.

Luke was surprised to hear Grimsley answer his phone on a Saturday and even more surprised to find he already knew about the cattlemen's plan. The Mountain Cattlemen's Association of Victoria had emailed the VPP.

'They think they're being courteous and playing fair by telling us,' Giles said over the phone. 'But they don't appreciate the number of headaches they're giving us. They acknowledge it's an illegal action but still they do it! They have no idea of the paperwork and costs this will generate. It's taxpayers' money they're wasting!'

Giles's card in his hand, Luke ran his index finger over the embossed VPP logo.

'Can I do something to help?' he asked.

'I'll have your Heyfield supervisor call you first thing Monday.' Giles began to outline the plans they'd put in place.

'Darren is drafting a Coordinated Incident Plan and formulating a Risk Management Assessment of the potential situation in regard to the proposed protest. Then he's compiling a rostered crew of staff, both in the Heyfield offices and on the ground and is going to liaise with the DLSC&EL Corporate Communications Unit at every stage and formulate a Remote Media Unit outlet. I'll have him draw me up a flow chart of the Departmental Responsibilities for each unit during the protest. That way we can notify staff right from the top, starting with the Deputy Land Stewardship and Biodiversity Officer down to the Forest and Biodiversity Utilisation Unit.

'But as you're just a ranger on the ground, you don't need to worry about any of that, Luke. You're not yet adequately trained. Darren at Heyfield can guide you.'

'So he'll phone me Monday?' said Luke, his head swimming from all the government lingo.

In Melbourne Giles Grimsley tapped his teeth with his finger as he thought. He wondered whether he should roster Luke on to the Protest Response Strike Team. But the boy had such limited training it could be a risk. He was yet to complete his 4WD training unit, his unit one fire combat block or his minimal environmental impact camp-out instruction. At the interview he had seemed like a bright young man, but it could be risky to take someone so inexperienced out into a volatile situation. Giles cursed the cattlemen again for all the trouble they caused, and for the disruption to his own weekend.

He recalled that Luke had been a farm boy and felt a glimmer of disappointment over this fact. Agriculture was such a simplistic pursuit, and country people were often dimwitted and narrow-minded, he found. Still, he rationalised, at least the boy had a university degree.

'Yes, Luke, Darren will set up a conference call first thing Monday morning. Nine o'clock.'

He thanked Giles and hung up. Nine o'clock was first thing? Luke laughed to himself, remembering his old life on the farm. Nine o'clock there was time to come in for a cup of tea after two hours' work.

'Well? How did you go?' Cassy asked him. 'You didn't say much this end.'

Luke shrugged.

'It's all sorted.'

She propelled herself off the ute and stood close to him.

'Got anything to eat at home?'

'Hadn't you better be getting back to Melbourne?' he said. He could tell Cassy was winding herself up for another pounce. He had to get her out of here.

'Luke, I'm starving. I need food!'

Back in his house, he opened the cupboard.

'Baked beans. Or tinned baby corn spears.'

Cassy rolled her eyes and reached for the baked beans. Luke didn't feel like talking to her so he picked up the documents Emily had left him and sat down heavily in the chair.

'What are you reading?'

'Nothing,' he said. Cassy turned her back on him.

The first document was Tasmanian. He frowned, wondering how that was relevant to the mountains he was about to caretake. He flipped to the next. It was a submission to the Victorian Government after fires in the area in 2003. Emily had marked a page with a sticky note and highlighted the text in green. The extract had been written by descendants of the original cattlemen. They talked about their ancestors in the thirties who would throw out a match into the vegetation every couple of hundred metres along the ridgelines ahead of the snow season, so that fire would not be able to burn too hot in the area come summer.

Luke looked up to see Cassy stirring the saucepan on the stove top. Her face was set. He could tell from her expression she was gearing herself up to drive away after this last pathetic meal. He felt sorry for her, but could no longer offer her comfort. He went back to his reading, thinking of Emily and her pigheaded relative Bob. Was it a simple truth that the once open, rolling grassland in the area had been taken over by scrub only since grazing and burning controls by government?

How could these stubborn, proud, uneducated people be making claims like this? During his degree course Luke had studied CSIRO findings that proved livestock grazing in alpine environments was not, in his lecturer's words, 'an effective fire mitigation tool'.

He wondered now who had run the studies and where the truth lay. Luke could understand the cattlemen's frustration with the whole process, but why did Bob have to be so aggressive? He threw the paperwork on the table. It was all too confusing, and at the heart of his confusion was Emily.

Cassy set down two plates of baked beans.

'Our last supper,' she said, and then began to cry.

Luke shut his eyes. He just wanted her gone from his life. And now, with the clash of information swirling in his head, he wanted the whole cattlemen debate, even Emily along with it, gone too.

Twenty-six

Emily shifted in the saddle as the young gelding plunged through the dogwood scrub towards the Wonnangatta National Park. The bush around her smelt sweet from the overnight shower. Thirty other riders were following her, their horses pausing to step over high logs or weave around trees. Rousie had his tongue fully out, front paws up on a log, ears pricked as he watched the small mob of Hereford cows ahead lumber steadily down the slope.

There were no roads into the Wonnangatta National Park, just hair-raising tracks that four-wheel drive enthusiasts tackled in the summer holiday season. Before the ride, Emily knew there would be screamingly steep mountainsides to slide down into the station and over a dozen deeply gouged river crossings to forge.

Snowgum's injuries still made her unrideable for such a long, tough trek. Emily had wondered if her own body would take the rough riding, and if she'd be able to handle Luke's young horse, Bonus, who was still green at moving through and around trees. But once sitting in her old stock saddle on the beautiful young chestnut, she felt as if she'd truly come back to life. He was so steady, had such flex and was so obedient Emily found her fears giving way into joy.

Packed in her saddle bags was an entire apothecary supply

of Evie's natural prescriptions. There were vitamins, tonics, rubs for sore muscles, drops for every conceivable thing. Emily had to admit that, thanks to Evie, her body was feeling surprisingly good . . . so far. Evie had even shown her how to connect up to universal energies to help heal different areas of her body. The first time Evie had shown her how to do a 'healing' Emily had almost burst herself inside out trying not to giggle. She kept opening one eye to see what Evie was doing and if any bolts of lightning were coming out from the sky or spiking through the top of her head. But after a time, her giggles dissipated and Emily began to feel the strangest sensation throughout her body. Evie started to talk of things she simply could not have known about Emily, and at the end of the experience she felt utterly altered.

At first Emily felt fearful, then amazed, and by the end of Evie's healing session found herself to be a true convert to something a few months ago she would have scoffed at and ridiculed. Now here she was on a horse, a cattleman's daughter, in the middle of nowhere, thinking about energetic healing. Emily laughed at herself and the changes within her as she rode through the bush on the biggest adventure she'd ever had with her family.

The plan of the Mountain Cattlemen's Association was to take three groups of cattle – ten in each herd, from three different mountain regions across Victoria – into Wonnangatta as a media stunt, to convey publicly the message they hoped would reach the men and women in the Victorian Parliament.

'What's the worst that will happen to us by going in there?' Emily asked her father.

Rod shrugged. 'We could be fined a thousand dollars a head but I doubt there'll be arrests. The police and the Parkies know it'd be public-relations suicide.'

Hang the fines, Emily thought. The land mattered more. Before taking on the last steep ride into the valley the group stopped to take photos of the Hereford cattle rubbing their sweaty ears on the treated pine posts of a Park sign that read:

Welcome to Wonnangatta National Park – No firearms, no domestic animals permitted.

'The cattle can't read,' Emily joked, and they all laughed, but she could feel the group's nervousness. These men and women astride their horses weren't law-breakers, or trouble-makers. They were just passionate about the land.

Emily had thought guiltily of Luke then as she watched the cattle lumber forward into the designated Parks zone.

Flo reined her horse to the left to hasten the mob as they slowly pushed through the overgrowth.

'I remember when there were bridle trails all over these hills,' she said.

'All gone now,' Rod answered as he slid down an embankment on his horse, twisting out of the way of a branch. He turned in his saddle so that Emily could hear him. 'You were just a little tacker when I last came in here on the drive to take the cattle out. Just shows you how quickly the scrub gets overgrown.'

'And there hasn't been a fire in here for decades, by the looks,' she said, touching one of the clean, upright trunks of the eucalypts with her fingertips as she rode past.

Rod grimaced.

'Makes me nervous just bringing people in here. If I were the VPP, I wouldn't let the public near the place. Alight, it'd be a deathtrap.'

Emily pulled her horse to a halt at the top of a rise and looked down across the massive valley that ran ahead of them as far as the eye could see.

The river-flats were yellow with Saint John's Wort weeds. The dirty-blond swathe of tall, rank grasses, which whispered in the wind inviting fire, was only interrupted by the large darker-leafed domes of blackberry bushes dotting the plain. In places, particularly near the winding creek bends, the black-berries had joined together in clumps, some as high as a house.

Her father pulled his horse up next to hers and followed her gaze.

'*That* is a National Park?' Emily said amazed. 'We're going to be hard-pressed to drove the cattle through that. The weeds are as high as the cows' horns!'

She could see the Park contractors had slashed away a small area of grass around the site of the old homestead and camp grounds. They must have made the difficult journey over the tracks with a ride-on lawnmower tied to the back of their ute. What an absurd thing to do when there were thousands of acres of overgrown valley flats. Getting a tractor in would be a nightmare, but if grazing weren't used to control the overgrowth, tractors and chemical sprays were the only other options.

Emily looked at the site of the homestead that had been built by the pioneering family who'd farmed this area over one hundred years ago. The house was all but rubble now, burnt down by vandals over the years. Now composting toilets and neat Park signage dotted the small area for the comfort of holidaymakers. Tents sprang up here in summer for idle days to be spent at a place where men had once toiled and tilled and women had birthed and raised children in the hard slog of a life spent in total isolation.

Emily felt like crying. This once-beautiful property was going to ruin. The overgrowth all around was testimony to the fact that government money and a handful of staff couldn't manage this land properly, no matter how good their intentions.

'Dad,' she said, 'doesn't anyone *notice*? Are they that blind to this? Or don't they care?'

Rod shook his head. 'I don't think it's about lack of care. You know most of the Parkies are really good fellas. Take that Luke . . . I reckon he's all right. But I think they're all constrained from the top down. By both money and mindset.'

Emily felt a buzz run through her, hearing her dad say Luke's name.

Rod talked on. 'The VPP boys on the ground are already stretched. They're relying on funding to trickle out from

214

Melbourne for sprays, staff and equipment. While they wait, the weeds are taking hold. Darcy said the last straw for him was when the funding policy changed. Because some clown in Melbourne deemed there wasn't enough money to do anything about the huge blackberry problem, they made another weed a "higher priority". Darcy couldn't believe it.'

Emily wondered how Luke would fare in the midst of such a system. Would he be absorbed into the culture of the giant organisation and swamped, like her dad said, by the mindset? She knew he'd be pressured by locals to do more burning off, but fires were also controlled by the heavy weight of bureaucracy.

When the winds and the temperature were perfect locally, the opportunity for a safe, cool burn was often lost because of the official process required. To start any burn-off, Luke would need the go-ahead from Melbourne. It was so costly once they got 'dozers, fire trucks and men on the ground, plus helicopters on standby, that only a small percentage of burns proposed ever took place.

Gone were the days when men like her grandfather would expertly feel the air temperature on their skin, the breeze on their face, and then cast an eye around the bush to see if the time were right. Then her grandpa, riding along on his horse, would simply puff on his pipe and drop a match here and there and let the slow trickle of flames do their work. In her grandfather's day, one person was able effectively to manage thousands of acres of healthy bushland, rejuvenating it in the way Nature intended. Gently, with expertise and care, like the Aborigines had done. Now in the hands of a giant bureaucracy, burning-off cost millions and its effectiveness was disputed and doubted by academic 'experts'.

Emily realised how close they were to being locked out of their own high-country station. Seeing Wonnangatta in this state filled her with despair.

'So, is this what our land on the high plains will look like soon?' she asked her father, voice cracking with emotion.

Rod reached out and gently pulled the rein of his daughter's horse. The gelding took a step nearer him and Rod laid a hand on Emily's knee.

'C'mon, Em,' he said. 'They'll have to see sense. This place proves what we've been saying to the bureaucrats, politicians, scientists and public all along. How can they not see that grazing helps manage land like this?'

'But what if they don't see, Dad? What then?'

Emily's face mirrored her father's sad expression. All his life he had lived with the discrimination that came from being a Flanaghan, a cattleman. It hurt to see his daughter go through the same distress.

'It's okay, Em. You just pull your hat down tight and keep on riding. That's all we can do.'

'But why are they so quick to condemn us, Dad? Like we're just a bunch of uncaring old ratbags and rednecks, raping and pillaging the mountain country? Seems they're quite happy to have hydro schemes, ski villages, logging and tourism all over the mountains, but they're making our grazing cattle a crime! The government gives its blessing to bulldozers and chainsaws up here, but not our cattle.'

'It's just how it is, Em. You can't let it get to you. It'll consume your life.'

'Like it has yours?' her eyes sparked, challenging her dad. She knew he had all but given up. Resigned to his fate, she could tell he was just going through the motions on this protest ride. His heart was no longer in it.

'C'mon. We've got to keep moving,' Rod said, pressing his horse away with his heels.

As they rode closer to the valley floor and the cattle eagerly made their way to the flatter, grassy creek flats, Emily looked back to where they had come from. The track had the steep pitch of a church spire. Some riders were leading their horses down, half sliding and hanging on to the branches of trees.

216

There were calls of excitement and laughter in the air, knowing they were almost safely there. Clipped to Rod's belt the two-way radio crackled to life.

'This is the Mansfield mob. We've sighted you Gippslanders. Can you see us?'

Far off to the north, against the backdrop of a giant mountain, were the tiny specks of cattle and riders.

'Welcome to *Weed-angatta*, Mansfield mob,' Rod answered. The riders let out whoops and cheers. To their left on the steep bank came another call. There, the Licola riders were picking their way down the hill on a treacherous zigzag track, letting their cattle find their own way down.

'*Weed-angatta*, here we come!' the Licola group called on the radio.

As the sound of helicopters throbbed overhead, a crowd was gathering near the ruined homestead on the valley's floor. Four-wheel drives appeared from the hills. Campers, too, made their way over and gathered, all looking skyward to watch the helicopters descend. As the choppers landed, they stirred the air and whipped the heads of grasses back and forth in a manic dance, like eddies in a flooding river. The crowd of bushmen, campers and cattlemen watched the media crew tiptoe their way through the grass. Women in office clothing and dainty shoes, men in white shirts with ties. The crew, wearing standard arty black, lugged camera tripods, boom microphones and heavy shoulder-bags. The media pack looked so at odds with the landscape that some people laughed.

As the crew set up their gear, each party of drovers was given the cue to move its herd forward. As the three small herds came together the cows were too weary to bother much with pecking orders. They all grouped as one and began to graze while horsemen ringed them. Rod rode forward carrying a microphone and the Australian flag upon his tall chestnut horse.

With the cameras rolling he delivered his heartfelt speech.

217

Emily wondered just how many passionate words had been spoken or written on this subject over the years, with no changes to the outcome. She fingered her leather reins as she listened to her father's words.

'Mr and Mrs Average have it so good that they don't worry much about tomorrow. Well, I think Mr and Mrs Average need to take heed of what's going on in the wider world. The assumption that we can turn on the telly for our entertainment, drive to the supermarket for our sustenance, keep up the consumer spending, use fossil fuel as if it were there forever, needs to be addressed.

'Up until now the public conscience has dictated that someone else should do something. The government, for instance. This has resulted in government policies that are formulated purely to placate the voter. Kicking a few cows off the high country fits comfortably into this approach for many politicians. But *we* say an uneducated majority of voters has no right to promote the "lock-it-up and let it burn" approach to public land management. This approach will only result in massive flora and fauna decimation with the hottest holocaust of bushfires to come – as, with certainty, they will.'

Emily shivered. She had seen her fair share of firefighting in her young life, though never anything too serious. But as the years rolled past and the bush around them never saw the gentle lick of a cool-flame burn, she started to wonder when that apocalyptic fire would arrive. Now it was autumn, they had most likely survived for another year, but all the bushmen knew there was a fire disaster waiting to happen.

Redgum shifted his back leg and rested a hoof, and Rod paused from speaking until his horse stilled.

'How is it that early mountain cattlemen families survived bush conflagrations when the only fire control they had was a hessian bag, a bough off a tree and a box of matches? The Aborigines before them had even fewer control measures. But they knew how to use fire at the correct time. They did not put out all the natural fires until the fuel build-up on the land became massive. And now look about you! Look at this mess. All the Elvis helicopters available, the thousands of well-trained firefighters with millions of dollars-worth of state-of-the-art firefighting gear, cannot be effective here once a major fire gets underway.'

Emily felt her eyes sting with tears. She had witnessed her own part of the high country going that way with cool-burn bans and now, having seen Wonnangatta, she could foresee the Flanaghan station in the same state – a riot of weeds and fallen-down fencing with just the rutted wheelmarks of four-wheel drives carving through the guts of the country. She backed up her horse and rode away, keen simply to be on her own for a time, overwhelmed by the hopelessness she felt. She thought of her girls at Evie's house and wished she could hold them close for comfort.

A woman reporter with a notebook and shiny patent-leather shoes stepped out in front of her, wary of her horse.

'Having a good day?' she asked. Emily looked down, noting that her face, although pretty, was covered heavily in makeup and that there were sweatstains on her white blouse. Her streaked blonde hair looked windswept and no longer chic.

'It's not exactly a picnic, but it's close enough,' Emily said, trying to sound cheerful.

The reporter looked about her. 'This place is beautiful, isn't it? Look at the flowers and all that grass.'

'Beautiful?' Emily wondered aloud. This? Yes, the setting was beautiful, but the management of the land was shocking. Appalling. Heartbreaking even. Didn't this woman see it too?

Emily looked at her smiling, squinting face and realised she didn't. She just saw trees, grass and sky. It looked *pretty* to her. Emily suddenly realised that people with no knowledge of the land *couldn't* see – not even when trouble was staring them right in the face.

They saw green so they thought there was no drought. They saw grass and flowers but not the toxic weeds. They saw creeks not dull lifeless water; steep hills but not the erosion on them. Then they saw cattle and dung in amongst high-country flowers and thought it was bad. They didn't realise that over thousands of years this grass had evolved for grazing, offering up the sweetest parts of its leaves so that they were mown by the animals to exactly the right length.

They didn't realise the cattle were time-controlled and lightly stocked on the plains area so that the land had months and months in which to rejuvenate. Emily saw for the first time that they didn't know what they were looking at, and they even didn't know what they didn't know!

'Want to have a ride?' she said. The reporter hesitated. 'He's very quiet.'

Emily was off, already out of the saddle, grabbing the reporter's bag. Offering her the stirrup. 'On the count of three,' she said, bunking her up before she had the chance to say no. Then she led the woman into the deep grasses.

'See this grass here?' Emily said, running the palms of her hands over the tops of the seed heads. It was well over waist-high. 'This will all fall over and rot. It's just one species. All the native grasses have been buried alive underneath it. They don't stand a chance if this other stuff isn't kept in check. That's what grazing usually does. And see this yellow stuff? Pretty though it is, it's a weed – Saint John's Wort. Toxic and highly vigorous. No native orchid stands a chance when this stuff's about. And you know blackberries, don't you? Just look at that creek over there. That dark vegetation . . . all black-berries. You can't even get to the water.'

The reporter began to nod.

'Yes, I see.' She looked around the valley. 'It's everywhere! This grass, those weeds, the blackberries . . .'

'Not so beautiful really,' Emily said.

'Well, no. Not when you point it out like that,' the jour-nalist said. 'Now I see what you mean.'

Good, thought Emily. Another seed sown.

*   *   *

At the same time, in a Bairnsdale hospital, Clancy was holding Penny's hand as her Chinese-born ultrasonographer friend, Lin, squirted lube on to her abdomen. Clancy was thinking what he'd really like to do with that lube. Penny looked so cute lying on the bed with her top pulled up and the buttons of her jeans undone.

He bent forward and kissed her on her freckled nose, thinking he couldn't wait to get her home with some lube of his own. He had surprised himself by really enjoying this trip to the hospital. He hadn't been in for Emily's scans, making sure he'd been away in the truck. The baby stuff and hospitals had freaked him out then, but this time round he vowed he'd do things differently. It was like a second chance. This time too he was sure it would be a boy. A boy to take fishing. To drive trucks with. To go to the pub with. To kick the footy with. A boy. He hoped not a red-headed boy, but a boy nonetheless.

In the dim room, they turned their eyes to the monitor and watched expectantly for clarity to come to the swirling grey and black blobs on the screen.

'Oh, my,' said Lin as she pushed her glasses higher on her nose. 'You have been a busy boy! There's the baby, see?' She extended one finger to the monitor and pointed out the tiny heartbeat. With her other hand she swivelled the probe that slithered over Penny's flat belly.

'And . . . there's the other one.'

'The other one!' Penny almost shouted.

'The other one?' echoed Clancy.

'Yes,' said Lin. 'You have sowed not just one wild oat, Clancy, but two! You are having twins!'

Twenty-seven

L uke sat uncomfortably in the back seat of the VPP four-wheel drive next to Giles Grimsley, who had been cursing the number of grass seeds in his socks. While Luke's Heyfield supervisor, Darren, tackled the last steep pinch on the track into the Wonnangatta Valley, his workmate, Cory, continued to play with the satellite navigation equipment in the front passenger seat. Through the canopy of leaves, on the saddle of a giant hill, they had seen the TV news helicopters arriving.

'We'll wait until the television crews have left,' Giles decided. 'The less potential for confrontation with the cattlemen, the less airtime the story will get.'

Luke knew the government's media department had given Giles a clear brief should they get caught by any reporters or journalists. He had watched him rehearsing his statement over and over on the trip into the Wonnangatta. He didn't seem to be taking in the bush around him at all.

For Luke the trip had been amazing. The river crossings they drove through had been gouged deeply by four-wheel drives over time, but the beauty of the ribbon-like river winding its way through the valley was staggering.

Now, nearing the crest of a hill, with only a few short steep kilometres to go to the Wonnangatta, Luke felt his excitement rising. He was getting paid to do this! His first days on the job had been like one big adventure. The only downside was that he would no doubt run into Emily and her family. He didn't want to see her in this context but what was he to do? He had a job now. He had a house in the township. He was aware how touchy things were between the VPP and the cattlemen and he knew now it was best to leave things well alone with a cattleman's daughter. But still he hoped to see her. Just one glimpse.

'There they go now,' said Darren, pointing to the helicopters lifting up from the valley floor. 'Leaving just in time to meet their broadcast deadlines. Looks like you won't get your mug on telly after all, Giles.' Darren glanced at his boss in the rear-view mirror, smiling. Luke could tell Giles was disappointed.

'There'll probably be newspaper journalists travelling with the cattlemen,' he said. 'But only I'm to give the statement, okay?'

'Right you are,' said Darren, winking at Cory.

Giles checked his watch.

'With the choppers gone, now's the time to find the cattlemen's camp and get a count on the cattle.' He swung about to see if the police four-wheel drive was close behind them. 'Thank God we've got the Bairnsdale boys to back us up if things turn nasty.'

Nasty? Luke wondered. He had seen the worst of the cattlemen, Bob Flanaghan. Angry and rude though he was, Luke didn't think Bob would be violent. Still, Giles had been at this job for decades. Perhaps he had seen nasty.

As they drove into the Wonnangatta, Luke was shocked to see the level of flammable vegetation that covered its thousands of acres. He'd heard the VPP boys recounting their difficulty in bringing a slasher over the goat tracks and for an instant had wondered why they hadn't burnt or grazed the area. It would have been much cheaper and faster. He saw the weeds all around and alarm bells began to ring in his head. This place was a shambles.

223

As they lumbered their way over the valley, they saw smoke drifting up lazily from an afternoon campfire. Heading towards it, they found the bulk of the cattlemen camped over by a river bend on a large bare area of ground.

'No sign of the cattle,' Giles said, scanning the scene. 'Looks as if they want to play funny buggers with us and they've hidden them.'

There was no sign of Emily either, thought Luke, as he surveyed the campers and scanned the horses for a sight of his young gelding.

'Stick around while the cattlemen are interviewed by the police, then you'll have to go and look for the cattle. If we can't locate them, we can't fine the owners.' Giles sighed and shook his head, his fists clenching. 'Ignorant mongrels! Now remember, boys, be professional at all times. Say as little as possible to them.'

Luke noticed that the cattlemen barely glanced up at them from what they were doing. Some men boiled billies, others sat around the fire drinking tea or beer. Some of the women, hot from a day in the saddle, were towel drying their river-wet hair after a swim. They didn't look like a bunch of protesters. More like people comfortable with each other, and the land, simply out in it camping.

Rod Flanaghan stepped forward. 'Afternoon, gentlemen.'

A young policeman tipped back his hat and nodded, while the older rotund sergeant with a clipboard returned Rod's greeting. Luke stood among his khaki-clad cluster of colleagues and listened.

'We have reason to believe you have cattle on a designated VPP area,' the sergeant said. 'This is an illegal offence and such an action would constitute a fine of $1000 per head for the owner.'

'You have to find the cattle before you can fine us,' Bob said. Rod cast him a glance to silence him.

'Don't play smart with me,' said the sergeant. 'We know there are cattle here. Who owns the cattle and how many are there?'

'If there are cattle, they'd be owned by each and every person here. And if you want to find out how many, I suggest you count them yourself,' said the Cattlemen's Association President, who stood next to Rod.

'How many cattle are here?' the sergeant asked again, while Giles Grimsley gave an audible sigh.

'I think you'll find the ear mark is different on each hypothetical beast and that if you want the owners of the hypothetical cattle, you'll have to take the names and addresses of everyone at this camp,' the President said.

The policeman nodded and handed his clipboard to Rod.

'I want all the names and addresses listed. If cattle *are* found in the Park, each person will be charged accordingly.'

'Certainly, sir,' said Rod.

In silence, each man, woman and child wrote their name willingly on the paper. The VPP men looked on. Luke could feel their nerves settling now they could see the group wasn't interested in conflict.

He wondered how many dollars and man-hours had been spent on trying to calm this particular storm in a teacup? Wouldn't government money and energy have been better spent on the land itself?

Hidden in the trees, Emily and Rousie kept watch on the cattle. Next to them Bonus was dozing, his head dropped, lip hanging, back foot hooked upright, Emily holding on to his reins while she listened out for vehicles or voices. She felt sorry for the horse. It was such a big trip for a baby, but he'd risen to the challenge. More and more she could feel a bond developing between them, and with it came reminders of Luke. Emily let these thoughts be a welcome distraction from the situation with Clancy and the now pregnant Penny.

Not far away, Flo was also keeping watch, gazing out over the ti-tree to the river-flats below. The plan was to keep the cattle out of the rangers' sight until morning. When it was nearly dark they'd find a flat spot and run some solar-electric tape round the cattle to keep them contained overnight, but for the time being they'd keep them on the move. Tomorrow, at dawn, they would drive the cattle up the steep bridle track to the east of the valley and on to the edge of the Park, to a logging road, where portable yards and a semitrailer would be waiting to cart the cattle back to their respective owners.

'Rawhide one, are you on channel?' came a familiar voice.

Sam? Sam! Emily couldn't believe it. He'd been adamant that he was staying home. She was thrilled to hear his voice and to find him stepping back into their cattlemen's world. Maybe at last she was getting her funny old brother back.

'Copy. This is Rawhide one. Is that Cowpoke two?'

'Yes! This is Cowpoke two. Papa Bull has given me your location and me and Curvy Cow are bringing you some sustenance.' Before his voice was cut off on the radio Emily overheard a slapping sound and an 'Ouch!' from Sam.

She knew Papa Bull was Rod, but who was *Curvy Cow*? What was Sam on about?

Within a few minutes Emily heard his ridiculous bird call from the hillside above.

'Ki-ki-ki-ki-kick-off-the-cows! Kick-off-the-cows! Ki! Ki! Kiiiii!'

Emily repeated the call, laughing. Up until now, she had felt tense, worried that she might be the one caught red-handed with the cattle, even though feisty Flo was there to dress down the authorities if need be. But now, with Sam here, this was beginning to feel like fun.

Emily squealed when she saw not just her brother coming towards her but Bridie also, her face lighting up at the sight of her friend. 'Curvy Cow! What are you doing here?' Emily called.

'We're the inside intelligence,' Bridie said. 'Dargo was all but dead after you guys rode out of town. So Sam and I raided the black and brown in the makeup box and went commando, black beanies and all. We staked out VPP headquarters and found out what they were up to. We couldn't leave you down here like sitting ducks.'

Sam and Bridie high-fived, their eyes shining.

'But you two hate each other.'

'Internal feuding ceases when external foe approach,' Sam explained.

'Yeah, whatever,' said Bridie. 'He still annoys the crap out of me.'

'You love me,' he said, digging a finger in her ribs.

'Piss off! Don't touch the fat.'

'She loves me,' he said again to Emily just as Bridie gave him a good shove, sending him sprawling down the hill.

Sam stood up and brushed himself off.

'The police are listening in on the radio so we're to use it only for emergencies. They've taken everyone's names and it's yet to be seen if they'll collectively arrest us or just fine us. The police and Parkies are out now looking for the cattle. They went to the north and south ends of the valley, not in this direction. One of them even got bogged in a creek crossing and the Mansfield mob had to winch 'em out! It was a classic.'

'Yeah?' said Emily, hoping like crazy it wasn't Luke who had bogged the vehicle but thinking he was too much of a farm boy for that.

As Sam talked, Bridie unpacked a thermos and some food from a backpack. Emily let out a low whistle and Flo, who had failed as a sentry, shook herself awake, clearly surprised to see Sam and Bridie. She began to make her way over.

'Is new ranger boy there?' Emily asked casually.

Sam shrugged. 'Couldn't tell you. Bridie and I kept the vehicle in the trees on the south side and walked our way up the creek. I haven't laid eyes on them. Just seen their vehicles. Why . . . does it matter?'

'Oh,' she said, squinting, 'it just feels a bit rich. You know, taking the fella's horse on trial, then using it to bring cattle through his National Park in his first week on the job.'

'He'll get over it,' Bridie said.

'I s'pose.'

Once they'd eaten and tossed the scraps to Rousie and Useless, Sam stood up and stretched. 'Okay, Rawhide one, we'll go back to base camp. Are you right here for another hour? Then we'll send up a relief party.'

'Can Curvy Cow stay with me?'

'Why not? We'll send Hilarious Heifer back to Papa Bull and she can have more of a nanna nap in her swag.'

'Who are you calling Hilarious Heifer?' Flo said gruffly, but with a twinkle in her blue eyes.

And with that, Flo, Useless and Sam walked away up the steep bush-covered hill. The cattle were beginning to stir, wanting to browse the bush around them.

'We'd best mount up and keep them together,' Emily said. She helped Bridie on to Flo's horse, and went to block the lead cows, which were starting to take the herd towards the long grasses of the river flats.

Bridie tilted her head. 'Is that a vehicle I can hear?'

Emily paused, her ears straining to detect a sound. Yes! She could hear an engine far off in the trees below. Then she caught glimpses of a ute winding its way towards them.

'Let's push 'em up higher.'

Emily sent Rousie scooting around the herd and began forcing the cattle directly uphill. Ten minutes later, she paused for a breather, the cattle, too, stopping on a ledge on the hill-side. One cow bellowed.

'Shush!' Emily said. She called to Bridie: 'I think we've lost them.' Then, to her horror, she looked up and saw Luke standing above her on the mountainside. He had his hands on his hips and was decked out in the khaki of his VPP uniform. He wore shorts and sturdy walking boots, and Emily noted that his legs were muscular and tanned. His arms looked strong and delicious in his short-sleeved shirt. For days she'd wanted to see him. For days she'd longed to know if the spark she felt towards him was reciprocated. But now, at this very moment, he was the *last* person she wanted to see. He had caught them red-handed with the cattle.

Emily urged the gelding up the steep pinch towards him. As she neared him, she could see Luke's chest rising and falling and the sweat on his brow from his fast walk up the hillside in pursuit of them. Emily couldn't help thinking he looked gorgeous in his uniform.

She, too, was sheened in sweat, her checked shirt tied about her waist, the straps of her red gingham bra showing on each sun-tanned shoulder under her red Bonds singlet. As she slid from her horse to stand before him, their eyes locked. Emily waited for an angry reaction.

Instead, in an instant, Luke had bent towards her and was kissing her. She tasted the sweet salt on his lips and savoured the feel of his strong body pressed against hers. At last! she thought. She cupped his face in her hands and closed her eyes, not wanting this dream to stop. Her hands slid down his neck and broad, hot shoulders, then the curve of his long, strong back. His hands glided deliciously over her body as he kissed her again and again. She pulled back from him for a moment and they looked deep into each other's eyes. Both laughed at the ridiculousness of the situation, and kissed again, only this time it was softer, more tender.

'Umm . . . excuse me?' came a small voice. Bridie was sitting on Flo's horse down the slope with the cattle, staring up at them. 'Can you arrest me like that too?'

They laughed, and then Emily and Luke were kissing again.

'I'll just be here,' Bridie called. 'Don't mind me. I'll keep an eye on the cattle. But I must say, that is one thorough frisk job you're doing, Mr Ranger!'

Smiling, Luke took the reins from Emily and hitched the gelding to a fallen log. Then he took her hand and led her gently to the trunk of a giant granddaddy tree. Its great grey base was ringed with soft green moss, sending a delicious pungent scent into the still hot air. Her back, as she leant on its solid trunk, felt cool, while Luke's body pressed against

229

hers felt hot. Emily closed her eyes as they kissed and ran her hands under his ranger's shirt, feeling the smooth warm skin beneath, the trail of hair that led down his belly, the firmness of his horseman's waist.

'What are we doing?' he breathed.

'I don't know,' Emily said, stunned by the intensity of their passion.

'They'll be up here soon. The other rangers.' He kissed her again, but Emily felt him drawing away. 'I'll find you,' he said breathlessly. 'Tonight. I'll find you.'

He pressed his lips to hers a final time and then was gone, loping down the mountain. Leaping logs, swinging round tree trunks, looking in every way like he belonged here in the bush.

Emily stood at the top of the hill watching him go. Bridie glanced up at her.

'What was *that*?' she said. 'Tarzan?'

'I don't know, but I ain't no Jane.'

'Was it bush tucker man?'

'I don't know.'

'Was it the croc hunter?'

'I don't know! All I *do* know is that it was out of this world, and weird – and wonderful.'

Twenty-eight

Still breathless from Luke's kisses, Emily stood beside her horse as the police took their names and details. A group of cattlemen had gathered round. It all seemed so serious and so stupid, she thought. She bit her lip to stop a smile and glanced over at the rangers. They were scribbling notes on the incident and talking with each other, all except Luke. He was leaning on a tree, head bowed, arms and ankles crossed. He was looking down at the ground, but she could feel his presence like a burning white heat. When he glanced up and caught her eye, Emily's heart skipped a beat. She was utterly hooked on him. For a fleeting moment his face conveyed his secret attraction to her. Then he looked at the ground again, trying to hide behind a mask of indifference.

Emily felt a twinge of annoyance. Had he said something to his superiors about the disgraceful state of the Park? she wondered. He must be able to see, with his farm-boy eyes, that fining the cattlemen would be a bureaucratic joke. It should be the government being fined, she thought. Surely Luke'd have to let his boss know what he thought about the mismanagement of the land?

Now, with the police standing before her, she looked down at the scuffed toes of her boots as if she were a criminal. She felt the earth pulse under her feet. The life of the soil. This was what was driving her. This land. She decided to do as Evie had suggested and hold true to her promise to protect it.

She raised her head to gaze, not defiantly, but gently at the policeman with her large dark eyes. She summoned up all the energy of the earth that thrummed beneath her and, just as Evie had taught her and the girls, imagined a powerful beam of light pouring into her from the heavens, streaming right to the core of her being. Suddenly she felt strong and empowered in the calmest, most gentle way. It was like those moments when she had hovered over the treetops in that strange but surprisingly normal-feeling limbo between physical life and spiritual eternity.

'It's simple science,' Evie had once said. 'We are all simply energy, and our thoughts and emotions control the vibrations of that energy. It's just we have forgotten this fact.'

The policeman faltered as he read Emily her rights. In his job, he had developed a steely façade, but Emily, like a tiny flower pushing through concrete, had made it through his armour. He stopped speaking, shut his clipboard, and steered her away from the group.

'Look,' he whispered, leaning in close, 'we're just doing our jobs. And they're just doing theirs.' He indicated the Park rangers with a flick of his head. 'There's no way known the government would be stupid enough to proceed with charges against you. It would be a media circus and politically disastrous. So don't worry, okay? This is just for show. Just procedure. You'll be fine.'

Emily nodded. 'Thank you.'

The policeman shrugged. 'I know you're good people.' He cleared his throat. 'I know you're doing this for what you believe in, not to make trouble. I just have to do my job, that's all.'

Emily watched as the men climbed into their vehicles. Luke glanced up briefly and gave her an uncertain smile. From beneath the brim of her hat she half-smiled back, hoping no one else would see. For a moment she felt as if she were Juliet

232

and Luke her Romeo. Then she told herself to get a grip. Starting something with that man really would be playing with fire.

As the sun sank beneath the giant mountain and illuminated the hills, the cattlemen's campfire was cranked up so that flames danced wildly and sparks flew. Beers were cracked and platters of biscuits and cheese passed about. On another more sedate fire, bush stew was cooking in a giant black pot, and there was damper wrapped in shiny foil in the ashes.

Emily swigged on a stubby, laughing at the cattlemen's tall tales. There was an element of bravado about the people around the fire, but Emily felt sadness in each of them that they had been driven to such measures. None of them was a law-breaker by nature. She also felt unsettled about Clancy's move to Bairnsdale with Penny and their instant family. And there was that new feeling in her that Luke had ignited with his kisses. She felt her emotions soar then plummet then soar again with each new turn of thought.

The sound of laughter and squealing came from the nearby riverbank. On a small track leading through the trees, Bridie and Sam emerged from the half-dark. They were dripping wet and chasing each other. They made their way to the campfire and Bridie crouched down beside Emily, breathless. Her eyes were shining and her hair, normally styled and straightened to within an inch of its life, tumbled down in long blonde ringlets. She wore wet boardshorts and a bright-pink singlet, with an aqua bikini top underneath, curvaceous and gorgeous in the heat of the evening. She leant closer and whispered to Emily, 'Sam just tried to kiss me! Down at the river.'

'And?'

'I told him he couldn't.'

'Why?'

'Because I'd just eaten tuna and spring onions.'

Emily laughed. 'Why would you go and do a thing like that?'

'Because I'm trying to lose weight and the chops have been really fatty . . .'

'No,' Emily whispered back. 'I mean, why didn't you let him kiss you?'

Bridie looked down at her body. 'Because, look at me. He's come from that rock-star world of glamour girls who are stick-thin and gorgeous.' She grabbed a handful of flesh on each hip. 'As if he'd really be serious about a fatty-boombah like me.'

Emily reached for her hand. 'Oh, Bridie, you're gorgeous. You've just been reading too many magazines. Men love curves. There's no way those skinny girls can come near you once you unleash that wit of yours – not to mention those boobs. Any man would be hooked. Even country-music stars.'

'Yeah? You think so? You think I should kiss him?'

Emily grinned. 'Well, maybe after you've cleaned your teeth.'

At that moment, Sam ambled into the firelight holding his guitar.

'Who wants to hear a tune?'

The campers cheered, Emily the loudest. It had been years since the cattlemen had been treated to Sam's singing in this informal way. He'd been too busy with the bigtime. But now here he was, Rod Flanaghan's son, home from Nashville with a dinner-plate belt buckle and a fancy guitar, ready to play again. Her brother *was back*.

Emily shifted up on the log as her father came over to the campfire and sat down next to her, pride and love for his son visible on his face. Emily knew all the recent family support and the teachings of Evie had helped Sam in some way, but she could see a new energy in him tonight – he was falling in love. Sam strummed a few powerful notes and began to tune his Maton with a couple of twanging plucks of the strings. Then his fingertips hit the worn wooden face of the guitar and drummed a lively lead-in beat.

'A one, two, a one two three four . . .'

234

And he was away, Sam Flanaghan singing again. It was a new song, a song Emily had never heard before, but she was pretty sure she knew where Sam had discovered his muse.

'"Peachy bottom! Honeyed hair! You get about like you just don't care,"' he sang. '"When I see you sittin' over there, you make me wanna be your chair! Ouch, I love it when you treat me mean. Hottest lovin' mama, come and sit on me!"'

The campers let out a 'Woo-hoo' at his funny but funky song, spurring Sam on to another verse. Emily laughed while others clapped and danced, some joining him in singing the chorus, Bridie with a smile like the sun.

They grooved for two hours, Sam fronting a solo concert in the middle of nowhere. He made their eyes shine in the firelight and their hearts sing. Emily knew the joy and togetherness they felt that night was founded on generations of such nights shared beneath the stars. Friendship, food, music, bawdy jokes, a campfire and a love of the land, these were the constants, no matter what the day, the year, the era. Eventually the tired campers took themselves off to bed, covered in dust, spilled beer, tomato sauce and rum, but all with the warmth of community in their hearts. Emily was the last to kick the straying, smoking logs into the fire. Reluctantly she took herself off to her swag, the longing for Luke heavy on her mind.

As she lay in her tent she could hear the crack and tick of the bush about her. Her sunburnt shoulders were radiating gentle heat and she could feel herself sweating beneath her singlet and cotton boxers. She sighed. It had been such a big day, but her mind kept going back to that meeting, those kisses on the hillside with Luke. It just didn't make sense. His words ran round and round in her head: 'I'll find you.'

As if, she thought, rolling over angrily. He'd be tucked up in a rangers' camp somewhere with his boss sleeping just metres away. She shut her eyes and counted, but still sleep wouldn't come. Instead of tossing and turning, she dragged her swag out and pulled on her boots. She needed to cool off by the river and have some space to think. Rousie stirred at the entrance of the tent, stretched and made a comical noise.

'Shush, you,' Emily told him.

Outside, the night was exceptionally still and there was a sliver of moon in the sky. There was just enough light for her to see the swags scattered about in the camping area. Some slept in tents, others on the ground. No need to be huddled near the fire on a night like this. A little way off she could make out the paler-coloured horses as they dozed on nightlines amidst the trees. She could see Bonus's gleaming white socks.

She and Rousie made their way downstream to a grassy spot that jutted out into the river bend – perfect for a cool sleep beside the water. She thought the mozzies might bother her but was beyond caring. She lay there for a time, looking up at the gap in the gums to the stars beyond.

The river tinkled quietly over the rocks, a soothing sound. Emily called Rousie to her side and pulled the tarp over her head. For a short time she lay there. Then she heard Rousie's low growl, and a sharp bark. Flipping the swag open, she propped herself on her elbows and looked around, holding tight to her dog's collar as he barked. In the shadows stood a man.

'Emily?'

'Luke!' she said, happiness flooding through her. 'How did you find me?'

'I said I would.'

He stepped out of the shadows and came to kneel before her. But his handsome face was set like stone.

She frowned, her body suddenly tense. 'What's wrong?'

He paused, a deep frown slashed between his brows.

'I came to tell you the bill's been voted through parliament. You've been banned from your cattle runs.'

She felt the impact of the news like a blow. An awful silence followed. Luke desperately tried to fill it.

'They got word through on the sat-phone tonight. Emily, I'm sorry. I'm *so* sorry.'

236

Around her the night-bush murmured and beside her the river tumbled by. Far from here, in the plush carpeted rooms of Parliament House, a group of men and women in suits had just altered Emily Flanaghan's life, and reset her daughters' futures forever, with one stroke of a pen.

Were they really losing their cattle runs? Emily's eyes closed. After all that had happened. After she'd finally come home to the mountains. Her whole body shook as Luke drew her into his arms. Stroking her hair, he held her close as her tears soaked into his blue singlet. She could smell him, all clean from a river swim. Then he was kissing her tears away, and despite her grief, desire flowed through her and she began to kiss him back. She sought comfort in the warmth of Luke's kiss, the wetness of his mouth. She wanted to forget everything: the bans, the loss of her land, the empty, uncertain future. She just wanted to lose herself in him, there beside the river. They began to peel away each other's clothing and she felt the warm night air on her naked breasts.

She moaned when his bare chest pressed against hers, and began to cry again. He made a gentle sound to soothe her, then lifted her chin and kissed her softly, until the passion was rekindled. They began to kiss harder. Her breath fluttering, Emily slid her fingers to Luke's belt buckle, undoing it, then releasing the button of his jeans. All the while they kissed and kissed as the river slid by.

Luke kicked off his jeans and pulled Emily's shorts down over her strong, firm legs. They lay naked, pressed together, hands roving over each other's bodies. Desire quickened their breath. Luke gently pushed Emily's hair from her face as he kissed her on her forehead, behind her ears, on the fresh scar on her shoulder, and on her breasts. He pulled her beneath him and looked deep into her eyes, hesitating.

'Don't stop,' she pleaded. This was so different from Clancy. It was as if she were floating again.

As he pushed into her, Emily cast her head back, wanting this, wanting him more than anything.

237

He moaned as he felt her warmth and murmured, 'You're so beautiful, Emily.'

She ran her hands along his back and reached for his firm backside. She pulled him into her, deeper and then deeper still, breathing in the smell of him, pressing her face into the soft hollow of his neck. She was carried on the crest of a wave of desire as they moved as one, faster and faster, and clenched her teeth as she felt herself coming, stifling her scream. What they were doing felt illicit, like an affair. A betrayal of her clan. Luke, too, held his cry inwards as he came. They were each fraternising with the enemy. It was exciting. It was scary. It was confusing. But, Emily thought, as he kissed her gently all over her face, it was also beautiful.

She didn't want to think what lay ahead. She just wanted to preserve this moment for all time. She lay in Luke's arms, not speaking, gazing deep into his eyes in the faint moonlight as his fingertips drifted over her skin. Eventually, still wrapped tight in each other's arms, they fell asleep.

In the depth of darkness just before the dawn, the sound of screaming woke them. It wasn't a human scream but something more guttural, like the noise of a terrified horse. Luke and Emily sat bolt upright. There was no sign of Rousie. Emily panicked. She couldn't breathe, terror keeping air from her lungs. It was as if her ribs had been crushed all over again. Upstream they could hear the deafening sound of horses thundering along the river stones at full gallop. The crack of hooves on rock was unmistakable.

'The horses!' she said. 'Something must've spooked them.'

The horrible scream came again, like a stallion roaring for his mares. A wind came howling towards them downstream along the tunnel of the riverbed, creating an awful moaning sound, like a man gone mad. The gust hit them with cold fury and whipped the trees about, so that bark and grey finger-bone tree limbs were flung down around them. Emily and Luke grabbed for their clothes, the sound of the horses' hooves bearing down on them getting louder and louder. If they didn't move fast, they would be trampled. They dressed as quickly as they could, scrambling up the bank and sprinting towards the campsite to wake the others.

But when they emerged from the thickets, trembling and gasping for air, they were met by stillness and silence. They looked about. No one stirred. The air was calm. The horses all dozed peacefully on the nightlines.

From the heart of the camp, Rousie came towards them, cowering as he walked, his tail jammed between his legs. He whined and whimpered and pressed his wet nose into Emily's palm, as if to apologise for leaving her side.

'What *was* that?' Luke asked in a whisper.

'I don't know. I mean, it was horses. Obviously. Galloping in the riverbed.'

'Are these all your horses?' he asked, pointing to the cattlemen's mounts. Emily nodded. 'Surely they should be going nuts by now. They must've been able to hear or smell the other horses.'

A little way off they could make out the white faces of the cattle, all camped quietly behind the tape of a white electric fence, many of them lying down and chewing cud.

'Were they brumbies, do you think?' Luke asked.

Emily shook her head.

'There aren't any brumbies in this area. Maybe over Mansfield way, but none here – certainly not a whole mob like that.' She reached out for his hand. 'Luke, I'm scared.'

He pulled her to him and she pressed her face against his warm body.

'I know. It's pretty freaky.'

He began to stroke her hair. It gave her a little comfort, the memory of their lovemaking returning with his touch. He pulled back from her.

'I'm sorry, I have to go now. It's nearly dawn.'

'Yes,' she said, suddenly remembering their situation.

He bent to kiss her quickly on the lips.

'I'll see you again?'

It was a question more than a statement, and it sowed a tiny seed of doubt in Emily's heart. Then he was gone, jogging along the grassy flat towards the rangers' campsite at the homestead.

Emily sat in her tent, knees hugged to her chest, feeling the swell of mixed emotions in her. Fear, passion, devastation. She waited for daylight, knowing she would have to deliver the news that parliament had voted to ban alpine grazing. She curled up in a ball, dragging a jumper over her shoulders, and began to doze.

Before long she was woken by noises outside the tent. Bacon and eggs sizzled, billies boiled, tea stewed, and the clank and clatter of tent poles rang out as the campers packed up in the blue morning light. It was time to get droving and as saddle bags were stuffed with food, water bottles filled and buckets carried from the creek to the horses for a drink, Emily took comfort from the normality of the scene. She went to bash on the flimsy walls of Bridie's tent, pitched nearby.

'What?' came a deep voice from within.

'Sam? What are you doing in there?'

'Got lost, didn't I?' he said.

'Only packed one tent,' came Bridie's voice.

'Bridie,' Emily said, 'get your bodacious arse out here! I *really* need to talk to you.'

'Okay,' said Bridie, 'I'm busting for a bush wee anyway.'

'Oh, noiyce,' said Sam. 'She's all class, this bush chook.'

Emily heard a whack and then an 'Ouch!' from Sam.

'Don't smack me.'

'That's not what you said last night . . .' Bridie said.

'Oh, *please*,' said Emily. 'This is serious.'

Bridie, dishevelled but glowing, finally emerged from the tent wearing a red satin nightie with black lace trim enhancing her bosom.

'You brought *that* camping?' Emily said, momentarily distracted from the news she was about to deliver.

Bridie looked down at herself. 'Worked, though, didn't it?'

The girls drew each other into a quick hug and laughed. Then concern clouded Emily's face.

'What's wrong?' Bridie asked, pulling back.

Emily could barely say the words. Sam poked his head out of the tent, looking up at his sister.

'Luke came to find me last night,' she began, 'to tell me parliament's passed the bill. It's now legislation that we can't graze cattle up on our runs.'

Sam disappeared into the tent and quickly dragged on his clothes. 'Well, they've finally gone and done it. After all these years.'

'I know. Can you believe it?' she said. 'All that time and effort, and for what?'

'Does Dad know?' he asked. Emily shook her head, looking skyward. 'How do I explain how I found out? That I've been over in the Parkies' camp being sociable?'

Bridie shrugged. 'It doesn't matter that it came from Luke.'

'Oh, I think now it might.'

'I'll tell him,' Sam offered. 'I'll go straight away. You girls get packed up. We've got to be out of here in an hour.'

Bridie and Emily set out towards the place where Emily and Luke had slept. The sun had still not risen far enough above the hill to touch the riverbank. Emily shivered as they walked through the trees.

'Last night . . .' she began. 'There's something else I have to tell you about.'

Bridie turned to look at her.

'Something really weird happened.' Emily told her friend about the sound of galloping horses and the deafening roar and the wild wind. Bridie was about to make a joke, but when she saw Emily's frightened expression and heard the way her voice trembled, she drew Emily into a hug.

'Some really weird things have been happening to me since my accident, Bridie. I've been seeing stuff, and hearing stuff. And my head . . . it's as if I don't think the same way as I used to.'

'What kind of stuff do you see and hear?'

'You know, things from the past. Weird things like the horses. But also people.'

'You mean, like, "I see dead people"?' Bridie whispered, quoting the line from the movie *The Sixth Sense*.

'Yeah. Kind of.'

'Oh, well,' she said Bridie with false bravado, 'that's normal after such a big trauma. You know, your near-death thingy. You just need a bit of time.'

'I think I'm going mad.'

At that point they walked out through the ti-trees and there, lying open on the grass, was Emily's swag. She walked into the cold river water and waded upstream. There was no sign of hoof prints. No sign of tree limbs torn down by a violent wind. She waded back downstream and looked at Bridie with a questioning expression.

'You must've just dreamed it, Em,' her friend said gently.

'But,' Emily said frantically, 'Luke was here. He heard it too!'

Bridie shivered. 'C'mon, darls. Let's have a quick wash and get back to the others. I'll fix you up so you'll look real flash on that beautiful horse of yours. Despite what those city dickheads have done, today can still be a celebration, the end of a beautiful era. Don't let them ruin your day or your life. See this as a positive. It's almost a relief that it's over. No more fighting. No more protests.'

As Emily dunked herself into the fresh, freezing water, she gasped. But her goosebumps weren't just from cold, they were also from fear. She wanted to feel exhilarated about being with Luke but it was all so clouded now. Their new love had been overshadowed by their terrifying night, and the cold hard fact that she was now an evicted cattleman's daughter, and he a Park ranger. Emily splashed ice-cold river water over her face again and again, and tried, as best she could, to wash the memory of Luke and the night away.

PART THREE

Twenty-nine

Gradually the days grew shorter on the Dargo High Plains and a chill came into the evening air. Winter was approaching and it was time to move the cattle from the alpine runs down to the lower slopes of the mountains. This time the job was weighted with sadness for Emily and her family, because it would be the last of their mustering and droving trips.

Emily stood up in the stirrups, dropping Snowgum's reins.

'Saaaaalt!' she called across the empty plain. 'Saaaalt!'

Sam repeated the cry from his bay brumby. Their voices rolled out over the snow-grass clearing and through the twisted white branches of the trees. Flo and Rod joined in the cattlemen's cry.

Away in the bush, the cattle turned and flicked their ears in the direction of the sound. As the calls came again, cows lowed gently to calves and tossed their heads as an indication to move, some mothers bunting their large babies impatiently. As the cries of 'Salt' continued, the Herefords began to move faster through the bush, reaching a jog, crashing through the ti-trees and ducking under low-slung snow-gum branches.

On the salting plain, Emily heard them coming. It was always so rewarding to see the healthy, round-bellied cows emerge from the snow gums.

On the grass at the cattle camp there were bare patches where the Flanaghans had laid salt piles in the summer season and the cattle had persistently licked at the salt until it was all gone. The soil up top was salt-deficient, so to keep the stock in good health and to make them quiet and obedient to their calls, salting was a regular practice for the cattlemen.

Emily normally loved salting, rain, hail or shine. But today she was wracked with sadness. This would be the last time they mustered this run, the last time the call of 'Salt!' would ring out across the high plains. This land was now a Park.

She felt the presence of her forebears. They would have seen the same sights, conducted the same process, with gear not much different from her own, the salt wrapped in hessian sacks, rolled and tied to the front of the saddle.

Emily dismounted and began to unhitch the sack. It was heavy and damp from the early-morning mist, and her ribs twinged as she heaved it on to the ground. As she bent to tug at the hayband knot, water on the brim of her hat tipped out suddenly on to the ground. The weather had been coming in all morning. Alongside her father, she walked around the plain, tipping out little hillocks of the coarse salt.

The cattle were coming fast out of the bush, their calves gallivanting in little skips and letting out snorts of excitement. They carried their tails up and skittered about in babyish fashion.

As they reached the invisible bubble that was their flight zone, the cattle stopped abruptly, skidding to a halt and bumping into each other, to sniff at the air. Then the boldest, a big deep-red cow, thrust her head down and ambled forward, bursting the bubble, closing the flight zone in around the riders. She extended her tongue out to the salt, then shoved her nose right in so that white granules stuck to her moist pink nostrils. Other cows came forward, too, tossing their heads at Rousie, who lay panting not far off, the lure of the salt too great for the cattle to be much bothered by a dog.

Emily retied the bag and flipped it back over the saddle, while Flo counted the cows.

'Fifty-six. That's less than a third of 'em,' she said.

'Let's shut the gate on these and go see if we can find the rest down at Shepherd's Hut,' Rod suggested.

Emily legged Snowgum about and rode on beside her family, pulling her collar up and her hat down against the weather coming in from the east.

Since Wonnangatta, Luke had called her father's house several times, leaving messages. At first Emily had toyed with the idea of meeting him, but as the letters from the bureaucrats came in, notifying the Flanaghans of the revocation of their grazing licences, she felt that old anger simmering in her, even against Luke. After all, he was a VPP man. He was part of the eviction process. He could never be a part of her clan. He might have made love to her by that river like he meant it, but hadn't he stood aside, mute, right when Emily needed him?

Flo came to ride beside her.

'You know, we'll be out of range for the next two days once we get over this ridge. You'd better call the girls.'

Emily smiled at the thought of Tilly and Meg tucked up warm beside Evie's woodstove, happy in her calm aura and kindliness. Emily pulled out her phone from her oilskin pocket just as Flo added, 'And you'd better give that Luke a ring, too. Put the poor bastard out of his misery.'

Emily flashed her aunt a glance. She had left a cheque covering the cost of the gelding at the store with a short note to Luke that gave him no reason to hope. No clue as to their future at all.

'You can catch us up,' Flo said, urging her horse away. 'Do the right thing, Emily,' she called after her. Sitting on Snowgum, Emily sighed and looked down at the phone's screen. She was surprised to see that a message was waiting for her. As she listened she heard Bridie's bright voice on the recording. Just the sound of it made Emily smile.

'Hi, it's me. I hate leaving you this news on a message but I thought you'd best find out sooner rather than later and hear it from me rather than the grapevine.'

Emily's smile faded as she braced herself for the rest.

'I'm hoping you'll see the funny side,' Bridie's message continued. 'I've just heard from Trace at the Dargo hospital that Penny and Clancy found out the sex of their babies. And . . . guess what . . . girls! Two of them! Huh! So Tilly and Meg will have two half-sisters. It seems Clancy is on his way to breeding a whole netball team! Hope you see the funny side, darls. By the way, your brother's hot, but don't tell him I said so. Say hi to him from me. Love you!' Bridie made smooching noises before her message ended.

Twin girls. Emily sighed. She remembered Clancy's sullen anger at her when Meg was born. The second baby was supposed to be a boy. Emily wondered why she wasn't feeling angered by Bridie's news. Instead she found herself thinking that God had a wonderful sense of humour. There was no way Clancy could escape learning about women now. Not with all these daughters to steer through puberty and beyond.

Emily suddenly remembered what Evie had told her when she'd returned from the Wonnangatta, still stewing over her experience there. Evie had said mildly, 'Carrying around the energy created by an argument with someone is like carrying around a bloody great anvil in your pocket. It simply won't serve you. It's much better to clean up the messes you make and get rid of those anvils!'

But as the winter approached, Emily still felt several anvils weighing her down. Clancy was one big one and now it was as if she were dragging the idea of Luke with her everywhere she went, too, even though he was the last person on this earth she wanted to be infatuated with. He was a ranger, sent to evict her from her runs. She had better end it at once. Flo was right. She had to call him, finish things properly before they'd even begun. No more carting anvils about.

She didn't have his number in her phone, so with icy fingers she dialled a connection company and asked for the VPP's Dargo office. As she sat astride Snowgum in the misty rain, it took Emily a while to realise she'd been put through to head office in Melbourne. She sat listening to a slick advertising recording being played over and over on the other end of the VPP phone line.

By the time Emily had been waiting fifteen minutes, she was seeing red. She knew she'd have to canter Snowgum hard down the steep and slippery track to catch her family, though she didn't want to push the mare. She was sound in every way, but if the deep wound beneath her girth opened again, Emily would be riding home bareback and slowly in this cold, fickle weather. But she hung on the line, knowing she had to clear things up with Luke. She listened to the over-cheerful advertisement selling passes to the 'great outdoors' as if the bush were just another commodity, like a six-burner gas barbecue or a new PlayStation.

'But I don't want to find out about kayaking or rock climbing or bloody fishing,' she muttered. 'I just want to talk to a human being!'

Emily pictured herself carrying another heavy anvil with her. The vision stopped her from pressing the off button on her phone. Finally the crisp professional voice of a VPP staff member came on the line.

'Umm,' Emily began uncertainly, 'I was after Luke Bradshaw at the Dargo branch.'

'I'm afraid I don't have that number. I only have the Heyfield headquarters. You'll have to call them out there,' the woman from Melbourne said.

Just the way she said 'out there' stirred Emily's blood. Surely, given the woman worked in an organisation whose job was to care for the land, she should not think of Dargo and Heyfield as 'out there', but as the very reason for her job.

'Perhaps you have his mobile number on a staff list?' Emily suggested.

'I'm sorry,' the woman said, not as an apology, but as a

barrier. 'Under the Privacy Act we cannot disclose the mobile numbers of employees.'

Emily wasn't used to such officialese. She clenched her teeth. How could Luke have chosen to join an organisation like this?

'Never mind. Thank you for your help,' she said, and tried to tell herself the woman was only doing her job.

Emily sat contemplating calling the branch at Heyfield, but didn't want to leave a message. It would have to wait until after droving, she decided. Instead, she dialled Evie's house to tell the girls she missed them, and that she'd see them in a couple of days.

'Also,' she added, as brightly as she could into the recording machine, 'Bridie has just told me Daddy's new babies will be girls. So you will have two baby sisters! Evie will explain about the machine that tells you if it's a boy or a girl! Love you both and see you soon.'

She hung up, thinking back to the time she first broke the news to Meg and Tilly that Clancy would be living with another lady who was having his baby. The girls were so confused to hear about the baby they asked the same questions over and over, until Emily felt exasperated.

Then poor Tilly had cried out, 'So he's not coming back to us and has a new family!' Meg had frowned still trying to make sense of it, then had laid her hands on Tilly, saying, 'It's okay. Daddy will let us see the baby, won't he, Mummy?' Emily, with tears in her eyes, had reassured her girls this meant a bigger, better family for them, and they would have a new brother or sister, but as the days drew by without Clancy visiting them or returning their calls, Emily's heart broke on behalf of her daughters. She was also furious her husband had left it up to her to explain the situation.

By the time she'd delivered the news to them that Penny was having twins, both girls seemed to have come to terms with the scenario. Meg even seemed excited that there would be not just *one* baby but *two*. Emily guessed that slowly the girls were relinquishing the presence of their father from their daily lives. She hoped they would continue to cope.

She pulled up her collar and rode on. On the lee side of the mountain the rain had stopped, but when gusts of wind shook the trees, big fat droplets spilled from their leaves on to Emily and Snowgum as they passed underneath. The horses' hoof marks ahead of her had cut grooves into the muddied track. Emily had to ride quickly to catch up but she also wanted to savour the landscape. Once the cattle were mustered, there would be no reason to ride this way again.

She squeezed Snowgum into a canter, praying the wound could handle the rubbing and called Rousie along with a whistle. He leapt over logs, ears pricked, and fell in behind Snowgum's hocks on the track to Shepherd's Hut.

Emily reined her horse from the four-wheel drive track on to a shortcut, a narrow trail only the cattlemen, cattle and wombats knew. She rode past trees that had been blazed by men a hundred years before. Despite its remoteness, this place had once been alive with the sounds of people and their toil. They had laid whole hillsides bare with their mining and dug channels for miles to bring water to the crush. They had cut trees down to stumps on the tops of hills so as to build shelters and yards and rough bush furniture. Many had starved or otherwise perished when the mist or snow bamboozled them, but a few wily pioneers made it rich from the gold they found in the alluvial creekbeds and in the heart of hillsides.

In those earlier days, the sound of axes had rung out across the still bush. Bullock drays, anchored steady by sawn logs, gingerly scuffed their way down precipitous slopes carrying heavy loads of mining equipment. The creekbeds and the hillsides had been alive with men. Some went mad from the isolation, some were driven mad by the fleas and flies. Others, like the Flanaghans, had stayed and thrived.

What did those shiny-bottomed city bureaucrats know of this land now? No Park ranger had ever been on this track, Emily thought angrily. She knew it would only be a few seasons before tracks like these became impassable. Without regular traffic and a day out with the chainsaw clearing the way now and then, the secret places, like the fairy dens near hidden springs, would no longer be found. They wouldn't even survive. The gentle filtered sunlight would be blocked by the overgrowth of robust grasses and weeds. The mid-storey dogwoods and wattles would grow unchecked and smother the open grassy areas. And as more and more snow-gum boughs fell from the weight of winter snow and the bans on gathering firewood and burning were enforced, the land would become choked with fallen tree limbs. That limbs dropped in winter was the natural way of things; the government policy of putting out the fires resulting from electrical storms, and so preventing the land from clearing some of its overgrowth, wasn't.

Every year, as Rod, Emily and Flo had travelled down here with heavy backpacks to spray weeds, they'd commented on the fire policy, and all of them had predicted an inferno to come, if not this coming summer, then the next. They could all plainly see disaster looming. A fire that would be hotter than Nature intended. A fire that would utterly destroy, not one that would breathe new life into the seeds of gums, so that the land grew afresh with saplings and wildflowers.

Emily shut her eyes momentarily as she rode, feeling Snowgum's steady gait beneath her. She'd read the accusations in the papers that it was the cattlemen and their cattle who had brought the weeds here, and perpetuated them. It was so easy for the ignorant to point the finger and accuse them. She reached out and pushed away against the firm trunk of a tree so she did not collect her knee on it. The trunk felt cool and strong. She sensed the energy at its heart and in her mind said farewell to it. Those men in the city were locking her out from all this.

Then, like a ray of sunshine through the tree canopy, she remembered Evie's words: 'If you focus on the bad things in your life, you'll get more of the bad. You reap what you sow in your thoughts and actions.'

Emily suddenly realised she was being negative again. Her whole family was. Maybe they had spent so long focusing on the bad, on the bureaucrats, they had in some way created this situation themselves? Maybe it was time to start thinking differently.

As Emily and her silver-grey mare slipped down a steep bank, the vegetation began to alter from screens of snow gums to groves of woolly butts. Soon they were trotting across a green meadow towards a small hut. Named Shepherd's, it had been built by her great-great-grandfather and was now shared by rangers, shooters, bikers and four-wheel drivers. This time of year there was nobody else about, and there wouldn't be until summer came again.

Emily could see smoke curling up from a campfire and her family sitting on sawn-off stumps watching the flames. The time to start the change was now, she resolved as she rode towards them. She undid the girth and slid the saddle from Snow's back, pleased to see the extra padding had protected the puckered freshly healed flesh.

'What took you? Sam's eaten your share of the jam sandwiches,' said Rod.

'You bugger!'

Her brother grinned at her.

'How'd you get on with your phone calls?' Flo asked.

'Bridie left a message. Clancy's twins are girls.'

'Both girls?' Rod said.

'How funny,' said Flo. 'He'll have to groom one of them to take on the trucking business. Poor bugger will have oestrogen overload by the time he's old and grey.'

They sat quietly, all of them thinking of Clancy and his lost dream of having a son. What use were twin girls to a man like him?

Flo broke the silence.

'And?'

Emily shook her head. 'And nothing. Couldn't get through to Dargo VPP.'

'Ahh,' was all her aunt said to this.

As Emily dumped her saddle bag down she said, 'You know, I've been thinking . . . '

'Thought I could smell rubber burning,' Sam interrupted.

She gave him a shove so that he almost fell off his log, then sat down next to him. Rod handed her a pannikin of tea and she wrapped her hands around it and blew at the steam.

'We're all moping around as if this is the last drove ever,' she said. 'I say, let's choose to enjoy this trip and not see it as an ending. Let's see it as a beginning.'

'What are you talking about?' Flo asked her.

'Never say never.'

'Isn't it never say die?' Sam objected.

'Whatever!' Emily said, laughing. 'But maybe, just maybe, if we all start to think positively, act positively, and begin to live like we know that they'll ask the cattle back here to help manage the runs, it might just happen.'

'You reckon?' Her father was shaking his head doubtfully.

'I know it sounds like it's done and dusted,' Emily began, leaning forward, 'but once the grazing stops and the snow grass and scrub get away, eventually there'll be a fire here too hot for the land to handle, then soil erosion will follow, then river pollution, and the weeds will run rife. Now, I know none of us *wants* that to happen to our land, but we all know that a huge fire is on the cards. How can a Parkie on a budget look after all this? One day, they'll *have* to ask us back to help.'

'Hah!' said Flo. 'In your dreams.'

'They'll even pay us for it.'

'You reckon?' her aunt added sceptically.

'Yes! If we start putting out positive energy, thoughts, words, actions, it'll come back that way. We reap what we sow.'

'She's got in your head,' Sam said.

'Who?'

'Those words you're saying. They're not yours, they're

Evie's. She's talked you into thinking you can do anything. Be anyone. But look at you. Look at us. We've lost.'

'No, we haven't,' Emily said, turning to him. 'Do we look like people who have lost? We've got our health, each other, our animals. Look what I've been through, and I've survived. The girls haven't just survived, they've bloomed. We might not have *all* our land but we still have some, and isn't this the best life in the world? We can still continue to have it this way. I'm done with being a sad-sack about it all.'

'There's just one thing you're forgetting, Emily,' Rod put in. 'Income. Now the bans are in, you know as well as I do that we'll have to sell two-thirds of this herd. How can we all survive financially on that?'

She tossed more sticks on the fire. 'There's still Bob's land. He might help us?'

'And pigs might fly,' muttered Flo.

'And there's Sam. If you get out there again with your music, you'll have the media hanging on your words. We could use that as a positive way forward. Not pushing an anti-government line, but a pro-environment one.'

He frowned. 'I know what you're saying but isn't it too late? They've kicked the cattle off.'

Emily knew her brother didn't want to cloud his music, his one joy, with all the negativity that had come from being a cattleman, but surely, if they took it from a new angle, and gave the public their side of the story in music, things might turn around.

'I'm not saying continue on with the same old fight. I'm saying continue on, but this time light the way for people.'

'Praise the Lord, hallelujah!' Sam said in a Nashville accent. 'You ought to go on one of them big American happy-clappy religious TV shows. You'd be rolling in greenbacks, the way you're talking!'

'Sam,' said Rod, toning him down, 'Emily's right. It's all about finding the positive spin, and I guess when you're in the middle of something you tend to lose sight of the good stuff. I was like that for a long time after your mother died.'

Sam and Emily looked at their father's lined face in shock. He *never* talked about their mother. They sat in silence. He went on.

'Then I started to see the blessings she'd left behind. In you.' His blue eyes rested on Emily and then on Sam.

'It was actually at this hut, the first time you'd both come mustering on an overnighter. Remember? Your first night out here?'

Emily and Sam nodded. How could they forget? They'd ridden their ponies for hours on end, too excited to complain of cramps, rubbed calves from the stirrup leathers or freezing hands. Exhilarated to know they would be sleeping in a hut tucked away in the hollow of a massive mountain. Emily tried to recall how old she had been. Sam was at least five so she must have been almost seven. Her father had been swamped by a black cloud of grief before that time, until something in his mind lifted and cleared, like fog on a moonlit night.

'It was that night,' he said, 'around this campfire, with you sleeping in your little bed rolls and your ponies tethered to that very same tree over there, that I realised Susie was still here with us. I realised it was up to me to see the good, not the bad. That's when I knew I could keep going, no matter what. Even if I miss her every single day, still, I can see the good things left of her, in you.'

He tossed the remains of his tea into the fire. The family sat in silence, save for the hiss of the tea fizzing on the hot stones of the campfire.

Emily flung off her hat and moved over to hug her father. Flo smeared a tear over her cheek and patted Rod on the leg.

'Geez,' she said. 'Will you look at us? Talk about *Days of Our Lives* on the Dargo High Plains.'

Emily laughed, feeling the moment slide into history. But it lingered with them all. It was an ending, but it was also a new beginning.

Thirty

Two days later on top of the Dargo High Plains, in the blue hue of pre-dawn, Emily dropped the rails of the old chock and log yard to let the cattle out. They were beginning the last drove on the steep winding road that fell southward to Dargo. Rousie at the lead steadied the cattle as they made a rush for the long roadside grasses. The cows knew it was home time and were keen to begin their walk to the warmer climes of the lowlands. They set off at a cracking pace and Rousie, along with Sam on his brumby, worked hard to hold them up and get their heads down to settle them.

There were three hundred head of cattle, with a further two hundred and fifty of Bob's to collect from a holding yard on a lower ridgeline of the cattle run. Flo had the cattle in hand for her brother, who had rung to say he wouldn't be there for the muster or the drove. The family had taken the news with a collective roll of the eyes. It was typical of Bob.

Once the herd was settled, Rod called out from his horse, 'Sam and Flo, you take the front. Em and I will take the back.'

'As long as we can swap,' Sam said. 'Flo will want to yak all the time and I need to compose a few songs.'

'You're here for droving not composing,' she told him.

'And you're here for droving not yakking,' Sam said.

'You cheeky little sod!'

'We're all supposed to be in Emily's positive happy-land, remember?' he teased.

The family tactic of thinking positive had started out as a joke but it had kept them buoyant during the muster as they'd gathered and yarded the cattle across the mountainside.

'Fine,' said Flo crossly.

'Fine,' said Sam, but each of them had a smirk on their face as they rode away to the head of the mob. Useless watched his mistress go, then snuck into the back of the horsefloat near the yards, in the hope of snoozing there for the day. Soon, though, Flo's deep voice bellowed out, '*Useless*!'

'Wish them luck,' Emily said with a grin to her father.

'They haven't changed . . . Sam and Flo, pretending to fight but loving every minute of it.'

But it was going to change for all of them, Emily remembered again with a jolt. Rod and Flo still owned one hundred acres of private land surrounding the homestead on the high plains, but the loss of the government licence spelt the end of their cattle enterprise up here. A small number of cows could be trucked up next summer, but it really wasn't a viable proposition.

Bob, as the owner of nine hundred acres of private alpine land, was the only family member who could still make a living from the plains. Despite her efforts to keep her thoughts positive, Emily found it a crime that he should be left with good precious mountain land when he didn't look after it. Yet her father and aunt, who managed land with respect and love, had been evicted from theirs.

Emily looked at the red hindquarters of the healthy cows and their calves as they moved along the gravel road, the tops of their tails sporting little rolls of fat from spending months on the lush summer alpine pastures. Emily loved following a herd, getting to know each and every beast at the tail end. The one that would turn and argue with a dog, the old girl that would try to sneak off in the bush for a pick of green, the slow ones, the lazy ones, the stroppy ones who bunted others. They were all individuals and she loved each one of them. Collectively, cattle were peaceful, obliging and curious creatures.

Now most of them would have to be sold. Sorrow rose in her again when she thought of the letter Rod and Flo had received from the government, declaring they were entitled to compensation. They just didn't get it! No amount of money could compensate for the loss of their breeding herd.

These cows were special, for they held the memory of droving days past. They weren't so much 'trained' for the road, but had instead shared the journey along it with the humans and their dogs over the years. With their sale the herd's memory of each curve, each climb along the way, where to rest and where to drink, would be lost too.

With her emotions swinging again between joy and despair, Emily was suddenly grateful that her dad was here to ride with her on this last stretch, along with Sam and Flo, and soon her daughters on their ponies. Her family steadied her, made her feel calm within the storm of her life. Her family and Evie.

She knew Evie would be at the high-plains house, packing the back-up vehicle for the day, while the girls got an extra sleep-in. There was no sense in getting them up at the crack of dawn on the first day of the week-long drove. Evie, together with the girls, would act as a pilot vehicle, bringing the riders drinks and ferrying them to pick-up utes at the end of the day, where camp would be set up.

'You happy riding up the back with me?' Rod asked. Emily nodded. She wanted the distraction of the cows and her dad's conversation, rather than the isolated job of riding in the lead where she knew she would only mull over the situation with Luke. She also didn't want to think any more about what life would be like from now on with Clancy and his new girls and the cattle bans. All those anvils she was carrying. It was a wonder Snowgum wasn't buckling at the knees from the weight.

Droving was a lengthy, slow business. It sounded romantic, but the reality was that it could be a challenge mentally when the weather was rough. Emily had endured days where the cows began tonguing from heat or were frisky from cold, or they battled howling winds so wild it was hard to keep them mobbed. This morning, though, the weather was mild and the cows content to walk along.

She dismounted and led Snowgum for a time, checking the spot under her girth, worried the mare would not be up for the entire trip. There were spare horses, but Emily liked to travel the road with old Snowgum. She was an easy-natured creature who enjoyed the work, flicking her ears forward, looking about the bush, occasionally hunting in Emily's pockets for an apple. Other horses on droving days were not so obliging, wearing sour faces the whole way with ears pulled back, or baring their big, yellow teeth to bite at the rumps of slow-moving cows. Some horses jig-jogged or pulled when they were fresh. But Snowgum was made for the road.

Hours later, as the sun was getting low, the Flanaghan drovers made it to the Twelve-Mile yards, a cattle camp used for generations by the family. Sam, riding ahead, had already dropped the rails and the lead cows walked straight in.

With the sun gone, Emily's fingers felt like ice. Evie had already lit the fire outside the hut and Emily was looking forward to spreading her hands before the dancing flames. She knew Tilly and Meg would be camping in the old hut with her tonight and smiled happily at the thought.

As she unhitched Snowgum's girth she felt the mare flinch. Emily swore under her breath when she ducked her head to look at the old wounds from the race-day fall. The slight press of her fingertips made the mare stomp her foot and flick her tail, her ears pinned back in an uncharacteristic expression. Emily could see the proud flesh opening up again and bright blood freshly weeping from the wound.

'Flo,' she called out, 'come here.'

She indicated the mare's wound and Flo shook her head.

'Well, that's buggered that. Still, it was worth a try. I'll get Evie to run me back up to the plains and fetch me float and grab another from the mob. I'll see if I can radio her now. Get her to bring some of her goop to put on Snow's wound.'

'I knew I shouldn't have tested her. I should've left her longer to heal.'

'Nah, she loves it, don't ya, girl?' Flo said, giving Snowgum a good scratch on the neck. 'Tell you what, I'll get your new gelding, if you like. Good chance to give him some work. We've got to put a positive spin on it, remember?'

Emily smiled sadly. She no longer wanted the gelding because he was a constant reminder of Luke, but she knew this was a good chance to educate him as they went. Flo took Snowgum's reins from Emily. 'I'll see her right. You go get yourself warm.'

At dawn the next morning, Bonus stood still as Emily dragged the girth tight. She lobbed into the saddle and soon they were tailing the mob, her belly full of Evie's hot breakfast and rich coffee.

'You travelling okay?' Emily asked her girls as she looked down from Bonus to Tilly and Meg, riding by her side on Jemma and Blossom.

Tilly beamed up at her mum. 'Are you serious? *Yeah*!'

As the girls chatted happily to each other, Emily tipped her head back and let the swaying movement of the horse relax her. She gazed skyward to the azure blue that shone through the canopy of gum leaves. It was a glorious, gentle autumn day. Perfect for droving. Then she flopped forward, pressing her cheek to the gelding's neck. While she missed Snowgum's predictable calmness, Bonus was taking to the life of a drover's horse with ease.

By one o'clock, the cattle had reached Evie's house. Sam and Flo herded them into one of the house paddocks for the time being, while Emily helped the girls hitch their ponies to a nearby shady tree. They were expecting Evie to come out and join them, but to their surprise it was Bob who appeared from the house and scuttled down a side path.

'What's he doing here? The sly old dog,' said Flo to Rod, then she called after her brother, 'You here to do your share of the work, eh, Bob?'

He didn't look up. As he rounded the side gate, he nearly ran smack into Emily, who was stooping to fill a bucket of water for the horses from the corrugated-iron tank.

'Bob!' She looked into his face and was shocked to see the strain visible on it. He'd been crying, the tears still fresh, brow knitted in a frown, mouth slanted sideways. He said nothing, brushed past her, fired up the engine of his ute and was gone.

'What's with him?' Flo said, arriving on the ground with a thud as she slid from her horse.

'I really don't know,' Emily replied, still stunned from seeing her rough, tough uncle crying like a baby.

From behind the stone wall Evie popped up her head, her white hair almost glowing in the sun.

'Come in! Only the two-legged ones, mind. Not the four.'

Jesus suddenly went nuts, barking and leaping up and down behind the wall.

'*Jesus Christ*!' they chorused.

As she walked towards Evie, Emily asked, 'What was *Bob* doing here?'

'You and he, aren't . . .?' Flo wiggled her eyebrows up and down. 'I mean, you're not . . .?'

'*No*,' said Evie, eyes twinkling, 'we're not. Of course we're not. He came to me for a healing.'

'A what-ing?' asked Flo.

'A healing,' Evie repeated mildly. She turned and began to walk away, calling over her shoulder, 'Everyone needs one at some point.' Then she tactfully changed the subject. 'I like your horse, Emily. He's very handsome. Thought of a name for him yet?'

Emily jogged to catch up with her, shaking her head. 'Luke called him Bonus, but all I can think of is Trouble.'

'Trouble? That's not something you want to focus on or attract.'

'I know, but it's a name that keeps coming back to me. I just don't know what's coming. What my life's going to be like from now. I don't even need a new horse. Not now all this has happened.' She waved her arm about to encompass the cattle in the bush yards.

Evie looked at her with gentle green eyes.

'He's no trouble. He's a stud muffin.'

'Well, I can't exactly call him that.'

'A hunka-spunka? Hot stuff? Like his previous owner, eh?'

'Evie!'

'C'mon,' she said, linking her arm with Emily's as Jesus danced about their feet. 'You're all invited in for a quick bite.'

'Oh, Evie, don't worry,' Emily said. 'We've got tucker left over from yesterday. That'll do us for the rest of the day.'

'No, you're all my guests, please,' she said. 'Sam,' she called, 'lunch inside for you all.'

'We'll be along soon,' he called from where he stood with Rod, making hasty repairs to one of his stirrup leathers.

Evie walked Emily along the path where wild hollyhocks and lupins flowered colourfully amid her new plants. The girls ran on ahead, happy to have arrived at what had become their second home.

Emily kicked off her boots, stepped into the cool stone cottage and walked along the hallway to the back of the house where Evie had built a sunny kitchen.

She lifted a quiche from the oven and set it beside a fresh and colourful array of dishes: salads and homemade pasta in a free-range egg mayonnaise. Steamed new potatoes garnished with mint and drizzled with pale butter made from Evie's milking cow. Crisp lettuce, snow peas, carrots and cucumber set out on a platter. It looked so inviting.

'Yum! What a feast,' Emily said.

'If you're going to do great things with your life, Emily, you'll need your body to support you. Fuel it only with the good things.'

'What great things am I going to do? What now? After the cattle are taken down to the lowlands and sold, what then? Dad's already worrying about how we're going to manage. And me a single mum.'

Evie just smiled up at her as she sliced the quiche.

'You will know your path,' she said calmly.

Emily had become used to the way Evie spoke. At first it had unsettled her, then amused her, but now she knew there was truth in all that Evie said.

With the special meals Evie had cooked up at the high plains station, Emily had been amazed by the way the excess weight had fallen from her body. At Brigalow they had lived near a corner store, where ice-creams and chips and lollies were always a temptation. Eating Evie's meals, though, she and Sam had felt their bodies gradually detoxing of sugar and preservatives and the junk food additives they'd become accustomed to.

Their tastebuds had adjusted quickly to the simple yet delicious food Evie set before them. Even the girls seemed to have more energy, compared to their past life in Brigalow, and were shooting up into leggy young things. Emily continued to be surprised by how quickly her dark hair was growing longer and more glossy, the scars on her body smoothing over, her breath coming more easily, her bones meshed painlessly, her energy restored.

Sam came into the kitchen, followed by Rod and Flo.

'What a spread!' cried Flo. 'This is the best droving fare we've ever enjoyed.' She gathered up a plate and passed it to Rod.

'Thank you, Evie,' he said, 'for *everything*.' There was weight in his words. He wasn't just thanking her for the lunch, but also for her care and love of his daughter and granddaughters.

Emily looked around the clean, tidy kitchen. There were herbs hanging from rafters and tomatoes growing on the windowsills. On the counter top a big bowl of fresh apples, a jug of homemade lemonade, and a special plate of honeyed natural sweets for the girls. From the old wooden chairs to the well-worn kitchen table, the whole house had the same serene energy that radiated from Evie.

As Emily bit into the nutritious food, she could taste Evie's love in it. For the first time it felt as if she had a mother caring for her. How ironic was it that someone like Evie had at last come into their lives, on the last drove?

With the meal over, Rod, Sam and Flo stood and thanked Evie, giving her warm hugs, Rod's embrace lingered longest of all. The girls, eager to get back on their ponies, danced down the hallway and banged their way out through the screen door. On the way down the path, Jesus had a go at Flo's leg, his teeth meshing with the cloth of her jeans. She responded with a high kick that sent the little dog sailing into a snapdragon patch. He rolled over, wagged his tail and jumped up on to the stone wall to bark at her with a dog's grin from ear to ear, as if it were all a game. Flo passed him, muttering profanities.

Inside the cottage, Emily started gathering up crockery and stacking it neatly in the sink.

'You're a good girl, Emily, but I'll do that. You go on with your family. Enjoy the rest of the day.'

'Part of me doesn't ever want this day to end. Part of me knows that once these days are over, this is it.'

'Are you thinking in negatives again?'

'Oh, Evie! I just can't seem to stop my thoughts from running away with themselves.' Such was the challenge of being a soon-to-be jobless drover, Emily thought, with miles of dusty road ahead and endless space for thoughts to run riot.

'You need time, my darling.'

'Time for what?'

'To truly heal. You can see Snowgum's still not wholly healed. Well, neither are you, my dear.'

'So what should I do?'

'Go where your heart and soul calls you.'

'You mean, up top?' Evie nodded. 'For the winter?'

Emily had seen photos of the old-timers in their snowshoes, as if they wore tennis racquets strapped to their feet, outside the high-plains homestead. Looking at the pictures, she had shivered to see they were wearing not much more than waistcoats and jackets over their usual clothes, but their smiles radiated a warmth all of their own. Emily imagined being there with her daughters, skiing or riding in the snow down to Evie's little cottage.

'It's doable, and it would do you good.'

Emily sat contemplating a winter on the plains. It would be tough, but no tougher than living in the tiny town of Dargo and wondering each and every day if she might bump into Luke. Or, if she ventured further afield to Bairnsdale, if she would see a very pregnant Penny. There was no telling what she would do to Clancy if she encountered him. The anger she had felt towards him for his long list of betrayals and put downs had been dealt with, she believed, through Evie's patient coaching. But she still nursed fury towards him for his neglect of his girls. She could see how it hurt them. Emily wondered if taking the girls up there would stop Tilly longing for her father to visit, as the snow would clearly make that impossible. Evie came and sat down next to her.

'There's something else on your mind, isn't there?'

Emily nodded.

'A man? Two men? The old and the new?'

She nodded again.

'Until you truly love yourself it isn't wise to try to love another. Heal first, darling, then love.'

'I know,' Emily told her. 'Deep down, I know that.' She looked into Evie's eyes and felt such utter trust that she was suddenly blurting out the story of being down by the

Wonnangatta River with Luke and the terrifying sound of the horses.

'What does it all mean, Evie?' The fear was back in Emily's voice.

Evie smiled. 'It means you both have a gift. That your union created an energetic freedom for the earth. Horses mean freedom.'

Emily frowned, confused. 'But the energy felt dark.'

'You know there was a murder in the Wonnangatta and the station manager was chased to his death on horseback?'

Emily did know the folklore of the place, but had not connected the two incidents. She shivered.

'You and Luke share a special power. United, it's a strong light energy that draws out the dark and dissipates it.'

'So we should be together?'

Evie shook her head. 'Not if there's no anchor of self-love on which to tie your passion for him. Time, Emily, is what you need. You and Luke are for another time.'

From the hallway came a shout from Sam. 'Time to go, gasbagging girls!'

Evie gave Emily a quick hug and then Emily was gone, jogging along the hall, feeling altogether sad that she and Luke were not to be. Not this time.

Thirty-one

On the very last day of the drove, it poured. Instead of cursing the weather, Emily viewed the low grey skies and the heavy silver streaks of rain as a gift. A good autumn break would set them up well for winter on the lowlands. But she knew that just one good season on their former mountain runs would be enough to fuel fierce fires next summer, given the right conditions . . . For the umpteenth time, Emily tried to shove these negative thoughts about the fate of her beloved mountain landscape from her mind.

With just a few steep bends to go, she was riding alone at the back of the herd with no one to distract her. Think positive, she told herself.

The cattle were travelling well. Her father was riding slowly ahead on the gentle curve of the road. He was close enough to steady the lead cattle and far enough on to warn oncoming traffic to slow down. It was nice that it was just the two of them today. Emily could savour these last hours of droving in solitude. Just her and her dad, and the bliss of rain.

Sam, who could only ever tolerate droving in short bursts, had absconded a couple of days before to see Bridie, restless to get the songs he'd thought of on the road down on paper. Evie was minding the girls at Tranquillity and cooking up an end-of-droving feast for them all. Emily knew that by this afternoon she and Rod would have the herd tramping through the township of Dargo and into a paddock there. Then a big dinner by the homestead fire.

Rivers of rain fell from the brim of her hat and cascaded down the back of her oilskin. She wore waterproof trousers, but beneath her wet-weather gear she was damp right through, her clothes steamy against her skin. But at least her body and limbs were warm. At one point the rain was so heavy some of the cows stopped, pinned their ears back and turned about, looking at her as if to say, 'Are you mad? How can you make us walk in this?' She answered their query with a loud crack of her stockwhip. The leaders jolted, mooed, then turned to walk forward once more.

So loud was the rain, Emily didn't hear the vehicle approaching from behind until it was almost upon her. The gelding danced a sideways step at the sudden sight of the white four-wheel drive, but she soon had him steadied.

Emily drew in a breath. There in the rain shone the bright VPP logo on the door of the four-wheel drive. The lairy green paint was at odds with the muted sodden bush surrounding them. She steered the horse around to the driver's side. Luke wound down his window, frowning at the rain that dashed inside.

'Hi,' he said. 'Wet enough out there?'

Emily looked at his handsome face. He'd cut his hair short, which gave him an almost military look in his khaki uniform. Gorgeous though he was, when she saw him sitting there in that flash four-wheel drive, with its bells and whistles, all she felt was sadness and resentment. How could she ever love her way around the fact that he worked for the very organisation that had just derailed her life?

So far, not one actual person had been brave enough to speak to the Flanaghans about the bans directly. Instead, life as they'd known it had been brought to a halt by letters sent from Melbourne on weighty, expensive paper. The responsibility for evicting them from the mountains was never delegated to a single man. It was dished out collectively by men who could stand behind each other and argue that it was not all down to one person.

'Have you come out to make sure we've got all the cattle off the mountains?' Emily said coldly. She saw the shock on Luke's face before he covered his response with a smile.

'No, I trust you. I was just out doing the flood monitoring. Might have to close the Lower Dargo Road if this rain keeps on.' He looked skyward, then glanced back at the horse. 'How's he going?'

'Good,' said Emily, not giving Luke anything but feeling guilty nevertheless, knowing the horse was far from good. He was brilliant, and she should tell Luke so.

'Thought of another name for him yet?'

Emily squirmed. 'Not really. Not officially. Evie nicknamed him Hot Stuff.'

'Hot Stuff, eh?' Luke gave her a wink. 'Like Salsa. Bit like how you danced in the pub that night.'

Oh, God, Emily thought. He's flirting with me. Part of her was delighted. Part of her devastated. How could he flirt when here she was, taking cattle down the road for the very last time? Didn't he get it?

'I think I'll just stick with Bonus,' she responded dully.

Luke picked up on her continuing coldness, realising he wasn't going to warm her, realising the gap between them was too huge. He fell silent for a time, the rain drumming on the roof of the vehicle, the gelding shifting his feet, ears back, rain trickling down his already soaked rump, not happy to be standing still.

Emily whistled Rousie and growled at him to stop hassling the cows, who were now also standing, resting, steam rising from their backs.

'I tried to call you,' Luke said softly.

'I know.'

'Should I try again?' he asked hopefully.

Emily shook her head and rain spilled off her hat. 'No. Don't.'

'Okay,' said Luke. 'It's your call.' He started the vehicle and the gelding jumped a little. Luke looked out through the fogged-up windscreen waiting for Emily to speak. She didn't. She sat staring ahead at the big herd of beautiful cows they would be forced to sell.

'Well, I'll leave you to it then,' he said. His voice was cold now. There was hurt in it too. He drove round the cattle, tooted the horn at Rod, who was waiting at the top of the hill for Emily and the herd to keep coming, and then was gone from sight.

'C'mon, Mr Bonus-Salsa,' Emily said to the unhappy, rain-soaked gelding, 'move your hot arse. We got cows to yard and boys to forget. We're almost home.'

On the river-flat road into Dargo the rain eased and a cold wind came racing through the grasses. The autumn leaves of the giant walnut and elm trees that flanked the main street were falling like silver confetti. The iridescent leaves stuck to the dark wet road so it looked as though the cattle were walking over a pathway of shining coins.

As Emily and Rod drove the herd through Dargo and past the pub, some locals came out to the verandah, beer in hand, toasting the cattlemen's last drove.

Across the road at the general store, Emily watched a tourist who was hellbent on taking a thousand photos. Disgruntled, she neck-reined her horse about and hunted the cheeky, curious cows in the mob away from the store's gardens and outdoor coffee tables. In the town's heart, the cattle were perky, knowing they were close to home. They trotted for a few hundred metres before Emily and Rod guided the leaders into an open gateway that lay between an old miner's cottage and the river. It was one of the Flanaghans' paddocks and flush with fresh grass.

The cows instantly had their heads down, grabbing up great mouthfuls of feed. Emily sat listening to the rhythmic sound of the cattle eating as they tore at the sweet grasses that had been rested over the summer months. She observed their

271

glossy coats and knew they would make top dollars in the sale yards in such condition, but she had no desire to see them go. It broke her heart to know that these quiet beasts, bred selectively over generations in the mountains, would now go elsewhere. Perhaps to slaughter, perhaps to another farm where they would not be treated kindly and with respect. She shook the thoughts from her head and chose to think instead about the night ahead with her family. Emily manoeuvred the gelding around the gate and swung it shut, marking the end of an era.

Thirty-two

Passing by the dining-room window of the Flanaghans' family homestead, Emily looked in and smiled. There were Tilly and Meg, bright-faced, helping Evie carry dishes for tonight's feast over to the old red-gum table. It was decked out with fine old crockery and silverware, and at the centre stood a candelabra ablaze with white tapering candles. Emily recalled that her grandfather had won the candelabra with a Hereford bull at the 1955 Bairnsdale Show. The light from its flames cast an angelic glow over the girls' faces.

At the old sideboard, Rod was pouring port into delicate crystal glasses, also trophies won by long-gone livestock at a long-gone agricultural show. Emily hadn't seen some of these old things in years, they had mostly been shoved to the back of the sideboard cupboard, but Evie had declared tonight was special.

So things had been dusted off, polished up and were now being used and enjoyed. Even the big old dining room, normally shut off from the rest of the house and used as a storage place, had been cleaned out and restored to its former glory. The open fire burned brightly, illuminating the beautiful big painting above it of a cattleman's hut, and there were fresh flowers in the vase on the sideboard. Evie had brought the house alive.

Hungry now and keen to get her jobs done so she could join the others inside, Emily walked over to the feed shed and scooped dog pellets into a bucket as the kelpies danced in their pens. Flo's cat, Muscles, wove in and out of her legs, miaowing up at her.

Above her, the stars were bright in the crisp night air. She felt tired from droving, but exhilarated that her body had coped so well. It was her mind that had not. Not since seeing Luke today on the road.

In the near-darkness, she rattled out biscuits into the dogs' bowls, talking to each of them but making a particular fuss of Rousie, as she always did. Then she made her way to the shed, swung her leg over the four-wheeler bike and revved it into life, Muscles leaping on to her lap for his moggy joyride. Zooming away down the road, she travelled the two kilometres to Bob's house.

There were no lights on inside. Flo had said he'd shot through again, though no one knew where to. When Bob left, they always took it upon themselves to check his animals. He'd been known to leave horses in yards for days without food or water so that they chewed the top rails down to thin splintery sticks. Once he'd left his dog, DD, on the chain for so long in the summer that the animal nearly perished from thirst. Emily hated going to Bob's house. It was snaky and spidery and a constant reminder to her of the loss of her grandparents, who had kept the garden as a child's paradise.

She remembered a pond with golden fish swimming lazily in sparkling water, and stepping stones leading to a soft, ferny fairy glen. There were flowers and windchimes and special places to sit. But since Bob had lived there, he ran the crossbred killers in the yard and the garden was all but gone now. The place had a depressing feel to it.

Tonight, as she approached the house, she frowned. DD wasn't bouncing madly up and down on the end of his chain. Emily shone the headlights over to the empty kennel. Tied to the upright star-picket on which the dog was normally tethered was a piece of cardboard torn from a beer carton. On it, in Bob's scratchy hand in permanent marker: *Thank you, but have sent DD on holiday.*

Emily sucked in a breath. Surely he didn't mean he'd shot the dear old dog? Mad though it was, it was a character and so much a part of the place.

She frowned and made her way to Bob's henhouse. Again, a message on a ripped-up beer box. *Gave all the girls away to Donna.* Emily took in the dark interior of the empty chook shed. She marched over to the paddock where Bob kept his riding mare. Normally Emily would throw her a bucket of chaff when her uncle wasn't about as he kept the mare in a sparse and weedy paddock and she often looked ribby, her coat dull. Another piece of cardboard was inside the feed-bucket that hung from the fence. *Gave the mare to Kate.*

What was going on? Emily ran over to Bob's house and a sensor light flicked on. She saw that the back lawn was mown short, and all the rubbish on the verandah had been taken away. The curtains were drawn. The place looked completely deserted but, more surprisingly, it also looked clean and tidy.

Emily jumped back on the bike, waited for Muscles to join her and then sped along the drive to the homestead. Just as she was heading inside the house she saw headlights. Sam's sporty ute drew up, and he and Bridie tumbled out, laughing.

'Hi, drover!' Bridie called, looking stunning in a red top worn with funky black jeans. Sam, all in Johnny Cash black, gave Emily a quick hug.

'I can see you've made an effort,' he teased as he took in Emily's old farm clothes.

'What do we do with her?' tutted Bridie, her blonde hair swept up Jayne Mansfield-style in a thick red ribbon.

'What's wrong with this?' Emily said, looking down at her chunky woollen work jumper.

'We are going to pick out something for you to wear. You're not coming to our special dinner looking like that!'

'What a bossy pair you make,' Emily said, as they rambled along the big hallway into the heart of the house.

Once they were all gathered at the dining table, Emily, now wearing a pretty checked cowgirl shirt, couldn't hold back her news any longer, 'I think Uncle Bog's in trouble. I'm really worried about him,' she blurted out.

Everyone turned to look at her.

'We've been worrying about Bog for years,' said Flo dryly.

'But this time it's different. There's no sign of any of his animals and he's left all these strange notes and the place is *tidy*. I mean, *really tidy*.' Emily twisted her hands together in her lap. 'You don't think he's done himself in?'

'No, of course he hasn't,' Evie soothed her. 'Bob's been coming to me for healing.'

'Geez!' said Flo, recalling seeing him leave the house. 'The only healer Unky Bog would have ever heard of is a blue heeler, not a spiritual one. Evie, how did you get the man to come to you?'

'I didn't. He came to me voluntarily after the bans.'

'Yeah? Why?' Sam asked.

'I can't tell you why,' she said, 'but I can tell you he's okay. He's not going to do anything silly . . . well, I can't guarantee *that*, but you know what I mean. He's not going to do himself in.'

'Phew!' said Emily.

'Let's drink a toast to Bog then, wherever the flock he may be,' Flo said, the pre-dinner port already warming her up. And they raised their glasses.

'To Bog!' they toasted. 'Wherever the flock he may be!'

Emily sat watching her family eat by the flickering light of the candles and the open fire. Evie's roast beef and vegetables kept them all so busy that for a time the conversation was slowed to a series of 'Mmms' and 'Oohs' and 'More, please!'

But as they finished their dinner, Evie looked at each of them in turn. 'What now?' she asked?

276

'Dessert?' said Tilly hopefully.

'Yes, darling, but first I'd like to hear from each of you. What now for your lives? Rod, how about you go first?'

He set down his glass and cleared his throat. He laced his fingers together before him and thought for a time.

'First, we'll sort out the cattle. Keep a third of the best and sell the rest of them. Then . . . I don't know. I thought I could go fencing and slashing. There are plenty of hobby blocks round here that need a handyman and the Melbournites who own them aren't short of a penny. It'd tide us over financially until we find something else. Might even be a nice little business.'

Emily could hear her father talking himself into this new way of life. She felt a prick of sadness, but she was also proud that he was open to trying new ventures after a lifetime of being a cattleman.

'Flo?' Evie said.

'Mmm, well . . .' she began, 'I've had a proposition from Baz.'

'Not another one!' said Sam cheekily.

'Not that sort of proposition. Well, yeah, I've had plenty of *those* sorts of propositions from Baz. But he's goin' into live-stock cartage and wants me to run a truck this side of the mountains for him.'

'Flo's going truckin'!' cried Bridie delightedly. 'Can I be your stylist? You've *got* to look good. You'll get more clients that way. I'm thinking translucent tops, tight jeans, sexy boots. But still classy . . . kind of like Nicole Kidman in *Australia*. Oh, Flo, your business could boom.'

'Look out! We'll have a heap of understocked properties round here 'cause all the blokes will be selling their animals in the hope they get lucky with the truckie,' Emily teased.

'That sounds great!' Evie said. 'Now, Sam, you?'

'Well,' he began, eyes shining as he gathered up Bridie's hand, 'I'll have to answer for Bridie here too because . . .' they looked at each other joyfully, 'we're moving to the New South

Wales north coast – the hub of country music! She's helped me write enough songs for a new album and we want to record them. We've booked a house and a studio for the winter there. Once I've done some demos, Ike's going to look about for a really good contract. We've written some great stuff.'

'All written lying down, I presume,' Emily joked, and Sam kicked her under the table hard on the shin. The pain in her leg wasn't enough to cloud her happiness at hearing his news. But as all eyes fell upon her, she felt the pressure.

'Your turn, Emily,' Evie said.

'I-I,' she stammered, 'I don't really know.'

'C'mon, Emily,' said her brother.

'Well, I'm thinking of heading up to the plains for the winter. Just the girls and me.'

'Yay!' cried Meg, 'We can live in the snow!'

'I don't want to live in the snow,' said Tilly, pouting and folding her arms.

'We won't *live* in the snow. We'll live in the house in the snow,' Emily explained, but still her eldest girl scowled.

'It'll be fun, Tilly,' she said uncertainly. 'You'll see.'

Rod looked concerned. 'Are you sure? It could be tougher than you think.'

'I know, but Evie'll be down the way. We can ride or ski to her. We're only likely to be snowed in for three weeks max. It's not like a Flanaghan hasn't lived that way before.'

'Are you sure you want the girls in such isolation?'

'Yes, I'm sure! I *need* the isolation. I'm not like all of you. I haven't got a clue what I'm going to do next. I had my heart set on being a cattleman. Now I need time to figure out what else to do.'

They all sat contemplating Emily's words. They knew she was still healing emotionally. Still recovering from her broken marriage, Clancy's desertion to another family, and the loss of her dreams. None of them, save for Evie and Bridie, knew the full extent of her confusion over Luke, though, and the part that he played in her wanting to bunker down in the snow.

'Tilly,' Emily said, 'if you really don't want to go, we can ask Daddy if you can stay with him if you like? Or else you can stay here with Grandpa Rod and Flo, if you really, really don't want to live up there. But Mummy has to go. She just has to. I can't explain why, but it has something to do with that dream I told you about.'

Tilly screwed up her mouth as she thought. They all looked at her.

'C'mon, Tilly,' Meg cajoled. 'We can build igloos. And snowmen. And we can take our ponies, can't we, Mum?'

Emily nodded.

'Okay,' Tilly said in a small voice, 'I'll go.' Relief flooded through Emily. There was no way she'd wanted Tilly to go to Clancy's or to stay here by herself, even if she was in the care of the family. She got up and went to hug her elder child.

'Then it's settled,' Rod said at last. 'Emily, off you go into self-imposed exile with your girls. But please, please, remember you can always come back before the spring, if it gets too much.'

'We'll be fine, Dad. I'm sure.'

279

Thirty-three

One week later, on her first night on the plains away from her family, Emily couldn't believe the depth of her loneliness. In the darkness, she led Bonus and Snowgum from the float to the stable. She could feel the wind bite into her lips, so cold she had to pull the neck of her jumper up over her mouth. With just the low gleam from her head torch lighting the way, she put the horses in a stall and returned to get the girls' ponies, who shared the third bay of the float. Her breath hazed before her in a chilly mist.

Her fingers were numb with cold as she fumbled around in the dark for the heavy horse rugs. She shook the imagined spiders from them and took them to the stable to heave on to the horses' backs. Each of them snorted contentedly and got down to the business of chewing their chaff. As Emily shut the stable door, she caught a brief impression of another woman's hand on the latch and felt energised by the connection.

'Emily?' she said aloud. She could feel her ancestor's presence, there in the darkness of the big old sheds. Fear ran through her then. Wind railed, far up in the treetops, but down here on the ground, it was dead still, giving the bush an eerie feel.

The sudden loud tap of a branch broke the silence. It startled Emily and she whirled about as if there were something out there in the darkness. A wild dog? A hunter? A ghost? The noise of the phantom horses in the Wonnangatta still haunted her. She felt panic rise in her chest.

Control your thoughts, she told herself. Her great-great-grandmother had spent many nights alone here, in charge of her eleven children while her husband went off in search of gold in those cold, lean years. How brave and tough she must have been to have created a welcoming home on top of an isolated and sometimes hostile mountain.

Peering into the blackness of the bush, Emily realised that, with time, she would no longer flinch at the eerie sounds of the night. They would become part of her world. But right now she felt daunted. She felt a sudden urge to rush inside and huddle close to Meg who always slept so still and warm compared to Tilly's thrashing limbs.

Emily summoned up her courage, though, and forced a smile to her face. She had wanted this ever since the accident, and here she was at last. Blissfully alone, with the energies of her forebears floating all about in this most precious, most beautiful place. The wind whipped up again and Emily heard a snow-gum limb crack and fall. She pulled her hat down low and made her way back over to the house.

The warmth from the kitchen didn't extend as far as the bedrooms, so when she checked the girls they were still covered by old featherdown quilts and their beanies were jammed on their heads. In the candlelight, the gentle fog of their breath pulsed steadily, in and out, in the icy air. Emily agonised again about her decision to bring them to a place so cold and remote. Was she doing the right thing? Could she and the girls remain here the whole winter? This first night she'd doubted it, but then she had thought of Evie and the comfort of knowing she was nearby.

On their arrival, late and in darkness, they found that Evie had left the fire smouldering, a giant new candle alight, freshly baked bread on the table and a pot of wallaby stew, made tastier with bacon, warming on the stove. She had also stocked the big old meat safe with spuds, onions, carrots, swedes, flour, rice, apples and pasta and filled the cupboards with tins. Emily had brought food, too, so she knew that if they were snowed in, there'd be plenty of rations. Evie had left a note: *Time heals and so do good thoughts. Enjoy!* Emily had sent her a silent 'thank you' in the night for all her care. Now she fell heavily into bed and eventually drifted into a fitful sleep, wakened from time to time by the ghoulish sounds of the wind moaning about the homestead.

'What have I done?' she said aloud in the darkness in the dead of night, feeling utterly lost.

Just then the shrill ringing of the radio-phone shattered the silence.

It would be her dad. Emily dived along the hall and grappled for the receiver in the kitchen.

'Hello!' she said, trying to sound as bright as she could.

'How dare you take them up there without asking me!' Clancy's voice lit a fuse in her.

'*Ask* you! Ask *you*? You've not returned any of my calls. Don't be such a bastard, Clancy! And spare me your stupid games. You're breaking the girls' hearts, do you know that?'

There was silence on the other end of the line. Then: 'You'll be hearing from me. That piece of shit of a house isn't any place for kids in winter.'

'Since when did you know what is or isn't good for kids! *And* you're drunk. You only ever call when you're drunk. Loser!' The storm within Emily raged stronger than the one outside as she slammed down the phone.

In the morning she woke to complete silence, the wind blown out and gone along with her own fury at Clancy's threats. She lifted the blinds and gasped to see the fairytale landscape before her. The whole scene was white with snow, soft and peaceful. She leapt out of bed. Her clothes felt damp, even icy, when she pulled them on. She hurried to cajole the woodstove alight and set Meg's and Tilly's clothes out to warm. Was Clancy right?

When she went to the toilet, she realised the pipes would be frozen and the water had been drained from the cistern. Flo had warned her she'd have to bucket water from the well to flush the toilet, and to keep it empty so the porcelain didn't freeze and crack. The seat was so cold it burned the backs of her legs like a freezebrand. Her feet and nose stung from cold. When she went to make tea in the icy kitchen, she realised there was no running water. She'd have to scoop up buckets of snow for the stovetop. Emily was about to cry, Clancy's words haunting her, then she made herself laugh instead. She had a lot to learn, that was all.

Heading outside with a collection of saucepans, she enjoyed the crunch of snow underfoot. She shooed Rousie away from where she filled the pans. The snow seemed to lie the deepest on the eastern side of the woodshed, but all about her was a white-coated landscape. The calls of crows and currawongs rang out from the snow gums. Rousie barked with the excitement of this cold, strange world, and the sound echoed through the bush.

When Emily went back inside, the kitchen felt cheerier, the fire lively now and spilling warmth into the room. Hearing Tilly and Meg talking in their beds, she rushed into their darkened room and whipped up the blind.

'Look! Snow!'

Both girls shrieked and jumped up to dress. Outside, they ran about and tossed snowballs in the air, which Rousie leapt and snapped at with a Tassie-devil clack of his teeth. They built snowmen, using sticks for arms, gum leaves for smiles and gum nuts for eyes. Soon, though, Emily cajoled them into leaving the snow-family. There was work to do. In the stables she handed a hay fork to Tilly and pushed a wheelbarrow into the stall.

Emily was shocked to hear her elder daughter say sulkily,

'I don't want to pick up poo.' Never when she'd trailed behind her mother picking up Snowgum's dung at the Brigalow block had Tilly objected to helping. She'd been such an easygoing kid. Now Emily realised that her eldest was testing the boundaries of this new life. Emily didn't want to be one of those mothers who said scathingly 'You're so like your father!' in exasperated tones, but Tilly share certain traits of Clancy's that jarred with her, made all the more apparent in isolation. Respond, thought Emily, don't react.

'You don't have to help, Tils, if you don't want to,' she replied calmly, 'But it will mean you don't get hot chocolate with marshmallow when we go inside.'

Emily turned away to let both horses and ponies out into the day yard. Outside the horses slung their heads down low and snorted at the snow. Bonus pawed the ground, then trotted around the powdered paddock. Emily took in the way the drift had settled on the poa grasses and the horizontal limbs of the trees. The whole world was soft and crisp. It was paradise. But so, so cold! Inside, she heard Tilly set to work while Meg chattered on, helping her sister.

By the time Emily had fully unpacked the ute, the sun was arcing up over the treeline and the gum boughs were pelting down ice whenever the wind blew, making a sound like hail.

The roofs of the homestead and stables, glaringly white, were now beginning to reveal the grey of the corrugated iron beneath as the snow melted, pouring down from the roof and spilling on to the ground. Small holes had been punched in the tin to allow water into the guttering beneath it, but most of the melt fell like rain. As the sun warmed the paddocks, the grass began to reappear and the world turned from black and white to full colour again.

They traipsed inside, Emily stripping the wet clothes from the girls. They shivered, feet and fingers red raw from the cold, stinging. Meg cried and Tilly whinged, but Emily soon had them huddled by the fire, dressed in fresh dry clothes, and feeling content. She set the mountain of wet clothing to hang beside the fire, then cooked a bacon-and-egg brunch to warm them. As the girls ate, Emily sat with a cuppa and began to make a list.

Lived in over several generations, this place had begun to look tired. For the past twenty years the family's energies had been focused chiefly on attending a constant round of meetings in order to keep their grazing runs. The Flanaghans' enterprise had been built on brothers and sisters, mothers and fathers, all working together as one unit. There might have been hired help now and then, but most of the work they did themselves. One legacy of their constant battle with bureaucracy was that time for them was always in short supply. The high-plains base had suffered. Jobs started there were rarely finished.

Emily saw these next few months as her chance to put things right. She was the custodian of this place now. The woman in her dreams had told her that. All the huts and dwellings, painstakingly crafted by hand by her forebears, would crumble into the soil if she didn't look after them. She would still care for this place, even if she no longer had cattle to run here. The government be damned!

She picked up a pen and began to write a list.

> *Fix Block Paddock fence*
> *Rebuild Lanky's corner strainer*
> *Clad northern stable wall*
> *Nail loose tin on woodshed*
> *Re-swing door in stable*

And so it began. A blueprint for the winter days ahead. The jobs would be crammed in around the labour required just to run the home. There was still mothering to be done, Tilly's home-school lessons to supervise, the cooking, cleaning, firewood to be fetched, and animals to be tended to. And there was the constant, niggling worry that Clancy could show up out of nowhere and destroy it all. But as Evie had taught her,

Emily grappled to control her thoughts, so that the moment she thought of Clancy, she banished him from her head and instead focused on the beauty around her, including her amazing children.

Many of her domestic duties were not so different from those she'd had in suburban Brigalow. But up here the work took on a whole new meaning for Emily. It was another link to the women of the past, Emily and then Joan, who had raised their children here. She sensed them around her now. She felt their grief at losing children to accidents and illness. She felt their pride as they watched their children thrive and grow into fit and competent adults. She felt their mixed emotions when their children moved away to have families of their own.

All that lay in front of her still with her own girls. Always, in the Flanaghan brood, there'd been one or two children who loved the place so much they put down roots here, despite the harshness of the climate and the landscape. Like old Emily's son Archie who had brought Joan to the plains as an eager bride. Emily knew that she was one of these. The one who simply had to remain in this wild beauty. She couldn't tell yet, but Meg or Tilly might have that in them, too. This period of exile, she reasoned, could just be the making of them.

Or the breaking. As the days wore on, cabin fever set in and Emily was tested to the limits by her girls. They were good kids, but their endless banter began to get on her nerves in the tiny rooms. She found herself saying over and over, 'Not so *loud*!'

There was no sending them off to their bedroom to play. It was just too cold. So they all squashed into the kitchen and annoyed each other.

Meg was at first fascinated by the candles on the table and was always blowing at them, making the flames flicker and waver. Tilly's most irritating habit was to pick at the hot wax, sometimes spilling it on to the table surface.

'Ow, ow, ow!' she'd say, flicking her smarting hands. Emily

286

would stifle a scream inside herself, trying as best she could to humour them to bed early, rather than hunt them, just to give herself some space.

When they did at last fall asleep, she would sit down to read a book only to find dissatisfaction brewing in her again. She glanced up to the gas mantel above her that constantly hissed like a pot simmering on a stove. Reading beneath that noisy, dim light was not as pleasurable as reading in a warm, modern, brightly lit home. She told herself not to be so fussy.

She had many, many more luxuries than the Emily long before her, who had first lived in a two-roomed hut on the King's Spur. It made her realise how spoiled she had been in the suburbs, with food nearby at the store, and light and heat at the flick of a switch and running water at the turn of a tap.

Emily struggled, too, with the ever-present dull smell of smoke. It was in her hair, on her clothes, in the house. The fires in the kitchen woodstove and the dining room had to be kept going at all times or the house became an iceblock. Socked feet still froze on the cold linoleum, so they had to wear slippers always, and some nights Emily sat on the couch in the dining room in two jackets, dozing off from exhaustion but unwilling to move away from the fire.

She dressed and undressed as quickly as possible, and never was it warm enough to lie naked between the sheets. In that big, icy bed, she longed for another body to warm her. To have Luke beside her, naked. Instead, she was covered neck-to-toe in thermal underwear, pyjamas, socks, and even a beanie. There was no shower. The cold bathroom only had a tub, the water heated in a small wood furnace. Baths were now once a week only. Emily vaguely realised she was getting fitter and leaner from the constant work of carting wood from the shed and water from the well. In bed occasionally she ran her hands under her clothing, feeling her belly firmer, her waist more slender.

'"Ahh, ah ah, thinking about you naked,"' she sang in her best Sunny Cowgirls voice. She had another flashback then of Luke and herself at the river. All the quashed desires that lingered deep within her came rushing to the surface. A longing came over her so powerfully she thought she would suffocate if she couldn't touch him again. She could visualise him here in this very bed, lying with her, both of them naked. She exhaled and ran her hands gently over her skin beneath her pyjamas, giving herself goosebumps, feeling pleasure rise.

She began to sing again. '". . . and I'm sweating from head to toe just from dreaming 'bout that shirt of yours on my bedroom floor. Undressing you with my eyes – tell me, baby, do you read the signs? Oh-oh-oh, thinking about you naked."'

Emily recalled the sensation of Luke's body under her fingertips. The way she'd slipped her hand down his belly and been delighted by his firmness. How she longed to experience the weight of him pressed against her, the skin on their bodies touching, feeling the electricity flowing between them. Their breath coming fast from passion. It had been so different with Clancy. Luke's lovemaking was generous, his moves so in line with the needs of a woman.

'"Oh, and here you come, stirring naughty thoughts around this head of mine. Leave me breathless, restless, you do. Oh, honey, if you only knew. Oh, oh, thinking about you naked . . ."' she sang.

Then Emily sighed. She grabbed a pillow and shoved it over her head. She had to stop thinking like this!

She exhaled and forced herself to picture Andy from *Little Britain*. Or Dame Edna. She began to sing a medley of Rolf Harris songs. Anything to shake Luke from her mind. But there he was again, in her mind's eye, lying on a mossy riverbank, kissing her. Naked. His buttocks moving rhythmically under her hands as he pushed into her . . .

'Arrgh!' she cried out in frustration. She began to recite nursery rhymes, and an hour after she'd gone to bed, finally found sleep.

Deep in the night, the curtains stirred. No window was open and there was no breeze outside. Emily was not awake to see, but as something gentle drifted by, only Rousie lifted his head from where he lay by the fire and flopped his tail once in a lazy wag.

In a brand-new house in Bairnsdale, Penny stood barefoot on the plush peach carpet clenching her fists.

'Arrgh!' she cried, her ice-blue eyes wide with fury. Clancy stood on the porch beneath the faux Cobb & Co.-era gaslight, his coat half on, his keys in his hand, looking sheepishly at the petite woman who stood angrily before him.

'If you go, Clancy, I promise you, I'll do appalling things to your truck! And I'll lock you out of the house forever!'

'Oh, baby,' he said, his face twisted in confusion, 'But shouldn't I just go once? To see if they're okay up there? I won't even speak to *her*. I'll just see the girls, then come straight home.'

'Oh my God!' screamed Penny, 'You idiot! Every time! *Every time* you get full of Jim Beam you do this.' She waggled her head as she parodied his deep voice. 'My girls! My girls! I have to see my girls!' Her speckled hand ran over the curve of her stomach beneath her sheer baby-doll pink negligee. 'What about *these* girls, huh, Clancy?'

Her nails were painted the same colour as her nightie and her red hair, longer now, fell about her slender white shoulders. He took in the spectacular way the light behind her shone right through the nightie so he could see her entire outline, even the bits between her legs. Penny saw where his gaze was fixed. It was her cue. Her voice altered. She spoke more softly.

'Why drive up there now? Drunk and in the dark. You're being a bit silly, aren't you, Clancy?'

He looked down at his boots, one on, one off. He knew that what she was saying was true. Then she said his name, softly, purring it like a kitten. She tilted her chin downwards but looked up at him with those come-to-bed eyes. Slowly her hand slid along her upper thigh lifting her already short nightie even higher.

Before he knew it, Clancy had kicked off the other boot,

slung away his coat, and was pressing Penny up against the freshly painted wall, and she was pressing her crotch hard against him.

'If you really want to go,' she said, panting, rubbing her hand over the insistent erection in his jeans, 'I'll go with you tomorrow. I promise, baby, I promise.'

'Don't worry about it,' he murmured, kissing her neck and cupping his hands over her perfect tiny breasts. 'I'm home now. I'm staying with my girl. My girl.' As he dropped his pants, picked her up and thrust into her, he repeated over and over, 'My girl. My girl.' Penny responded with porn-star moans.

When he was done she smiled, cupping her hands around his beautiful face, kissing him over and over. Men were all the same, she thought. Especially this divinely gorgeous one. Nursing had taught her more than just caring for patients. Working in the big city hospitals and her shifts out in the bush had shown her men at their most vulnerable, taught her their basest needs. She'd had many of them, but for her Clancy was a dream come true. Good-looking beyond belief with only one major need. Once it was fulfilled, he could be steered in any direction.

'Oh, I love you,' she said. 'You make me *so* happy.' And as Clancy kissed her back he let his guilt about his first family melt away. He pushed the thought of Meg and Tilly from his mind. As Penny began fall to her knees in front of him, he realised he was happy too. For the first time in a long while.

Thirty-four

A fter weeks of living in snow, the horses and ponies now picked their way through the rocky, icy-white landscape with sure-footed certainty. Emily, Tilly and Meg rode out most days on adventures across the mountains. Today the fog had lifted early, leaving them with relatively warm, settled weather.

Emily was keen to teach the kids all she knew of the mountains. She had a hunch that the roads from Dargo would be closed after such a heavy overnight fall. It had been a relief for her to be so isolated. It meant the niggling worries that Clancy could turn up any moment to challenge her over the girls could be forgotten.

Today, also, she knew she wouldn't be caught by the rangers taking Rousie on to Parkland. They were on their way to the Long Spur, where she would show the girls one of the conservation reserves their great-grandparents had established.

As they trotted over the snow plains, it was a joy for Emily to see Meg's and Tilly's faces bright with exhilaration. Their little ponies looked comical, like Thelwell cartoons, leaping the tufts of grass and dodging rocks, while her girls stuck to their backs with ease. There had been a couple of spills in the early days, but the soft cover of snow over spongy snow grass had broken any falls, so that now, young though they were,

Tilly and Meg were confident and happy to ride for hours at a time. Tilly especially had altered since her horse had become the focus of interest for her. She mentioned her father less and less; seemed so much more settled.

In the natural snow-grass clearings, they paused to study high mountain tops, watching clouds race towards them in great tumbling walls that would eventually obliterate the views. Some days were perfectly still, others perfectly wild, an icy wind whipping the horses' tails into a frenzy, wrenching hats from heads. Most days were a mix of both heaven and hell, the weather forever changing – and changing fast.

They rode with scarves wrapped about their faces to stop the icy sting of the freezing air entering their lungs. Emily carried a backpack of food and, tied to her saddle and to Bonus's pack saddle, her cattleman tools.

She was training the young gelding as a packhorse. He might as well be versatile. She had strapped her grandfather's old saddle packs to him, weighted evenly to either side. Inside them she stored a chainsaw – not so big as to be a real nuisance but large enough to slice through any limbs of trees that had fallen across the fencelines. She also stored loops of high-tensile wire, some fencing pliers, staples, a hammer, a hatchet, a small shovel and some strainers. Bonus was a steady-minded horse and had taken to his job well, trailing Snowgum happily on the end of a lead rope. If the gear caught on a tree, he wouldn't spook but would plant his feet and wait patiently for Emily to come and unhitch him. Despite his being a constant reminder of Luke, Emily was beginning to love the horse as they journeyed together over the snow-topped mountains.

Some of the fencelines she checked as she rode were those that separated the Flanaghans' own small acreage of private land, but most of the fences ran between paddocks now classed on the map as National Park. A large portion of the land had never been fenced so there was some work to be done if Emily and her family were ever to run a small token herd up on the home paddocks and State Forest areas of the now diminished and divided station.

When they reached the Long Spur track, Emily saw that snow had settled quite deeply. She pointed out the Mount Hotham and Dinner Plain ski-fields on the ridgeline opposite to the girls. Tiny black dots of skiers, like ants, could be seen weaving this way and that down the mountainside, surfing the white snow drifts. At the end of their skiing day, the holiday-makers would head to the showers, the bars, the restaurants and the bands, or even flick on the TV or surf the internet for entertainment.

Emily found it amazing to think she could see such sophisticated 'civilisation' from where she stood. The stillness here was in stark contrast to the busy, self-obsessed and distracting buzz of the ski-fields.

Here she sat on her horse, with her daughters, in land that was still beautiful after one hundred and fifty years of controlled cattle grazing. This spur was one of her favourite places and a particularly lovely lunch stop when mustering . . . apart from that grating view of the ever-expanding ski villages and communication and electricity towers opposite.

The Long Spur ran alongside a majestic cliff-face that dropped down into a massive valley full of bush below that was known as Devil's Hollow. Emily sat trying to get her head around the fact that while her family and their stock were banned from this place, on the opposite mountain thousands of skiers were welcome to run riot over the landscape.

She had nothing against the skiers, but she did feel enraged by the developers who profited from their use of the land-scape in such a way. As she watched the swarms of people skiing over the mountainside and the sunlight reflecting off the ski villas that poured sewage out into septics that seeped down the mountainside, the government decision to ban the cattlemen, while encouraging the ski developers, weighed heavily on her.

What the skiers never saw was the massive scarring their

winter recreation left behind. They were never up here in the summer to see the way the land was compacted so that the vegetation struggled to grow. Even when the snow melted and the soil was watered back to life and warmed by the sun, slopes that should have been shooting green remained brown and undernourished.

She could see the scars of roads, the runways of an airport, and soon a pipeline for a sewage-treatment plant and dams for more water supplies would mar the mountainside. She could see the sharp-angled roofs of private villas huddled together in cul-de-sacs like transported suburbs. Abruptly she turned her horse away from the sight.

'C'mon, girls, let's go light a fire and have a hot drink. We're almost there.'

Despite a new VPP sign declaring everything was now banned from this land, including domestic animals, firearms and fires, they continued riding towards a brand-new bright yellow boomgate. It hurt Emily to see it there. She set Snowgum at a canter and, leading Bonus, jumped over the low rail. The girls' ponies, small enough to squeeze around the strainer post and a boulder, followed their mother, Meg's knee catching on the post.

'Why'd they put that there?' she said in annoyance.

'Because a man in Melbourne said they had to,' Emily answered.

They rode on a little down the eastern ridge until the snow became so deep they opted to turn back towards her grandparents' reserve. Emily had wanted to see the plain where she and Sam had last salted cattle, but decided it would be best to keep closer to the ridgetop. The weather could close in at any moment.

On the ride back up to the boomgate she ducked off the track. There she pointed out a sign her dad had made.

'It says, Flanaghan Reserve Number Five,' she explained.

'What's a reverse?' Tilly asked.

'A *reserve*,' Emily corrected her. 'It's an area of land protected from people and some animals, to help keep it healthy. This one is a sensitive spring that we don't want four-wheel drives or cattle or people in.'

'Why is it a five?' asked Meg.

'Because it's the fifth reserve your great-grandparents set up. They made ten reserves on this mountain.'

Emily's grandparents had opted to enclose special areas of the mountains nearly sixty years earlier, long before the term 'conservation' was thought of in government departments. In some places the fences had also kept the four-wheel drive enthusiasts at bay, since they seemed to like to carve their vehicles through boggy patches, steep slopes prone to erosion, and river crossings just for fun. While the cattle might never return to this ridgeline, the four-wheel drives that came in their hundreds from the city and surrounding regions were still permitted into the Park in summertime. Preservation of the economy at all costs, thought Emily wryly.

As they rode towards the reserve, she was disappointed to see that a tree had recently fallen, knocking a fence post sideways. The reserve's fence wire lay slack, flung back against the earth. Emily drew the horses up.

'Shall we fix it for old Pa and Ma?'

Tilly and Meg nodded.

'It shouldn't take long,' she said, glancing up at the sky, knowing the rough weather would eventually come.

The girls dismounted and tethered their ponies as she lit them a small fire and put the billy on it, scooping up clean snow and placing it inside the tin. She set out cups and filled each with a spoonful or three of Milo and a dash of sugar.

With the girls settled and drinking happily, Emily examined the damage done by the fallen tree. Soon the sound of her chainsaw cut through the air, shattering the peace of the mountainside as she separated the twisted old snow gum from the fence. As it cracked and splintered away and she kicked it with her boot, she saw that the old post her grandfather would have dug into the ground was shattered too.

'Bugger,' she said. A new one was needed. That job would take a little longer. Still, Tilly and Meg were warm by the fire and it was a while before dark. They had a good two hours' ride back to the house, but the horses were fit now and well used to the cold, as were the girls. She also knew there was a hut just half an hour's ride down the eastern slope should they really get stuck.

Emily cast her eye about. No suitable trees on the former cattlemen's side of the Park. One was too twisted. One would split at the knot. The others were too small or too big. She took an axe and the chainsaw and soon found her tree. It was close to hand, the perfect diameter. She set about felling it.

As Luke Bradshaw and Giles Grimsley inched their way over Lanky's Plain, Luke tried not to think of the word 'wanker' every time his boss finished speaking. But he had to concede that some of the stories Giles had told him about the cattlemen's antics, and the scientific data on grazing he'd given Luke to read, almost convinced him their eviction was necessary.

Luke and Giles had spent the day together at a VPP luncheon-conference on the Hotham snowfields where Luke had met some more interesting VPP colleagues, confirming there were some really bright people in the organisation. They were people of around his own age, who were fun and enthusiastic about their work. They'd all filled their bellies with food and enjoyed a couple of glasses of wine or beer before Giles announced it was time for them to leave.

Although the High Plains Road over to Dargo was closed due to snow, Giles had insisted on travelling home over it with Luke as part of his four-wheel-drive training component. Giles was proud to announce that, as VPP-registered staff, they were permitted access to the snowfall areas of the Dargo High Plains in times of closure. Luke knew Giles's role as acting region manager was coming to an end soon and he was making the most of it. He had talked several times about the benefits of having a vehicle and time to travel about away from his Melbourne desk. He'd also been crowing about the trip to Wonnangatta, the fining process still underway, and about the new legislation and plans for the Park.

'It's been a pleasure to take you under my wing,' he said, nose still red from the lunchtime wine. Luke endured his condescending mentoring with good humour, in the same way as he'd endured Cassy's bossing. He reasoned it was only for a couple of days. Soon Giles would return to Melbourne, slipping back down the ladder. Luke would then be left in peace in his new job, which so far seemed to involve a lot of driving to the Heyfield office and not so much work out in the bush.

The road back towards Dargo had been reasonable until they reached Mount Freezeout, where snow had begun to thicken and the tyres started spinning, even in the four-wheel drive. Giles was clearly excited to get the new chains out from his off-road kit.

'We'll be late getting home tonight,' he said to Luke. 'But don't worry. You'll be paid overtime.'

Luke cast him a glance. It had never crossed his mind he should be paid extra for being late. On the farm, they'd worked until dark or beyond until the job was done, and there was no talk of overtime. At the VPP, however, everyone reminded him to work exactly seven hours and thirty-six minutes a day. Apparently the extra six minutes earned him a Rostered Day Off every fortnight. But Luke still couldn't understand the prompt laying down of tools once the clock ticked over, even if the job was an hour shy of getting done. There'd been no RDOs on the land.

They were travelling where the snow lay thickest on top of a ridge when Luke saw smoke curling up from the trees into the clear winter-blue sky.

He pointed it out to Giles.

'What in the devil's name? Campers out *here*! This time of year . . . during Park closure? Turn off, boy! Turn off!' he said as if about to embark on a Hornblower adventure.

297

They spotted the little girls first, sitting beside the campfire. Luke was as shocked to see them there as his boss was.

'Fancy bringing children out under such dangerous conditions!' Giles huffed. Then they saw Emily wielding a chainsaw a little way off in the trees.

'She must be *mad*. And she's cutting down a tree on Park land! I think it's the same woman who hid the cattle from us in the Wonnangatta. A typical Flanaghan. Trouble!'

'Yes, I think it is,' said Luke, feeling the blood drain from his face.

Rousie pinned his ears down as the chainsaw droned away. The noise was enough to mask the sound of the approaching vehicle which had pulled up at the boomgate. By the time the tree fell, with a loud crash that echoed out across the massive valley below, the ranger's vehicle, with chains on its wheels, had rolled to a halt not far from the campfire. As Emily cut the chainsaw engine she heard the sound of doors slamming and looked up, startled.

She breathed in sharply when she saw it was Luke, feeling excitement and horror run through her. Then she noticed the older VPP man, the red-haired one who'd been at the Wonnangatta, with the same serious look on his face. She was about to call out a greeting but saw how Luke avoided her eyes, busily pulling on his coat, a hat and gloves, and grabbing a notebook from his pocket.

Together the men made their way towards her, following the tracks made by the horses. They looked so official and serious, marching through the trees in uniform.

'What do you think you're doing?' asked the red-haired man.

Emily was about to begin her explanations and excuses when she felt the earth pulse beneath her boots and warmth radiate through her body, filling her with a fiery strength. She thought of Evie then and of her great-grandmothers, Emily Flanaghan and Joan Flanaghan. She held her head high, and in a strong but friendly voice replied: 'What am I doing? Why, I'm introducing myself to you in the polite, old-fashioned way, as bushmen always do.' She held out her hand. 'Emily Flanaghan, very pleased to meet you, Mr . . .?'

The man looked down at her hand as if it stank of dead fish.

Luke interrupted. 'Emily, this is Mr Giles Grimsley, acting region manager for the VPP.'

He couldn't believe his misfortune in finding her here. Her daughters looked at him with wide possum eyes, clearly scared their mother was in trouble. Luke saw the gelding he had sold her laden with packs, work-fit but well-fed, standing calmly hitched to a tree. He swallowed nervously. He could tell this was going to get ugly.

Now Giles stood in front of Emily, casting daggers with his gaze. 'You do know it's an offence to fell trees in a National Park? What do you think you're doing?'

'Isn't it obvious?' she said, gesturing to the broken fence. 'I cut a tree down because I needed a new post. For the reserve.'

'But it's an offence to cut down a tree from a National Park.'

Emily looked at him incredulously and then towards Luke for help. His eyes, she thought, were reluctant to meet hers.

'I'm hardly likely to duck down to Bunnings to get a post, am I?' she protested. 'Not when there's a perfect one just there in the bush!'

'You are not responsible for fencing in this area,' Giles told her.

Emily looked again at Luke but still his eyes would not meet hers. Was he just going to stand there and say nothing?

'Excuse me,' she said, anger creeping into her voice, 'but I *am* responsible for this fence. My grandparents put in that reserve to protect the spring in that thicket there. I figure it's my responsibility to preserve my family's work and continue to protect the spring.'

'Your family no longer has any claim over this land,' Giles said with satisfaction. He'd had years of battling these cattlemen from his office. To be out in the field with one now and experiencing such arrogance face to face was enough to make his blood boil.

'I don't want to *claim* this land,' Emily shot back. 'I just want to *care* for it.'

'Care for it by cutting down trees?' Giles said sarcastically. 'You cattlemen only *pretend* to be environmentalists. If you really cared for the high country, you'd take your kids, your horses and your cattle, and get off this mountain!'

Emily's mouth dropped open.

'You arsehole,' she said, the words escaping her before she could help herself. She saw his jaw clench and a flash of hatred on his face.

Giles steered Luke away, talking quietly. Luke nodded, frowning, and wrote something down in his notebook.

They both came back.

'If you continue to abuse me, this will become a matter for the police,' Giles announced. 'Plus, you have endangered the lives of your children by bringing them into such a remote and rugged area when the Park is closed. Which begs the question whether you are fit to be mothering these children at all.'

Emily was speechless with rage. Didn't this man know that the Flanaghans had taken their children all over this mountain for generations? Didn't he know that some of the Flanaghan boys had worked packing horses in the snow, to help get mail and supplies through to hungry miners, from as young as nine years of age?

How dare he insinuate that she was risking her children's safety? She *knew* they were safe. She had plans and provisions for every scenario. She had her animals with them, too, and they had the best bush skills of all. Rousie and her horses would guide them home no matter what. She stood quivering with fury at the arrogance and ignorance of this government desk jockey.

Giles stepped back. 'Now my colleague Mr Bradshaw will inform you of the Park regulations you have breached.'

And Luke, his face dark and closed, began to read from his notebook. Emily looked at the face she had once thought was beautiful, and the lips she had kissed and dreamt of kissing again, as he read on and on in a monotone.

'Dogs are prohibited on Park land. You will be fined for breaching this regulation under Park policy. You will incur a fine for riding horses on Park land without an out-of-season permit. You are in serious breach of Park policy in the felling of a tree. That too will incur a fine. You are in breach of Park safety regulations in venturing into an area that is closed to the public. The presence of children here is also a serious act of negligence and the police and Family Services will be informed of this.'

'Now wait a minute!' Emily interrupted, 'My children? You're saying I'm neglecting my kids, Luke? You can't report me for that! What if . . . you can't . . .' her voice wavered.

'Ms Flangahan, silence!' Giles barked. 'Let my colleague continue.'

Emily couldn't believe she was hearing this. Her eyes filled with tears as she searched desperately for one kind look from Luke. Instead, he kept reading from his stupid green notebook.

'The lighting of fires in a non-designated campfire area is also a breach of Park policy. The total of these infringements will amount to $2,312, pending a hearing.' He then began to read her her rights. When he had finished, he tried to maintain his steely expression, but Emily was sure she could see shame underlying it. He still wouldn't look her in the eye. She felt fury rise within her. An icy breeze whirled snow about and brought with it a white mist that began to blanket everything about them. Inside Emily, anger and distress were swirling in her too.

'How can you do this? How can you be like this?' she said softly, the question addressed more to Luke than to Giles

Grimsley. She was devastated. She was only trying to do the right thing: by the land and by the people who had cared for it before her. She paid her taxes. She respected others. And she truly did care for the land. How could Luke threaten her and her children like this? And how could Giles Grimsley say that cattlemen weren't environmentalists when most of her family had lived as environmentalists long before it became trendy to do so? Yet here she was, being treated like a criminal in her own sacred place. And to threaten her girls too! Here was Luke, siding with Giles and kicking her when she was lower than low. For weeks she'd heard nothing from Clancy – as if his girls no longer existed for him. His lack of support still stung. And now Luke was treating her the same way. Did the fact that they had been lovers count for nothing?

Emily called out to Meg and Tilly, 'C'mon, girls. Let's leave these gentlemen to their *Park*.'

'You'll be hearing from us, Ms Flanaghan,' Giles Grimsley said, holding out the fine documentation.

Emily snatched the paper from him. As the weather worsened, Giles retreated to the warmth of the four-wheel-drive cab and waited for Luke to join him. But he remained out in the freezing snowfall, watching Emily pack away her gear on the gelding he'd sold her. He felt the immense pressure of his superior's eyes watching his every move. The way Emily had said his name had surely given away the fact that he had been fraternising with the locals. He watched, scowling, as her girls efficiently put out the fire, packed the billy and pannikins into their saddle bags, and swung up on to their ponies. Emily quickly stashed her tools into Bonus's packs and expertly hitched them tight again. Then she lobbed up on to Snowgum. She grabbed up her reins and rode right past Luke, nearly knocking him over. She set her eyes on the man in the vehicle who stared back at her with contempt.

Knowing she should guide the men back to the main road in this weather, but too angry to offer, she kicked Snowgum into a canter and popped her and Bonus over the boomgate.

Her girls, in a rush of bravado, followed their mother at the jump, the littlest pony just clipping the yellow boom with the tip of her nearside rear hoof. Then they jogged away as fast as they could through the snow, keen to leave the strict and scary men behind. As they veered left off the track into the snow gums, Emily fought back tears. But she had little time to let her emotions get the better of her. It *was* a total white-out. They couldn't see more than a metre in front of their horses. Stuff them! she thought. Emily tugged her hat down low and flipped her collar up. She smiled. She knew that if she simply gave Snowgum her head, the old mare would guide them all safely home along the winding bridle tracks. This was her place. This was her home.

Thirty-five

When they at last reached the homestead, Emily and the girls were surprised to see Evie's little four-wheel-drive Suzuki parked in the shed, the chains on the wheels still crusted with snow.

'Evie!' Meg shrieked.

'You go on inside and get warm,' Emily said. 'I'll fix the ponies.' She didn't want her girls to see her cry, but that was all she wanted to do right then.

'Thanks, Mum,' said Tilly, eyes aglow at the thought of their very special visitor. Then the girls were running inside to the warmth of Evie.

When Emily came in, red-eyed and red-nosed, she found the visitor dishing up steaming soup to Meg and Tilly. They were already scoffing chunks of fresh bread coated thickly with dobs of Evie's homemade butter.

'What are you doing here, Evie? The snow! I thought you'd come up after it melted.'

'I didn't know we were going to have such a season! Plus, driving in snow is easy-peasy compared to driving in bull-dust in the desert,' Evie said with a wink. As she sat Emily down in front of a steaming plate of delicious chicken and vegetable soup, Emily realised she knew almost nothing of her friend's past. She knew Evie was a nurse, knew she had worked in Aboriginal communities in the desert, but didn't know where she came from, about her family, even if she had any children.

Emily was about to ask when Evie said, 'You look like you've had a tough day.' Emily felt a wave of despair then as she recalled Luke's strained face and cold voice. She bit her lip and looked down. Evie patted her hand. 'One moment.'

She pulled out a platter of chocolates from the meat safe and passed them to Tilly.

'There you are, my darlings. You go sit by the fire and enjoy these. We'll bring you a hot chocolate in just a moment.'

'Thanks, Evie!' Meg said.

The girls gone to the next room, Evie drew up a chair next to Emily's. 'Tell me,' she said, her green eyes blazing.

So Emily told her about Giles Grimsley, who had acted so superior, who had come on to her family's sacred place and made her feel like dirt, like she was an outsider in her own heartland.

'To top it all, Luke was there,' she said, 'and he did *nothing* to help me. Instead he threw the book at me! They're going to fine me and inform some other department that I'm not a fit mother!'

'They're not! Oh, Em,' said Evie, drawing Emily into her arms. 'What a load of rot. You're a fine mother and a fine bushman.'

'But what if they take the girls from me, Evie?' She was crying now.

'Emily my dear, they won't. It's just men asserting their power. Don't feed it any energy. Don't think about it. It will blow over. You know the truth – that your girls are getting the best upbringing any child could have! Teaching them to be part of this wilderness and not fear it is a gift. Unconventional nowadays, so the authorities may not understand, but Luke does. He gets it.'

'But why didn't he do something! Say something to his boss!'

'He was just protecting himself.'

'But worrying about a *job* ahead of what is morally right? I thought he was so much better than that.'

'Oh, I think you'll find he is. But perhaps Luke was protecting himself from something else.' Emily looked confused. Evie lifted her eyebrows. 'My dear, can't you see? He was protecting himself from you.'

'From me?'

'Yes. He's in love with you.'

The words seemed to hang in the air. Emily frowned. 'But–'

'There are no buts. He has a soul connection to you that runs so deep it frightens him. And the time isn't yet right in this lifetime for you to join him.'

Emily almost rolled her eyes but something stopped her. She could see such conviction in Evie that she began to allow her words to sink in. Evie never tried to *prove* her theories to her and Sam. She just spoke as if things simply *were* as she said they were.

'We all have a body, right? And inside that body is a soul that, when we die, leaves this planet for the non-physical realm. Sometimes those souls come back in other bodies. That's why sometimes when you meet someone new it feels like you've known them for an age. You get that feeling because you *have* known them for an age! Sometimes for thousands of years over many lifetimes. Sometimes there are advanced souls in the non-physical world that guide you in the physical one. That's how it is for all of us. The more you're tuned in to it, the more you'll see it.'

Emily shook her head. Until meeting Evie, until her accident, she'd never contemplated stuff like this. Some days she was up for Evie's strange notions. But tonight she was tired. Her face felt raw from a day spent in the bitter cold. She felt deeply hurt by the encounter with Giles Grimsley, and by Luke's coldness. A log in the kitchen woodstove moved, making her jump.

'My God,' said Evie. 'You're a mess, girl! C'mon, I'll make

you a hot chocolate as well,' she offered, getting up from the table. 'I think I'd better slip some of your Aunt Flo's harder stuff into it too. Now get up off your backside and on to that couch in the sitting room to snuggle with your girls. I'll bring it in.'

'Thank you. Thank you so much, Evie,' Emily said wearily.

She dozed off before Evie arrived with her hot chocolate. She dreamed of cattle in the snow, plunging deeply through drifts, Tilly and Meg following them on ponies. Emily was screaming at them all to stop, but no sound would come from her mouth. The snowy landscape was silent despite her internal screams. She watched in horror as the girls, their ponies and the cattle all tumbled over the cliff, bodies thudding violently against rocks as they fell. On the mountain opposite, the skiers watched and toasted the sight with shining glass flutes of bubbling champagne.

She woke suddenly to the shrill ringing of the radio-phone. Evie must have put the girls to bed as they were no longer with her on the couch. She grappled on the mantelpiece for matches and lit a lantern. In the armchair beside her, Evie was stirring awake.

'Who could that be?' she said sleepily.

Emily hurried to the phone.

'Emily?' There was a delay as the radio-phone beamed its signal to the satellite tower and back.

'Dad?'

'Just had a call from the VPP. Any sign of two rangers up your way? It seems they're missing. Were due back this afternoon in Dargo, but there was no show.'

She asked her father the time.

'It's after midnight.'

'Yeah, I've seen 'em,' she said.

'Where?'

'Out on the Long Spur.'

'When?'

'Dad,' she broke in, 'it was awful. They tried to ping me

307

on all fronts – when all the girls and I were doing was fixing a bloody fence at Ma and Pa's reserve at the spring! They reckon they'll fine me or take me to court. And they said they'll get Family Services in – that I'm not a fit mother. Just for . . . for . . . I dunno what! So I left 'em. Out there on the Long Spur, at some new boomgate, in a white-out . . .'

'Oh, Emily,' her father sighed.

'I thought they'd be right! They're supposed to be rangers. They weren't far off the track.'

'That young bloke is brand new and wouldn't have been up there more than once or twice, and you know it! And the other fella – well, he's from Melbourne. Plus, you know it's a black spot for radio reception that side of the range.'

'The trees were blazed – I even did a couple of fresh marks myself on my way through.'

'They wouldn't know to look for the blazes.'

'I know,' she said quietly, feeling guilty that she hadn't guided the men out to the main road where modern snow markers of orange plastic flagged the worst parts of the snow-covered route. 'I was so mad, Dad. I'm sorry.'

'I'll have to tell the authorities. If they're really lost, there could be all kinds of enquiries and you could find yourself more than fined!'

Emily fell silent, fearing again for her girls. She resolved she'd do something. She'd go find the men . . . but as she did her father predicted her thoughts.

'Don't rush out in the morning,' he said. 'The weather's not meant to lift until mid-morning anyway. I'll call you then. Chances are they'll send a chopper across from Hotham at first light.'

'A chopper! Are you serious? They've only been gone one night. They'll be okay if they stay with the vehicle and I know at least one of them has the sense to do that,' Emily said, thinking of Luke.

She bit her fingernails. She was so confused by his behaviour. He was a farm boy, but he'd been touched by a government culture that seemed to skew his perception of real life. She thought of him reading aloud that list of infringements, his voice a monotone, devoid of any emotion. Was a job so important to him that he couldn't speak up for her?

When Emily put down the phone, Evie was standing behind her, her hair sticking up on one side from sleeping in the chair.

'You must be like a sapling,' she advised.

'A sapling?'

'Yes, not a rigid tree trunk. Saplings bend with the winds of trouble and bounce back quickly when times are still. But trees that are inflexible in the wind are simply blown over. Try not to resist what life throws at you, Emily. You must be flexible and bend with it. Be in the flow. And, remember, never shrink to be a tussock.'

'A tussock?' she said, leaning forward and hoping for more pearls of wisdom. 'Why not a tussock?'

Evie looked her in the eye and Emily saw a twinkle in her friend's eye. 'Because dogs and wombats crap on tussocks.'

Evie began to laugh then, and so too did Emily.

They both made their way back to the dining room where they stoked up the fire and resettled themselves under blankets on the couches. There was no way Emily could sleep now, knowing Luke was still out there, probably with the engine running for warmth, shut in the four-wheel drive with only his boss for company. But, she thought angrily, he deserved it.

The next day, despite what Rod had said, Emily set out early with the wind whipping about her. Evie stayed behind with the girls, who for the first time were not begging to come out for another ride. Even though the weather was rough, Emily knew their reluctance was mostly because they didn't want to go near the grumpy man again. Meg had mentioned Giles Grimsley several times last night, saying in Evie's words that he had an 'angry energy' and even had 'angry hair'.

Emily didn't want to go near Giles again either, but as she

rode Bonus towards the Long Spur, she knew she was doing this for Luke, no matter how awful he had been to her. Suddenly, the clouds parted and sunshine poured down upon the snow. She thought about Evie's view that Luke loved her. If he did, surely he would have stuck up for her yesterday. With the warmth of the morning sun on her face, Emily realised now that she couldn't help but feel something very strong for Luke too. No matter what he'd done. She thought of Evie's talk about souls last night and 'other lives', past and future. If she and Luke couldn't be together in this lifetime, Emily decided now, she would look for him first in her next life.

She felt comforted by that thought and urged Bonus on faster. He was breathing heavily, as the effort of walking through deep snow was great, but he was also fit and lean and completely bonded to Emily. Even though she was riding out to find two lost men and the situation could be serious, Emily felt lightness within her. She was enjoying the solitude, the first time in weeks she'd had time off from being a mum, just her and Bonus. Her one link with Luke. What a gift he was.

As she rode, she recalled a story about her grandfather's bushman's knack for finding people who had become lost on the vast ridges of the high plains. On one occasion he'd ridden right up to a large log in a gully where he figured the bush-walker might have wandered, hopelessly lost. Sure enough the walker was there, lying asleep on the lee side of the log, cold but none the worse for wear. The walker was woken by the deep voice of Emily's grandfather saying, 'So, do you want to be found today, boy?' It seemed only fitting that here again, Emily was looking out for stranded people on the mountain. Ironically enough, VPP employees in the year of the bans.

On the last zigzag pinch on to the track, Emily pulled her horse up short in the cover of the trees. There they were, and with them a further three vehicles that had travelled from Mout Hotham and Dargo. There were rangers and SES crew everywhere, laughing and chatting. In the huddle stood Luke and his boss. Relieved for him, Emily watched for a while.

She was about to swing her horse around when Luke looked up as if he'd sensed her there, sitting astride the big young chestnut amidst the snow and the twisted limbs of the trees. She saw his face open up fleetingly with a flicker of warmth, then he shut it back down again. She too tried to mask her hurt with a haughty expression but then she remembered the warmth of his touch at the river and couldn't stop the tiny glimmer of a smile from passing across her face. She cast her eyes down, grappling to regain her composure, her breath as visible as a dragon's, quickening from the mere recollection of his kisses. When she looked at him again he was smiling back at her. The most gentle, beautiful smile. He slowly shook his head and mouthed 'Sorry' to her. Emily tried not to return his smile, but knew her face betrayed her.

He's not for me in this lifetime, she told herself again. She would be beholden to no man. And she was no longer only a cattleman's daughter, but a cattleman in her own right. She was a strong woman who could survive on her own, living a rich, wonderful life. Like a sapling, she would bend to any troubles that came her way. But for now, no more men.

'Goodbye,' she whispered. 'See you in another life.'

She turned and urged her horse on, sliding, laughing and tumbling her way down the track, enjoying the bright clear warmth of the sun but keen to be home again, with her girls and Evie.

Thirty-six

Weeks later, Emily was surprised to see a solitary yellow daffodil blooming beneath a sprinkling of snow beside the stable. Spring had arrived on the mountains, and this one special winter with her daughters was coming to an end.

After that first bloom, spring began to reveal itself all around them. Emily pointed out to Meg and Tilly the shoots of granny bonnets emerging from the icy soil. Above them, bright green, red and blue parrots skittered overhead, flirting in their own private mating ritual. Mother Nature was nudging Emily to accept that her self-imposed isolation was over. It was time to pack up and go back to the lowlands, time to make a new life.

As she carried bags out to the ute, Emily held within her a sense of accomplishment – she had not merely endured the winter here, but had thrived in it. She had ticked off many of the jobs on her list and also added more, knowing she was free to come and go from here as she pleased. It was her home. She was no longer answerable to any man. She felt altogether changed.

She now had a lean, fit body, and her mind was sharp too. The only thing worrying her was how she was going to earn an income. She had no formal qualifications. But she pushed the worries away and focused on the positives.

Tilly and Meg had also thrived in this wilderness and as she watched them now, dragging their backpacks on to the verandah, she saw they were very different children from the meek little ones she'd mothered in the suburban house in Brigalow. She realised how withdrawn they had been there, hunkering down in front of the television if Clancy was in a rage. But now, they rarely asked after their father, and seemed so alive and engaged with the world around them that they offered to help with everything and asked questions all the time.

There was no need to pack everything up. The horses would stay in the vast home paddock and the food could remain in the pantry as Emily knew they'd be back soon. She now planned to live between the two houses – her father's on the lowlands and here. She was heading down now to enrol the girls at the school for next year, then would travel back up for the summer holidays. Perhaps she could get a job in the pub or the store so she could pay the bills that would no doubt follow now they were heading back to the modern world.

Soon they set off down the mountain road. They called in to Evie's but she wasn't about. As they reached the foothills of the mountains, the rivers were fresh from snowmelt, the water rushing and burbling over rocks. On the road into Dargo, the giant walnut trees, once winter skeletons, were beginning to shoot huge green shady leaves. The gums frothed with flowers.

Emily drove past the church and the school. She held her breath when she passed the ranger's office, both wanting and not wanting to see Luke. But his vehicle was not there, and she laughed at herself for the mixture of relief and disappointment that swirled in her.

Tranquillity's driveway was flanked prettily by walnut trees and elms in true Dargo fashion. Emily drove past Bob's house, surprised to see DD back on his chain and bouncing up and down. For the first time ever the dog's coat was glossy and

313

he was actually fat. Bob's lawn was mown, not grazed, and the daffodils in the garden beds that had survived from her grandparents' days had been joined by other bright spring blooms that had obviously been *planted*. Emily frowned. Had someone else moved into Bob's?

She had barely switched off the vehicle before Meg and Tilly were out, bounding up the verandah steps. They ran into the house calling out, 'Grandpa, Grandpa!'

There was no one about. The house was silent, the kitchen empty. They came banging back out through the big wooden screen door their faces subdued.

'No one's home.'

Emily frowned again. She'd rung to say they would be here around lunchtime.

'They're probably out working,' she said. 'We'll see them later. Come on. Help Mum with the bags.'

The girls, a little grumpy now, lugged bags into the homestead. As they walked along the hallway they heard a noise.

A snickering.

'Shush,' Emily said to them. 'Did you hear that?'

Meg's and Tilly's eyes lit up. 'They're playing tricks!'

Suddenly they could hear Jesus Christ barking madly from behind the one closed door in the house, the dining room's. Swinging it open, they were met with a chorus of voices shouting, 'Surprise!' Jesus Christ bounded up and down on the spot and made snuffling noises instead.

The Flanaghan family stood around the table, which was laden with a lunchtime feast that was clearly Evie's work. Emily was amazed to see Sam there with his arm around Bridie. His cheeky handsome face glowed with good health and Bridie beamed a welcoming smile at Emily. Evie stood beside Rod, who radiated love and pride for his daughter and granddaughters. Next to him stood Flo, towering over Baz, one arm slung about his shoulders. And beside them, to Emily's astonishment, stood Uncle Bob.

He had lost weight, shaved his head, and had a fresh tattoo

314

of a flaming comet on his forearm. He was wearing tight black jeans with a silver studded belt and a black T-shirt with one of Keith Urban's funky country rock designs on it. He even wore an earring!

Emily, tears brimming, rushed to hug each and every one of them as they told her how fit and strong she looked and how beautiful the girls were. They began to trip over their words and conversation ran this way and that as Emily tried to take in all their news.

'Sam's album will be out next year,' Bridie told her. 'Ike reckons Compass really like the demos we recorded and they'll sign him!'

'And Bridie's going to get paid as my PA and wardrobe assistant,' Sam said, clutching her hand, clearly proud of her.

'Stylist,' she corrected him.

'*Stylist*. That's it! Couldn't do it without you, babe.'

'And we couldn't do it without Bob,' Bridie added, casting him a wink.

'Bob?' said Emily.

'We needed cash fast to help pay for the rental house and the studio, so Bridie coaxed me into a couple of pub gigs,' Sam explained. 'Before long we had bookings every week, not just weekends either. I started to feel a bit, you know, over it. With that pressure back on I was about to turn it down and give it all away again, when Bob walked into our lives.'

'He was touring up the coast,' Bridie said, 'weren't you, Bob?'

Uncle Bob nodded. 'I blew a fuse in me head around the time of the grazing bans. Thought, I can't do it anymore.' He shivered at the memory, but his eyes lifted and settled on Evie who smiled at him.

'Luckily Evie suggested I go walkabout for a bit. To find what really floated my boat. I was just about to give up when I bumped into Sam and Bridie in a pub in Coolum.'

'Man, did we do some drinking that night!' Sam recalled. 'And some D&Ming. We sorted out all the crap between us.'

'In the finish,' Bridie said, 'Bob came on board as Sam's

315

band manager and roadie. He's the one who rounded up the best musos to play with Sam on his pub gigs, and he's the one who's organised all the travelling between venues. It frees Sam up and takes the pressure off me.'

'He's a natural,' Sam added. 'One of the best show managers I've worked with, and still a new kid to the muso game!'

Bob grinned. 'You can't help but be good, doing something you love!' His round red face softened for a moment and he looked earnestly at Emily. 'I've worked out I hated being a cattle farmer. Hated it with a passion but felt obligated to do it. And that's why I was crap at it. I'm just sorry I've wasted so much of my life, and wasted so much of other people's time, before I figured that out.' Emily was about to smooth things over, but he held up his hand to silence her.

'I've been an arse. But with things taking off with Sam in the next twelve months, we know the three of us are finally going places. United States or bust!'

'And this time we're doing it drug- and dickhead-free,' added Sam.

Emily smiled at him.

'There's more, though, isn't there, Bob?' Bridie prompted.

'You bet,' he said, turning back to Emily. 'You're good at what you do because you love it too. I can see you're a bloody good mum and a bloody good cattleman. That's why I'm leasing you my land up on the plains and down here on the lowlands. If you'd like.'

Emily's mouth fell open.

'You don't have to say yes right away,' her uncle said. 'You do your sums, work out if you can make a go of it. The lease payments won't be huge because one day I'll be leavin' the lot to you and your girls anyway.' He shrugged. 'You're the one the land deserves. That's why old Hughie upstairs spared your life after that horse accident. Least, that's what I reckon.'

A smile lit Emily's face. Bob was giving her a go on the land. She loved the way he'd put it too; that the land deserved her. Not the other way round, that she deserved the land. It didn't

316

work that way in her mind either. The land did deserve someone who not only loved it but could read its messages, understand it and above all respect the balance needed in its management.

'Thank you, Bob,' she said, tilting her glass towards him in a toast. 'Thank you so very bloody *much*!'

Emily beamed. Her dream was alive again. The life of a cattleman now stretched out before her, like a road suddenly cleared. She glanced over to her father and smiled at him. He was never one for noise or fuss, but Emily could see the happiness he felt.

She looked at Evie and she, too, had an expression of calm satisfaction on her face, as if she had orchestrated the whole thing. Then, suddenly, Emily realised that in many ways Evie *had* made all these miracles happen.

'A toast,' she proposed. 'To us! The Flanaghans – that includes you too, Evie.' And they all chorused a reply and drank.

When the meal was done and the table cleared, Rod delivered a pile of mail to Emily.

'Welcome back to the real world.'

'Gee, thanks, Dad,' she said dryly as she flicked through the envelopes.

The first she opened had neat lovely handwriting on it, like a party invitation. Emily tore it open and was shocked by what she saw. There was a photograph of two tiny babies swaddled in pink, their faces puckered, eyes like slits. They were being held by Clancy, who sat perched proudly on a hospital bed, a grin from ear to ear. Emily stared at the photo. Then she slowly unfolded the letter which Clancy had scratched out in his uncertain hand.

Dear Meg and Tilly. Here is a picture of your new sisters, Dimity and Renee. You might want to come and live with them, if you like. Love Dad and Penny. xxx P.S. Tell your mum I got one of them letters too.

That was all the note said. What letter? Emily wondered. Then she saw one in the pile that caught her attention. The black lettering on the envelope read *Family Services Department*. Her heart thuddeed. She tore the envelope open anxiously and began to read.

She sat staring at it in silence as the rest of the family buzzed about the kitchen, washing up, stacking plates. Skylarking. It took them a while to notice Emily's reaction.

'What is it?' Bridie asked eventually.

'This,' she said, placing the photograph of the newborn twins on the table, 'and this,' holding up the official letter.

'They want to investigate me as a mother,' she went on. 'They say I've put the girls in danger and I have to go into Sale for an interview, next week.'

'Are you serious?' Bridie said. Flo grabbed the letter. Evie read it over her shoulder.

'That's a shocker,' Flo announced. 'You couldn't get a better mother than Emily. How could they? Bastards!'

'It's understandable,' Evie soothed. 'Anyone who doesn't do the conventional thing is a threat to bureaucracy. Emily doesn't fit into a neat little box. This is just the government men throwing their weight around, trying to justify their pay packets. It's a storm in a teacup. Once the girls settle into school next year at Dargo, they'll pipe down.'

'But that's not the point! Those mountains are our way of life. How can they condemn her for that?' Flo objected.

'They'll let it go. It's just a power play by that man who saw her on the mountains. It's a rap over the knuckles because people like him are jealous of Emily's freedom and oneness with the land.'

There was that word again, Emily thought angrily. *They*. She knew she was lucky to live in this country, but the era of the public servant was upon them and to Emily it felt stifling after being away from it all for months on the high plains. Here was another letter in her hand in cold bureau-speak, threatening her very existence.

'Well, I've had it with "*them*". I'm going to find out just who started this.' She thought of storming into Luke's office over it, but knew it was the men in Melbourne pulling all the strings.

Evie shook her head. 'Let it lie, Emily. Let them dig their own graves. You don't need to jump in and finish the hole for them. Fight this with positivity.'

Emily nodded, but Evie's coaching gave her little comfort now. If she lost her girls, her life wouldn't be worth living. Could the government do that? Take her daughters from her?

'Let me deal with it,' Rod said, 'I'm ringing Clancy.' He stalked from the room like a giant grumpy bear.

'Dad, just leave it,' Emily begged, 'Don't.'

Deep in the night Meg came in and quietly curled up with Emily in her bed.

'Go to sleep,' Meg said, resting a hand on her mother's forehead.

How did Meg know she'd been lying awake in the darkened room for hours now?

'Okay, darling,' she said, pulling her daughter to her. 'I will.'

'Sweet Mummy,' Meg said sleepily. 'The granny will be happy about Uncle Bob's land.'

Emily opened her eyes. 'What granny?'

'The granny that helps you.'

'You mean Evie?' She felt Meg shake her head.

'The granny that follows you in the snow. The one that watches you when you split the wood.'

'What granny?' Emily said.

'You know,' Meg said. 'You know, Mummy.'

Thirty-seven

As she got out of her father's ute, Emily swivelled to tug down her skirt and in the process nearly turned her ankle in the high heels she wore. The cement in the car park radiated heat so intensely she had to squint from both its warmth and the glare. Rod, dressed in the clothes he reserved for cattlemen meetings, walked beside her as they made their way to the Bairnsdale government office. The glass doors slid open and they were enveloped into what felt like a fridge.

'Which department?' a woman with black-framed glasses enquired from behind the high front desk.

'Ah . . .' started Emily, reaching for the appointment letter.

'Family services,' Rod said, 'Emily Flanaghan to see Marjory Pitts.'

'And you are?'

'The grandfather,' he said. 'Mr Rod Flanaghan, but you can call me Rod – or Granddad, if you like.' He winked at Emily as the receptionist, slightly miffed, fumbled for the phone. 'The . . . er . . . Flanaghans are here to see you.' She surveyed them both, clutching her cardigan across her chest as she listened to the person on the other end of the line. 'The grandfather too,' the receptionist said. 'Yes? I'll tell them to wait.'

Despite the air-conditioning Emily's legs sweated against the uncomfortable vinyl of the waiting-room chairs. For the

320

first time in weeks her shoulder was aching. What was it Evie had about shoulders and emotions? Something about them representing her ability to encounter experiences in life joyously. How on earth could she make this experience a joyous one? She was about to be grilled by some woman on how she was raising her children. Then she was struck by fear again as she wondered if she could even lose them. She knew how obstinate government workers could be with regard to rules. Could Family Services take her children from her? Emily sighed nervously. Her dad frowned at her.

'It'll be okay, Em. I promise.'

'Thanks, Dad,' she said, wanting to believe him.

She settled back in her chair, but before she had time to pick up a magazine and blindly flick through it, the doors slid open and Clancy appeared. He was pushing a double pram containing two tiny babies swaddled in pink. Beside him stood Penny in a pretty floral summer dress, looking ultra-slim, as if she had never been pregnant.

'Clancy!' Emily said as cold panic swept through her. *Was he here to claim the girls?* He simply nodded at her then offered a hand to Rod who shook it.

'Congratulations to you both.' Rod gave Penny a courteous smile then stooped to look in the pram.

'They're tiny! Meg and Tilly are busting to see them.'

'Yes,' said Penny. There was an awkward pause.

Emily stood dumbfounded, watching the scene unfolding around her. She hadn't expected Clancy would be here today, let alone Penny and the twins! He'd shown so little interest in the girls in the past months, why would he come now? And why bring Penny? Emily swallowed down the bitter taste of fear.

'You'd better introduce us,' Rod said, breaking the silence. Emily was grateful he was keeping it courteous, keeping it light, even though she could feel the undercurrents of the situation tug at them all.

Clancy's cheeks flushed a little as he stooped over the pram.

'This one is Renee and this is Dimity.'

'Other way round,' said Penny.

'Oh, yes, that's right,' Clancy said.

As Emily peered into the pram, a feeling of warmth over-took her. They were *gorgeous*. Little half-sisters to her own girls. One had the same colouring as Penny, the other had the dark blue eyes of her father. Emily felt emotion well in her. It was so surreal and strange to meet them. Clancy's daughters. It hurt to see them, but at the same time they held such fascination. Surely these little girls would be enough for Clancy. He simply wouldn't want to take Meg and Tilly from her now, would he? Emily was about to ask him if that was his intention when a short, round woman with brown hair cut into a helmet shape trundled out into the waiting room, carrying a file under her arm. Her dour expression opened up into a smile.

'Penny! My goodness, what a lovely surprise! And your babies! I heard. How beautiful!'

'Hi, Marj,' Penny said hugging the woman briefly. 'Good to see you.'

'And you, my dear girl. I'm sorry I don't have more time . . .' the woman said '. . . but I believe these people are my next appointment.' Her nose twitched like a rabbit's and she blinked from behind her glasses as she looked Emily up and down.

'Yes, I know,' Penny said, 'We don't mind waiting.'

'Oh?'

'Clancy is the father of the girls on your file,' Penny said, indicating the folder in the woman's hands. 'He'd like a word with you, too. Afterwards.'

Marjory looked up at Clancy and then at Emily.

'I see. So you're here to discuss custody?'

'Yes,' said Clancy, and held his head high, jutting out his chin.

'No,' Emily said.

'I see,' Marjory said again, the friendly tone gone. 'We'll

start with you then.' Turning to Rod and Emily, she indicated her office door. 'This way.'

As Emily took a step forward her whole world spun around her. *Custody*? She felt the air catch in her lungs. If it weren't for Rod steering her by the elbow, she thought her legs would buckle beneath her.

Emily didn't know how long the interview went on for. She sweated in the air-conditioned room, her mouth dry as a gravel road, while Marjory Pitts outlined the report submitted by Giles Grimsley.

On and on the questions flowed about the girls. What school would they attend? Had the elder child had home schooling on the plains? What was Emily doing for income? Did she have a *de facto* partner? Had she endangered her children at other times? Was she using drugs?

At times, when Emily stuttered or faltered, Rod would answer for her. He kept his voice calm and steady. There were times too when Emily felt she would explode at the woman and tear her file from her, but mostly she was frozen with terror. If she did one thing wrong, said one incorrect thing, this woman had the power to tear her life apart. At last Marjory stopped asking questions and closed the file.

'Thank you,' she said, still making notes and not looking at Emily. 'That will be all.'

'But . . .?'

'You will be notified by mail.'

'Notified of what?'

Marjory sighed. 'I thought I'd explained. The authorities will assess my report and contact you with regard to custody of your children.'

'Sorry?'

Marjory stood up briskly and waved her hand out towards the door, 'I have already run through the process with you, Ms Flanaghan.' She looked at Emily as if she were a simpleton. How could Emily explain to this woman that her mind had spun into such a panic that the interview had made no sense to her? How could she say that she didn't understand the offi-cial language Marjory Pitts was directing at her? Emily could feel her whole body shake.

'If I am to interview your former husband too, I'll need to keep moving. I don't want to run over time into my next appointment, so if you'll excuse me . . .'

In a blur Emily passed Clancy and Penny in the waiting room. Clancy wouldn't meet her eye. One of the babies squawked and he jiggled the pram.

'Come in, Penny,' Marjory said. 'Let me help you with the baby bags.'

In the carpark, Rod opened the door for Emily. She lifted her gaze to meet his steady blue eyes and felt the tears come.

'I can't believe this is happening.'

Rod reached out and held her. Emily could feel the sweat on his back beneath his shirt.

'It might not be.'

'What?'

'Your worst fears might not happen.'

'But . . .'

'Don't think about it anymore, Em. Come on, get in. I'll buy you a drink.'

In the café, while Rod ordered coffees at the counter, Emily sat hanging her head, turning a paper tube of sugar end on end. She wondered if that woman did plan to take her chil-dren from her. Her bureau-babble had made no sense. Emily felt the tears rise again and reached for a paper napkin which she clenched in her fist, willing herself not to cry.

Outside in the baking street a shiny four-wheel drive pulled up behind Rod's ute. Emily noticed the baby shades on the rear windows and a colourful clown hanging down. Penny slid gracefully from the passenger seat and smoothed down her short summer dress.

She said something to Clancy, sitting in the driver's seat, before slamming the door.

Emily ducked her head when Penny opened the café door,

letting in a breeze of soupy hot air from outside. She stood for a time, allowing her eyes to adjust from the bright sunshine to the dullness of the café. When she saw Emily, Penny set her mouth in a thin line and made her way over.

She slumped down in a chair before Emily.

'It's so hot out there,' she said, pushing back a strand of red hair from her high forehead. Emily stared at her.

'Look,' the other woman said matter-of-factly, 'I just came to tell you that it's all okay.'

'Okay?'

'Yes,' said Penny. 'We sorted things out with Marjory.'

'What do you mean?'

'We've asked her to close the file.'

Emily tilted her head on one side. 'Close the file? I'm not sure . . .'

'You won't have any trouble from Family Services again.'

'But . . . the girls? I thought you and Clancy were seeking custody.'

Penny's eyes widened.

'God, no!' she said. 'I mean, Clancy thought he did want that but . . . well, you know. He doesn't know *what* he wants. And really he doesn't, if you know what I mean.' She glanced out of the window and sighed. Turning back to Emily, she said in a softer tone, 'He knows the twins are enough for me. And besides, having Clancy is like having another kid.'

'Tell me about it,' Emily said dryly. The women exchanged a glance. Emily's rich dark eyes and Penny's ice-blue ones locked for a moment. It was unsaid but Emily felt a new understanding pass between them.

'I'm sorry,' Penny said gently.

'I know you are,' Emily murmured.

'I'll make sure he visits them more, though. I promise.'

'You do that,' Emily said. 'The girls . . . Meg and Tilly, I mean . . . would like that very much. They still need a father. You stay on his case.' Both women smiled then and Emily was surprised when Penny reached out and squeezed her hand.

'It's good to see you looking so well after . . . after all you've been through.'

'Thanks,' Emily said quietly.

And then Rod was there, standing above them with two cups of coffee in his hands.

'Can I get you one?' he asked Penny.

But she was already standing, scraping the chair back across the floor, shaking her head.

'No, thanks,' she said, her voice strangely choked. As she exited the café Emily watched Penny swipe away tears before she got back into the four wheel drive.

When they had driven away, Rod looked up from his coffee. 'Funny girl, that one. Reminds me of an apricot-brindle whippet.'

'Oh, Dad,' Emily laughed, then sighed. 'She's all right.' Suddenly Emily felt overwhelmingly tired.

'Should I ask what that was all about?' he said.

'She came in to tell me they're not after the girls. She talked that Marjory Pitts into closing the case against me.' Emily rolled her eyes and put her head in her hands. 'I went in there thinking the worst was going to happen.'

'Miracles do occur, if you allow them to,' Rod told her.

'Thank God they do,' Emily sighed.

She closed her eyes as she sipped her drink, feeling for the first time in a long while as if everything was going to turn out fine.

326

Thirty-eight

'Take it steady,' Flo said as she hauled herself up next to her niece in the truck. 'You gotta glide the gear knob gently into place, as if you were holding your fella's precious one-eyed trouser snake. No grating gears, okay?'

'*Okay*!' Emily rolled her eyes and noticed Flo's concerned expression in the early morning light. She flicked the gear-stick into neutral.

'You gotta go easy on the clutch, too. Double-clutch in the bends.'

Emily looked at Flo, beginning to regret asking to borrow Baz's stock truck and trailer to take cattle up to the high plains. Flo was acting like a mother hen with their precious new red DAF.

'I've got my licence. I know how to drive it! Stop panicking.'

'It's not an *it*!' Flo told her. 'This big revvin' baby is my Hugh Jackman.' She patted the truck. 'Aren't ya, gorgeous? Huge Jack-man!'

'If you're so worried, you drive it . . . I mean *him* . . . and take the cattle to the plains for me!'

Flo shook her head. 'No, you go on alone. I trust you.' She carefully shut the truck door and Emily wound down the window and looked over at her father's house.

'Tilly! Meg! You coming or what? Hurry. We've got a big

day ahead,' she bellowed from the cab. The girls slammed through the screen door, their packs in their hands and smiles on their faces as Flo helped them up into the DAF.

'Don't you go spilling food in Auntie Flo's cab, you hear? Or put grubby fingers on the windows.'

'Flo!' barked Emily.

'All right.' She threw up her hands in the air. 'I know you'll look after him.'

As Emily pulled on to the Tranquillity driveway she deliberately bunny-hopped the truck for a few metres, watching the horrified expression on Flo's face. Then she let rip with two good blasts of the air horn and stuck her middle finger up at her aunt before rolling the rig away down the drive.

Since she'd taken over the lease of Bob's land, Emily hadn't stopped working. She had set out to restore not only his land, but also her father's tired old Dargo house.

Any spare time she had was spent scraping flaky paint from the walls and puttying, sanding and painting. On the plains she began fencing, and on the lowlands ripping trenches for poly-pipe in a new watering system that would keep the cattle out of the river that ran through Bob's Dargo property. At night she tallied cattle sums, trying to work out how much she could make to spend on the land, and during sleepless hours tried figuring out drought strategies. In between it all, she was forever busy with the girls.

Instead of worrying about Clancy, Emily now worried about running into Luke and went to all kinds of measures to avoid him. So far, so good. As she rolled along in the truck, the girls singing to an Adam Brand CD, Emily's mind was miles away. In a good year she could still run three hundred head on the lowlands. But that was in a good year. Since the rain in autumn and only a few inches in spring, no more had fallen and the landscape around Dargo was barren, with dams in some paddocks running dry. It wasn't even December yet, and already they had endured some hellishly hot, windy days.

In a year like this she could run, at a stretch, two hundred head of cows on the lowlands, but she needed to help Bob's land on the plains to recover. She planned to stock it lightly in the first two summers with just a hundred and fifty cows. She didn't want to stretch her lower country either, so had opted to sell fifty head. The cows were in good nick and the extra money would go towards fencing up on Bob's. Now was her chance to make amends to the run up there. To set it right.

Instead of droving, Emily had chosen to truck the one hundred and fifty cattle up in several trips, so small were the numbers now due to the bans. While she was sorry they weren't droving, Emily reasoned she could use her days more efficiently this year by fencing cattle out of areas that needed rehabilitation. She told herself they could always return to droving once the seasons were more generous and Bob's land was in better shape.

She looked out at the garden that would swelter once the sun was up. Yesterday the girls had been playing in a pitiful few inches of water in an inflatable pool beneath a weeping willow. There wasn't enough water in the tanks or the river to warrant the sprinkler being on much at all, but the garden from the road looked like an oasis of green in the frazzled landscape. At least the prospect of an intense fire season had allowed them to justify running the taps a little around the house for the girls to play with. That small buffer of green could be their saviour should fire come this summer. She revved the truck up a gear and rattled on to pick up the cattle from the yards.

Luke Bradshaw frowned when he saw the giant dusty red truck with a stock trailer pulled over in the middle of seemingly nowhere. He stopped the VPP vehicle behind the truck and looked about, sniffing the pungent waft of cow dung coming from the empty truck. He heard a dog bark to the west of the road and saw someone over by a stream. He started striding over the tussocky plain towards them. Soon Emily's black and tan kelpie was bounding over to greet him, a big kelpie-grin on his face and his tail wagging frantically.

Luke saw Emily standing beside the stream. She looked gorgeous in her grubby jeans, a thick leather work belt and tight blue singlet that showed her curves. Her brown shoulders, wet from the river, glistened in the warm afternoon sun. An Akubra hat shaded her pretty face. Luke knew she would be nervous she'd been 'sprung' with a dog in the National Park. Her tousle-headed girls looked up from their panning and he could read the fear on their faces that their mother was about to get in trouble again.

Luke wasn't going to play by ranger rules today.

'Hi!' he said, trying as best he could to convey a friendly casual air. 'Struck gold yet?' He stooped and ran his hands over Rousie's ears.

Emily tilted her head and answered cautiously, 'Nope. Not yet.'

'How have you been?' he asked gently.

'Fine.'

'Er . . . I'm sorry. Okay? About last winter. *Really* sorry. I put in a report with recommendations they should drop the charges. Grimsley got shafted downwards in the department, so they were happy to drop it. I hope you didn't hear anything more.'

Luke stood before her, apology written all over his face. He looked gorgeous in his shorts, his fit, strong legs a deep brown, lace-up boots looking worn and rugged. She stared into his dark eyes and saw the kindness in them.

'I've left it too long, I know, but I . . .' His voice faded away.

Emily stepped back. 'I don't think you've ever met my girls properly,' she said, changing the subject quickly as she took in his apology. She watched as he crouched down to greet Meg and Tilly.

'My name's Luke. What are your names?'

The girls looked at him, but remained silent.

330

'Luke's a friend of Mummy's,' Emily told them. 'Say hello!' The two girls blinked at the man before them. He seemed nice now, but after their day in the snow with that cross old ranger, they were wary.

'This is my youngest, Meg, and this is Matilda, but we call her Tilly,' Emily said, speaking for them, her tone a little forced.

'Hi, Meg and Tilly!' Luke moved over to the stream. 'You going to show me how to pan for gold?'

Emily ushered them both over to the stream and, reluctantly, they set about dipping their pans into the water. But soon they were laughing, splashing and chatting with Luke. Emily joined in cautiously, though part of her was still hurt by his presence there in uniform on what had once been Flanaghan land. She knew Evie would say 'forgive and forget'. Perhaps she should put the memory of that day in the snow behind her and allow herself to feel joy that he was here, being so kind. She was grateful he hadn't mentioned the fact she had a dog and a stock truck in the Park. He seemed to understand now. Standing near him by the stream Emily felt her heart flutter again. She had stifled her feelings for him long enough.

The sun was dipping down beneath the treeline and the cold came in quickly.

'Well, it looks as if we won't find gold today,' Luke said finally, winking at Emily but talking to the girls. 'It's time for me to go. We'd better all go.'

'Can we go panning with Luke again tomorrow?' Meg asked, grabbing hold of her mother's hand with wet, cold fingers, her eyes bright.

'He has to work. And you're going to Evie's for a visit, while Mummy goes fencing. Maybe another day.'

'Oh!' Meg said, stamping her foot. 'Mummy! You must let this nice Luke into our life. He's one for keeps, like you said about the hairy guinea pig when we got him!' She frowned up at her mother and Emily, shocked, frowned back at her.

'Back to the truck, *now*!'

Meg stomped off with Tilly in tow, while Luke, grinning, stacked up the pans and passed them to Emily. Their hands touched momentarily. Emily shivered. He caught her eye. 'It's Saturday tomorrow,' he said. 'I'm not working.'

'Well, I am,' she said.

'What are you doing?' he asked cheerfully. 'Maybe I can help?'

Emily couldn't believe it. Here he was, part of the group that had taken this land from them and now he was offering to help! But Meg's words stuck in her head. Let him in, Emily, she thought.

'I'm riding out round Bob's run to check the fences and do a few patch-up jobs.'

'You got a spare horse? I could come with you. Learn a bit about the place.'

Emily looked at him, amazed he would want to. Hesitantly, she nodded.

'Yeah? You could ride your gelding, if you like. He's coming along really well.'

'I would like,' Luke said. 'I'd like that a lot! See you first thing, then.'

And before Emily could change her mind, or warn him away, he was gone, jogging over the snow-grass plains towards the truck. There he cheerfully helped the girls into the cab and waved to Emily as he got into his vehicle and revved away.

'He's really nice, he is,' said Meg, when Emily came and clambered into the driver's seat.

'Shut it, Meg,' she snapped.

'But he *is* really nice,' Tilly added.

'You shush too,' Emily said, her nerves dancing.

'Why is Mummy so cross about Luke?' Tilly said, rolling her eyes and folding her arms across her body.

'Because she likes him but she thinks she's not allowed to because he's a ranger,' Meg said wisely. 'And she's worried about giving us a new daddy – when we still have an old daddy.'

'But Daddy has his new babies, so Mummy should be able to give us another daddy.'

'All right, you two! Yes, I like Luke. Okay, I really like him and your old daddy will *always* be your daddy. You don't just swap daddies. But can you please stop talking now?'

'You really, *really* like him?' Meg asked.

'For a boy, he's really nice,' Tilly said again.

'Yes,' Meg said. 'For a boy. He'd make a nice other daddy.'

'Will you two just be quiet?' Emily said, lamenting the fact that she hadn't said no to Luke. She was as nervous as if it was a first date. She began to run through what daggy work clothes she'd packed. Then she realised the only clean pair of undies she had with her were the bright-green ones with the white lettering that read *Plough my patch* and an arrow pointing to the crotch. Too late to rinse her most normal pair, which had a puppy on them with *Bury your bone here*. They would never be dry in time. The green ones it would have to be!

'Oh, *God*,' she groaned, wondering why she was thinking of Luke and her undies at the same time.

'It's okay,' Meg reassured her. 'God knows, Mummy. He knows everything.'

Thirty-nine

As Emily pulled on her clothes that morning she berated herself for having worried what undies she was going to wear. As if Luke Bradshaw would even get a look in! She wasn't going to show him, even if he was interested.

Outside, the sun was gently hitting the eastern walls and roof, so the high-plains homestead was alive with creaking. It was going to be a warm day. Emily could hear the girls waking, stirring, talking to each other, slowly remembering that today was the day they were going to Evie's, who was taking them into Dargo to do the shopping. Before excitement set them jumping out of bed, Emily made her way along the hall to the bathroom to clean her teeth. Fresh breath in case he kisses me, she thought, before shoving the thought away.

In the gloom of the bathroom, she stared at her reflection in the mirror. Her eyes, big and wide and dark, her glossy dark hair, longer now, framing her face. Her skin was clear and smooth. Perhaps Luke could like her . . . As she bent forward to reach for her toothbrush she caught sight in the mirror of a woman standing behind her. A flash of white nightgown, a sweet smile, long, dark grey hair hanging softly around the woman's face. Emily spun around, knocking over the cup of brushes and toothpaste with a clatter.

There was no one there.

'Okay, Emily,' she said, calming herself. 'It's just normal nowadays. Get used to it. Granny Emily, I know you're there. But what is it you've come to remind me about? Is this the work I'm supposed to do? Playing tour guide to a VPP ranger?'

Sleepily, Tilly pushed open the bathroom door. 'Who are you talking to, Mum?'

Emily blinked her way into the here and now.

'The granny, silly,' Meg said as she bumbled her way past Tilly and picked up the toothbrushes from the floor. 'You know, the one that watches over Mum. She's happy about the nice man, Luke. She wants them to work together.'

'Oh, Meg,' Emily said. 'What are you on about?'

'You know, Mummy.'

Emily crouched down and hugged her. 'You just know stuff, don't you, my little one?'

Meg shrugged and began squirting Shrek toothpaste out of the tube.

'Hey! Not so much,' Emily told her.

As she sat with the girls eating breakfast she shut her eyes and pictured how things could be. She and Luke working together, deciding which part of the Park needed grazing and which should be left for another year. Which areas needed cool burning and problem areas that required weed control. Could life really be like that? she wondered. Perhaps old Emily was telling her it could. Maybe these mountains were their work together, hers and Luke's? Fantasy land, she eventually told herself.

After dropping Tilly and Meg at Evie's, Emily was inside again checking her face in the mirror when Rousie barked to tell her someone was approaching. She watched Luke drive up in his old WB, thumping along the rutted track. She was relieved to see he was out of uniform. When he got out and stood before her in his Wrangler jeans, boots and a woollen work jumper, Emily felt weak at the knees.

'Morning,' he said, reaching for his wide-brimmed cowboy hat and jamming it on his head.

'Good morning,' she said nervously. 'Like a cuppa before we go?'

Luke shook his head.

'Nah, let's get cracking.' He rubbed his hands together. 'Can't wait.'

'I was hoping you'd say that,' Emily said. 'I'm not one to sit about either. Follow me.'

'With pleasure,' Luke replied with a broad smile, and she could hear flirtation in his tone. This could work, she told herself excitedly. She led him over to the stables, her heart racing.

Inside the old stables, she watched as he ran his beautiful hands over the old upright posts that met with sturdy bearers beneath a lofty shingled rooftop, which had been covered over on the outside with roofing iron to preserve it.

'This building is *amazing*. Look at the timber work!'

Emily glanced up as she gathered the bridles from carved wooden pegs.

'I know. They were pretty handy in those days.'

'Pretty handy nowadays too, from what I can tell,' Luke said, catching her eye and hoping she'd catch his compliment as well.

'Granddad built these stables, and out here . . .' she said, stepping through a side door '. . . is where Granny used to keep her goats.' She pointed to the solid post-and-rail fence that cornered off a high-plains meadow. 'That old stone wall was part of the piggery. And this head bale here is where Granddad used to milk the cow when he was a little tacker.'

They rested their elbows on the yard rails, looking through them at the view of Flanaghan Station with its old shingle roof outbuildings and the homestead at its heart.

'This place is awesome!' Luke said.

'It's pretty special, yeah. You're the first government bloke that's been on the place in decades, you know. It's not that we don't ask you blokes here, it's just none of the others seem

336

to want to come and see for themselves. It's like they're not interested in the history of the place. I think it's easier for 'em if they pretend all this isn't here.'

She turned to look at him, the morning sun lighting up her smile. 'It's good to have a government bloke come in and see first hand what heritage the bans are destroying.'

'Emily,' he said, turning to look into her eyes, 'I'm not a government bloke and I'm not out to destroy anyone's heritage. As long as you're here, no one can take this place from you.' He frowned. *'Government bloke*? Ouch! That hurts.'

'But you *are* a government bloke. You work for the VPP.'

'It's a job, Emily. A ticket out of the city for me. It isn't who I am. I was chucked off my land, remember? The government caused that too. All those tax rules that let outsiders buy in for so-called carbon credit tree-farming . . . it's as ludicrous as what they've done to your family. The only difference is, my dad gave up. Yours hasn't.'

Emily frowned at him, suddenly seeing his point.

'Sorry,' she said. 'You're right. We're in the same boat. I won't call you that anymore.'

'Good. I'm glad.'

There was a moment when she thought he might lean over and kiss her but Luke drew away.

'Now, let's go catch these horses. I can't wait to see more of this place!'

As Luke threw the heavy stock saddle up on to the gelding's back and reached under for the girth, he watched Emily as much as he could without being obvious. He was intrigued by her. She was so self-contained. Tough, even. Not angry and hostile like Cassy, but resilient, like the landscape about her. He saw how she saddled her grey mare, the way it was second nature to her, her movements swift and confident.

She talked as she tacked up, explaining how she'd liked the name Salsa that he'd mentioned on the road back in autumn but she'd settled for Bonus instead. Her chatter was fuelled by nervousness, Luke could tell. He couldn't take his eyes off her pretty face and her competent hands that were as strong as a man's yet still beautiful. She was being very formal, almost old-fashioned, with him. It was as if their encounter at Wonnangatta had pushed her further away rather than brought her closer to him. He had to find a way to relax her somehow, find the unguarded version of Emily within. As she bent to clean Snowgum's hooves with a hoof pick, Luke caught a glimpse of bright green underpants lairing out from the top of her jeans.

'Whoah! Interesting colour choice,' he said, grinning.

Emily set Snowgum's hoof down, looking at him and frowning.

'What?'

'Your undies.'

'Oh, God!' Emily flushed red as she tugged up her jeans. 'Sorry. They're foul.'

'Don't be sorry. I love green. It makes me think of grass.'

'You don't want to know about my undies, honestly. It's a long story.'

'Well, I like long stories and we've got all day,' he said, grinning, as he led Bonus from the stable. Emily was still rolling her eyes with embarrassment and smiling when she swung up on to Snowgum.

Seeing her astride a horse, looking so much a part of the scene, Luke could barely keep track of her words as she explained where they were headed. All he caught was something about Bob's runs and the western side of the road. He nodded, dumbstruck, wondering how he could get closer to this girl. He was besotted. But the VPP thing still seemed to hang between them like a great silent shadow.

'You right to trot for a bit?' Emily asked, and was off before he could answer, sitting easily in the saddle, the stocky mare rolling along the track, curving in and out of snow gums. The gelding beneath him was moving well, too. She'd done a good job on him. Bonus was responsive yet steady, and he moved over the rocky, twisting track with ease and confidence. Emily must be some horsewoman! More admiration rose up in Luke for the extraordinary girl riding in front of him.

On the way, she pointed out trees with stories to them, plants he hadn't heard of, and access to tracks that had never been marked on a map, nor ever would be. She told him of old-timers who'd had huts out here and of the best places to tickle a trout or look for gold. They rode up gentle hillsides and slid down steep tracks, Emily knowing where each fence curved away.

Every place she took him was breathtakingly beautiful. As they journeyed farther into the heart of the high plains, Luke felt her opening up to him. She was forgetting his ranger status and talking to him now as a friend. She spoke of Bob's inability to farm; the way he'd done wrong by the land. She spoke of her own plans to rehabilitate it. As she talked, Luke's admiration for Emily began to grow. His feelings for her mounted to such a height that, as the morning moved on, it felt as if desire for her might burst him apart.

By the time the sun was high and hot, Emily had led them to a mountain brook shaded by a dappling of snow gums. The water ran across a grassy plain and then bubbled and splashed down over a small waterfall. Emily hitched Snowgum's reins to a sapling and unbuckled her saddle bags from the mare.

She'd packed a very special smoko. Normally she'd just shove in an apple and a bottle of water, but today, knowing Luke would be along, she'd rummaged around for as many snacks as she could find. She clambered down a small embankment and settled herself on a mossy bank beside the deep pool. Luke followed and settled next to her, watching as she took a thermos from the saddlebag and offered him a cup of tea or coffee.

'This is a flash smoko spot *and* I get a choice of what to drink?' he said with a smile.

'You could have Milo too, but there's only one sachet so you'll have to share it with me.'

'I don't mind sharing with you,' he said invitingly.

Emily lifted her head and looked into his eyes. It was a moment when she knew she could have leant over and kissed him. But she wanted to savour this opportunity. To test him a little. She quickly poured him a drink and passed it to him.

'Thanks.' She could feel his frustration, the desire barely leashed. Now she could tell he wanted her. Now she knew she wanted him. It was time to have some fun. To let Luke in. She kicked off her boots, pulled off her socks and stood up suddenly, unbuckling her jeans and whipping them down to her ankles.

'What are you doing?' he said, looking up with a mixture of delight and confusion on his face at the sight of her tanned bare legs.

'It's tickling time.'

'Tickling time? I didn't know you were into fetishes,' he said with a grin.

'The trout,' Emily said, pulling her shirt down over her loud green underpants.

'Isn't that illegal?' Luke stood and took off his boots and jeans too. 'It's out of season. You'll need a fishing licence and you're not using the right equipment. You're just heading for trouble, young lady.'

'You'll have to arrest me then,' Emily said, wading into the stream.

'Only if I can frisk you again first.'

That sparked a memory of Wonnangatta, and their first kiss, in both of them. Emily smiled at Luke as he followed her into the mountain stream. She bent down, sliding her hands deep under the water. Her fingertips felt about on the unseen rocks below the surface until she found what she was searching for. As she expertly scooped the trout up into the air, its silver, spotted body glistened in the sunlight.

'Got him!' Luke said, smiling at her.

'Got her, you mean.'

'What are you going to do now? Eat her?'

Emily shook her head. 'Nah. Set her free.' She gently placed the trout down into the darkness of the rocky ledge. 'Put her back where she belongs.'

'She's like you,' said Luke, facing Emily as they stood thigh-deep in the cold mountain stream. 'You belong here.' He took her hands and held them both, then leant towards her and gently, cautiously, pressed a soft kiss to her lips. His mouth hovered near hers, waiting for her to return the kiss.

She answered by moving close, pressing her body to his, kissing him deeply. The relief of touching him again was phenomenal. Electricity sparked between them as they ran their hands over each other. Breathless, she led him back on to the mossy bank. They lay next to each other there, the earthy smell of life rising up around them. Luke drank her in with his hands and mouth. He pulled her shirt and singlet from her and expertly unclipped her bra. Then, with sunshine on her skin, he kissed her neck and her breasts, moving his mouth down over her stomach.

'Mmm. Plough my patch, eh?' he said from where he lay, running a finger along the elastic of her undies playfully.

'I thought, you being a wheatbelt boy, that'd crank your tractor.'

'You did, did you?'

Emily bit her bottom lip and nodded.

'I'm not into ploughing. It's not so good for the soil over the long term,' he said, slowly, tantalisingly, easing her under-pants down over her curvaceous, firm hips. 'I prefer direct drilling.'

'Direct drilling, eh? I don't mind a bit of direct drilling myself,' Emily said, running her fingers through his hair and looking skyward to the blue.

'Don't you now?' continued Luke as he began to draw her knickers down. 'I find direct drilling is gentler, slower, and lasts much, much longer.' As he slowly delivered each word he punctuated it with a kiss to her thighs, her belly and then beyond. Emily arched with pleasure at his deft, practised

341

touch. Never had she felt a man perform so expertly, with such assurance. The quickness of his fingers, the dance of his tongue on her, the confidence in his moves. He sent her heavenward on a wave of pleasure to the very last gasp.

He came to lie on top of her, and continued kissing her. Emily, a dreamy smile on her face, ran her fingernails gently up and over his back beneath his T-shirt. She nuzzled in his neck and pulled him closer. She wanted him inside her. She dragged his T-shirt over his head and the press of their naked torsos, skin on skin, awoke a new surge of desire in them. Luke pushed into her and they bucked against each other, the pungent mossy bank releasing its perfumes all around.

They were lost now. In each other. In the landscape. They rolled over so that Emily sat astride Luke. He was the one lying back now, she the rider. With Luke deep within her, Emily moved as if at a gallop. Luke, teeth gritted, eyes half-closed, grabbed at her beautiful hips and urged her onwards. As they both came in waves he reached up to her breasts and cupped them, then Emily fell forward, her hair brushing his face as they breathed and kissed and kissed and breathed.

'I'll always remember this special place,' he whispered.

'If you think this place is special, wait till I show you Mayford one day.'

It was getting late by the time Luke and Emily made it back to the homestead. Their faces were flushed from the heat of the day, their races over plains, the laughter that had spilled constantly from them as they bantered, flirted and joked.

She left him to rub down the horses in the stables and ran inside to ring Evie to apologise for being late in collecting Tilly and Meg. When she picked up the phone there was a message waiting for her, and Evie's kindly voice came over the line.

'No need to get the girls. They begged me to stay for a sleepover at Auntie Bridie's. We'll see you back on the plains at my house tomorrow afternoon. No hurry, my darling girl. You enjoy the solitude.'

Solitude? Emily thought, smiling. She wondered if Luke would stay.

That night they moved about the kitchen as if they had belonged in each other's company for an age. There were no inhibitions anymore. No off-limits topics. Emily spoke of the effects of the bans, and Luke of the adjustments he'd had to make within the job. He sketched out his family situation, and he spoke about Cassy. In response Emily told him about Clancy.

They kissed in front of the open fire in the lounge room and made love there again. Afterwards, snuggled up naked beneath a blanket, they lay in front of the fire, Emily flicking through the old photo albums and telling stories of life on the high plains. At one point she stopped mid-sentence to find Luke gazing at her. He brushed her hair from her face gently. 'You are so beautiful,' he said.

'And so are you.'

They kissed again and then, holding hands, walked down the hallway to the bedroom. She pulled him down on to her cattleman's bed, where they loved and tasted each other again and again throughout the night.

The next day they rode out together again. A ride out on a mountain ridge. Making love in a cattleman's hut. A picnic by a stream. Then, as the sun sank beneath the line of the snow gums, Luke gathered Emily up to him in a final hug and gave her one long kiss goodbye.

Watching him drive away down the mountainside, Emily felt like he was crossing back over that divide, the one that would see him back in his uniform and on the job on Monday morning, while she returned to her life as mother and cattleman, set apart on the mountainside.

Forty

Outside the pub, Cassy Jacobson swung the wheel of her new little green Jazz. She was furious. She'd driven all this way only to find that Luke wasn't home. Now she was searching the town for the ranger's office.

Her eyes narrowed at the sight of the giant four-wheel drives that lined the road by the pub. She frowned when she read the sticker on the back of one of them: *Fertilise the Bush – Doze in a Greenie*. The cars were also plastered with chainsaw stickers. She couldn't believe Luke had chosen to live in this bloody town. She couldn't believe he was still dicking about in that dump of a house by a mosquito-infested river.

Cassy dragged off her hat, which looked like a crocheted green tea-cosy, and ran her silver-ringed fingers through her spiked-up hair.

The store was closed and no one else was in sight along the street. If she wanted to find Luke by nightfall, she'd have to go and ask in the pub. But she just couldn't. Those rednecks would probably eat her alive. Carnivores! she thought. She glanced up the quiet street again. This place really was too much.

A few hundred metres away from the pub Cassy saw a sign swinging from a wooden pole. She started the engine of her little green car and drove closer. Squinting, she saw that it read *Beauty in the Bush*. She parked outside the tiny cottage and went through the picket gate, knocking on the squat white door.

Evie answered, calmly assessing the girl wearing what looked like the Aboriginal flag fashioned into a caftan and boots that could crush a cat's skull.

'Hello,' said Evie. 'If you're after Bridie, she's taken the girls to the river to fish.'

Cassy looked at the woman with the strange green eyes. She was wearing very daggy clothes and had her long grey hair in braids.

'No. I just want directions to the ranger's office.'

'Oh,' said Evie, 'come in then.' She opened the door wide and stepped back against the wall.

'I don't need to come in for directions, do I?' said Cassy, almost rudely.

'No, but I do need to sit. My leg is giving me hell,' lied Evie.

Before she knew it, Cassy was perched on a white couch with a huge fluffy ginger cat on her lap and a cup of camomile tea in her hands.

She was fuming. She just wanted to find Luke, but this old woman seemed like one of those desperate, lonely kinds. She probably shared the cat's food out of the tin and wore the same undies for a week. Cassy decided she'd endure her for just ten minutes.

'You're lonely,' Evie pronounced.

Cassy's eyes widened. '*Me*? Lonely? No!'

'Then why travel so many hours to see a person who's no longer your boyfriend?'

Cassy stiffened. Bloody small towns. Everyone knew everything about each other.

'That's none of your business.' She set down the cup and pushed the cat off her knee. 'Now, if you'll just give me directions, I'll be going.'

The woman looked levelly at her. 'My name's Evie. Would you like me to do a healing for you? No charge.'

Cassy shook her head but Evie stretched out her hand to her. The moment her palm came to rest on the girl's bare forearm, Cassy felt a tingle race along her skin and in an instant she was crying. Crying like a baby. She let Evie gently put her arm around her shoulders and guide her back to the couch. Evie offered her a tissue and sat quietly while Cassy blubbered.

Years of hurt welled up from within Cassy. Her father leaving her; the manipulation of her mother who had tried to buy her love every step of her life; the way the negatives of the world had weighed upon her since she was a little girl. She realised it had been the purity of Luke's spirit and his open-mindedness that had captured her. Now, she saw he didn't love her. More importantly, she realised she didn't love him. She'd just loved the idea that she was cared for by him. That simple fact had made her feel less intense, not so anguished. Not so much her hateful, hopeless self. Twisting the tissue, Cassy watched as Evie shut her eyes. The old lady's eyelids began to flicker and she inhaled deeply through her nose.

'God says you are loved.' This statement prompted a torrent of further tears from the girl. 'He also says to get a sense of humour.'

Cassy looked at Evie, wanting to slap her, but there was something about her that made the girl realise this woman was for real. She was connected to something. Though what that was, Cassy couldn't say. She certainly didn't believe in God. She looked up at the white pressed-tin ceilings of the old cottage. She was beginning to get the creeps.

'There is nothing to fear,' Evie said in a voice that sounded strangely altered. She was silent for a time and Cassy wondered if she had finished what she had called the 'healing'. But then Evie spoke again.

'God is showing me injured wildlife. Burnt wildlife. You are there. In the centre of them all, caring for them.'

'Wildlife?' Cassy queried. She'd never had much to do with animals, really, except for dressing up as them for the protests.

'God says your path lies with the animals.'

'The animals? But what about Luke?'

She watched Evie's eyes roam from side to side behind her eyelids as if scanning something.

'God says I am not a clairvoyant and if you want one, go read *Cleo*.' Then Evie burst out laughing, her eyes still closed. 'Oh, he's a funny bugger, this God!'

Cassy stood up. 'You're taking the piss out of me. This is all crap. I can't believe you sucked me in.'

But Evie didn't respond. She sat with her eyes still shut. 'God says, remember your sense of humour. He says you will do good in the world, but this town is not your place. Luke has a soul-connection to another.'

Cassy once again felt her emotions rise and tears well. This woman was right. What the hell was she doing here? She'd been hanging on to Luke for months now, and he'd been trying so gently to let her down, to lose her. She shut her eyes. When she opened them Evie's intense green eyes were fixed on her.

'Okay?' she asked gently. Cassy nodded. Evie gave her a glass of water and then, without another word, ushered her from the cottage.

'Travel safely,' she said.

On impulse, Cassy gave her a quick hug and thanked her. Then she got in her car and drove away from Dargo, feeling all of a sudden enlivened and empowered. She had asked for directions, and Evie had certainly given her those! Wildlife. She would work with injured wildlife and she would start this summer during fire season. She squealed with excitement and turned up her CD of world music full-pelt.

Forty-one

For the following week, Emily wasn't sure if she was feeling lethargic from the unseasonal heat or from love. Her thoughts constantly ran to Luke and her body felt listless and languid. The mere recollection of their lovemaking caused her to flop down on the nearest chair or log, and sigh. Never before had she been so physically and mentally affected by a man. She wondered how on earth she'd cope with her girls' energy and the work she had in front of her, longing instead just to wallow in her blissful memories of Luke.

She'd only talked to him once since their weekend together. He'd phoned to say he'd been called into Heyfield for a week of fire training. Their conversation was brief and to the point, he was in a rush, but Emily could hear the underlying excitement in his voice. As she set down the phone she knew her feelings were reciprocated.

Now, though, as she thought of him, she wondered where he'd be. Today was going to be bad for fire. She could tell by the way the summer storms rolled past the homestead, crackling fiercely with thunder then sparking with lightning across the purple mountain tops. No rain followed to quench the storms and douse the lightning. Instead the wind was warm and gusty, and already the daylight was taking on an eerie hazy feel. The bush was limp after days and days of heat.

Luke would have to bypass fire training on a day like today, Emily thought, and be ready for the real thing – on a fire crew. With dry electrical storms threatening and the air heavy with heat, there would be no more time for her to dwell on thoughts of him. Emily called Tilly and Meg over from where they were playing on a gum-bough swing near the house.

'There are going to be fires about,' she said, trying to keep her voice light. 'So I'm going to send you down the mountain to Evie while I get the cattle closer to the yards. Granddad Rod and Auntie Flo will pick you up from there.'

The girls nodded solemnly. They knew not to argue with their mother when it came to talk of fire. All their relatives belonged to the volunteer fire crew and they had heard the serious grown-up talk about fires their whole lives.

Here at the high-plains homestead, the ute already had the firefighting unit on it with the boxy water tank, as it did every summer. The girls had been helping their mother rake leaves and clear tree branches and bark away from around the house for weeks. They'd even been allowed to tether their ponies to the verandah posts, to keep the grass extra short round the building.

Over the winter, Emily had done a good job of reducing the fuel load around the homestead as she'd burnt many of the loose sticks and bark in the house fire. But snow gums were messy trees, and seemed to toss an endless scattering of bark and branches down come summer and spring, so that the work renewed itself each day.

'Your great-grandparents always said, "Firefighting is done in the spring and autumn months",' she told the girls. 'No use doing it in the summer. It's too late then.'

She glanced out across the treeline to the mountain. It would be too late for most of the government country. She thought with frustration of the constant pleading by local fire crews to get the all-clear from the Melbourne authorities for fuel-reduction burns in the autumn. But they were either out of money in the budget or the ideal weather conditions for burn-offs had passed by the time they were organised by head office. The people living in the mountains did the best they could on their own country, but lived nervously, knowing that the fuel loads on the government-run lands and investment-scheme plantations around them were dangerously high.

Now Emily could see from the weather that she'd have to put their own family fire plan into place, hoping she'd done enough to protect the homestead. But she felt that sinking feeling again when she considered that none of the run country's new spring growth had been kept in check by grazing this year since the government cattle bans.

Hundreds of acres of spring snow grasses would now be tinder dry. The weeds too, once kept down by the cattle, would also be shoulder-high and rustling their dry stalks and seed heads together, kindling for the flames. This was country that couldn't handle hot fires. She worried for it. But for now she must worry first about her girls, getting them down to Evie's and then to the lowlands at Dargo. She went inside to phone her dad at Tranquillity.

'I don't like the look of it,' Rod agreed, gazing out from the homestead towards the ridges of the Dargo High Plains. There, great leaping forks of lightning radiated down from the heavens and clouds massed blackly to the north. Behind him, the screen door banged as another gust channelled cool air into the hot belly of the house.

'I'm taking Meg and Tilly to Evie's now,' Emily told him. 'Could one of you pick them up and run them down to Bridie and Sam in Dargo? And can Flo bring the stock truck and trailer up for the cattle while I go muster the cows?' She swallowed nervously, knowing there was so much work to do. 'We'd better get everything out of here, Dad, before we get called away to a fire. It's not looking good.'

'They've already issued a high alert and we're all on standby here. The forecasters got it so wrong, *so wrong*,' he said.

From the weather patterns, Emily and Rod knew they'd be kept busy in the coming days as volunteer firefighters. It was a frustrating job as it often took them away from their own land and families, but if they could make sure their cattle were in Dargo along with the girls, they would at least be freer to fight fires in other regions.

All the locals knew that if fires threatened, the government would spend millions and call in the army for heavy equipment and manpower to protect assets like the city's water catchment, the ski fields, roads, and power and communications infrastructure. They'd ship in crews from interstate and overseas, setting up entire tent cities to house hotshots from the USA, firemen from Canada, specialist teams from New Zealand. Fire was big business if it affected big business. But if it was just wilderness that was under threat, or a few private houses, like their own homestead on the plains, firefighting was mostly left up to the locals.

Emily could hear lightning cracks over the line.

'I'd better go, Dad. See you soon.'

'You take care, you hear?'

Rod Flanaghan put down the receiver and jumped as thunder suddenly boomed, loud as a cannon, above his house. He stepped on to the verandah to watch the rain arrive, slowly at first in giant lazy drops that landed, splat, on the green garden outside. Then it began to teem down, steam rising up from the hides of the bulls that stood in the house paddock, listless and uncomfortable in the summer heat.

Then, as quickly as it had come, the storm passed. The cold air pockets moved on and the wind once again felt like a fan heater on high. Rod looked up and saw what he had expected to see. Thin coils of smoke were drifting up in the mountains already as fires from the lightning strikes took hold.

He shook his head, fear settling in the pit of his stomach. Everyone round here knew the government land had a fuel load on it – so high that an inferno was on its way. He tried to count the decades since the area had been burned.

Once again he cursed the department policy putting out every lightning strike, instead of allowing some naturally lit fires in the cooler months to trickle along harmlessly and burn away the vegetation that created such a volatile environment come the summertime. His daughter was up in that.

As he ran outside to find Flo and get the stock truck and trailer on the road, all he could think of were the stories his father had told him of the '39 fires, when eighty or so people had died. His father had told him how the stables on the high plains had almost burnt, a dog escaping when the rope he was tied with smouldered right through. Three times the family had managed to save the homestead and yards. But in that '39 fire, seven hundred Flanaghan cattle had perished.

Rod had fought many fires, although never a monster like the one of '39. But today he knew something massive was on its way. In their inability truly to see and read this land, white-fellas had been creating the conditions for this fire for decades. And now, thought Rod Flanaghan, shuddering, they would all have to pay.

Forty-two

It felt like an age to Emily before they were winding down the mountain bends towards Evie's cottage. There was so much to do in such a short time, and as the day grew hotter, the winds stronger and the haze thicker, she felt fear driving her on, faster and faster. On the radio the callers' fire reports were becoming increasingly urgent.

She was relieved when she at last saw Evie, waving from behind the stone wall of her lush garden. There was less haze on the northern side of the mountain and, with all its shady greenery, this place seemed unlikely ever to burn. Emily tooted the horn and watched as Jesus Christ went nuts, barking and chasing his tail in manic circles. Leaving the ute to idle, Emily leapt out, helping the girls with their bags.

Meg and Tilly hugged Evie, and Emily gave her a quick kiss on the cheek.

'Thanks so much for minding them.'

'My pleasure, my dear. They'll be safe here, for the time being.'

'Dad should be about three hours getting the cattle, then he or Flo will collect them. I'll be along after with the horses.'

'Right you are.'

'Are you going to come down with us when we leave? I don't reckon it's a day to be staying behind up here,' Emily said, looking towards the smoke haze now spreading out over the landscape to the west.

'Try moving me,' Evie said.

'But . . .'

'I'm fine, love,' she said. 'I've done all I can to prepare.'

'We'll check you on the way down,' Emily said. 'If the fire's heading our way, I'll chuck you in the stock truck with the other stubborn cows and *make* you come, if I have to.'

Normally Evie would've laughed along with Emily at this point, but she seemed distant today, almost dreamy.

'You sure you're okay?' Emily asked again.

Evie nodded and her smile returned. 'I'm fine, really I am. You just go, and know that your girls are safe with me.'

'Thanks,' said Emily, giving her a hug. 'I'd better go. Got cows to get in.'

'You'll need to run with that at your back,' said Evie, looking up towards the smoke, 'but God will carry you along the way.' She raised a hand to Emily's cheek. For the first time, she noticed a tremor in Evie's touch. 'Goodbye, dear.'

'See you soon!'

Emily gathered both her girls to her and kissed them.

'You help Evie out, okay? Granddad will be along soon. And I won't be far behind with the horses in the float.'

As she climbed into the ute she smiled to see Evie's arms go around Meg's and Tilly's shoulders as if she were draping her wings over them. She truly was an angel. On impulse Emily wound the window down and yelled, 'I love you, Evie!'

Faint on the wind came Evie's reply: 'And I love you, my girl.' Then she was gone, out of sight, as Emily roared the ute away around the bend.

She rushed inside the homestead and gathered up the boxes of precious things they had already packed during long hot nights that week. She took down the old family photographs that had hung on the walls for years and wrapped them in a blanket, the face of old Emily staring up at her from one picture with her lively dark eyes.

'I know,' Emily said to the photograph. 'I know you're watching me, and I'll be careful.'

She had been through the fire drill several times before during scorching summers like this one. She knew the procedure and moved like clockwork. She and Sam had done this many times as kids. All the Flanaghans were fire-aware. Ever since the early-1900s, when the government had restricted the family from pre-emptive burning, they had tried to come up with other ways to protect themselves should a fire break out.

After the fierce '39 fires, the Flanaghans had built a fire bunker near the homestead. It was still there and the family checked and restocked it every year. Emily's grandfather had called it their 'life insurance policy', and Emily knew it was one of several such bunkers he'd built on the mountain, such was his conviction that a raging inferno would come one day.

She glanced at her watch as she loaded the boxes and some old handmade furniture onto the ute and drove it all quickly to the bunker.

Inside in the gloom she shone the torch about. It was damp and cool in there. Rousie flopped down on the dirt floor as if to say, This is the place to stay. She set the boxes down and whistled him out, sealing the bunker up behind them. As she did, she imagined what it would be like actually to use it one day. She and Sam had only ever gone in there to tell ghost stories and scare themselves witless when they were kids. She shivered at the thought of being in there while a fire rampaged overhead.

At the homestead, she disconnected the gas and dragged the canisters away from the buildings. She checked a small pump at the water tank and hooked it to a hose that ran up on to the roof.

After climbing a ladder, she quickly plugged the gutters with rags, her boots screeching on the tin. She checked that the line leading to the roof sprinklers was still nailed securely.

From the peak of the homestead, she looked around at the beautiful high-plains trees and the home meadows, grazed short over the summer by the horses. The snow gums were listless from heat, stirred occasionally by erratic blasts of hot wind. She loved this place and would hate to see it burn, but it wasn't the first time the Flanaghans had faced the destruction of fire and Emily knew it was all part of choosing to build a house in such a place.

Suddenly the wind dropped. She stood for a moment on the roof, staring up at the sun, which was now a sinister orange ball in the sky. As she did, she was sure she could hear the faint sound of a woman calling out. Old Emily? She shook her head. It was nothing, she told herself, nothing but the wind. She had to hurry. She climbed down the ladder.

In the shed she dragged out several big old dusty signs that were hand-painted in Flo's sloping text. Emily propped one up next to the pump. The sign read: *Hi CFA, If you make it this far, please start this pump.* Then she set the other white signs along the drive. They had thick black arrows painted on them and pointed to the water tank and pump. This was the family's 'Plan B', and they hoped one day in a fire, it might work.

Back in the house Emily skolled a big glass of water, threw on a long-sleeved woollen shirt and ran to hitch the float to the ute.

She paused, sticking her head inside the cab to listen to the radio as people keeping watch in the fire towers reported the locations of columns of smoke. It seemed the winds were fanning the fires away from them. Relieved, she continued with her tasks.

She jogged to the horse paddock to catch Snowgum. Bonus followed them into the yard, where she put the pack frame on him and strapped heavy water backpacks on to him. Ready to ride, she whistled Rousie to her as she swung herself up on to Snowgum. At the house the ponies whickered to them from the ends of their tethers and trotted in half-moons as they passed.

As she rode out towards the snow-grass plains, Emily could

smell the smoke. Although it was barely past midday, the day was growing dark. She swallowed down her nerves and got on with the job of finding her cattle out on the runs.

On the Block Paddock, where the cattle had last been moved, she checked the two knapsacks hitched either side of Bonus's pack frame. The gelding took the weight well. He'd done plenty of packing over the winter, but his ears flicked nervously as he listened to the slosh of water following him with every step. At a trot, the sensation of the water moving its weight independently unsettled him. He shifted sideways and tossed his head.

Emily tried to soothe him, but when he continued carrying on, said sternly, 'If you don't like it, mate, you'll just have to lump it. This is an emergency!' She tugged on his lead rope a little. He seemed to take her gruff tone and sharp check as a message to behave, and knuckled down to his job.

After trotting north for about half an hour, Emily found the cattle hiding in the shade of a thicket of snow gums, on the fringe of an open plain. The cows cast their ears forward at the sight of the rider and some ambled out curiously, sniffing the air, made nervous by the smoke. Emily sent Rousie out around them and followed his cast in a canter, leaping ditches and logs.

On the end of the lead, Bonus put in a couple of bucks as they travelled, still not liking the weight and feel of the knapsacks, but after another growl from Emily settled again. Thankfully the straps on his pack had held. She knew they could not afford to waste time. Emily soon had the cows and calves mobbed, but a quick head count told her it wasn't the full one hundred and fifty. She grimaced.

'Twenty-five short,' she said. The open plain gave her a view to the east where the sky was clear, but to the west there was a wall of smoke. Heartened that the breeze had dropped, she decided to take the cattle she had back to the yards. Some was better than none and she might have time to search for the others afterwards. The truck would still be half an hour away and the wind was fanning the fires to the south-west, in the direction of Wonnangatta.

At the yards, Emily bustled the cattle into the pen nearest the loading ramp. Around her, day had turned to a creepy untimely dusk and the wind was gusting every which way. Every now and then a blackened leaf spiralled down and landed on the ground, like confetti from hell. One burning leaf or a windblown ember could spark a fire.

She remounted Snowgum. If she could just take one last look for the rest of the cattle, she reasoned, just one gallop across the plain, she might find the remaining cows and calves. She had heard horror stories about how cattle fat burns hotter than trees, so that firefighters had discovered eerie white shadows cast on the ground, caused by the radiant heat of a burning beast. She just couldn't leave her cattle to die like that. The sooner she found them all, the sooner she could get out of here. And then she'd be back in Dargo with her girls, shouting them a lemonade at the pub after this fiery day was done.

She swung Snowgum about, Bonus following at a canter, and rode away from the yards.

'Find 'em, boy,' she said to Rousie and he bounded on ahead, nose to the wind, eyes keen, despite the ever-thickening haze of smoke.

Forty-three

At the high-plains homestead yards, Rod and Flo peered through the thick fog of smoke to find most of the cattle in the pen. There was no sign of Emily. To their horror they saw flames sparked by embers beyond the treeline beginning to chew up the grassy plain. They knew she would be searching for the remainder of the herd there. Rod's eyes watered from the smoke.

Surely he couldn't have lost her again, he thought in anguish.

'Emily!' he screamed to the empty bushland. Flo, her face set, got on with the business of loading cattle on to the double-decker truck and trailer.

'Where *is* she?' Rod implored as Flo swung the inner door of the truck shut.

His sister looked out towards the smoke-filled plain. 'I dunno.'

Rod was furious. How could she do this? How could she leave him and her girls? How could they endure losing her again?

As time passed and they loaded as many of the herd as they could on to the truck, then the trailer, in a scramble, Flo began to see her brother's eyes fill with panic. He looked about desperately, calling out Emily's name over and over, climbing high on to the top rails of the cattle yards, bellowing until his throat was ragged. He had no means of looking for his daughter. No way of finding her. He knew he should never have let her muster the cattle alone, but he had wanted her to be able to step out from his shadow. He'd wanted her to see she was so much more than just a cattleman's daughter. Now he cursed himself. Flo came over and tugged on his arm.

'Rod!' she screamed above the roar of the manic wind. 'We have to get out of here!'

'No, I won't leave her!'

'We have to get Meg and Tilly out. We have to leave. *Now*!'

As Rod saw his sister's terrified expression, he began to pray. Over and over he prayed, the same way he had last summer as he'd sat outside the operating theatre of a Melbourne hospital, praying for the life of his daughter.

'Rod,' Flo told him, 'she knows the country. She knows to go to Mayford. She'll be fine once she gets down off the King's Spur. It's our Emily. She'll survive. It's her girls we have to worry about now.'

He nodded. Numb and mute, he clambered up into the truck while Flo let the remainder of the herd that wouldn't fit on the truck out into the biggest, barest yard, in the hope they would survive. As she drove on towards Dargo at a madman's pace to beat the fire front, she radioed through that Emily Flanaghan was missing. Her words jabbed urgently into the radio and each one pierced Rod like a knife.

Shaking, Flo turned him, hunkered down in his seat. We *can't* lose Emily, she thought. Not again! She began to feel the panic rise, then shook some sense back into herself. She had to comfort her brother.

'Emily's savvy. She'll be right, I know she will. Any minute now she'll come riding through the trees on her fat horse with her gangly goofy dog and we'll be on the whisky in the Dargo Hotel . . . after you've given her a proper flogging, and then one from me to follow for scaring the crap out of us. Again!'

Glancing up from the steep winding mountain road, Flo was

crushed to see her brother crying as his eyes desperately searched the smoke-filled landscape around them. She jammed the gearstick into second as she took on the first of many bends down the mountainside, praying Emily would find her way. Praying the fire wouldn't beat them to the girls at Evie's house.

Emily had at last spotted a red hide in the trees in the distance. The cows were in the farthest-flung corner of the paddock. She swore. She'd already put far too much distance between her and the yards for her liking. The smell of smoke was now definitely a taste and even Snowgum was getting twitchy, throwing her head and jiggling her bit in her open mouth. Her mood was infectious, and Bonus was sweating from nerves as well as the oppressive heat. But Emily couldn't leave her cattle. She urged the horses on.

The cows and calves were stirry in the hot gusty wind, with the haze of smoke all around them and the sky so dark it took Emily and Rousie a while to mob them. So focused was she on the cows that it was a shock to glance up and see the swirl of smoke moving towards her. Emily realised then that the wind had altered course.

The flames on the horizon advanced fast, gobbling up kangaroo and poa grasses in an instant, gnawing on the bleached skeletons of snow-toppled trees. In the distance, the fire was exploding, fizzing and whining like fireworks as it ignited the oil from green gum leaves. It consumed everything in its path. The fifty-degree temperatures created thermal eddies in the air, and burning bark and embers were sucked up into the sky.

Fire was now spotting the plains ahead. Emily knew there was no way she could drive the cattle into the wind that way, towards the yards.

She had to think quickly. Then a voice came into her head. *Breathe slowly, regain your calm.* Instantly, she thought of the gully to the north-east, which would take her to the King's Spur and then down on to the Little Dargo and Mayford.

She knew fires burnt more slowly downhill, and the wind, if she was lucky, would push the main front beyond it. Mayford, she thought suddenly. The valley she'd seen in her dream after the accident. The place where old Emily's hut had stood years before. Mayford, she thought again, where another of her grandfather's fire bunkers still was, and the big deep pond in the meandering river that was spring-fed and always full. She knew there was an island in that deep pond. She and Sam had swum to it as children. Mayford. Mayford. Mayford. It became like a mantra to her. If she and the cattle could get there, she knew they would survive.

Forty-four

On the Little Dargo River, as Luke set down his back-burning drip torch and reached into his vehicle for a bottle of water, he froze. A woman was on the radio repeating over and over that Emily Flanaghan was missing on the Dargo High Plains. Her voice was full of fear. Although the words were barely audible above the noise of two 'dozers, which were putting breaks in to protect Dargo, he was certain he'd heard Emily's name.

Luke didn't pause to tell his fellow crew members where he was going. He jumped into the VPP vehicle and swung it about, driving straight for the High Plains Road through Dargo.

At the base of the mountain road a police car was parked with hazard lights flashing, their reflection bouncing eerily off the smoke haze. A policeman was setting out signs saying the road was closed. A volunteer fire crew member was helping him.

'Sorry, mate,' the cop said. 'It's no go. Not even for rangers. The mountains are alight. It's deadly up there.'

Luke got out of his vehicle.

'But there's a girl missing . . . Emily Flanaghan. We gotta get up there!'

'I know, mate,' said the firefighter. 'We gotta get to a lot of places, we gotta get to a lot of people, but the clowns in Melbourne say we gotta stay here and protect Dargo. A whole town is more important than one person.'

'But Emily's missing. Her family need help!'

'The Melbournites ain't going to pull a unit out, not when there's a whole township in the firing line. I'm sorry, but there's nothing we can do right now.'

Luke looked at the well-meaning fireman. He knew this kind of dilemma faced them each year, given the hierarchical nature of the firefighting organisation. They knew the lie of the land, how the fires would run, how the weather changed . . . but the shots were called by people further up the ladder. Luke could tell this firey was jaded and worn out. Of course he cared about the Flanaghans, but he'd seen it all before.

'I'm going up,' Luke told him.

'No, you can't . . .' the policeman was saying just as a big red stock truck came roaring into sight on the other side of the road block. They heard the driver change the gears down as it slowed and at last hissed to a halt. The pungent smell of cow manure greeted them as cattle bellowed on the back of the truck.

Luke recognised Emily's father and aunt as they got out of the cab, then felt a pang of sorrow when he saw the white faces of her girls staring out at him from the windows of the truck.

'You've got to help us!' Rod pleaded, running over with arms outstretched. 'My Emily's out there . . . Please!'

The policeman stepped forward, a frown on his face.

'I'm sorry, sir.'

Rod turned to Luke who flinched when he saw the fear in the cattleman's blue eyes.

'Luke,' he said, grabbing hold of his upper arms and clutching them so hard his skin bruised, 'she's still out there! We've got to send a crew up.'

He looked across at the firefighter, who shrugged.

Flo stepped forward to put a calming hand on her brother's

arm. 'Rod, please. They're not going to send a crew into that and you know it.'

'Just give me a truck and I'll go myself!'

'Rod,' Flo told him, 'you know they can't. If she makes it to Mayford, she'll be fine.'

'Mayford,' Luke repeated, looking at Emily's girls again, and then he was running, leaping into the VPP vehicle. Before they could stop him, he was gone, revving over the bank beside the road, sending up a cloud of dust in his wake.

Up on the high plains Luke struggled to find the homestead gateway, so thick was the smoke. When he realised he'd overshot it, he reversed back. Perhaps she was there? He bumped along the driveway and got out. It was almost dark around the house. He called out, 'Emily!'

No answer. The girls' ponies trotted about urgently on the ends of their ropes next to the house. Luke frowned. Emily would have come back to get them. She couldn't be here.

Then he saw the signs. The arrows. He ran in the direction they pointed, hoping he'd find her, but instead discovered Flo's instructions on starting the pump. He flicked the switch and ripped on the cord. The motor shuddered to life and Luke watched as water from the tank spurted up through the hose and out through the sprinklers on the rooftop. Silver jets spouted up and over the building, filling the gutters, dousing the house in a cooling film of water. The ponies, soothed by the spray that fell like mist upon their sweaty coats, settled a little. Luke threw them each a biscuit of hay and left the pump running, knowing the big tanks would run like that for a good few hours. He got back into his vehicle, now thinking only of Emily. Mayford, he thought. He would find her on the Mayford track.

Back on the road, he flicked on the headlights. They shone on a warped, eerie world of dull, dirty brown. Adrenaline coursed through him. He was shocked to see how quickly the fires had been and gone in places. Trees were still burning high up in their trunks, leaving the under-storey of the bush-land black and smoking. He had to veer around several fallen logs that smoked and sizzled. Near the creek where he and the girls had panned for gold he had to chainsaw through a still smoking fallen tree so his vehicle could pass.

Dead birds littered the road along with smouldering walla-bies and possums. Some, still alive, hulked their bodies along painfully. Their suffering was so tangible he felt his heart lurch and race within him, and sweat was pouring from his body. The smoke made it hard for him to breathe, but so, too, did his fear.

There were still patches of unburnt bush. A fireball could alter course with the wind and swing back to devour him in one of those patches of tinder-dry deadwood and grasses. He was still so new to this country and realised he had been stupid to come – but how could he leave Emily alone up here?

Through the smoke he saw the VPP sign for Mayford. He swerved the vehicle as best he could with the water load on it and lumped his way over the ridged track. So stuffy was the air in the cab that he pulled his T-shirt from beneath his overalls to cover his nose and mouth. He squinted along the track, beginning to lose hope of ever finding her.

Luke travelled slowly in this way for nearly forty minutes, panic rising in him. At last, in the gloom, he saw a smattering of cow dung: a clue that raised such hope and relief in him he almost cried. She had to be here with the cows! The dung was fresh and the country that he travelled through was Park land. But what if it was just dung from a stray cow that had pushed through the fence?

As he began to cave in to doubt, suddenly there she was in a clearing ahead. Emily Flanaghan. She was standing beside a new fence that, until a moment ago, had divided the Park from her family's cattle run. The gleaming wires were cut and flung back against the grass. Six strands of silver, like broken guitar strings. Behind her stood her mare, dancing nervously where she was tied, flicking her charcoal tail against her flanks

366

of snowdrift-white. Next to her stood Bonus, laden with knapsacks, moving about but obviously lame in the offside rear leg.

To the right, a mob of glossy, white-faced cows and calves spotted Luke and lowed, as if pleading for help. He looked over at Emily, who was smiling at him in amazement. Luke jumped out of the Cruiser, his strong legs propelling him quickly over the tussocky plain. Crying with relief, she ran to him. Together they embraced, kissing each other, tasting the sweat, the tears and the soot.

'Luke! You can't be here!' Emily held his face in her hands and gazed deep into his eyes. She was so relieved and yet so horrified to see him here in the mountains that were engulfed in flames. It felt so wonderful to hold him, but it came with the horrific realisation that it was not just her life at risk now, but his too. 'We've gotta get out of here!'

'I know! Come on,' he said, taking her hand, starting to lead her towards the VPP vehicle. She pulled her hand away.

'But, Luke, I'm not leaving my girls,' she said, gesturing towards her cattle. 'And I'm not leaving Snowgum or Bonus.'

'Are you crazy?' he said. 'Emily! You've cut the fence. Let them go. They'll find a way out on the tracks.'

She shook her head.

'Not through that mess they won't,' she said, and instantly he knew what she meant. He looked with shame at the long rank grasses and weeds that had grown up on the Park side of the fence since winter.

'Emily, I can't let you . . .'

'Can't let me what, Luke? Damage Park property? Take cattle on to a restricted area?'

'No. I can't let you go.'

'Well, nor can I! *You* have to come with *me*,' she said. 'You're crazy to go that way. I reckon we've got half an hour before the hottest fire from hell hits this place. I'm telling you, if you go that way, via the road and the ridge, you're fried!'

'But where is there to go from here?' He looked about at the wall of trees and grasses.

'A special place,' she said.

'Emily,' he cautioned.

'Luke, you've got to trust me. If you try and go back on the road, you're dead.'

She jogged over to Bonus and took one of the water packs off him.

'Here, spray this over me.'

Luke pumped the spray unit and together they showered each other with water, drenching their clothing. They sprayed the horses too and gave Rousie a quick drink out of Emily's hat. Then she gathered up Snowgum's reins and lobbed up on to the grey. The mare swished her tail and bowed her head, keen to move on, away from the onslaught of the furnace-like wind. Emily grabbed Bonus's lead rope and let rip a piercing whistle to her kelpie.

'Bonus is lame. You'll have to dink with me.' She held out her hand to Luke. He looked from her to the vehicle that still had the fire unit on it.

'Safer to go this way,' she said, looking into his warm, dark-chocolate eyes. She saw beyond the fear that shone in them. In his eyes was love. Pure love. He took her hand and electricity sparked at their touch. He swung himself up behind her.

Emily's quick-footed dog was soon round the cows and calves. Small blackened twigs were falling all around them now. Ash drifted down, sticking to their wet skin. Then a furious wind hit them full force at their backs. It whipped Luke's hat from his head, and flung it away into a patch of thick young dogwoods. The cattle were panting as they crashed through the bush, hot tongues hanging out so far they looked like a butcher's shop display. The heat, the stress and the smell of the fire caused them to roll their eyes in panic.

Fireballs ignited and exploded on the tinder-dry ground. Where the grasses were grazed on the cattlemen's side, the flames only trickled along, but on the Park side they leapt and noisily licked at seedheads whipping wildly in the wind, then jumped from the mid-storey dogwoods and began to climb the trunks of trees, burning bark raining down like liquid flames.

'Hang on,' Emily called over her shoulder as she urged Snowgum down the mountainside. She had unclipped the lead on the gelding who was still following them, nose pressed to the tail of the mare.

Luke tightened his arms around Emily, feeling some comfort from being so near to her, though the fear still pulsed through them all: horse, humans, dog and beast. Emily steered the mare from the road to an unseen bridle path. Visibility was very poor and Luke was amazed that she knew where to turn. He sent up a silent prayer for forgiveness that he had ever doubted this girl and her connection with the land. She was an amazing rider, a true bushwoman. He felt her strong body flexing to the jolts as the horse moved over the rough terrain. He berated himself for ever listening to the VPP stories about the cattlemen. This girl, for one, was incredible. He listened to her talk to Snowgum as they dropped down through the scrub on a southerly slope, the mare responding to her calm, gentle tone.

Externally Emily seemed to be in control, but inside adrenaline coursed through her. Her eyes stung, her chest burnt, both she and Luke were coughing in dry, rasping gasps, the pain in their lungs intense. Snowgum was breathless too. Her sides heaved against their legs and blood was coming from her nostrils. Ahead of them, in a dark haze, the cattle half-slid down the slope, Rousie hunting the ones that tried to veer off in a different direction. He was overheating too, and Emily was terrified he'd cramp and then she'd have to carry him.

She spoke encouraging words to the dog and was relieved to see him respond with a small flicker of his tail. She was relying heavily on him to get the cattle down. He'd turn to look back at her every now and then, as if to tell her this was madness. She urged him on. She knew that it was madness, that she shouldn't have gone back to search for the strays.

But there was no turning back from this now. At least Luke had seen the girls, safe in Dargo.

Suddenly the mare slipped and lurched sideways, righting herself just as quickly. Luke clung with his legs and held on to Emily's waist, only just staying on. To the left, a large bough cracked, loud as a shotgun, and plummeted to the ground. The mare shied violently but again the riders stuck.

The trees whirled madly about in the hot wind and more ash showered down. Embers stung their skin like wasps. They could hear a roaring behind them. Fire or wind, they weren't sure, but there was no looking back. The mare called out in a shuddering whinny, her black eyes rimmed white with fear. A choking dryness to the smoke-filled air starved them of breath and their eyes stung and watered.

Ahead of them, the cows were half-sliding down the track, bumbling through bushes. The froth about their mouths trailed down to the dry ground. The day was becoming as black as midnight, Emily relying purely on her animals' intuition to guide them all down the mountainside.

At last the vegetation began to thicken and change. The greenness brought on by damper soil appeared around them. The slope levelled off and soon they were pushing their way though thick ti-tree. Here, the world felt slightly cooler and the air clearer. They ducked their heads to avoid the fretwork of twigs.

With relief, they emerged on the other side into a clearing. Emily pulled up her horse and watched as the cows and calves splashed into the shallows of the river. They began to draw in water in great, lengthy draughts. Rousie lay in the shallows, panting and lapping furiously. Emily flicked her leg forward over her horse's neck and slid to the ground, letting Snowgum drink. Luke stared down at her.

'Thank you,' he said.

'Oh, we're not out of it yet,' she said. 'We could still boil alive in these shallows. We have to take the cattle further up. There's a big rock island there. We'll have to swim them. If

Rousie can hold them on there, they might just make it if the fire jumps the river.'

'And us?' he said. 'Do we get in the river?'

Emily shook her head. 'I have a better plan. C'mon, there's no time to talk. You'll have to walk upstream. I'm going to need my horse for this.'

And then she was riding again, splashing into the shallow, fast-running river, swinging her stockwhip about her head, letting fly with a loud crack.

'Get up, girls!' she called, and soon the cows and calves were stumbling upstream. It seemed to take so long. The air was easier to breathe near the dampness of the river, but it was dark as night in the gully, and fear still drove them on.

In her mind Emily was transported back to the night at Wonnangatta and the terror she and Luke had felt when they'd heard the ghost horses galloping past. Now she realised it had been a kind of warning. A glimpse of what had been coming in their own lives.

She urged the cattle on, and most of them plunged into the wide, deeper pool. Rousie was swimming too, barking in the water as best he could at the stragglers. At last the final cow and calf heaved themselves up on to the island the river held at its heart. A giant old willow had taken root there many years before, offering a green canopy of shelter, but the cows still bustled and called out beneath the terrifying blacked-out sun.

The heat all around was intense.

Emily and Luke turned at a thundering roar high above them on the mountain top, interspersed with explosive cracks as tree trunks succumbed to the inferno raging on the ridge above. They stood transfixed as spot fires began to ignite all about them and the oxygen was stolen from the air. The mare tossed her head and clashed her hooves on the river stones as the fire hunted wallabies, possums, lizards, snakes and other bush creatures to the riverbank. More fearful of fire than of humans, a wallaby darted right under Snowgum's belly, its breathing quick with panic and its docile brown eyes alert with terror. Bonus stuck close to the mare, too fearful to trot away.

'C'mon!' Emily shouted at Luke as she hitched Snowgum's reins and Bonus's lead to the willow tree. She undid the knapsack from the saddle pack, slinging it on the riverbank with a heavy thud. 'You have to get wet,' she told Luke.

She led him into the shallows and at her touch, he felt his own hands shaking uncontrollably. He was almost blind from the smoke.

'After this we're going into a fire bunker, okay?'

'Yep,' croaked Luke, amazed that there could be a fire bunker here in this remote river-bend. He wanted to ask her about it, but no sound came. He could barely speak, barely swallow. Emily pulled him towards her.

Frighteningly warm water rose up over his clothing and, close to blind in the smoke and the darkness, he began to panic. Then he felt Emily's quiet, steady hands on either side of his face as she gently dragged him down. He felt like he was in the presence of an angel. As the fire front hit the ridge directly above them and began to race downhill towards them, its terrifying roar was muffled as they both plunged underwater.

In the mountain stream, Emily pressed a last kiss to Luke's blistered lips before they surfaced to find a hail of burning bark and leaves fizzling out in the water around them. Smoke curled over rock and ripples. Luke gulped at the thick, poisoned air and found himself coughing uncontrollably as they stumbled blindly from the river, Emily grabbing up the water pack.

All the while he felt her other hand leading him. Choking in the smoke, they half-crawled up an embankment, the soil hot under their palms, the screech of green gum leaves crackling above their heads. He heard Emily grunting with effort as she tore away old grasses, rocks and tin. Then she ushered him into the dark quiet space of the fire bunker, which had once been a Flanaghan goldmine.

It smelt of cold earth, of worms, of death and decay. But it was cool and the air, though musty, was easier to breathe.

Luke couldn't speak. All he could do was lie on the cool, hard earth trying to drag tiny breaths into his bleeding lungs. His whole body was stinging in agony where embers had burnt him like cigarettes.

'Here,' Emily said. 'Drink.' She placed the nozzle of the backpack into his hands and he felt a trickle of water pass over his dry lips but could not swallow.

'The horses,' she said. 'I'm going to hobble them in the river. I'll be back.'

Luke tried to lift his head to protest but felt a rush of giddiness and simply had to lie there in the darkness.

'Emily,' he whispered, knowing she would soon be back in his arms. 'Emily Flanaghan.' Then he passed out.

Forty-five

A sudden noise in the pitch-black bunker jolted him awake. His head throbbed with pain. His mouth was so dry and his tongue so swollen he could barely swallow. He reached blindly for the nozzle of the spray pack, his hands grappling helplessly in the darkness. He knew from the silence that the fire had passed, but how long had they lain here?

'Emily?' he croaked, conjuring up her face in his mind, reaching out in the darkness to hold her. 'Are you okay?' Joy came over him then, knowing they had survived and would be together. 'You are the most beautiful cattleman I've ever met.'

She didn't answer. Maybe she hadn't heard him? He heard the tin being tugged open at the entrance. A strange, gentle light touched his eyelids.

'Emily? Emily?' Luke stretched out his blistered and blackened fingers and felt around on the bare earth for her, then he reached out towards the light.

'It's all right,' came a man's voice. 'We've got you, buddy.' Luke felt a hand on his shoulder. 'Can you see?'

He shook his head. 'Emily? Where is she? Emily!'

He began to scramble about on all fours, terror wrenching his heart, his mind crazy with questions.

'Mate, there's no one else in here. You are one lucky bastard, though.'

'But . . . Emily?'

'I'm sorry, mate,' the rescue worker said as he shone the torch around the cavernous den. He could see an old mine shaft, boarded up long ago. 'There's no one else here.'

Despite searing pain, Luke tried to open his eyes. With blurred vision, he could only just make out the fluoro overalls and hard hats of the SES men who crouched down next to him. Outside the bunker, the blackened world looked as if an atomic bomb had hit. The crash of a falling tree prompted a sudden burst of rising embers from the charred landscape. The pain was too great. Luke had to shut his eyes again.

'C'mon, we've got to get you out of here. It's dangerous for us all.'

'But Emily? Emily?' he yelled, until his voice again gave way to just a croak. 'The cattle!'

'Cattle?' the rescue worker said, barely able to make sense of his speech.

As the men radioed out that their three-day search was over – the ranger had been found and needed medical help – Luke became angry. They must have been flown in from another region, with no idea Emily might be in the area, let alone that she was missing. How could the rescue be so uncoordinated? he wondered. They'd been instructed to find the government employee but not the cattleman.

'But, Emily. The cattle,' he tried again. It hurt to talk, but fury was rising in him.

'There's no cattle here, mate. This is Park land now. The cattlemen were kicked off it. This must've been a cattleman's mine and fire bunker. How the hell did you find it? We only found *you* because your vehicle's burnt to a crisp up top, and the track and the ventilation shaft that sticks up outta the ground stand out like dog's balls now it's all burnt.'

Luke sat up, ready to roar, but no sound came. He was giddy.

'Settle, mate. You're in shock. Calm yourself. The medicos will be here with something good for you in just a little while.'

What the worker didn't want to tell Luke was that there was no sign of the cattleman's daughter. He didn't like to say that the fire which had just destroyed a million acres of Park land was still so hot, no one could discern if the fine white ash now blowing in the wind was that of cow, horse or human. White dust, like the powder of angels' wings, taking flight over vast areas of charred mountain wilderness.

On the chopper ride out, Luke pressed his fingertips to the cool cotton pads that covered his eyes. He felt the pain of trying to shed tears from eyes that had none left. As they flew over the black-faced mountainside, he didn't see the big metal VPP sign hanging twisted and singed. He didn't see the burnt matchstick trees, seared from top to bottom. Lingering flames still glowed on the breeze-side of the tree trunks and in the guts of hollow stumps. But Luke didn't see them. He didn't see the way the fire had crawled to a stop within metres of the Flanaghan homestead, as if God had finally had some hand in this gigantic scene of desolation. He didn't see the rubble of the old hotel, which had been Evie's leafy green haven. She too was gone. To ash and dust? No one knew. The only colour in the garden now was the striped tape of the coroner's investigators.

What Luke *did* see in his mind's eye was the bravest, most beautiful girl he'd ever known. A girl on a ghost-grey horse, standing in a thicket of snow gums. The land was written on her palms and fingertips and, he knew now, the land had been written in her heart.

As the chopper landed on the Dargo oval in a cloud of dust and ash, Luke heard the paramedics groan at the sight of the media hovering nearby.

'They all want the scoop on the ranger who went to rescue the cattleman's daughter. I'm sorry, mate,' said the pilot.

Through puffy eyes Luke could make out the cluster of journalists and a sombre group of people watching in silence as they wheeled him into the waiting ambulance to take him to the bush hospital. He knew that if they'd found him and

Emily alive, there'd have been whoops of joy. But his home-coming was so weighted down by the tragedy of losing Emily he wished he'd been taken by the fire too.

They settled him into a hospital bed in a room that faced the main street. Through the curtains he could see Betty, the receptionist, shooing away the pack of reporters who hung about like hyenas on the scavenge.

He looked up at the ceiling while Tracy, the nurse, checked his vital signs. He recoiled from the cool touch of her pudgy hands on his stinging skin. The only human touch he wanted was Emily's. He thought of their night in the high-plains homestead, by the fire, when she had told him about her mother dying in this very hospital. And now Emily was gone too. Seeing his distress, the nurse fussed over him with extra care.

The sun had faded to just a small patch at the foot of Luke's hospital bed when Flo led Rod into the ward. The old cattleman was bent over and almost shuffled. It was a shock to see Emily's tall proud father so broken by grief.

Behind them stood Bridie and Sam, but Luke was shocked, even horrified, to see that it was Clancy who ushered Tilly and Meg into the room. Luke could see they'd all been crying, even Clancy. Emily's usually wild-haired, smiley children were now pale-faced and silent. Their eyes were full of fear and confusion. They looked utterly lost without their cheerful, busy mother. Luke's breath caught in his throat.

Rod came over to him and drew Luke up in a hug. The two men held each other, both unafraid to cry for Emily. Their bodies shook. The hearts of those who watched twisted in agony.

There was a whole life still ahead of them, without Emily. Rod pulled back eventually.

'Thank you,' he said, 'for going to look for my daughter.'

Luke, his face contorted, shook his head violently.

'It was my fault. I should've made her stay. But I . . .'

377

Rod put a hand on his arm, and Luke could feel he carried the same strong energy within him that Emily had.

'You can't make Emily do anything she doesn't want to do.'

Luke smiled, comforted by Rod's talking about her in the present tense.

Once they saw Luke's smile, the girls ran from Clancy's side, clambered up on Luke's bed and held him tightly.

'Don't go, Luke,' Tilly said.

'No, don't go. Mummy thinks you're really, really nice,' Meg said. 'She wants you to stay with us.'

And at that point Luke's heart broke for Emily Flanaghan's daughters.

The next morning, when Donna from the pub began to scream, Kate downed what she was doing in the general store and ran out to see what was wrong. The old men on the bench seat muttered that Donna had clean gone off her rocker. They watched her standing with her hands held up to her face, frozen in the middle of the main street, gazing towards the river and yelling, 'Oh my God!' over and over.

Donna's cries rang out, the sound making it to the Beauty in the Bush cottage along the way. There, Rod, Flo, Bob, Bridie and Sam were quietly going about the strained business of organising memorial services for Emily and Evie, while Meg and Tilly sat numbly watching *Play School*.

For the past few days Bob and Sam had been trying to contact Evie's family, but it was as if she had no past, no contacts. They could find no traces of her previous life. Nor could the media, who were hounding them, looking for something more on the old lady who'd died in the fires. It was as if Evie had blown in from nowhere. And since no body had been found in the debris of her house, it was as if she'd just blown right out again.

With all the leads on the stories about the two missing fire victims going cold, the city journalists were packing their gear

378

into the boots of their cars at the motel when they heard Donna's screams.

As the Flanaghan family ran down the main street to Donna, they followed the direction of her gaze across the river to the winding Lower Dargo Road. They couldn't believe their eyes! There, at the bridge, rode Emily, swinging her stockwhip over her head. The crack rang out as the lead cow gingerly walked on to the wooden bridge. In front of Emily, twenty-five footsore, scorched and blistered cows and calves took the agonising last steps to home.

Emily was crying through swollen, stinging eyes as she made her way towards the crossroads at the pub and the store. Her clothes were singed rags, her eyelashes burnt and gone, her lips blistered, her Akubra hat, once cream, now mottled black with holes where embers had landed. Snowgum, head down but ears cast forward, let out an exhausted whicker, her lips blistered red and weeping. Emily sat bareback on the mare leading a hollow-gutted Bonus, his pack saddle hanging over his back as he limped along.

Tilly and Meg sprinted towards her. Rod, Flo, Bob, Bridie and Sam all followed, calling out with joy and disbelief. They ran right through the herd towards Emily, dispersing the cows. Relieved no longer to be driven, the beasts began to browse the rich green grass of the Dargo Hotel beer garden. Rousie, footsore, flopped down in a patch of long green grass, his job done.

A frenzy erupted around Emily. She was covered with burns, bruises, scrapes, blisters, sunburn and cuts, but felt no pain as she swept her precious girls into her arms. She held them to her and felt their tears of relief and joy on her face.

Tilly and Meg breathed in the smell of their mother. She smelt scary and wonderful all at once. She smelt of fear and fire and long days and nights in the bush. She smelt of dogs and horses and cattle. But she also smelt of home and of love.

Then Rod was hugging her, Flo and Bob too, and Sam and Bridie, beaming with joy. As they all clustered around her, firing questions, they didn't notice Meg slip away. Nobody saw how the little girl ran towards the bush hospital as fast as her legs would carry her.

Luke was up from his hospital bed. He was dressed. He was leaving, going back to his bush block to begin a life without Emily. He could barely imagine how he was going to do it. As he pulled on his boots he looked up, surprised to see Meg standing in the doorway, framed in golden light from the corridor.

'Hello. What are you doing here?' he said softly.

She held out her hand.

'Come with me,' she said, her big, brown eyes the mirror of her mother's, looking up at him with urgency.

He frowned, but took her hand.

'Hurry!' Meg said, as she trotted down the main street towards the pub with him in tow.

Luke saw the cattle first, singed and footsore, ambling about the lawn behind the building. Then, on the fringes of a crowd of townspeople, he saw Kate from the store holding two horses. A chestnut and a grey. Emily's horses! His heart began to race. Meg squeezed his hand as she looked up and smiled at him. Then he knew. He knew that at the heart of the crowd he would find Emily. Emily was alive!

He swooped Meg up and carried her over, pushing through the onlookers to stand before Emily, breathless. He set Meg down, cupped Emily's face tenderly in his hands and looked deep into her eyes.

'You!' he said.

'Yes, me.'

He stooped down and kissed her so gently, so lightly, like a butterfly passing over her skin. Her lips were red-raw, her skin burnt and blistered. But she was alive. She was here with him.

They held each other, and Emily felt more butterflies flutter and tumble inside her.

Their peace was shattered as the media stormed them,

cameras flashing in their faces, microphones pressed far too close. The thrill of finding such a scoop stripped away any pretence of courtesy as the journalists fired off questions in a frenzy.

'How did you survive?'

'How long have you been travelling like this?'

'Did you think you were going to die?'

'Do you have a message for the Victorian Government on alpine management and fires?'

Emily turned to the city media pack and, as best she could with her stinging eyes, looked down the barrel of one of the cameras.

'You don't need me to deliver a message. It's written all around us, in what's left of the land and the wildlife.'

As she turned and stepped back into the warmth of her family, and Luke's arms, Emily wasn't to know that her image and her message were about to be beamed around the world.

When they walked away along the main street, Emily felt her father's hand on her shoulder. 'I think we'd better get you to the hospital,' he said.

She shook her head.

'No way, Dad! No more hospitals! I'll stick with Evie's remedies.'

The family looked at each other, their faces falling. Someone had to tell Emily. But she caught their looks and smiled sadly.

'I know she's gone.' Again she felt her family enclose her with their love.

'How do you know?' asked Rod.

'I just know,' Emily told him.

Settled on Bridie's couch, she watched as her family rushed to fill a bath for her and fetch her drinks and food. In the back garden Luke and Sam were tending to the horses, who now stood resting beneath a shady walnut tree. Bob was offering Rousie a fat steak on the porch. Rod was on the phone, relaying the news to Clancy who was now back with Penny and the twins in Bairnsdale.

Meg and Tilly sat with her on the couch and Emily draped her aching arms over them, just as Evie had done on the day of the fire. Emily rested her head against each girl alternately, breathing in their smell, kissing them over and over with her painful swollen lips.

'What happened, Mummy?' Tilly asked.

'You don't want to know,' she said. 'Let's just say, I'm having a bad run with trees!'

'Tell us, *please*,' Tilly prompted again.

'Not today, darling. One day soon I'll tell you. Just give Mummy a rest now.'

She lay back and shut her eyes, conjuring up a vision of the giant burning gum that had crashed down in the winds gusting through the river bed. She had been about to hobble the horses and lead them into the deep hole of the river bed before returning to Luke in the bunker. But as she picked herself up from where she had fallen, Emily found the sparks, smoke and dust from the falling tree had blinded her.

Thankfully, when the tree fell, the horses had shied but not bolted. She grappled to find Snowgum, and held tight to her reins. She knew she had to stay with them. Blinded, she had no way of finding Luke. Shivering from the memory, she opened her eyes and reached for Meg's and Tilly's hands.

'Thank God I'm home!'

'Bath for madame,' came Bridie's sing-song voice as she held out a robe.

In the steaming tub, as she washed the soot from her tender skin, Emily's hands shook. Shock was setting in. She could still feel the fire around her, and her own conviction that she would surely die. She had clambered up on Snowgum and the mare had set off at a jog amidst the roar of the fire in the mountains above. At first Emily had panicked, trying to rein the mare towards the deeper hole, but she had resisted. Eventually Emily heard a voice in her head saying 'Trust'. She let Snowgum have her head.

She could hear Bonus limping along behind them in the

river bed, calling out madly if he fell behind. Her lips were so parched she couldn't whistle Rousie – had had no idea where he was. She had lain flat to Snowgum's neck as she trotted along the river bed, water splashing cool on Emily's legs while the fire raged above them. Low-cast branches scratched her back. Falling embers burned her skin.

Emily had no idea how long they travelled like that. She just felt Snowgum moving beneath her as she pressed her face into the mare's hot, sweating neck. She could smell her own damp Akubra smouldering and hear Snowgum grunt with effort as she stumbled over boulders in the river bed. Emily clung so tightly to the reins her fingers curled and cramped as if in a death-grip.

Gradually the bush around them quietened. The wind settled. Still, Emily could not see. The mare stopped and dropped her head. Emily heard Bonus come to stand beside her and let out a slow snort. He too was easing himself down for a rest. When the horses began to doze, Emily knew they were safe.

Still blinded and lost, she knew Snowgum would eventually take her home. She tried to call Rousie but her throat was so swollen she could not speak. Soon, though, in the deadly hush of the burnt bush, she heard a crack, a crash, a splash, then miraculously a dog's bark. Rousie was bringing the cattle along to her! Emily could hear them crossing the river. Goosebumps trailed from her legs up to her scalp.

'Good boy,' she croaked. 'Good boy.'

Then, in her mind, she began to call up her girls, 'C'mon, c'mon, c'mon!' Her beautiful, beautiful cows were with her still.

Bridie knocked and came into the bathroom.

'Okay?'

Emily nodded as her friend tenderly pressed a cool cotton pad on her eyes.

'Ouch!'

'Sorry.'

She settled back into the bath.

'Want to tell me about it?' came Bridie's voice, sounding strangely far away in the tiny steamy bathroom.

Emily shook her head.

She didn't want to recall out loud how she had slid from Snowgum at the riverside and stooped to wash her face. The water was thick with ash and she could only just peer out of her swollen eyes. As she bent over the river and swirled away grey-and-white powder, a pattern formed. Curious, Emily stared at it. She gasped when she saw the image. It was Evie's face. She reeled backwards, slumping to the ground with the sudden, horrible realisation that her friend was gone.

'Oh, God,' Emily said, her voiced cracking. 'Oh, God, Evie, no.'

She had hunkered down there on the riverbank and howled. Rousie had come and lain next to her and she had pulled him to her and held him for comfort.

In the cottage, Emily sat in a fluffy white robe after her bath, her family all around her, Luke by her side, when suddenly their conversation was interrupted by a burst of wind. It blew the door open with a terrific bang, sending Bridie's cat tumbling from the couch and Muff barking at the leaves that skittered over the lawn.

'What was *that*?' Sam exclaimed.

'It was just Evie,' said Meg. All eyes turned to the little girl as she nonchalantly continued to eat cashews from a bowl. 'Evie and Jesus Christ.'

Epilogue

A t the Mountain Cattlemen's Get-together at Rose River, Luke and Emily lay sweltering in the afternoon heat of their two-room dome tent, watching insects crawl on the roof. Luke interlaced his fingers with Emily's and stared into her eyes happily. She sighed, enjoying their siesta, listening to the constant thrum of a generator nearby and the giggles of Meg and Tilly who lay beside them.

In the river next to the tent, kids screamed and splashed. They heard the deep *plop* of a heavy rock as it was tossed and swallowed up in the swimming hole. Then the generator coughed itself out of diesel and the silence that followed was blissful.

On the other side of the tent, they could hear Snowgum and Bonus chewing chaff steadily, squealing every now and then as they bunted the girls' pesky ponies away from their tucker.

Above the tent, birds moved busily in the leaves of the riverside gums and the water bubbled over rocks beside them.

Rolling over on to their stomachs, Emily and Luke looked out through the gauze from their tiny shell of privacy as riders on fit stock horses ambled past, pausing to offer their horses a drink at designated spots along the river. Some horses had kids on ponies in tow, like little round dinghies trailing behind bigger boats. One big black stock horse was so impressively fit and sleek, Emily's gaze lingered on him and the rider.

'Do you wish you were in the race tomorrow?' Luke asked her.

Emily shook her head. 'Not at all. I'd rather spend the Cattlemen's with you!' She nuzzled into him.

She thought back over her day so far. For the first time ever, Luke had set up a VPP display for the two-day get-together. It was not so much an information booth as a place where information could be freely exchanged.

Old, bent-kneed cattlemen shuffled up to tell VPP staff about bothersome patches of weeds. Could something be done? Young men came forward to report sightings of wild dogs in areas they'd never been seen before. Others came to say they worried about the lack of burning along rivers, where delicate populations of galaxias that lived in the shade could be at risk. Could a cool burn be arranged? After some initial prickliness, each side had begun to listen to what the other had to say.

Luke and Emily were on the stall the entire day. Meg and Tilly came and went on their ponies, begging money for ice-cream or chips, with their little entourage of friends in tow. And as the day wore on, Emily could see excitement building at the potential of this new partnership.

A year ago this exchange would not have been possible, but the devastation of the fires had forced a rethink. Old mind-sets had to go. Already a contract was on its way from the VPP to employ Emily and another high-country family to graze cattle in the Wonnangatta National Park for fuel reduction. The mountain cattlemen had also been asked to be part of grazing trials on some of the burnt country as it recovered.

This turnaround in attitudes was incredible and happening so fast. But Emily knew she was being guided from above. As she dozed in the tent she daydreamed about Evie. Her friend had talked to her about death and how souls and love were eternal. She'd said death was not such a final thing as people would have you believe. And wasn't that what Emily herself had found out a year ago, when she had temporarily left this earth? She was jolted fully awake by Tilly. 'Mummy! Look!'

Outside the sun was disappearing behind a high wall of clouds that hung together in great swollen clusters, like fat grey balloons poised to burst.

'A storm!' the girls called excitedly, clapping their hands and bouncing up and down on their knees.

'The ute windows!' Emily said, ducking out of the tent, Luke following her.

They wound the windows up as the wind moaned in the trees. Horses were shifting about, working out which way to place their rumps against the coming onslaught. Emily felt warm turbulent gusts of wind on her bare limbs. Huge, fat drops began to thud to earth, bending blades of grass and turning the dust on vehicles into muddy rivulets. The storm flung tarps about so they whip-cracked in the wind. Card tables were turned topsy-turvy, spilling sauces and salt shakers. People ran for cover. Emily bent down and checked Rousie under the float. His ears were pinned down and he looked miserable.

'C'mon, fella,' she said. He hunkered his way out, tail between his legs. She unclipped him and invited him into the tent.

'Give him a cuddle, girls,' she said to Meg and Tilly.

'Can I put him in my sleeping bag, Mum?' Tilly asked.

'Maybe not. Just wrap him in a towel. He'll like that.' She had to shout above the wind that boomed in the treetops surrounding the valley. 'Luke and I are just going to tie the tent off tighter, then I'll be back.'

But the girls didn't answer. They were already offering Rousie a muesli bar and putting Meg's Winnie the Pooh coat with the fur hood on him. He looked very pleased with himself.

The rain hit like a fire hose and within seconds Emily and Luke were drenched. People scurried for cover all around them, but they stood in the torrential downpour, arms around each other. They lifted their faces to the sky. Raindrops fell from heaven into their laughing mouths, and a blissfully warm wind on their bodies made them feel alive.

Emily and Luke kissed. Emily felt a rush of gratitude for this man in her arms. For his amazing energy, his spirit, his knowledge that the land was sacred. He belonged with her in the mountains. She leant her head on his chest and listened to the steady knock of his heart and knew that their love was eternal.

Later, when the clouds had cleared and stars shone in bright swathes across the mountain sky, Emily looked heavenward as she spun about, dancing with Luke while Sam played with his band from the back of a semi. Above them on the hillside moths danced in the gleam of the generator lights that lit the bar area. People milled about, gathering before the makeshift stage. Under the lights sat Clancy, rocking a double pram back and forth, while Penny, wearing the shortest mini-skirt ever seen, laughed and chatted with a group of her nursing friends. Thinking back to the last Mountain Cattlemen's Get-together, Emily shivered. How far she had come, through the fire. Now here she was, with Luke, her daughters, Bridie, Rod, Bob, Flo and Baz. All of them rocking to Sam's music as he belted out new songs in celebration of the cattlemen and their life on the mountains.

Amidst the rabblerousing crowd of blokes and chicks in hats and singlets, the Flanaghan family stomped their boots the hardest and sang the loudest. From the crush of boozers and boppers, Emily gazed up at her brother. Beneath the spotlight he was the image of country-cool. A cluster of young girls at the front were calling out his name, but there, on the side of the stage, stood Bridie, her hands resting on her swollen belly. She was radiating even more beauty now that she was pregnant. Every now and then Sam would turn his head slightly and give her a quick glance, a wink or a smile. Beside

Bridie stood Bob, in an earpiece, ready to run on from backstage to check amps, feeders and foot pedals. He gave Emily the thumbs-up and she returned the gesture.

Luke spun Emily around and she held his hands and looked into his shining eyes. He nodded his head, a big grin on his face, as they took in the comical sight of Baz getting down on one knee in front of Flo, a bit drunk and wobbly, but nonetheless offering up a plastic ring from a six-pack of stubbies.

Then Emily watched as Rod danced with his grand-daughters, the love and laughter between them shining brightly. The future and the past of the mountains was embodied in them.

Emily gazed up at the stars and thought of the two people she knew who would be watching them tonight from above: Evie and Susie. She saw the brightest star wink, and suddenly Emily realised they were one and the same. The splicing of two souls. Her guardian angel, her mother, come to earth in the form of Evie.

As Sam's first song ended and the crowd cheered, Emily felt a rush of pure joy at the wonder and mystery of life. She thanked her stars she had seen the face of death in the horse race all those months ago, and that it had opened up her mind and her heart.

Her brother grabbed the microphone from the stand. In his fancy alligator-skin cowboy boots he stood at the very front of the stage. Everyone fell silent as he set his feet apart, his hands falling by his sides, a beautiful smile on his face. He looked straight at Emily and spoke clearly into the microphone. This next one's for Evie,' he said.

Author's End Note

It was Ian Stapleton's book, *From Drovers to Daisy-Pickers*, that gave me the courage to write a novel based on my family's eviction from the mountains. I'd like to share a section of it with you now. It makes me cry every time I read it. Thank you, Ian, for allowing me to reproduce it here.

As I write this book, the Victorian Government has just announced that it will not be renewing the grazing licences held by any of the families whose leases lie within the Alpine National Park. This decision effectively brings an end to 150 years of grazing, and has of course delighted some people, whilst devastating others. Some say it was inevitable in a changing world. But, regardless of your views on the relative impact of grazing and the role of the mountain cattlemen, few would surely not be saddened to see so many of the family names that have become synonymous with the mountains for so long, be hounded en-masse from their traditional High Country haunts. So many of them have been such tremendous contributors to life in the mountains, and such wonderfully colourful characters to boot. They leave behind not only their famous huts and names of many landmarks, but also a fabulous collection of stories and memories that will always be part of our mountains. Like so many others, I have been blessed with their friendship and support, and I only hope that books like this can help to dispel the prevailing urban myth that these families are being driven from the mountain in some sort of shame or disgrace. Our generation will never know the impact of another 150 years of ski village expansion, tourist development, road building, National Parks and bureaucratic management will be, but it would be enlightening indeed, to be able to briefly wind the clock forward 150 years for just a quick glimpse into the future, before too many hasty judgements are passed.

Author Research

While a little family folklore has crept into *Through the Fire*, this novel is not an historic or present-day account of the Treasure family. The Flanaghan family, the government organisations and all the characters, events and shenanigans in this book are fictitious. However, I have used my own experiences at protest rides through Melbourne and Wonnangatta, and droving cattle on the Dargo High Plains, for inspiration. Another 'real-life' event is the Mountain Cattlemen's Get-together, which happens every January in Victoria – see you there!

Other sources of research are:

Attiwill, P. M. *et al.*, 'The People's Review of Bushfires, 2002–2007', in *Victoria: Final Report*, The People's Review, 2009.

Brown, Terry, 'Mountain Folk Gather to the Fray', *Herald Sun*, 10 June 2005.

'Call for Action on Fire Management', *Bairnsdale Advertiser*, July 2008.

'East Gippsland Fires: A Retrospective', *East Gippsland Newspapers*, 2006/07.

Environment and Natural Resources Committee, 'Inquiry into the Impact of Public Land Management Practices on Bushfires in Victoria', Parliament of Victoria, June 2008.

Grand, Danielle, 'Plea for Big Attendance at City Rally, "Back Us"', *Weekly Times*, 8 June 2005.

Hay, Louise L., *You Can Heal Your Life*, Hay House, 1984.

Hicks, Esther and Jerry, *Ask and It Is Given: Learning to Manifest Your Desires*, Hay House, 2004.

Holth, Tor with Jane Barnaby, *Cattlemen of the High Country: The Story of the Mountain Cattlemen of the Bogongs*, Rigby, 1980.

Leydon, Keith and Michael Ray, *The Wonnangatta Mystery: An Inquiry into the Unsolved Murders*, Warrior Press, 2000.

Marino, Melissa and Garry Tippet, 'Alpine Grazing: 500 Horsepower in Support of the Lows in the High Country', *The Age*, 10 June 2005.

Memoirs of Charles Langford Treasure, family collection of writing, provided by Ken Treasure.

Roberts, L. (ed.), 'Black Friday, 1939' from *The Gap*, 1969.

Stapleton, Ian, *From Fraser's to Freezeout: Colourful Characters of the Dargo High Plains*, Ligare Printer, 2004.

Stapleton, Ian, *From Drovers to Daisy-Pickers: Colourful Characters of the Bogongs*, Ligare Printer, 2006.

Stephenson, Harry, *Cattlemen and Huts of the High Plains*, Viking O'Neil, 1980.

The Voice of the Mountains, Journal of the Mountain Cattlemen's Association of Victoria, Mountain Cattlemen's Association of Victoria, 2007.

Tomazin, Farrah, 'Minister May Yet Give in to the Cattlemen', *The Age*, 10 June 2005.

2006 Emu Committee and the Gippsland Grammar Foundation, *Is Emu off the Menu?*, E. Gee Printers, 2007.

69 Days of Fire: A Gippsland Community Perspective.

Acknowledgements

There are so many people to thank for the journey of this book, and if I've missed you, I'm sorry – I'm trying to brainstorm without Bundy! Just know I am grateful.

Deepest thanks to the world's greatest writing mentor, Rosie de Courcy and the team at Preface Publishing, UK. My Aussie Penguin editor Belinda Byrne – big sister and best friend. Thanks to Ali Watts, for giving me wings with your feedback! To my other Penguins, Sally, Dan and the crew, thank you. To my literary agent, Margaret Connolly, you are my safety net, mentor and dear friend. To my webmen, Allan Moult and Mat Tattersall. Thanks to the Tasmanian Writers' Centre for renting Kelly Street cottage to me at the crucial stages of this book. Thanks to my Hobart writer girlfriends for ongoing inspiration, and to Mev and Sarah – your love and friendship are constants. Thanks to the Woodsdale Women, Levendale Ladies and Runnymede Rum'ens for giving me a life rich with laughter. (Sorry about the prank calls!) To Kathy Bright, thanks for teaching me so much – about God, the Universe and Everything – and inspiring the character of Evie. Thanks to the Tate family for taking me trucking – a day that sparked the idea of our fodder fun factory. I'll never forget those saggy silage bales, Ben! Special thanks to my Tasmanian Public Relations Renovator of mind and soul, Helen Quinn of She Management.

Thanks also to Roweena for minding the kids at crunch time. To KJ, for looking so inspiringly gorgeous in your ambo uniform. To Luella, for waddling with me until we both learnt to fly. To Manty, my text buddy and third musketeer. Thanks to Heidi – my special phone-a-friend. To my Richmond team of oomphers, Judy, Danny and Helen, thanks. Thanks to Lou Loane for Emily's inspirational underpants collection (Tractor Fat Inc.). To Margareta, you shine like a star for me, thank you for your early feedback on the manuscript – I'll be sure to do the same for you. Thanks also to Kathy, Jess and Pru. Thanks always to the Williams family, Maureen, Tubby and Jake, Grant and Brodie (à la Beauty in the Bush) – you are my biggest support and I couldn't do any of it without you.

And now to my treasured Treasure family, you are the reason I've written this book. Thanks especially to Father-in-law, Doug, for the use of your MCAV speech within this book, and to the Gippsland crew: Mary, Anna, Paul, Kate, Ben, Fee, Ken and Lynette, Linette, Christa, Rhonda, Bruce, Alan and the entire clan. Thanks to the cattlemen's daughters, Lyric Anderson, Kate Treasure, Kate Stoney, Anna Treasure and Rose Faithful, for being beautiful girls and giving me the basis for Emily. To Marc and Andrea, Rod and Leeanne, Sharon and Rob, your help during visits to Tassie made all the difference at tricky times. Thanks to the MCAV for ongoing support. My gratitude to Parks Victoria, Heyfield – especially Mick – and Department of Environment and Sustainability, Bairnsdale, for help with research for the novel. I hope this book helps to create a new page in the history of the mountains.

To my Tassie clan, Miles 'the rock star' Smith, Kristy and Val and Jenny, again eternal gratitude. To my darling farm animals – especially Edith, Rousie and our Hereford bovines – thanks always for your inspiration. The biggest dose of gratitude to my husband, John – thank you for sharing your family's life on the mountains with me and for letting me leave so often for 'planet novel'. To my little one, Rosie, thanks for inspiring the character of Meg. You are a gift to the world.

To Charlie, thanks for loving your mummy so much – you are a cattleman and a character in the making. So thank you, dear family and friends, for giving me the riches of life in the form of love, laughter and chaos.

And, lastly, thanks to Ian Stapleton, who is generous, humble, yet great. Ian, your life and your writings are inspirational. Your wisdom highlights the balance needed not only in the mountains but in life. You gave me the conviction that this story needed to be told.